Getting Rid of Mabel

By Keziah Frost

Allegra Books

Hinsdale, Illinois

Allegra Books, LLC
15 Spinning Wheel Road
Suite 417
Hinsdale, Illinois 60521
www.keziahfrost.com

Publisher's Note: This is a work of fiction. Names, characters, places, and incidents are a product of the author's imagination. Locales and public names are sometimes used for atmospheric purposes. Any resemblance to actual people, living or dead, or to businesses, companies, events, institutions, or locales is completely coincidental.

Book Layout ©2017 BookDesignTemplates.com

Getting Rid of Mabel/ Keziah Frost. -- 1st ed.
ISBN 978-1-7338237-0-8

Getting Rid of Mabel

Praise for *The Reluctant Fortune-Teller* by Keziah Frost:

"Delightful. Norbert Z is warm and real and we rejoice in his growth throughout the story. This is a real comfort read in an uncertain world."—Rhys Bowen, *New York Times* bestselling author

"Insightful, charming and intriguing, Norbert Z shows us that it's never too late to change the cards that life deals us."—Phaedra Patrick, author of *The Curious Charms of Arthur Pepper*

"An extraordinary book."—Benjamin Ludwig, author of *Ginny Moon*

"A warm, charming story you read with a smile."—Catharina Ingelman-Sundberg, #1 bestselling author of *The Little Old Lady Who Broke All the Rules*

"A charming book that leaves you with a lot to think about in the end…" –Lucy Burdette, author of the Key West food critic mysteries

"I loved this charming and heartwarming story."—Lynda Cohen Loigman, author of *The Two-Family House* and *The Wartime Sisters*

"…charming, warm, and wittily told."—*Kirkus Reviews*

"A heartfelt story of coming-of-age late in life, *The Reluctant Fortune-Teller* is a poignant reminder that we're never too old to learn new tricks."—*Biz Hyzy, Booklist*

Getting Rid of Mabel

Dedication

This book is dedicated to the memory of
my fifth grade teacher, Mrs. Dorothy Kean
of Glen Rock, New Jersey, as promised.
Thank you.

The Universe began to conspire against Carlotta Moon on a Tuesday afternoon in June. She could not have known, as she patted her silver hair into place and smiled at herself in her rearview mirror, that the events that would lead to her downfall were already on the march.

On this sparkling day in Gibbons Corner, New York, her oldest friend was inhaling the fragrance of a bar of sandalwood soap. A man she didn't know was buying a bus ticket. A tourist was unsteadily riding a bike through the charming streets of Gibbons Corner. And Carlotta, in blissful unawareness of her impending undoing, was driving to the bank.

Gibbons Corner, New York, was a picturesque small town of winding roads, surrounded by hills, and set, like the proverbial jewel, on the edge of Lake Ontario. A fresh breeze blew from the lake and washed over the town. In the summer light, a hazy warmth floated in the air, and the gulls screeched overhead.

Carlotta parked her well-cared-for burgundy Ford Fusion and walked into Community Bank Finance and Trust. She headed to the desk of the new "Client Service Manager." She liked the plaque on his desk, announcing the trustworthy name: Michael Ernest.

The young man looked away from his computer screen to his crisp and stylish customer as she sat down.

Before Carlotta's bottom hit the chair, she quipped, "'It has always been a girlish dream of mine to love someone whose name was Ernest.'"

Alarm registered in the young man's eyes.

Carlotta sighed. How often had she lamented to her friends the burden she bore, everywhere she went, always being the smartest person in the room. Her friends tolerated her intellectual vanity good-naturedly, because they also considered her the smartest person—at least when she was in the room with them. Which was endearing.

Carlotta looked deeply into the darting gray eyes of the young banker, willing him to make the connection.

"*The Importance of Being Earnest,*" she explained.

Nothing.

She leaned forward to give him one last hint. "Wilde!" she beamed, encouragingly.

Alarm on the young man's face was replaced with horror, fear.

Which led Carlotta to reflect briefly on the twenty-somethings of today. She felt that young people saw her across a great divide, as a different species. She wondered now if there really wasa species difference between someone like her and someone like "Michael Ernest." What kind of orangutan doesn't know the plays of Oscar Wilde?

Carlotta would have a good laugh about Michael Ernest later with her sidekick, Lorraine. Lorraine, Carlotta's senior by four years, was back in town where she belonged after a year-long sojourn with her son's family, who had migrated to England. Carlotta, who had never been to England, had at first been on guard lest Lorraine use her European experience as a claim to superior culture. Both culture and superiority were Carlotta's own domains and everyone in the Club knew it. Lorraine had not forgotten this, and came home saying, adorably, "You know what? You can take the girl out of New York." And she had let Margaret and Birdie fill in: "But you can't take New York out of the girl!" Carlotta's friends were vain about New York State, reminding each other all the time how lucky they were to live among the winding roads, hills, woods and verdant fields. And if they were proud of their state, they were downright conceited about their charming little tourist town of Gibbons Corner.

With one half of her brain, Carlotta conducted her routine bank business (simply managing her "wealth," as she liked to think of it) with the literal-minded and unimaginative Michael Ernest, while the other half was busy amusing itself. This dismal fellow actually had thought she was a crazy old lady, flirting with him. The idea was so funny, she had to suppress her laughter, and could only think how she could use this scene later, with her friends. Material for her comedy seemed to keep rolling in from everywhere.

People are so droll.

-2-

Meanwhile, as Carlotta was suppressing her mirth at the desk of the banker, her dear friend Margaret was being accosted on the bus by a persistent elderly man.

Margaret Birch, eighty-seven years old, had been a petite and stunning "knock-out" in her twenties and had never gotten over it. She was riding home on the bus from Edwards Cove after a busy morning visiting the shops. Most residents of the area avoided the boutiques and souvenir shops during tourist season, but Margaret happily threw herself into the fray when expectant vacationers flocked to Edwards Cove and Gibbons Corner looking for unique finds and fun things to do.

The "elderly man," as she thought of him, was probably about seventy-five—younger by more than a decade than Margaret, but she always thought of herself as her younger version. Sometimes she found it odd that she, as a young and beautiful woman, had so many white-haired friends, until she remembered that she was older than all of them. It was always a jolt.

The man had looked up at her when she got on the bus, and immediately jumped from his seat and sat down in the one across from her.

"Mabel! Am I glad to see you again! How are you feeling today?"

Margaret drew herself up to her tallest extension, but measuring merely four feet, eight inches, her toes dangled above the floor. "You have me confused with someone else. My name is not Mabel."

The man chuckled, "Such a kidder, eh, Mabel? I don't think there could be two good-looking women like you in the state of New York. You're Mabel, all right."

Margaret had been used to approaches by strange men many years ago, and her power to rebuff was still automatic and quite firm. Her cornflower-blue eyes (she had been told once that she had cornflower-blue eyes, and never forgot it) turned to azure ice as she met the gaze of the grinning man and warned him: "If you continue to harass me, I will tell the bus driver. I will make a police report."

"Geez, Mabel, okay, okay. Calm down. I guess you're still mad at me about last night. Sor-ree. I didn't mean anything."

Margaret stood and marched to the front of the bus and in a loud voice told the driver, "That man is bothering me."

The driver motioned to Margaret to sit in an empty seat near him. Margaret did not turn to look at the annoying man again. She waited for him to get off in Gibbons Corner before she left the bus.

When he filed past her, he mumbled apologetically, "Sorry, Ma'am. Just a case of mistaken identity."

Margaret stiffened, sniffed, and stared out the bus window until she could be the last person to descend into the sparkling summer twilight. That irritating man was nowhere in sight. She'd just take her purchases (a bar of sandalwood soap and a new sketchbook) to her condo a block from Main Street, have a bite to eat, and get on her painting clothes. It was Tuesday: "Oil Painting with Carlotta" tonight. She began to rehearse the version of the man-on-the-bus incident she would tell her friends.

-3-

The Gibbons Corner Art League had been standing downtown, at the intersection of Main Street and Quaintance Court, for fifty-seven years. Always, from its inception, it benefitted from the allure of the nearby art-and-tourist town of Edwards Cove and received its share of the disposable income of seekers of unique "finds." Margaret and her friends were all avid members of the Art League, having happily discovered painting talent which had lain latent through the first seven decades of their lives.

Margaret walked with purpose toward the League, passing the storefront window displaying a sampling of the works to be found inside: watercolor angels bearing the neatly-lettered signature of Birdie Walsh; an oil painting of the rolling hills of New York State signed by "C. Moon;" a large ceramic plate with Native American-ish markings; and a sprinkling of handmade beaded jewelry.

As she pushed the door open, a bell jingled. Past the spinning display rack of handmade greeting cards, she saw ever-smiling Norbert at the back of the store, head down, tidying up the framing area. Near-sighted Norbert, thin and sinewy, had placed on the counter the usual white box of kolaczkis from Gloria's Bakery next door, which he offered to all members of the League, and which he himself never touched. Margaret passed him with a greeting and a brief pat on the head for his

Chihuahua, Ivy, who stood up in her basket and wagged her whole body at Margaret's approach.

Margaret went up the stairs at the back of the gallery, which smelled pleasantly of turpentine. The art students were already there, setting up their canvasses.

Margaret's friend Carlotta had been painting mainly in oils for ten years. She had won some prizes for her work. Her oils—along with Birdie's watercolors—were among the hottest sellers in the gallery. Lorraine's and Margaret's paintings sold sometimes, too.

Students in the oils class this summer session included two high school students, a young mother, and the core group that signed up in perpetuity for oils: Lorraine, Birdie, Margaret, and Norbert.

Carlotta was standing next to one of the high school students and tilting her head appreciatively at his canvas. As Margaret passed, she stole a glance and saw that young Liam was working on an abstract blue heart wound all about with barbed wire, and dripping crimson blood. He seemed terribly shy and protective about his gruesome work. Carlotta was such a good teacher. She didn't offer suggestions or reactions, but only asked if he had questions.

"I would like the blood to look more liquid," he mumbled, glancing at Carlotta. Margaret smiled, guessing that Liam hoped he was shocking the old people. "I'd like the heart to be a little shiny." Carlotta helped him to achieve the effects he wanted, not touching his painting but guiding him with words. As he saw his painting take on the life-like qualities he desired under his own brush strokes, he continued his work, absorbed.

Margaret set up her painting-in-progress of a cottage scene from a magazine picture. Norbert had followed Margaret up the stairs and was now setting up his portrait-in-progress of a grizzly bear from a *National Geographic*, and Birdie was painting a still life of orange roses she had arranged on the table before the wall of windows. Carlotta strode by with words of encouragement.

Over the whole studio was a spirit of calm, quiet industry, a sense of peace. Even wise-cracking Lorraine's face was relaxed and gentle.

Margaret prepared her narrative. She wanted to have a good story to tell. She had always been the not-smart one. *Beauty and not brains,* her parents had always told her, smiling fondly, as if this were a good thing. She had always wanted to be smart as well as beautiful; she had always hoped to become smart by association with Carlotta. Margaret read what Carlotta read and pursued Carlotta's interests in hopes of growing her I.Q.—or failing that, at least creating the impression of intelligence. Throughout the years, Margaret had suffered the sting of Carlotta's condescension. Lorraine, it seemed, did have the ability to keep up with Carlotta, and to spar with her on her own level. Carlotta and Lorraine were always the ones telling stories. Margaret suspected them both of embellishing those stories quite a bit, but because of their entertainment value, no one challenged them.

Margaret had been considering various openings for her story. She had mentally practiced: "Something so disturbing happened to me today," and "Some people!" and "Well, watch out if you take the bus!" and "I don't want to frighten you, but...." Unable to choose among these openings, she resolved to use them all.

She cleared her throat.

"Well, I don't want to frighten you, but watch out if you take the bus! Something so disturbing happened to me today, coming back from the shops in Edwards Cove. I swear, the nerve of some people!"

Birdie stopped painting and looked toward Margaret with her steady, dreamy gaze that made Margaret wonder if she was registering what was being said, or looking at her aura. Birdie was a wispy and mysterious creature who, as Lorraine often observed, seemed to "receive no earthly input."

Lorraine, her artistic reverie broken, whined with false anxiety, "Margaret, you're scaring us all to pieces. What did they do to you?"

Margaret, sensing sarcasm but proceeding anyway, began, "It was a man—."

Lorraine gave a little shriek. "A *may*-un? A *may*-un? Oh Lord! Where?"

"Lorraine, don't be so insensitive," said Carlotta with unexpected empathy. "Can't you see Margaret's trying to tell us something that happened, something that is bothering her?"

Carlotta and Lorraine were a team within the Club, always playing off of one another. They seemed to have their own signals that Margaret never caught.

Lorraine winked at Carlotta and returned her attention to her canvas.

Carlotta encouraged Margaret to proceed. "Go on, Margaret, what happened?"

Margaret stepped up to the figurative microphone and took the floor.

"*Well!* ... A man came and sat right by me on the bus and started talking to me and wouldn't stop. I turned my wedding ring toward him and I looked away, but he kept on. Even at my age, the men never stop!"

Lorraine opened her mouth to say something, but Carlotta was quicker, quoting: "'Age cannot wither her, nor custom stale her infinite variety.'"

Birdie supplied, dreamily, "*Antony and Cleopatra.*"

Carlotta affirmed, "Yes. The Bard. Go on, Margaret."

"He tried to act like he knew me. He called me 'Mabel,' and said he was 'sorry about last night.' I told him that my name is not Mabel, and he wouldn't believe me. So then I told him in no uncertain terms--."

"Maybe you have a double, Mrs. Birch." A surprised pause followed this suggestion. The Club members looked around, and saw that it was the teenager Liam who had spoken up. "They say everyone has a double. There's a German word for it —."

"A doppelganger!" chimed in Norbert, peering at everyone through his thick spectacles. "You have a doppelganger."

The high school girl piped up, "That is so cool! I wish I could meet *my* double. I'd go places with her and pretend we were twins!"

The young mother exclaimed, "I'd hate to meet mine! Someone who looks just like me? Oh, I'd never want to meet that person, or know anything about her. That would freak me out."

Liam chuckled with play-malice, "Yeah. Now that I have found you, Doppelganger, you must die! Ha!"

Everyone turned to stare at Liam. He blushed and went back to work. Liam was an unusual boy. He never mentioned video games or friends his own age. He had his own quiet place in the painting class, and seemed comfortable there.

After a little silence, Carlotta nodded toward Lorraine and then turned to Margaret.

Carlotta said, "I think I saw her today, Margaret—your double—at the bank."

Margaret—and everyone—stopped mid-brushstroke and looked at Carlotta. Carlotta seemed to warm to her subject.

"It was the strangest thing. I've known you all my life, and yet I really could have been fooled. I knew she couldn't be you because of the way she was dressed and the way she was behaving." Here, Carlotta seemed a little shocked and embarrassed, as if remembering the distressing details. "She was wearing a bathing suit with shorts. I saw her and thought, 'What's happened to Margaret? I hope she hasn't gone mental.'"

Lorraine's chin jutted forward and her eyes sparkled. Margaret wondered for a fleeting moment if she were being set up.

Carlotta continued. "And before I could run up to you—I mean, her—I saw that she was flirting—*flirting!* —with that poor dim young bank manager, Ernest, I think his last name is. Oh yes. She was cackling and flirting. The poor young man didn't know where to look—and neither did anyone else in the bank. Which was *packed* at the time, for some reason. She was laughing this crazy laugh I've never heard before, and so I knew it couldn't be you. Unless, as I said, you'd gone mental. Then, she turned her head in my direction, and I saw that she had a noticeable birthmark under one eye, so at that point I was sure it wasn't you. Well, she was carrying on like some kind of burlesque entertainer. I just got out of there as quick as I could."

Birdie, swirling a bit of Blue Windsor into a sea of white on her palette, said dreamily, "And you didn't mention it until now, because..."

Carlotta shot a look at her that Birdie didn't seem to perceive, and snapped, "Because I'd forgotten about it! Anyway!"

Margaret stood transfixed, paling, and looking back and forth between Birdie and Carlotta. This couldn't be a set-up. It was too detailed.

Birdie then intoned, "I saw her, too, I think, riding a bike down Main Street...maybe?" and drifted back to her painting, seeming to hear no more.

Margaret sputtered, "Riding a *bike?* I haven't ridden a bike since Eisenhower was president! Is this woman my age?"

It was bad enough to have a scandalous double, but to have a scandalous double who was in better physical shape than oneself was really too much.

Lorraine lobbed the ball. "People in their eighties can ride bikes, you know. Carlotta rode her bike here today. Of course, Carlotta's unusually vigorous for her age." Lorraine considered, standing back from her canvas and squinting her eyes at it. "Skin tones are so tricky.... Well, I wasn't going to mention this, but I guess I saw her too." Lorraine continued painting as she spoke. "Last night she was stumbling out of the Alibi Bar and making a scene all down Main Street."

Margaret let out a squeal.

"You weren't going to *mention* it?"

"Well, Margaret," Lorraine looked around furtively at the non-Club members in the class, and then said in a hoarse stage whisper, "I thought she was *you.* I was gonna talk to you alone about it when I got the chance. As a matter of fact, I was surprised to see you walk into class this evening all recovered, looking like you hadn't been out carousing last night."

Carlotta and Lorraine exchanged glances.

"But who *is* this woman?" cried Margaret at last.

Lorraine and Carlotta answered together: "Mabel?"

"But where did she come from all of a sudden? This is a small town. She wasn't here before! Is she a tourist? What if people think she is me? Wearing a bathing suit to the bank and getting drunk at the Alibi?"

Margaret caught a twinkle in Lorraine's eye and a twitch at the corner of Carlotta's mouth.

"Is this a joke?" she demanded, her blue eyes flashing fury.

Instead of answering directly, Carlotta reassured her oldest friend: "Don't be upset, Margaret. We'll get to the bottom of this. This—Mabel—or whoever she is—can't just come into town and turn your reputation upside down. We'll make a plan. In the meantime, try not to think about it."

"What kind of a plan?" asked Norbert.

"Well, *I* don't know. That's why I said we'll *think* of one." Carlotta looked annoyed.

"Well, Margaret," said Norbert, "everything dark eventually comes to light. That's what my Aunt Pearl used to say."

Margaret hoped that Norbert's Aunt Pearl was right, and that this Mabel person would come to light quickly. She didn't know how much more of this she could take.

-4-

Wednesday afternoon at one o'clock was Birdie's Watercolor Class. Because of Birdie's hands-off and absent-minded style of "teaching," this was a class that struggled with enrollment. Only the core Club members signed up dutifully, every six weeks. Today, Margaret did not attend.

The Club was feeling guilty. That is to say, Lorraine and Carlotta were feeling guilty. Birdie's feelings were always a mystery.

Margaret had left the art studio last night serious and silent. Was she fighting back tears?

Should they tell Margaret they'd just been kidding her? But how could they go back now, after evading her question about whether the whole Mabel story was just a prank? Or was the truth that they did not want to go back yet—that they were still having fun with it?

Lorraine wiped the sleeve of her smock across her brow, leaving a streak of terra verde paint. "Margaret is not an imbecile."

Carlotta lowered her chin and peered at Lorraine over the top of her glasses.

"Well, OK, maybe she is. But she did know we were just joshing her."

Carlotta twisted her mouth and gave her brush a vigorous swish in the coffee can.

Lorraine continued. "Or at least, after thinking about it, she would have to realize we were kidding. The stories we made up were too crazy to believe." Lorraine picked up a bit of Lemon Yellow paint from her ceramic tray. "Anyway, I, for one, refuse to feel guilty about having a sense of humor. I *refuse.*"

Carlotta saw the guilt and defensiveness fighting each other under the green stripe on Lorraine's forehead.

"We could tell her the truth now," said Carlotta.

Birdie, seeming to rise up from the mists of her alternative universe, asked, "The Truth?" They could hear the capital "T" in her "truth."

Lorraine and Carlotta, as often happened, had forgotten that she was there—or that she could hear them.

"Yes," said Carlotta patiently, "the truth. About Mabel. That she doesn't exist—or at least, none of *us* has seen her. *That* truth."

"Oh. Really?"

Lorraine burst out, "Oh goddam it, yes, *really,* Birdie. None of us saw Margaret's double. We were only joking!"

Birdie, stripping away the tape that had been securing her watercolor painting to the table, seemed to be concentrating on music only she could hear.

"I swear, that woman's on a never-ending acid trip," murmured Lorraine to Carlotta as she ran the faucet over her brushes.

Norbert popped his head around the door frame.

"Kolaczkis, anyone?"

-5-

Norbert enjoyed giving advice. It was what he did best, as he had discovered late in life. It was only recently that people had begun listening to his advice, after Carlotta and her Club set him up as a fortune-teller. The arrangement was meant to be a temporary solution to his financial crisis. It turned out that at seventy-three, he'd at last found his true calling: sitting *tête-à-tête* with a customer (or "querent," the term used in the fortune-telling book he'd memorized) and offering guidance in confidential tones. He'd gone from being a person that others talked over to being the wise man of the town. People made appointments to consult with him, and paid him one dollar per minute. His money worries had dissolved, and he had never had more fulfilling work, as he counseled tourists and residents alike on their personal concerns big and small.

Coming up the stairs with his trademark box of Polish pastries, he'd heard Lorraine's outburst. It sounded like the Club was in need of counseling.

Birdie said, "Norbert! It's as if you were sent at this very moment by the Universe!"

Lorraine said, "What Universe? He works downstairs in the frame shop, Birdie. And yeah, I'd love a kolaczki. Sugar calms my nerves."

Norbert gave her the box. "Anything I can do to help? Sometimes talking things through...?"

Carlotta laughed her tinkling laugh. "Oh, Norbert. I have everything under control."

Birdie said rebelliously, "Read our cards, Norbert. Carlotta and Lorraine have made a mess, and now they don't know how to fix it."

"A mess, Birdie? Of all the ridiculous things to say. I have never 'made a mess' in my life. And I'm certainly not about to consult the cards about it. You know I don't believe in fortune-telling," Carlotta said as she sat down at the table, and held out her manicured hand for Norbert's deck of cards. "You are so entertaining, the way you misunderstand everything. But, yes, Norbert. Just for fun. You may read our cards." She smiled benignly upon him, like a queen bestowing a great honor on a commoner.

Lorraine, Birdie and Norbert sat down, too. Norbert drew his deck of playing cards from his inner vest pocket and handed the deck to Carlotta, who began to shuffle and give Norbert the required seven cards one at a time. Norbert placed them in the horseshoe spread.

Four heads regarded the cards in grave silence.

And then Norbert began.

"We have here the Nine of Spades, the Ace of Spades and the Three of Hearts. The message is very clear: your own recklessness leads you into danger. Try to learn from this. You must take care to avoid a disaster that has been building."

Carlotta laughed a short, dismissive laugh, but continued to furrow her brow at the cards.

Norbert continued. "Five of Clubs. Handle issues delicately or they might explode. Now, here is the Queen of Diamonds, a charming and controlling woman."

"That's you, Carlotta!" said Birdie excitedly. "I mean, the charming part, of course."

"Next to the Queen, which I do feel represents you, Carlotta, as Birdie says, we have the Five of Diamonds. A personality clash, and a power struggle. You may be shocked by someone's ingratitude. Whatever the unpleasantness turns out to be, your best course of action will be to walk away. You'll be glad you did."

"Such a depressing reading," said Carlotta lightly, trying not to show how seriously she really did take it.

Lorraine said, "But there's one more card: The Seven of Hearts. Hearts are always good, aren't they? What's that one mean?"

"In this case, it's not so good. It's yet another warning. Strife between friends. You should focus on your common goals. You should remember that you really are on the same side as your opponent."

"Opponent!" scoffed Carlotta. "What opponent do I have? No, Norbert, I'm afraid your reading is completely off. But it is such fun, isn't it?"

Lorraine said, "Cut the crap, Carlotta. Once again, Norbert's reading is right on, and you know it. I don't know who your opponent is, though. Maybe it's Margaret. But she's not an opponent; she's more of a victim."

"A victim? Now that is going too far. A victim of what, I'd like to know? And don't act like I'm the only one to blame here. You're as bad as I am. Every bit as bad."

Lorraine, ignoring this, asked Norbert, "Can you tell us something we *don't* know, Norbert? How do we fix it?"

"And the problem you need to fix is...?"

Birdie and Lorraine filled Norbert in on their practical joke-turned-sour.

"Ah. I was beginning to wonder myself what was going on here." Norbert studied the cards, searching for the solution. Not finding it, he was forced to ad lib. He had become good at this. "Honesty is always the best policy."

18

Carlotta said, "But--"

Norbert continued, "But in this case, you can't just tell Margaret outright that you've been lying to her and enjoying a big joke at her expense."

Birdie asked, "Because?"

"Because if you did, you would be exposing how gullible she is."

Lorraine said, "So?"

"So, try this. Why don't you keep exaggerating the stories, really go all out? Make the actions of this Mabel character so far-fetched that Margaret will *have* to see that it's all a joke. That way, *she* can call *you* out. She gets to save face. She'll pretend that she knew it was a joke all along. You'll admit that you've been making it all up, and everyone will have a good laugh together."

Carlotta and Lorraine exchanged glances.

"It's as if you're channeling the guardian angels of wisdom," said Birdie, looking around as if hoping to see them there in the art studio.

"Or," offered Carlotta, "as if you're suggesting that we do what I had already decided to do. Thank you anyway, Norbert."

-6-

Tuesday night at six, Carlotta's Oil Painting Class convened again.

Instead of revealing the joke for what it was, Carlotta and the Club found that Mabel was becoming a person in her own right, and they were now powerless to stop her.

Birdie's mystified voice announced, "I talked to Mabel today in Edwards Cove for five minutes before I realized she wasn't you, Margaret."

"Oh, really," snapped Margaret. Her jaw was set, the corners of her mouth turned down. She seemed to be on to the joke, and hurt that she was the butt of it. "Five whole minutes, Birdie, and you didn't notice the huge mole on her face, after knowing me for over fifty years without a mole?"

"Mole?" asked Birdie, maddeningly.

"Yes! Mole! Mole! Carlotta said she had an enormous mole under her eye."

Birdie said wonderingly, "I didn't notice a mole. It could have escaped my attention."

"Most things do," agreed Lorraine.

"Well," moderated Carlotta, "I wouldn't say it was an enormous mole. It was more of a beauty mark, you know, just below the outside corner of one eye."

Before the mole could be examined further, Lorraine interjected, "I saw Mabel, too. In Gibbons Corner. She was in the back seat of a squad car, singing hymns."

"Hymns?" asked Margaret.

"Yes, you know, 'Nearer to Thee,' that sort of thing. I'm sorry to add: she was not completely dressed."

Before Margaret could fully envision this scene, Birdie supplied, "I think I might have seen Mabel on the local TV channel."

"What?" cried Margaret.

"Or maybe," added Birdie, "I didn't. I wasn't paying attention at the time."

"This woman is impersonating me on *TV* now?" cried Margaret. "Someone has to stop her." She looked around at her best friends.

Carlotta and Lorraine locked eyes in a desperate stare.

The more they exaggerated, the more Margaret panicked.

Norbert's advice wasn't working.

-7-

On Saturday afternoon, Norbert and the Club gathered in the Gallery downstairs for Lorraine's semi-annual show. The door to the street swung open, bringing in a summer breeze with each potential customer.

Norbert, Margaret, Birdie and Carlotta were at the gallery, as they were for every show, to support their friend, Lorraine the Local Artist. Lorraine's colored pencil pieces were realistic portraits of children and animals, and on this day she had sold three of them, making the show a great success already. It was her personality that helped clinch the sales.

Lorraine had a circle of tourists around her. Norbert liked Lorraine. She had a way of pointing her chin at people as if challenging them to make a wisecrack. As a result, people always tried to say funny things to her. She made a surprising impression as an artist, coming across more as an interactive and improvising stand-up comedian. Lorraine created amusement around herself, the way Carlotta created inspired action, and the way Birdie created mist.

Sometimes Norbert had the impression that the Club now partially believed in Mabel—all to varying degrees. Even Carlotta, who started the whole thing, had told him that she found herself scanning the sidewalk on both sides of the street as she drove, looking for a woman who looked like her friend, but with a "beauty mark" added to her face. Each time she did, she would say impatiently to herself, "Oh, don't be silly!" Lorraine had said that she'd begun to peer into busses and cars and shop windows, wondering what outlandish thing Mabel would try next.

While Lorraine held court with kolaczki-eating art buyers, Norbert stood at the back of the gallery with Margaret, Carlotta, and Birdie.

Looking directly at Carlotta, Margaret said, "I went to the bank and spoke to Michael Ernest."

Carlotta's bright smile waned. Margaret, pulling herself up to the fullest length of her petite-ness, went on.

"I asked him if a lady about my age had been in the bank flirting with him."

Norbert saw the look of horror in Carlotta's eyes and guessed that she felt caught out for some reason unknown. He turned his attention to Margaret and her story. Birdie, while physically present, may have been focused instead on fairies flying around Margaret's white curls.

Norbert asked, "And?"

"And," answered Margaret, "unfortunately he cannot talk to me about other clients of the bank, or so he says."

Carlotta's smile returned, and her shoulders relaxed.

"But he did say," resumed Margaret, and Carlotta tightened again, "that an older woman had come in and said she was in love with him because his name was Ernest, and then she said something about being wild. He said it was pretty awkward. I asked him what the lady looked like, and what her name was, but then he clammed up and said he was sorry, but he really couldn't say any more, and probably had already said more than he should. Then he just went on about how happy he is to serve our community."

"Well, of course he can't talk about patrons of the bank!" exclaimed Carlotta.

"Yes," agreed Margaret, "But I think if I go back there and word it just the right way, he'll tell me. That crazy talk sounds exactly like something that Mabel-person would say. He seemed to want to talk about it."

Norbert squinted nearsightedly to peer out onto Main Street.

"Is that *her*?" murmured Norbert to himself. A tiny white-haired woman in a yellow dress was marching away through the meandering shoppers down Main Street. Was she Mabel? For a moment, he too had gotten caught in the illusion. Even he had forgotten that Mabel did not exist, and therefore could not be walking down Main Street. He grabbed Margaret's elbow and steered her to the storefront window, murmuring discreetly, "Look Margaret. I think I see Mabel."

Norbert, Birdie and Carlotta found themselves standing alone, watching Margaret, now out on Main Street, moving fast in the direction of the retreating yellow dress.

Within ten minutes, Margaret returned, out of breath.

"Norbert, that woman looked no more like me than you do. What's wrong with your eyes?"

Norbert pushed his coke-bottle glasses back on his nose.

"You know," said Margaret, "I'm starting to think about hiring a Private Investigator. Like Birdie's nephew, Reggie Di Leo, for example."

"A detective!" exclaimed Carlotta, dabbing at the powdered sugar left on her lips by a lemon kolaczki. "Why, whatever for, Margaret?"

"Well, to get to the bottom of this whole thing. A detective could tell me Mabel's full name, where she came from, where she's staying, if she's leaving soon, if she has a police record, who her associates are, and, well, details that could give me some idea of how to deal with this problem."

Birdie, looking over the heads of them all, said, "Reggie is highly perceptive."

Margaret, Carlotta and Norbert, suddenly remembering her presence, turned to look at her.

Birdie said, "Since childhood. He gets to the bottom of things. That's his special skill."

"Exactly!" agreed Margaret. "He was glad to help us once before. Of course, he's not the one who saved the day."

Norbert said modestly, "He would have, though, eventually."

The little group reflected for a moment on the previous winter, when Norbert displayed true heroism.

Returning to the matter at hand, Carlotta sputtered, "Oh, Margaret! You don't want to waste your money on a detective. What good will it do?"

Margaret's tone was decisive. "It will be worth the money. Enough already! I intend to find out who this Mabel is, and then I plan to deal with her!"

-8-

After all the others had gone, Carlotta and Lorraine found themselves in another tête-à-tête about Mabel and her destructive path.

Lorraine, high on the success of her art show, was full of energy and self-esteem. Carlotta was drained from the whole Margaret-Mabel thing.

"It's gone too far," said Carlotta. "Mabel's out of control. Not even Norbert knows how to stop her."

Lorraine arched an eyebrow. *"Mabel's out of control?"*

"Yes, she is. She's not a joke, Lorraine. She's a threat now. She could ruin our friendships. She just appeared out of nowhere—."

"She appeared out of your imagination," amended Lorraine.

"OK, sure, but she may as well have appeared in flesh and blood. She's become real somehow. We're all expecting Mabel to turn up at any moment. So, she does exist—in our minds. How do we manage Mabel now that she's here?"

"Tell the truth."

"No! Margaret will hate us!"

"It's just a joke that's gone on a little too long. That's all it is."

"Is it a joke? Or is it a mean-spirited lie?"

Lorraine hesitated.

It was Carlotta's turn to say, "Tell the truth!"

"Well, maybe it's both."

"Coward's answer!" Carlotta pulled the Gallery keys from her purse. "Margaret could forgive a joke. She's forgiven a thousand. But we've kept it up even when we knew she was getting upset. We were laughing at her—that's how she'll see it. You know how proud she is."

"So if we tell the truth—."

"It could tear the Club apart."

Lorraine pushed a box of tissues toward Carlotta. "And if we don't tell the truth—"

Carlotta dabbed at the corners of her eyes and inspected the tissue to be sure her mascara wasn't coming off. "If we don't tell the truth, then Margaret is scared and anxious, because she doesn't know what Mabel will do next."

Lorraine opened her dramatic eyes wide: "*Nobody* knows what Mabel will do next!"

"Stop that."

-9-

Carlotta was enjoying a croissant with tea and the company of her remarkable granddaughter Summer at the Good Fortune Café on Main Street.

Carlotta needed a pair of fresh ears, a fresh brain, to go over the facts of Mabel and to consider what was to be done. Although Summer was a mere baby at twenty-six, Carlotta thought she was smart for a baby. Of course, she would no more have sought advice from Summer than from the tomcat sunning himself on the sidewalk outside. Still, she needed to hear herself state the events to an impartial, uninvolved party. Besides, Carlotta loved any excuse to get her granddaughter one-on-one—she loved her youth, her clarity, her young-generation-lightness. Summer had helped Carlotta many a time with her cell phone, printer and TV. Summer, meanwhile, did not seek the wisdom of Carlotta's advanced age. Apparently young people had replaced the wisdom of their elders with Google. But she did pay Carlotta the compliment of admiring her sharp mind and laughing at all her jokes.

This whole Mabel-thing only started out of Carlotta's unceasing desire to create entertainment, to always be the amusing one, the smartest person in the room. Carlotta only ever meant to be witty, so everyone would love her. She never meant to be unkind, and certainly not to one of her most treasured friends.

It was supposed to be funny.

It *was* funny, dammit.

As Summer settled in for a good story, Carlotta looked around to be sure she would not be overheard. It was a quiet moment in the café. At a distance, in his booth, Carlotta's erstwhile protégé, Norbert, sat reading the fortune of a Hawaiian-shirted tourist. Norbert's little business was humming along. And it was all thanks to Carlotta, who had gotten him started in the psychic business. Surely that proved that she was a good person, didn't it?

As Carlotta told Summer about how she and Lorraine had set Margaret up, instead of presenting it as a dilemma, she found herself telling it as an entertaining story. She could not help herself.

Summer threw her beautiful young head back and laughed.

"God, Gramma," said Summer with respect. "You and your Club are such Mean Girls!"

Carlotta's smile faded, and her heart sank.

-10-

The next Tuesday evening at Oil Painting with Carlotta, Margaret announced to the whole class:

"You may all be interested to hear that I have engaged the services of Reggie Di Leo, Private Investigator."

Liam, not looking up from his canvas, chuckled, "Cooool!"

Birdie, tuned in to Earth's frequency for the moment, told the group, "My nephew Reggie has a nickname: 'the Human Lie Detector.' Ever since he was a little boy, he could see through people." She smiled, her face serene.

Was she playing cat and mouse? Carlotta wondered.

"Reggie sees beyond," added Birdie, focusing her dreamy eyes on the evening sky outside.

"Oh, *another* one who sees beyond! Great. It must run in the family," said Lorraine.

The young mother said, "That's just what you need, Margaret."

That silly young lady was on Carlotta's last nerve.

Adding insult to injury, Norbert continued, "You could maybe have him start by interviewing Ernest at the bank."

"Oh Margaret, why are you so stupid!" Carlotta burst out.

The class turned to look at her in surprise.

"I'm sorry. I do apologize." Carlotta hated to get flustered. "It's just that I feel we've had enough of the subject. I, for one, am tired of it. We've talked of nothing else for three weeks!"

"Well, excuse me for living, Carlotta," huffed Margaret. "But when *your* life is in an uproar someday, I think you'll appreciate it if your dearest friends don't get 'tired of the subject.'"

Carlotta wanted to apologize again, better this time, but Liam, his voice cracking with adolescence, squeaked, "Mrs. Birch, did you know? They say if you meet your doppelganger, you will die."

Now all eyes were on Liam.

"Repeat that?" Margaret squared her shoulders.

"I looked it up online. You never want to meet your double. It portends evil. And after you meet, you usually die."

Lorraine repeated with ironic emphasis, *"You usually die.* What are they teaching kids in school these days?"

The young mother spoke up: "I knew there was something creepy about meeting your double. I bet that's true. You're not going to meet Mabel, are you, Margaret? Please don't! If I were you, I'd hide in my house until she leaves town!"

Margaret, quick to anger (ever since, in the 1940s, a young man told her she was beautiful when angry), declared, "I most certainly will not hide in my house. *You* hide in *your* house, young lady! I never heard anything so ridiculous. And who's to say I'm the one who dies if we meet? Maybe she's the one who dies if we meet."

Liam looked stumped for a moment. "Uh, I dunno." He scratched his ginger head. "I think you both die."

-11-

Margaret marched with vigor and purpose to Birdie's Water-color Class on a Wednesday afternoon in July. She nearly tripped, clambering up the stairs, she was in such a flurry of excitement. As she entered the studio, she heard Carlotta and Lorraine drowning each other out and competing for center stage. She breathed deeply, knowing that in a moment, all eyes would be on her.

The delectable scent of honeysuckle was traveling in through the screened window. Carlotta had tut-tutted that honeysuckle was an invasive plant in New York, and the offending growth should be dug up, but Birdie had pleaded to allow it to continue blooming beneath the studio's north window. She claimed that its fragrance exerted a healing and transformative power. And Margaret, ever-proud of her Celtic heritage, had claimed that growing honeysuckle near your door warded off evil, according to Scottish folklore. Margaret argued that she, for one, thought it was always a good idea to ward off evil, whatever anyone else said. At last, Carlotta had "let" the honeysuckle stay.

Margaret put her supply box down noisily. She was about to make an impression. For once, she would be the one with the best story.

She waited until the Club filled their coffee cans with water and taped their Arches watercolor paper to the table. There should be no interruptions or distractions once she began. She waited for the room to fall quiet.

"Turns out," she said, and all eyes turned to her. She basked in the warmth of their rapt attention. Really, it had been very nice, these past few weeks, being the center of everything for once. It would be a pity to let it go. She took her time.

"Turns out, I called Reggie Di Leo off the case." Margaret thought that would be the correct P.I. term: to "call him off the case."

Carlotta exhaled audibly. "That was smart, Margaret."

Margaret thought how irritating Carlotta could be, always assuming that she was the one to judge who was smart and who wasn't.

"Yes," said Margaret, "it was. Because it turns out, I don't need him."

Carlotta and Lorraine exchanged glances.

Norbert appeared in the doorway, calling, "Kolaczkis!"

The four women glanced at him in a way that told him to put the bakery box on the counter and pay attention. The spotlight returned to Margaret.

"I don't need the Private Investigator, because I've met Mabel myself."

Margaret smiled. She hadn't felt this powerful in a very long time. Not since she was young and breathtakingly beautiful.

"When I left here last night, it was still light out. I just love these long summer days, don't you?" She was stalling. They waited.

"People were strolling downtown. I was noticing the big white ceramic pots along the sidewalk. What are those flowers they're putting in them now? Asters aren't they, and these leafy things. Someone said they're called 'ornamental cabbage.' Such creative arrangements they make nowadays. Oh, and all the shops were busy, and the breeze coming off the lake was perfect. Refreshing! Do you ever just feel amazed to be living in such a beautiful place?"

"Margaret?" prodded Carlotta, "Tell us how you met Mabel."

Margaret pretended to start with surprise. "Oh, yes! I almost forgot what I was talking about. Well, I turned down Quaintance Court, and there she was. Walked right into me. I guess it was bound to happen, in a town as small as this. I said, 'Mabel?' and she said, 'Margaret?' It seems she'd been hearing about me, as well. Although the stories she was hearing must have been very bland in comparison to what I was hearing about her.

"So we went to Renata's for pasta and wine. We dined on the terrace with little fairy lights lining the brick wall, and we chatted all evening. I had the best time.

"You should have seen the people looking back and forth from me to her and back to me. And she's a firecracker, I'll say! A bit crude, it's true, but such a good-looking woman." Margaret said this without a trace of humor.

"I wanted to give her what-for. She'd been going around town behaving terribly and letting people think she was me. But you see, she didn't know anything about me, at first. She was only being herself. It *is* a free country. She was very kind and flattering to me. Really, Mabel is the most charming person I've ever met."

Margaret let her audience envision two tiny identical octogenarians sipping wine at the Italian restaurant and admiring one another.

"I invited her to come here today. I thought we could offer her a complimentary watercolor class."

Carlotta, Lorraine, Norbert, and even Birdie all held their breath. Margaret loved the moment and couldn't bring herself to release it.

Finally, Lorraine shook herself free of the spell.

"Let me guess. Mabel can't make it."

Margaret reluctantly released a little of her power.

"No, she can't make it. For one, she says, art is not her thing. 'I'm not creative like you and your friends,' is what she said. Because I told her all about you. Of course. And secondly, by now she should be on her bus back to Rochester. That's where she lives. She was just here for a little vacation.

"I asked if she'd come back and see us, but she said, 'To be honest, Margaret, I really don't think so. This is the most boring and small-minded place I've ever seen. Life is too short.' So," said Margaret firmly, "we won't be seeing her around town anymore." She fixed them all with her bright blue stare.

Margaret was the first to lift her brush. Her friends were still gazing at her.

Mixing a little Titanium white with a little Prussian blue, Margaret delighted in the delicious thought, *Who's the smartest person in the room now?*

-12-

Carlotta was eighty-one years old the day she sat down to write her first book. She intended to live to one hundred at least, so she was in no hurry. She had been planning on writing her memoir since she danced the Hully Gully with the high school football captain in 1954, when she was eighteen. From that day forward, in preparation for beginning her manuscript, Carlotta had been collecting note cards and filing them under colored tabs marking the years.

Writing a book, thought Carlotta, *is one part inspiration and three parts organization. A place for everything and everything in its place.*

The note cards now filled four boxes. From time to time she would pull out a card or two and read a stimulating remark that she had heard from a passerby on the street in 1963 or a striking observation she had written about one of her friends in 1975.

Carlotta had every confidence in her literary power. She had earned her Bachelor of Arts degree in English from Grendel University in 1958, and had led lots of book clubs over the years. She had written many excellent letters to the editor of the *Gibbons Corner Gazette,* and they all had been published. As for intelligence, she was smarter than many people who wrote books: especially those who were writing them nowadays—of that she was sure.

Anyone can be an author. Nothing to it.

Her working title was: *The Golden Bonds of Friendship*. Carlotta was to be the protagonist and her friends, the props, in her own memoir—or was it to be an autobiographical novel? What was the difference? A memoir was supposed to be entirely true, wasn't it? An autobiographical novel, on the other hand, was allowed plenty of wiggle room.

It seemed to Carlotta, then, that this wiggle room would offer more opportunity for creative license, that is, permission to make things up about people. That, in the end, was what she was after. Yes, autobiographical fiction would be the more thrilling genre for her book.

Carlotta sat in her living room at her French provincial writing desk and wrote on blue paper. She had read somewhere that the French writer Colette wrote exclusively on blue paper. Carlotta wrote with a black calligraphy felt-tip pen, because she liked the flourishes she could make with it. The flourishes were elegant, and while she was thinking, some of them grew organically into tree branches and leafy vines. The composition itself, however, was not moving in a forward direction, and a forward direction, generally, was what one wanted.

Carlotta shifted operations to her dining room table, where she spread out her note cards and matched them with photographs pulled from albums. There, before her, was her wedding day, when she stood holding hands with Ed in front of the United Methodist Church, young and clueless as to the faithlessness of man. And there was a photograph of her little boys, angelic, immaculate and dressed like angry little models. And here were the early days of the Club, where she achieved that sense of being entertaining and the center of everything—that sense of importance which she so craved. A picture of Margaret, not yet forty, looking like a movie star with sunglasses pushed to the top of her platinum hair, and her three children clinging to her shirtwaist dress and looking like small bewildered refugees. There was a shot of Birdie in her twenties, wearing pink and purple concentric circles (it *was* 1967, but still, those colors, with Birdie's red hair?) gazing dreamily over the top of the camera; Lorraine in her late thirties, one hand fluffing up her plentiful black curls and the other making a peace sign. Photographs of other Club members—wearing turbans and bouffant hairstyles—who had come and gone. Photographs of all their children playing together. Photographs of oil paintings that Carlotta had won prizes for or sold. Photographs of vacations and adventures, of décor that had since been disposed of and replaced. The sheer volume of it all became unmanageable.

After two hours of pouring over the past and sifting through to separate the wheat from the chaff (and what was "chaff," she wondered, parenthetically), she was exhausted.

How would she ever organize all of this into a book?

Why, oh why, had she not begun this magnum opus the morning after dancing the Hully Gully?

Carlotta, going back to her blue paper, wrote down the names of her current supporting cast, leaving a space of a couple of inches after each name. Characters of the past (such as her late and disappointing husband, Ed) could be woven in as flashbacks later on. *If necessary.* For the present, she would concern herself with the people who filled her current daily life: Lorraine, Margaret and Birdie—her Club. Her niece Hope and her granddaughter Summer. And, she supposed, Norbert. One needs a male character, for contrast. There might be a cameo role for her white miniature poodle, Toutou, she reflected, as Toutou approached her with her red leash and dropped it at Carlotta's feet.

"No one is to know about it," Carlotta told Toutou, who wagged her tail encouragingly.

Carlotta had read that a writer must not dissipate her creative energy by discussing her work-in-progress with others. For the moment, her literary labors would remain a precious secret. Although her friends would be atingle to know she was writing about them, she must wait for the right moment to make the reveal.

The Golden Bonds of Friendship would be all about Carlotta's Club and their cultural pursuits in the lovely little town of Gibbons Corner. It would touch on the storms of her youth which were all, thankfully, behind her now. She would present those gusts and squalls in a way to add excitement and interest, while framing them to show her in her very best light. Her friends would be impressed with her writing talent and thrilled to see themselves brought to life on the page.

Carlotta saw, in her mind's eye, a display of her volume in the window of Butler's Books downtown. She would humbly agree to do a book signing there. She would accept an invitation from the library to speak to admiring groups of would-be writers. She would graciously encourage them. She might even mentor one or two of them. She would wear her black sheath dress and her emerald green scarf. She did enjoy her green scarf. She would speak into a microphone. The applause would be thrilling.

Would her friends mind being featured in a bestselling book that would be read all around the country—and perhaps be translated into several languages? Of course not. *There is only one thing worse than being written about, and that is not being written about.* Carlotta wondered if she could use that sentence. It was really good. Or was that plagiarism?

If plagiarism is unconscious, does it count? Is it still plagiarism if you change the verbs? Anyway, Oscar Wilde is dead; what would he care?

No, her friends would be tickled to find themselves, under different names, of course, in *The Golden Bonds of Friendship*. It would be a *roman à clef*—a book about real people and real events, with only the names invented. What fun she could have creating new names for everyone. She could base their names on their outstanding characteristics.

Let's see: Birdie could be something ethereal like—Misty. Misty Seeker. That is a real possibility. What about Margaret? She should have "little" or "tiny" in her name. And the root of Margaret means daisy.... Daisy Little. Excellent! And as for Lorraine? Lorraine, bless her, is funny. She'd like to have a last name like "Witt," probably. But she's also tough. What is a good, tough name for a woman? Brunhilda? Very nice: Brunhilda Witt will be Lorraine's fictional name. And now for Norbert Zelenka. Near-sighted, stubborn man. Stubborn, because after Carlotta and her Club launched him in the fortune-telling business, he refused to be supervised by them. It was vexing. Carlotta flipped through a book of name meanings. Cecil meant "blind." And Giles meant "small goat." She was unsure why "small goat" seemed to fit Norbert. However, as soon as she saw the name "Giles," it snapped into place alongside "Cecil." Cecil Giles would be Norbert's new identity. And as for Carlotta herself?

Carlotta bit her pen. As the writer, it was her prerogative to choose the nicest name for herself. After all, she was the one doing all the work here. She would like a name that signified leadership. And also one that would communicate her selflessness and high intelligence. Now, Regina was a name that meant "queen." Carlotta had always liked the sound of it, as well. As for a last name.... Good? Goodman? ....No, on second thought, if it were a choice between *good* and *intelligent*, she would rather the world know she was intelligent. A quick search on the internet for "names that mean intelligent" yielded a list of possibilities. Carlotta's eye went immediately to the euphonious and dactylic name, *Cassidy*. In her writings, Carlotta would veil her-self (lightly) under the name Regina Cassidy—translating to "brilliant queen."

After the gratifying morning's work of getting some of the important names in order, Carlotta brewed a cup of English Breakfast Tea, and then, working from her outline, launched into her prose.

As she wrote, Carlotta entered that "zone" that is the natural realm of writers and artists. It was similar to the happiness of painting, and yet different. She enjoyed the music of her own words, attuned as she was to their rhythms and cadences as they fell into her graceful sentences. She read over her work and smiled with satisfaction. There was very little to edit, really. She was reminded of Shakespeare, who, she had read, "never blotted out a line."

She dragged her writing table (it didn't weigh much) so that it would be in line with the window. People walking their dogs on Clarence Avenue might glance up and see her frowning over her blue paper and wonder what she could be working on with such intensity. She said to herself, *I am in such a deep artistic trance that I have lost all awareness of myself.*

-13-

It was a fresh and cool summer evening, and fireflies were flickering their lights. The sky was just fading into darkness. Inside Carlotta's tastefully decorated home, she and Toutou were greeting Carlotta's dear ones: her twenty-six-year-old granddaughter, Summer, and her forty-six-year-old niece, Hope. Summer was a Spanish teacher at the high school, and Hope was the owner and manager of the Good Fortune Café downtown, where Norbert told fortunes.

Carlotta fretted about both of her "girls." Summer seemed to be coming out of a long depression at last, but Carlotta still worried that she wasn't getting out enough and making the most of her youth. And then there was dear Hope who had the most frustrating habit of getting involved with unsuitable men. Between the two of them, they drove her to distraction. Hope, always with the wrong partner, and Summer, always with no partner at all. Not that partners were all they were cracked up to be, as she knew from her own experience with her philandering late husband. But still. She'd love to see both girls happily "settled" in some way.

They had brought in their favorite vegan sandwiches from The Green Buddha Diner.

Summer was slipping off her shoes and petting Toutou, alternately. Summer was short and thin, and no amount of make-up would make her freckled face look her age. Her appearance was too youthful, and it held her back socially, Carlotta feared. She tried not to mention it too often.

"Come to the table, girls. Let's get settled for a nice dinner."

This really was enchanting, to have her lovely ones come over to share dinner and listen to her. Margaret was in New Jersey, visiting her daughter. That made Carlotta want to remind herself that she still had family, too. Carlotta unwrapped the sandwiches and set them on china plates. Jasmine tea bags were already steeping in the tea pot.

Carlotta knew she would do most of the talking, but she would put the spotlight on her dear girls first.

"Now, I want to hear *your* news. Summer? Anything—or any*one*—on the horizon?"

Summer rolled her eyes at Hope. They both hated when Carlotta did this, and Carlotta knew it. She just couldn't help herself.

Carlotta attempted to smooth over her intrusion with a compliment. "You've stopped biting your lip, dear! Oh, it looks much better. That scab was so unsightly. Yes, much better!" This didn't seem to please Summer either, so she turned her attention to her niece.

"Or you, Hope? Any—."

"Actually, there *is* someone on the horizon for me," said Hope.

-14-

Hope took in a deep breath, as if preparing to tell Carlotta something she wasn't going to like. But she was about to announce a young man! Was he somehow unsuitable? Or was she about to announce a young woman, instead? Carlotta was more enlightened than Hope thought, if she was worried about how Carlotta would receive that news. Or—surely it wasn't that slouch, Rudy. Hope had had a years-long relationship with a sluggard of a married man and had finally seen—after having her cards read by Norbert—the weasel's true nature, and had cut that unhealthy cord. Oh, Lord, let this announcement be anything but that. Not the return of Rudy. He had made Hope so unhappy.

Carlotta looked to Summer to see if she knew what was coming.

"Well who is it, Hope?" asked Summer, smiling. "Anyone we know?"

"No. It's no one you know. It's no one *I* know, as a matter of fact."

"You mean you're on an online dating site?" asked Summer.

"No," laughed Hope. "Been there, done that! *As you know!*" Hope smiled conspiratorially at Summer, and Carlotta felt the bite of being left out.

"Hope, dear, you're being mysterious," said Carlotta, trying not to betray the suspense she was in.

"Sorry. I don't mean to be. It's just—okay. I don't know how you guys are going to take this, and I really, really need your support."

Carlotta would never get used to being called a "guy."

"Spill it!" commanded Summer.

Carlotta braced herself.

"I'm going to become a mother."

"You're *pregnant?*" asked Carlotta, with a hand on her chest.

"No, Aunty. I'm forty-six. I don't think I would be a stellar candidate for pregnancy at this point, do you?"

"No, I do not," said Carlotta emphatically. Where was this going?

"But I always wanted to have children."

Hope rested her elbows on the table. Carlotta, due to the circumstances, didn't even object.

Hope went on, "Some women long for kids, and some don't. I'm the kind that longs. So I went on this website, Adopt US Kids, and saw all these children across the country who are 'in the system.' They're all waiting for a family. Some just wait there forever until they 'age out.' Something just clicked. Like destiny or something. I just knew. I have to do this. I need to bring one of those children into my home, and make a family for myself."

Ah, the tyranny of hormones. The impetuosity of youth. The imprudence of inexperience.

"Hope, dear. This idea is… well. It's very high-minded of you, that's for sure. It's so… altruistic."

"No, Aunty, it's not. I'm doing it as much for me as I am for my child."

Hope stopped and turned her head to the window, regarding the darkness outside. She turned back to her aunt, and Carlotta saw the tear trembling on Hope's cheek.

"*My child*," she repeated. "It means so much to me to be able to say, 'my child.'"

"Of course!" said Summer with warmth. "You're the most motherly woman I know. Of course you would want a child of your own!"

Carlotta, not to be outdone, said, "Yes, dear, I understand *completely*. It's quite natural."

Her true opinion was that if childless women knew how hard motherhood was, it wouldn't be such a popular choice. Of course it was fun to dress up little people in precious clothes. But all the rest of it? It took so much out of a person. She often wondered if she had missed something important in raising her own sons. She didn't remember it as a jolly experience. She recalled feeling worn out with the relentless labor involved. Keeping them clean was a full-time job. Then, when they grew tall and were no longer sticky and tearful, when they were at last capable of holding an interesting conversation, well, then, they moved across the country, or--. But she was getting herself side-tracked.

Carlotta fixed Hope with her sternest look: "I don't think you realize that *those* children are bound to have all kinds of... *issues*. It will complicate your life so."

"I need my life complicated, Aunty, I do. Complicated in a good way, that is. Goodness knows I've had enough bad complications. And I know all about foster kids' *issues*. I've been reading and reading on this for months. I'm ready."

"But, Hope, some of these children might be angry. They might, I don't know, swear and act up, that sort of thing."

Summer burst out laughing. "Hell, yeah, they *might* be angry, Gramma. Just a little bit. Being shuffled from place to place and feeling like no one wants them. Damn right, they might

46

swear. And we *might* survive that. They're *children*. God, Gramma you are funny!"

"When you say, 'they,'" said Carlotta, refusing to show how she was smarting from Summer's condescension, "how many are you going to take, Hope?"

Summer mocked, "Gramma, when *you* say, 'How many are you going to take,' you make it sound like Hope is adopting kittens."

"And," said Carlotta, "I think it is important that we all realize that this is nothing like adopting kittens. This is going to be very, very hard, Hope. Do you realize what you are getting into?"

"Yes, I think I do. You're the one that taught me that anything worth doing *is* going to be hard. I want a family. There's nothing I want more. There are thousands of kids who want a family, too."

Summer asked, "So you might really foster more than one?" There was excitement in her voice, as if this were a good thing that Hope was contemplating. If Carlotta were afflicted with a suspicious nature, she might almost think that Summer was toying with her.

Hope said, "I've told the caseworkers that I'm open to sibling groups, so a family could be kept together. I'm open to a boy or a girl, any race, and any age from six to seventeen. Since I have to work full-time, I thought school-age would be best. I've filled out reams of paperwork and had interviews and a home inspection."

Summer, smiling, shook her head. "Hope! How long have you been doing all of this without telling anyone? Why so secretive?"

"I applied about six or seven months ago. And why so secretive? I guess this is so important, so-precious to me. And I guess

I didn't want anyone to doubt or judge or try to talk me out of it."

Carlotta, who was now holding her hand to her throat, took this opportunity to doubt, judge and try to talk her out of it. "So this child—these children—they might be from different *backgrounds?*"

"Oh, Gramma!" snickered Summer. "Your white privilege is showing."

Carlotta waved at Summer as if swatting a fly away. "Do you really think you're *prepared* for everything this will entail? Do you understand what you are committing to?"

Hope went on, "I'm taking a course for foster parents. It's called 'Parents as Healing Hearts.' Maybe I'm more prepared than most parents ever are."

"Hope, I think this is wonderful!" said Summer.

Seeing Summer squeeze Hope's hand and Hope's look of gratitude toward Summer, Carlotta pivoted and pushed in.

"Oh! We're *both* happy for you, Hope. We'll both support you, if this is what you really want. And I'm sure I can speak for the Club when I say that they will support you, too. Your child—or children—will have lots of love. And so forth." She had stopped clutching her throat and turned on the charm. If there was no way to stop this bad idea from moving forward, then she would need to get out in front of it.

"Oh, good," said Hope, wiping away her tears and returning to her calm and business-like manner. "Because I'm going to need babysitters, after school and on the weekends, while I'm working at the café."

Carlotta pulled back as she envisioned herself, *babysitting.*

"Certainly. Just—do check on those issues the child might have."

"Of course, Aunty. I've already filled out a checklist on which issues I will and won't accept. There were some surprising ones, I'll say. Fire-setting, cruelty to animals, bed-wetting, rages, sexual acting out, developmental delays, self-injury, and medical issues like blindness, missing a limb, and juvenile diabetes. There must have been sixty items on that list. It went on for pages. It's really something to think of, all the troubles a kid might have."

As Summer and Hope stood at the front door, they wrapped each other in a long and warm embrace. Then Carlotta, not to be left out, embraced each of them in turn. Longer. And more warmly.

When Carlotta closed the door, she stood with her hand on the doorknob for a moment. She was lost in a vision of a mob of angry, swearing children burning down her house.

-15-

Butler's Books had been a Gibbons Corner institution since it was opened by a Butler ancestor in 1927. Arnie Butler's Aunt Edith owned it, and paid Arnie a handsome salary to run it, unconcerned about profit (she was an heiress) and more interested in offering Gibbons Corner an intellectual smorgasbord.

As such, an entire wall was taken up with religion and philosophy, and the subsections were labeled: Western Philosophy, Eastern Philosophy, New Age, Occult & Metaphysics, Christian Studies, Jewish Studies, World Religion, and Atheism. Customers stood in the aisle with one another, some of them casting sideways glances and wondering how on earth people could choose to believe outlandish and even dangerous things, while others hoped that neighboring customers were noticing the books they were browsing, and judging them to be either very bright, very pious or very evil.

Customers marched to the cash register feeling a sense of civic duty, voting with their dollars: *I represent what Gibbons Corner believes, just as well as the next guy.*

The opposite wall offered fiction, self-help books, and magazines. The center of the store had displays of best sellers, classics, biographies, "Arnie's favorites," and greeting cards. The children's section was divided similarly, and even had its own sections of White Magic and Bible Stories side by side.

Because of Arnie's refusal to declare the Bookstore's "brand" to be specifically this or that, the establishment evoked suspicion in many of the residents of Gibbons Corner. The manager and the owner could not have been less concerned, and provided a cheerful meeting room in the basement for an assortment of book clubs: The Cozy Mystery Book Club, The Feminist Literature Discussion Group, The Graphic Novels Affiliation, The Gibbons Corner Writers Workshop, and The Skeptics' Circle (which had begun as a group of skeptics, but had morphed into a trio of avid conspiracy theorists).

At the center of this base of the town's intellectual identity stood Arnie Butler, forty-six years old, a single man with a bit of a paunch, hazel eyes behind black-framed glasses, and unruly brown hair. Arnie was a friendly and talkative man, whose greatest skill was that of putting people at ease. Tolerant, easygoing, a great reader who was interested in everyone and everything, Arnie created about him an environment that attracted people who had passionate opinions on academic topics. Arnie, therefore, passed his days with people who desperately wanted to convince him of things. He enjoyed the rhetoric, and he drove fanatics to distraction by listening to them at length and with sincere attention and then remaining happily undecided. Arnie was a man who truly saw every side to a question, making it impossible for him to choose one belief as more valid than another. Or at least, that is what he professed to the public. What he actually believed in the privacy of his own mind, may have been another thing altogether.

Carlotta was not interested in Arnie's beliefs. She had popped in on this rainy August morning, shaking off her plastic rain bonnet and resting her umbrella by the door, to find out what he knew about the publishing industry. If, in the course of the conversation, he would somehow pull from her the admission that she was writing a book, well, that was not in any way her intention.

It is very difficult to keep an exhilarating secret to oneself.

Arnie seemed pleased that Mrs. Moon considered him an expert on the field of publishing, but was quick to admit his ignorance.

"I'll be glad to tell you what I *do* know, but it isn't much. I don't write books; I just read them and sell them, you know."

Dear, simple Arnie Butler.

"Well, let's suppose you—or someone—wrote a book. Which publisher would you send it to?"

"From what I understand, you don't send it to a publisher."

"You don't?"

"No. You have to find an agent first. The agent sends it to a publisher."

"Well for goodness sake."

"Yes. That's how they do it now."

"Well, how do you find an agent, then?"

"You really probably have to do it all online, Mrs. Moon. Are you online?"

"Of *course*, I am, Arnie. I move with the times. So, what do I type into the little rectangle thingy on the top of the screen?"

"The browser? Oh, you would type 'literary agent,' I guess."

Carlotta was writing in her small notebook. Now she knew the step to take after she wrote "The End" on the last page of her memoir. It was always best to be prepared.

"You know, Mrs. Moon, you should join the Writers' Workshop. They meet in the basement twice a month. They know more about this stuff than I do."

Carlotta smiled, "I'm not a joiner, Arnie." She added, to herself, *I'm a leader.* Carlotta did not join other people's groups. Other people attempted to join hers. And she decided who was to be let in. A writers' group would be for mere beginners. She had little patience for beginners. "And," added Carlotta aloud, "the Writers' Workshop is obviously a group for people who write things."

Arnie said, "Aw, come on, Mrs. Moon. I know you're not just making conversation. Aren't you working on a book yourself?"

Carlotta, unable to resist the thrill of sharing her excitement about the child of her brain, told Arnie about *The Golden Bonds of Friendship*. She swore him to secrecy. If what she knew about human nature applied to Arnie (and why shouldn't it?), the whole town would know she was writing a fascinating book by late afternoon.

Carlotta was halfway to the door when she stopped and decided to make this visit a double mission. She pivoted and returned to Arnie's counter.

"Arnie, you know that Hope always has had a soft spot in her heart for you." If this was a lie, it was a lie that could become true just by the chain of events that might happen by Carlotta's stating it, which therefore meant that it was not, strictly speaking, a lie.

Arnie looked very pleased.

"Well, no, I didn't know that. And I think very highly of Hope. Always have."

I know that already. Everyone does.

"Maybe you could lock the Bookstore up for a few minutes and just run down the street to stop in at the Good Fortune Café sometimes. She's very busy, you know, a hardworking businesswoman, but you'll see all the changes she's been making in there, and maybe you can chat a bit. Go at a slower time of day, say, ten or ten-thirty."

Arnie smiled. A handsome smile. What a mercy it was that he bore no physical resemblance to his weird Aunt Edith. He really was a nice looking young man. And he was so charmingly interested in her book.

Under the shop's awning, she opened her umbrella and smiled as she saw her literary future open before her.

-16-

A dramatic summer storm was lashing northern New York. Gibbons Corner residents were draped in hooded yellow raincoats, their heads down as they walked through the slanting rain. Norbert and Ivy were warm and dry in the Good Fortune Café when a new customer, face concealed behind a black scarf and body covered in a dark plastic poncho, marched toward them from the counter with a scone and a cup of espresso.

"May I?" asked the figure, setting down its order on the table, and proceeded to unwrap in the style of the Invisible Man.

That's when Norbert did a double take. Margaret was supposed to be in New Jersey, visiting her daughter Vivian. So what was she doing here?

As the petite white-haired woman sat down, Norbert's question stopped in his throat. *This* Margaret was subtly different from the Margaret he knew. Her forehead was narrower, and her nose had a small bump just below the bridge. Otherwise, she was strikingly like his friend. She even had Margaret's bright blue eyes.

Before he could stop himself, Norbert gasped, *"Mabel?"*

The little woman's eyes opened wide and her mouth formed an "O."

"You *are* a real psychic!" she exclaimed. "How could you know my name?"

"Actually," admitted Norbert, "that wasn't a demonstration of psychic ability."

Mabel looked disappointed.

Norbert explained. "You see, I'm a friend of Margaret's."

Mabel brightened. "Margaret Birch! Hey! She's *my* friend, too!" she asserted. "I've come to see her. *Surprise! Ha ha!* I might even decide to stay with her. But she's not home right now, I guess."

"Oh, dear. You didn't call before you came? You came all the way from Rochester?"

"Yeah. It's just an hour and a half on the bus. I wasn't sure I was coming here until I was already on my way. You know how *that* goes!" Mabel eyed Norbert and he felt she was deciding right then that no, Norbert didn't know how that went.

"And you don't have a cell phone?" asked Norbert.

"Oh, *God*, no!" said Mabel. "Whatever for?"

"Well, it's just that you could have saved yourself some inconvenience. You see, Margaret is in New Jersey visiting her daughter. She's due back in two days."

"No biggie," shrugged Mabel. "I'll wait. In the meantime, *I'll* find things to do," she purred with innuendo. "For starters, I'll have my fortune read!" She winked at Norbert. "You're a good lookin' fella," she added.

It had been a while since Norbert had had such a compliment from a woman. In fact, had he ever had such a compliment?

Mabel, glimpsing Ivy in her pink sweater, stretching and peering at her over the edge of Norbert's man purse, concluded, "Oh. But you're.... That's fine. Some of my best friends are."

"I'm sorry?" asked Norbert.

"Nothing to be sorry about, my dear. We're living in modern times, thank goodness. We can all be who we are! And *you* are a fortune-teller, so let's go!"

"Certainly. But let me just ask... Margaret said you thought Gibbons Corner was a narrow-minded small town, and that you would never come back here. What made you change your mind?"

"Well, hon, when I was here for a little vacation, I gotta say, I got the feeling it was a little judge-y. It's a cute town, but I felt like a chicken out of water. You know?"

Norbert saw this image in his mind, and it occurred to him that a chicken would be happier out of water than in it, but he only smiled and nodded.

"So, I got back to my apartment in Rochester, in my building where nobody knows nobody. All my friends are gone now. And I thought about Margaret, and the fun *she* has. How much she loves her friends and how much they love her. She belongs to some kind of—club, I think she called it—and it sounded like a riot. They get up to all kinds of things. And there I am, sitting alone in my apartment. I go to the bars, and I don't know anyone anymore. And finally, I said to myself, 'Mabel, old girl, what are you *doing*?' That's when it came to me. I wanna meet the Club."

Norbert pictured this meeting. It would create a sensation.

"What do my cards say about it?" Mabel wanted to know.

Norbert studied Mabel's horseshoe spread. The Queen of Diamonds and the Queen of Spades regarded each other in a murderous stare-down, while other face cards gathered around.

The Queen of Diamonds was Carlotta's card.

It seemed that the Queen of Spades had come to town.

The spread as a whole indicated a sharp personality clash and a merry adventure.

"I see here that you will have a lot of fun in Gibbons Corner, and make many new friends. There may be one person you have a little bit of difficulty with, however."

"Ha! Only one person? If I only have difficulty with one person, that will be a nice change for me!"

"Well! I think you will be quite the surprise! You're going to wait till Margaret comes back, and then you'll present yourself to the Club, eh?"

"Eh?" mocked Mabel. "That's cute, the way you say 'eh?'—like a Canadian. Yeah. I'll 'present myself to the Club,' as you say. After that—who knows? Maybe I'll feel like I belong here, and stay. I love clubs. Every club I've ever joined—I've always wound up being the leader."

Norbert put his hand to his mouth. He saw the future in a flash, and he felt a pang for Carlotta; he had come to like her so much. He shouldn't smile. But he just couldn't help it.

-17-

On this wet afternoon, Carlotta was at home, immersed in her literary labors. Her morning visit to Arnie at Butlers Books had inspired her. She cast her memory back over her life's history and wrote:

The advantage of being in a loveless marriage is that you do have your independence. You can do as you please. No one cares.

She stopped and read this over. Did it sound self-pitying? She thought it might. She struck it out.

She instead turned her pen to those aspects of her life which showed her in her best light. Those aspects, naturally, involved the Club. Through the Club, she had been able to realize her potential, exploring new horizons and new worlds with her friends scrambling behind her, trying to keep up. She had learned the deep psychology of leadership, how to make each person feel valued and appreciated, and how to give them all the impression that she was doing an enormous amount of work behind the scenes on their behalf to keep them entertained. As she led them toward continual self-development, she developed herself. Indeed, the Club was so much a part of her, it was her primary means of self-expression. It was her mirror into her own mind. Just as a person in a beautiful marriage might feel at one with the spouse, Carlotta felt at one with her Club.

As long as I'm the leader, I'm needed. My place in the world is clear and secure.

The Club had been together since 1967. Through the decades, it had lost many members to death, desertion and exhaustion. Only the *crème de la crème* remained: those thirsty for novel experiences, possessing above-average energy, and a sweet willingness to follow their leader. Whenever she sensed they were about to get bored, Carlotta would switch to a new passion, and they would all come running after her. It had been very gratifying.

It's easy to manage people. Just stay one step ahead of them, and give them projects they can't resist.

Lately, however, the Club had shown a nasty tendency toward independence of thought. They'd been a little too enthralled with Norbert and his fortunes, and she'd been afraid for a moment that he would become their new guru. Luckily, Norbert didn't want the position. They'd resisted learning French when she'd told them they had to. And then, without her guidance, they'd shown a stubborn interest in that odd woman Edith Butler at the Center for Deeper Understanding, and her past-life regressions. At the end of last January, Carlotta whisked her Club away to Quebec's Winter Carnival, where she did all the French-speaking for everyone, because they found French "too hard," poor things. (She had an app on her phone which translated for her. She was able to use it without their perceiving, relatively naïve to technology as they were.) They had returned, appreciative of Carlotta's organizational and linguistic abilities. Thanks to Carlotta, the Club felt young and adventurous. Since their return from Canada, she had been keeping them busy with intellectual and cultural pursuits. She had them all back in hand now, and all was right in her world. But they would have to be watched.

-18-

Margaret, breathless with excitement, phoned them all: Carlotta, Lorraine, Birdie and Norbert, to announce she was bringing a guest to the watercolor class at the Art League on Wednesday afternoon.

"It's not necessary," Carlotta said, "to let us know in advance, Margaret. You don't need permission." Really, Margaret, at eighty-eight, was such a child, reflected Carlotta.

Margaret gasped, "I know! But this is a very *special* guest. You'll never guess who it is! Oh! You won't believe it!"

"Well, by all means, don't tell me, then," indulged Carlotta. "Let it be a surprise."

Carlotta had smiled tolerantly, hanging up the phone. Who could it be? Some celebrity? One of Margaret's far-flung grandchildren? An alumna of the Art League? Silly Margaret and her girlish excitement.

Carlotta, Lorraine, Birdie and Norbert had all arrived for class on time, and there was a bit of buzz in the air as they started to work, while anticipating the arrival of Margaret and her mystery guest. Norbert appeared to know all about it already, and was avoiding eye contact with everyone. He stood smiling and bent over the work counter, organizing brushes by size, as if it were a task that absorbed all of his attention.

Norbert had been one of the more successful projects of Carlotta's Club. The Norbert Project had been her idea, and look at him now. The Club had brought him from retirement and poverty to a gainful second career as a psychic in Carlotta's niece's coffee shop.

Everyone was waiting now for Margaret Birch. Tiny at four feet, eight inches, and still retaining the sparkle of her glamour-girl youth, proud and emotional Margaret, thought Carlotta. Not the brightest crayon in the box, but her credulity had afforded hours of merriment for Carlotta and Lorraine.

Carlotta was just finishing putting her still life arrangement in order (fake oranges and daffodils), when there was a clambering on the stairs leading up to the studio from the gallery. It did sound like the steps of two people. Strangely, Carlotta felt her heartbeat accelerate. She was actually excited about Margaret's little "surprise."

"Close your eyes, everyone!" exclaimed Margaret. "Are they closed? No peeking, now! Are you ready?"

Around the doorframe appeared Margaret's mischievous face. Just her face. She kept the rest of her hidden. What foolishness. And then, around the doorframe, appeared a second mischievous face, just like the first one.

Carlotta reached behind her for a chair, and sat down with a thump.

"You can open them now!" announced one of the Margaret-faces, to eight already wide-open eyes.

One minute, Carlotta would reflect later, you could be running your Club and have everything nicely in control. And the next, a crude woman wearing a baseball cap could burst into your world and ruin everything. It was what Norbert the psychic might call "a reversal of fortune."

-19-

The two small Margarets came bustling into the art studio, smiling widely, eyebrows raised, and round, blue eyes taking in the astonishment they were creating. For one wild moment Carlotta thought they might begin singing "We represent the Lullaby League." The effect was surreal.

One Margaret said, "Oh! I have to introduce you! Everyone, this is Mabel Paine!"

Carlotta, dumbstruck, said nothing, for once. The fictional character now had a last name. Paine. Why did Carlotta sense that this surname was to be prophetic?

Birdie breathed, "Far out." She often responded like a hippie from the sixties. Perhaps because she was a hippie from the sixties.

Lorraine bellowed, "You gotta be kidding!"

Norbert, the only one who could remember to say the expected, said, "Hello, Mabel."

Margaret said, "And Mabel, let me introduce you to my friends! You've already met Norbert Zelenka."

Mabel said, in a voice that was gravelly and hard-living, not like Margaret's higher-pitched one, "Oh, Norb and I *know* each other, I can't say we don't!"

What on earth is the creature implying?

Mabel gave Norbert a wink, as he stood transfixed. "Norb read my cards the day I got into town, didn't you, hon?"

Norb? No one calls him that.

Suddenly Carlotta felt possessive of Norbert. This stranger insinuated that she and Norbert had had some sort of experience together. What right had she? Norbert belonged to the Club. That is, he wasn't a *member,* of course, but he belonged to the Club as one of their projects.

"And this is Lorraine Andretta. Lorraine teaches the colored pencils class. You were admiring her work in the gallery window just now."

Lorraine opened her mouth to speak, but no wisecrack issued forth, so she shut it again.

"And this is Birdie Walsh."

"Didn't I talk to you in Edwards Cove one day?" asked Mabel, scratching her head. "Sure I did!"

"Oh," said Birdie. "So you *were* real."

"I was *real? I am* real!" Mabel looked around the class for affirmation.

Margaret went on: "Birdie teaches the watercolor class— that's this one! Only, it's usually just us, so she doesn't have to teach so much; we just paint together, like we've been doing for years already. You can use my supplies, Mabel. It's easy—you'll see!"

Birdie looked as if she were seeing a ghost; but then, she always looked that way.

"And this is Carlotta Moon. Carlotta teaches the class in oil painting. She's won tons of prizes for her work. Carlotta's sort of the Leader of our Club."

Sort of?

Mabel seemed to take Carlotta's measure, her bright eyes moving from Carlotta's white salon-styled hair down to her classic navy canvas slip-on shoes. Carlotta took Mabel's measure, giving her "the elevator eyes," from Mabel's navy blue Yankees cap resting atop her white curls, down to her rain boots which she should have taken off to avoid making puddles on the studio's hardwood floor.

Remembering her role as head of state, Carlotta stepped forward and extended her hand. Mabel looked at it in surprise before pumping it.

"Welcome, Mabel. I'm afraid I'm a bit muddled," said Carlotta, only vaguely aware she was quoting Glinda from *The Wizard of Oz*. It was just that these two spritely little ladies put her in mind of Munchkins, unfortunately. They were so extremely short. "You see, we thought you were imaginary. That is, you *were* imaginary. We made you up, of course. But now you're here." A deep blush suffused Carlotta's cheeks, and she had the mortifying realization that she was talking like an idiot.

Mabel snorted. "The *hell* I'm imaginary! Pinch me!"

Carlotta took a step backward. She looked to Margaret for a way out of her bewilderment. "But Margaret, how can it be? I don't understand. I mean, all those Mabel stories—well, I'm sorry to say, it was all a joke. None of it was *true*. When I told you I'd seen a woman who looked just like you at the bank, flirting with the manager, and Lorraine said she saw you in a patrol car, singing hymns—none of that ever actually *happened*. You know that, of course."

Margaret raised her chin and her blue eyes shone. "You *lied* to me. I *knew* it. You and Lorraine lied to me."

Mabel, watching this exchange from the sidelines, grinned. "You people are real creative. Fact is, I don't even know any hymns. Can't say that I do. And wearing a bathing suit and shorts to the bank? Now, that's one thing even *I* wouldn't do."

Mabel had clearly forgiven all of the slander already. She was having a good time, as anyone could see.

Margaret kept her eyes locked on Carlotta's.

Carlotta said, "We're sorry, Margaret. Truly, we are. It started out to be a funny joke. You just didn't catch on." Too late, Carlotta realized her misstep.

Margaret's blue gaze became laser-like. "Once again, not as smart as you, eh, Carlotta? And you, too, Lorraine? *Et tu, Bruté?*" Despite the disagreeable circumstances, Margaret grabbed her opportunity to quote from *Julius Caesar*. Carlotta's Club appreciated classic literature.

"Birdie was in on it, too," said Carlotta, seeking safety in numbers. "She said she saw Mabel riding a bike down Main Street and then she saw her on the public access TV channel."

"Oh," inserted Birdie, twisting the excess of rings on her fingers, "but I really did see Mabel. *I* wasn't lying. Or—joking. I didn't know it *was* a joke."

"Yeah," offered Mabel. "I did go for a little spin on a rented bike one day. It's way easier to ride a bike in this one-horse town than in Rochester. And yeah, I got on Community TV one day—I love getting on television, don't you?" Mabel looked around at the group which was still struggling to catch up.

Lorraine threw her hands in the air. "Hold on! I'm missing something here. How could it happen that we made up a bunch of stories about an imaginary person, and then it turns out the person really exists? What the hell is going on here?"

Margaret stood up as tall as she could. She was the only one who could clear up the mess her friends had made. It was not often that she found herself at such an advantage.

"You may remember how the name 'Mabel' first came up? I was coming back to town from Edwards Cove after a day of shopping. A man on the bus approached me and acted like he knew me."

"That was Walter Strand," put in Mabel. "An old pal of mine. He's a womanizer; I can't say he isn't." She laughed and shook her head.

Lecherous woman, thought Carlotta.

Margaret resumed, "But I'd never seen him before in my life. He made personal remarks, and he called me Mabel. But when I came to the studio and told you all about it, you started saying *you'd* seen Mabel, too. Stumbling drunk out of the Alibi Bar. Et cetera." Here, Margaret took some deep breaths.

"Yeah," inserted Mabel. "I don't drink like that anymore. My doctor would kill me."

"Yes," admitted Carlotta, ignoring Mabel. "But then *you* came in one day and said you'd met Mabel by coincidence on the street, she was leaving town and none of us would ever see her again. I thought you were so clever, to think of resolving the problem that way!" Perhaps a little flattery would calm Margaret down.

Mabel and Norbert, both up to date and well-informed on the whole Mabel-Margaret episode, stood together watching the volleys between Margaret and Carlotta, their heads snapping back and forth.

"So you thought I made that up? About the dinner at Renata's?"

"Didn't you?"

"Of course not. Not *everyone* lies to their dearest friends, Carlotta."

Carlotta winced at the force of this backhand smash, and felt a flash of resentment. How dare Margaret make her look so bad? Lorraine jumped in to lob the ball from Carlotta's court.

"Oh, come on, Margaret! You never suspected we were putting you on?" Lorraine put her hands on her hips.

"Actually, at the end, I did. I'll admit, when I was able to tell you I'd met Mabel, I knew you'd be very confused. And that gave me *some* satisfaction."

"Which you deserved—after three weeks of aggravation!" Norbert spoke up.

Annoying man.

Ivy, Norbert's aged white Chihuahua, jumped out of her basket against the wall and came running on her skinny little legs into the middle of the fray, barking madly, and turning herself about. This was turning into a riot. Norbert picked her up and she went silent, but she continued to look accusingly at everyone as she trembled in his arms.

-20-

Six days passed quietly. Carlotta's book had been flowing from her pen, and she was in high spirits.

It was Tuesday night, and almost time for Oil Painting with Carlotta. Carlotta marched with her head high and shoulders back, through the mid-August twilight. It was only a block and a half from her Edwardian-style home on Clarence Avenue to the Art League on Main Street. As she walked, she enjoyed breathing in the fresh night air and soaking in the quiet. What an artist needs, thought Carlotta, is quiet, and lots of it.

As a painting teacher, Carlotta was popular. Striding about the studio, she gave plenty of individual attention, helping her students to achieve their own painterly aims. She had a knack for understanding what each student was hoping to achieve, and her suggestions helped many a budding painter to move up to the next level of achievement. She loved painting and helped her students to love it as she did. Along with her art instruction, she spooned out generous dollops of culture and personal philosophy.

The stillness of the small lakeside town was punctuated by a railroad whistle as a train lumbered along the tracks two blocks west of the Art League, reminding Carlotta that there were other places beyond the comfortable, peaceful world of Gibbons Corner. Nice places to visit, but everyone Carlotta knew agreed, there was no better place to live.

As she approached the entrance of the Art League, Carlotta saw Norbert with his white box coming out of Gloria's Bakery.

Norbert's four-pound Chihuahua peered out at Carlotta from his man purse/dog carrier.

"Good evening, Norbert. Good evening, Ivy," said Carlotta, as Norbert opened the door for her.

"Hello, Carlotta. It's getting to be a big class, isn't it?"

Carlotta nodded with satisfaction. She wondered if Margaret would bring Mabel again, and feared she would. Margaret had gotten so much attention by bringing Mabel to Birdie's class, she was bound to leverage Mabel again today. People who needed to be the center of attention were so tiresome. But it was of no consequence. They'd gotten no painting done when the doubles had burst into Birdie's watercolor class. Margaret had made such a scene. The little replica-woman Mabel was so awful, Carlotta could be sure of one thing: no one in their circle would like her. How could they? Loud, raucous, trumpeting specimen of a human being. Carlotta would be kind to her. And make sure to be seen doing so. And then the creature, seeing that she did not and could not ever fit in, would go away.

There were eight students on the roster, and such a large class would require Carlotta's full professional attention.

After hanging her coat and changing from street shoes to slip-ons, Carlotta mounted the stairs to the gallery and found most of the class setting up. Margaret had not yet arrived. Carlotta braced herself for another Lullaby League entrance.

Childish people, like real children, tend to repeat jokes after they are no longer funny.

The comforting aroma of turpentine filled the space. Carlotta flicked on a Mozart CD, and the stimulating strains of the opening scene of *The Magic Flute* began to build.

Carlotta, with her smattering of German, was satisfied to think that she alone of everyone in the studio understood the lyrics:

Oh, help me, oh help me, oh help me!
My mind is in danger!
The venomous monster will soon
Overtake me and I-- can't-- escape!

Well, it was *something* like that, anyway. Such a funny scene. Herr Mozart was such a genius, she thought. Such a gift for pointing out the ridiculous.

Lorraine, her black hair tied back, was hooking a photograph onto her canvas. Beside her, the young mother was turning her canvas this way and that, trying to decide: vertical or horizontal? The teenage girl took out her earbuds and gave Carlotta the "thumbs-up" sign as she set up her easel.

Ginger-haired, adolescent Liam, with his penchant for the macabre, was looking over Birdie's shoulder at her work-in-progress: an abstract, grey background, and faces peering at the viewer with intense oversized eyes, as if through some gauze-like material. *Dear, strange, out-there Birdie.*

"Cool, Mrs. Walsh!" approved Liam. "But you know what you should do? You should paint a bloody skull—right *there!*" He traced delicately with his pinky finger in front of the canvas where the improvement should go.

Arnie Butler, the manager of Butler's Books, was a recent addition to the class. The young man had the defect of excessive discretion, it seemed. He had not spilled the beans about Carlotta's literary work in progress to anyone, as far as she could perceive. Still, he was a nice young man and Carlotta wondered why her niece Hope didn't have the time of day for him. Not that young women today needed to be married. Not at all. Carlotta approved of the many choices available now to young people. Certainly.

The ever-smiling Norbert (the man had some unfortunate sort of tic that made him smile all the time, regardless of circumstances) was advising Arnie on art supplies.

"You'll be happier with your painting if you invest in the best brushes you can get," said Norbert.

"So true, Norbert!" said Carlotta, turning down the music to a faint whine, so that she could be heard by all. "A good brush makes all the difference between satisfaction and frustration. Buy the best, and take loving care of it," she went on, addressing the whole class as she began her slow and steady pace around the studio. "A cheap brush—or even a good one that has been allowed to dry with a little bit of paint in the bristles— will have unruly hairs sticking out that will ruin your work. As the poet Sara Teasdale wrote: 'Spend all you have for loveliness, buy it and never count the cost.'"

If Carlotta were to compose her own Ten Commandments, "Buy the best," would be one of them. Carlotta had never known want. Another of her Commandments would have been, "Take excellent care of what you have." Carlotta did not dispose of anything valuable, be it a high-quality, well-cared for old brush or friend. After choosing the best for herself, she valued what was hers, and she held on to it.

Where *was* Margaret? Carlotta wondered. No doubt she and that woman were planning to make a late entrance for dramatic effect. Carlotta would just detonate that bombshell right now.

"Most of you," intoned Carlotta as she strode, tilting her head slightly before each canvas, "were here in my Oil Painting Class last month, when Margaret started talking about having a double. She said this other woman who looked like her—."

Liam interrupted here: "Her *doppelganger!* Ha!"

Carlotta continued, "Yes. Her double, according to her, was going around town doing scandalous things."

Norbert's head shot up over his canvas. "Actually, Margaret was *told* that her double was doing scandalous things. Margaret was upset about it."

"Whatever," said Carlotta, borrowing a convenient term she had heard her granddaughter Summer use so often. "The *point* is, we all thought that the double was just made up."

The young mother wrinkled her brow. "Who made up the double?"

Carlotta stepped adroitly around this landmine, as Lorraine looked on with narrowed eyes.

"Apparently, no one. The double, in fact, exists," she said.

The class had stopped painting and all eyes were on Carlotta. She enjoyed the moment. Was there any better feeling than the sense of importance that came with being the center of things?

"You all may get to meet her very soon," said Carlotta, as if she were promising a birthday party to good children.

The teenage girl and the young mother chorused, "*Meet her?*"

Carlotta began, "Yes. Her full name is--."

"MABEL PAINE!" crowed a tobacco-stained voice from the stairs, and two tiny look-alike white-haired ladies stepped into the art studio.

Margaret and Mabel stood side by side, smiling at the class like giggly twin sisters.

The room fell silent, except for a barely audible screeching soprano that sounded like a mosquito circling the room. Carlotta clicked off the CD player.

"You look like *twins!*" thrilled the teenage girl, stating the obvious.

"Well, will you look at that," commented Arnie inanely, and Carlotta thought that Hope did well to not give him the time of day.

"You look exactly alike!" breathed the young mother, unnecessarily.

Margaret introduced her double to the young mother, the high school girl, Arnie, and Liam, as Mabel grinned and greeted each one. Mabel was clearly exultant as everyone's eyes ricocheted back and forth between her and Margaret.

Mabel crowed, "Aren't we a sight for sour eyes? Ha ha!"

Carlotta tried to conjure up an image of sour eyes, but was unsuccessful.

Liam enthused, "Wow. So, like, one of you could commit a murder? And, like, the other one could take the rap?"

"Aw, hon," chuckled Mabel, "I think we can have more fun than *that*."

"Which is which?" exclaimed Lorraine. "I mean, who is who?"

"But you *can* see differences," observed Birdie. Her maxi skirt swaying, she stepped toward the matched pair to get a closer look. Lifting her brush and outlining, as if she were about to paint a portrait of the two of them, she said, "Mabel, you are just an inch or two taller. Margaret, your forehead is wider. And Mabel, you have the smallest bump on your nose, just below the bridge--." Here, Birdie dabbed her brush into the air as if marking the spot.

Liam joined in, "But there's no mole."

"That's right," said Carlotta, "The made-up Mabel had a beauty mark, or a mole, as you say, Liam, under one eye. But the real Mabel doesn't."

"Who made up the mole?" asked the young mother, once again deviating into dangerous terrain.

"It doesn't *matter* now," said Carlotta, disposing of the mole once and for all. *"There is no mole."*

As the class threatened to ask more pointed questions, Carlotta steered them back toward their art.

"Margaret, you can help Mabel settle in. We need to get on with our painting." Carlotta lifted her chin, pretending to search for a quote she had actually memorized that morning: "As Vincent said, 'the only time I feel alive is when I'm painting.'"

Mabel asked, looking around, "Who's Vincent?"

"Vincent Van Gogh," said Carlotta, smiling widely. "A famous painter."

Mabel seemed to ponder. "The *only* time he feels alive is when he's *painting*? Man. That kinda limits a person, doesn't it?"

Lorraine twisted her mouth and shot a look at Carlotta. They would laugh together later about this uncultured woman.

Norbert offered, "There are kolaczkis on the counter. They're Polish pastries. *Koh-latch-keys* is how you say it. Help yourself, Mabel, before you get pigment on your fingers."

"Oh, I'm not here to paint!" exclaimed Mabel. "Painting would bore me to tears."

If this irritant thought she was going to close down another day's creative effort, she had another think coming. But then, Carlotta had to be seen being kind to Mabel.

"Mabel, how funny," said Carlotta in her tinkling voice. "You're in a painting class. What else would you do, if not paint?"

"Well, I could pose," Mabel suggested.

Carlotta stared at the woman's nest of white hair exploding from under her blue baseball cap and at her oversized tie dyed tee shirt. If she had Margaret's face and build, she certainly didn't have Margaret's sense of style.

Mabel, as if to help Carlotta understand the concept she was putting forth, added, "You know? Like a model?"

"Ah," said Carlotta. "But you see, everyone is already engaged in a work-in-progress."

"That's okay, Mrs. Moon!" said Liam. "We could put that work aside and grab a new canvas, y'know?"

Before Carlotta could squelch the idea, the room was in motion: a new canvas was settling onto each easel, and Norbert was helping Mabel to pull the light-weight wicker couch to the front and center of the room, so that all the painters would have a clear view of her.

As if she owns the place.

Margaret rushed to put on her smock and set up for this once-in-a-lifetime opportunity to paint a self-portrait of a model who was not herself.

"I always wanted to try modeling," said Mabel. "I've been a lot of things in my life…"

I'll just bet you have.

"But never a model. Try everything, that's what I say!"

Mabel experimented with various poses, taking direction from the class. Recumbent? Legs crossed? Arm up over the back of the sofa? Or arms folded?

As the art students disagreed with one another, Lorraine said at last, "Just make yourself comfortable, Mabel. Sit however you want, as long as it's a position you can sit still in for about forty minutes."

Mabel said, "Sitting still has never been my strong suit."

Lorraine assured her, "We can stop a couple of times for a break, if you need to."

"Oh, I'll be okay as long as I can talk. My mouth can move, right?"

"As long as you can move your mouth without moving anything else," said Margaret, thrilling with the spotlight that she and Mabel shared. "That can be trickier than you think."

Mabel adjusted herself, sitting comfortably on the sofa, with a perfectly good sofa cushion tucked firmly into her armpit (*Who does that?*), and then offered, "Do you want me to take off my clothes? Isn't that what you artists do?"

Carlotta leapt in. "That would be Life Drawing, Mabel, and no thank you. I don't think we are prepared for that today."

"Well," said Mabel, "if you change your minds, just whistle. It's warm enough in here! I don't have any hang-ups. I got rid of all my hang-ups in the sixties."

Mabel quickly mastered the skill of keeping perfectly still while talking. There was no stopping the woman's streaming monologue. She recounted stories that couldn't possibly be true about people who couldn't possibly be real. She filled the eyes and the ears of the class.

"In Rochester," she claimed, "there's a nudist colony, but it only has one member. Ha ha! It's just this one naked guy. He'll be sitting on a park bench in the center of town on a cold day. Everyone just goes, oh, there's the nudist! He's out again! Ha ha! Then he gets arrested. Poor fella. And they call this a free country?

"Speaking of nudists, many years ago, I lived in the woods in Georgia with a boyfriend who had no teeth. True story. We used to gather berries and bark to sell. In those days, there were a lot of people with no teeth in the woods doing that."

The young mother interrupted and sensibly asked, "Wait. Who buys *bark?*"

But Mabel just laughed, as if the young mother had made a very funny joke, and continued her rambling.

"My friend Zelda is ninety-seven years old and still cuts hair! I kid you not. She can't see, of course. Never could, actually. Her eyes are three inches from the scissors. It's kind of funny to watch her in the mirror. A haircut from her takes a pretty long time. But she doesn't charge much. And she does a real good job. I can't say she doesn't.

"Speaking of my friends, one was supposed to be a mermaid."

Lorraine asked, "Whaddaya mean, 'supposed to be?'"

"She was born with fish parts. They fixed her, at birth, *you* know. But the weird thing is, all her life she's been a really good swimmer. Life's funny, huh?"

Mabel's stories varied from humorous to off-color to something akin to magical realism. What kind of person makes things up about people? Was this woman even sane?

"I loved an artist once. In the early seventies, I had a boyfriend everyone called Smokey. Do I need to tell you why? Ha ha! He stayed at home and drew pictures of monsters while I worked to support us. Golly, I loved that man. He became a ventriloquist and left me.

"I never stayed sad after a breakup. I always said, 'there's plenty more ice in the sea.' I've had some good times! I can't say I haven't! Believe it or not, I was quite volumptuous when I was young." exulted Mabel.

Carlotta was reminded at once of Mrs. Malaprop, the character from a Richard Sheridan play who was famous for making up her own ridiculous words, and Chaucer's *Canterbury Tales*--especially the indecent ones. Really, there was young Liam to think of, and the teenage girl. After Carlotta had endured fifteen minutes of non-stop nasty narrative, she snapped on the CD player and turned the volume all the way up. She adored *The Magic Flute*. All right-thinking people did.

-21-

Much disturbed, Carlotta called Summer and Hope, who rushed over to her home to share in the gossip she had lightheartedly promised them. In truth, her heart felt anything but light.

"Tell us, Gramma!" said Summer. "It sounds so interesting! About Aunt Margaret's double."

(Both Hope and Summer always called the women in Carlotta's Club "Aunt.")

Hope asked, "So, what's she like?"

The young women leaned forward.

Carlotta smiled.

"Well, let me think how to put this."

Hope whistled.

Voicing Hope's thought, Summer said, "That bad, huh?"

Hope and Summer exchanged glances.

Carlotta said, "Well, my dears, you know the old saying, 'If you can't--."

Although their childhoods had been consecutive, being twenty years apart by birth, Summer and Hope had both received this doctrine from Carlotta. They chorused: " 'If you can't say something nice, don't say anything at all.'"

"Yes. Words to live by, I believe."

Then Carlotta launched, as her company knew she would, into a bitingly comical description of Margaret's doppelganger.

"So, like, no one likes her, right?" asked Summer.

The unkindness of youth!

"Summer, of *course* we all like her. Even if her ways are odd. She's just different from us."

"*Way* different," said Summer, refusing to be chastened.

"I don't expect she'll stay here long. It's not her kind of town, Gibbons Corner. We love it, but she's from Rochester. I guess quirky people don't stand out so much in big cities. Anyway." Carlotta poured the tea into the china cups. "She won't last."

"*That* sounds menacing, Gramma," said Summer.

"You know what I mean. She won't want to stay."

"And she's living with Aunt Margaret?" asked Hope.

"*That* won't work," predicted Summer, speaking with her mouth full of banana bread.

Carlotta reflected that years of instruction can amount to disappointing results, when it comes to table manners.

"Actually, Margaret seemed to be excited about the arrangement. She said she was looking forward to sharing her morning coffee with someone, after years of having only Myrtle the cat to talk to. And Mabel was excited about meeting the cat, and said they'd be 'the three M's: Margaret, Myrtle and Mabel.' As if she were planning on settling in for a while."

Hope said, "There's a lot more to sharing your living space than just morning coffee."

The three women paused for a moment, picturing the three M's in a domestic scene.

"How bizarre it must have been," said Summer, "to see Aunt Margaret and Mabel side by side in the art studio."

"Yeah," said Hope. "I'd love to see that."

"Me, too," said Summer. "What a sight!"

"I'm sure you'll see the pair of them soon enough," said Carlotta, realizing too late what she was proposing.

"When?" asked Summer and Hope together.

Carlotta was not sure why the idea of such a meeting displeased her, but it did.

"We'll have to arrange that—very soon."

She changed the subject.

"Hope, Arnie from the book store was just asking about you. He talks about you in the most flattering terms, you know. I really think if you just gave him a nod--."

-22-

Before leaving for lunch at Margaret's condo, Carlotta opened the end table drawer in her living room where her indispensable reference books lay concealed. Carlotta had not cared one bit for Mabel's easy commandeering of the Club's attention in her oil painting class. The entire room had seemed transfixed by this awful woman, and the more dreadful she became, the more entranced they were. It defied explanation. How could anyone like Mabel? And yet, it seemed as if they did.

Carlotta moved aside *How to Discuss Classics You Haven't Read,* to reach *French to Impress.* This was the volume that Carlotta wanted to peruse today, just for a quick refresher.

If there's one way to put a person in her place, speaking to her in a language of culture and refinement that she doesn't know, should do it.

What she wanted today were some conversational gems to throw in casually, to let Mabel know that Carlotta and her Club spoke to each other in French. If that didn't show her that she didn't belong, well, if that didn't show her, Carlotta would have to think of something else. Thinking of something else was never a problem for Carlotta's swarming brain.

A few expressions of delight would be easy to work into the discussion. Carlotta ran her red nail down a page.

C'est trop mignon! — "It's so cute!"

J'aime bien — "I like very much."

C'est merveilleux! – "It's wonderful."

Yes, these, along with the usual French greetings that her friends knew and responded to automatically now, thanks to her persistent tutelage, would be enough to make Mabel feel out of place. Not that Carlotta would ever be so lacking in manners as to make anyone feel out of place. But if Mabel didn't speak French, was that Carlotta's fault?

Carlotta was actually looking forward to dealing with Margaret's new roommate. Margaret had the distinction of being the Club's best cook, so an exceptional spread could be expected. Margaret had invited only the Club and Norbert.

"Gramma," Summer had said one day to Carlotta as they drank tea at the Good Fortune Café, "why do you always say 'the Club *and* Norbert?' Why isn't Mr. Zelenka a member of the Club by now?"

Summer had a soft spot for Norbert. She seemed to confide in him and trust him like a sort of father figure. And certainly, their relationship seemed to have brought about a wonderful change in her. She had become the more light-hearted girl she used to be, long ago. Carlotta had been able to worry a little less about her granddaughter, and she knew that was in some way thanks to Norbert.

Carlotta had laughed. "Norbert is a gentleman, Summer."

"So?"

"The Club is primarily about intelligent conversation, dear. Men, in general, are not gifted conversationalists, you know. Have you ever noticed? They tend to stall psychologically-oriented discussions. They want to talk about baseball and waste time. Men, just by entering the room, change the atmosphere. They introduce... a certain energy."

Summer smiled. "You sound like Aunt Birdie, talking about people's energy."

"Don't pretend you don't know what I mean. Men don't want to talk about what we like to talk about." Carlotta stirred her tea, even though she hadn't added cream or sugar. "And then...they tend to want to *run* things."

"Ah!" Summer had said annoyingly. "There it is!"

"It's always been a women's club. Since the sixties. That's a long time."

Summer had cast her eyes to the ceiling and said, "Oh, Gramma. Gender discrimination is so *passé.*"

Margaret's condo on Washington Street was an aesthetic abomination in rose pink and mint green, but friends didn't remark upon friends' shortcomings. Carlotta was the last to arrive, by plan. She wanted to give her friends the chance to talk about her and to look forward to the fun and direction she could be relied upon to provide. The anticipation would be nice for them.

She took a deep breath as she stepped over the threshold, preparing to ignore the kitschy clutter that was Margaret's home. At least, the clutter was always organized. (The phrase, *I can't say it isn't,* rose to her mind, and she wondered where that came from.)

The aromas of bread, potato and tomato filled the air encouragingly.

Her first act on entering this or any other room, was to scan the occupants for just a moment to take in what everyone was wearing. Part of the interest in going anywhere at all was in noticing people's clothes.

Margaret wore a green dress with small white polka dots, belted at the waist in matching fabric. She seemed to own a polka dot dress in every color. "Polka dots are so cheerful, aren't they?" she always said.

Norbert wore a white shirt and grey slacks, and good black shoes. Quite an improvement from the day she and the Club had gone to his house to persuade him to become a fortune-teller, and his shoes were falling apart. The fortune-telling trade was going strong, apparently.

Birdie fluttered in a maxi dress with capacious bell sleeves, and her earrings were swinging as she laughed with Lorraine, who had just delivered an amusing line. Lorraine wore her usual simple uniform-like outfit: black slacks and a smock-y white shirt.

And there was Mabel. In sweats.

Carlotta smoothed a hand over her own black and cream sheath dress that fell becomingly to her mid-calf, and smiled at Mabel with satisfaction.

Mabel smiled back.

"Hey, it's Carlotta!" she announced merrily. "You're late! Come on in!"

Of all the irritating things Mabel might have chosen to say, "Come on in" was certainly at the top of the list. As if she *lived* here in Margaret's condo. As if these were *her* friends.

"I'm so sorry I'm a bit late," said Carlotta, preparing to make the excuse she had invented. She needn't have invented it.

"No problemo!" cried Mabel. "We've been having a fine time without you!"

Carlotta looked around at the happy faces and saw that this was true.

"Don't take that the wrong way!" trumpeted Mabel, and the group giggled at her witticism.

"The *real* fun doesn't start until Carlotta gets here!" said Lorraine, loyally.

Dear Lorraine, thought Carlotta gratefully.

Lorraine went on, "I've been telling Mabel about some of the fun things to do around here. We oughta take her out and show her the sights."

Treacherous Lorraine, thought Carlotta.

Margaret called her guests to the table. The choice spots at any rectangular table, Carlotta knew, were the head and the foot. From either of those places, one could most easily control the flow of the general conversation. That had been her observation after years of paying close attention to such things. Margaret, in her own home, should have the head, of course. Therefore, the foot belonged to Carlotta.

Except that the foot was already occupied.

As Carlotta pulled the chair back from the white table cloth, she perceived a small weight on it. It was Myrtle, the monstrous black and white cat that Margaret kept. The thing lifted its head with a trill, and narrowed its eyes at Carlotta. Carlotta experienced a little *frisson* and gave a cry.

To say that Carlotta was terrified of cats was to state a bold-faced lie. Or was it a bald-faced lie? It was both. She would deny it until her last breath. Only the weak had phobias, and Carlotta took pride in her mental toughness.

"Oh, I'm sorry, Carlotta!" exclaimed Margaret. "Myrtle, get off that chair!"

Myrtle shot a look of surprise at Margaret, and then, one by one, glared at each of the human faces peering down at her.

"*I'll* get her," offered Mabel. "Myrtle and I are friends, aren't we, Myrtle?"

Mabel reached toward Myrtle, and Myrtle was up on her hind legs, anchoring her claws into Mabel's hand. Mabel drew back, and applied a white napkin to the stripes of red forming on her skin. Carlotta experienced at once an urge to laugh and a wave of nausea. She was at the same time both horrified and pleased at the cat's assault on their mutual antagonist.

"I'm so sorry!" cried Margaret. "No, Mabel, that cat is not anyone's friend, I'm afraid—except Carlotta's. For some strange reason, she loves only Carlotta. But Carlotta—."

Carlotta would not allow Margaret to announce to everyone—especially Mabel—that she suffered from a fear of cats. Because she didn't. To admit to a phobia was to show weakness. In fact, Carlotta thought, as she focused her attention on slowing her breath, this would be an excellent time to bring out her prepared French phrases. This would highlight her culture and education.

"*O, mais c'est mignon, Marguerite!*"

The Club and Norbert looked at Carlotta in puzzlement.

"You think she's *cute*?" asked Birdie.

"*Mais oui! C'est merveilleux!*"

"Marvelous?" asked Margaret. (Even Margaret could work that one out.)

"*Oui oui oui. Je l'aime bien!*"

"You really like her?" asked Lorraine.

Carlotta wanted to try to pet Myrtle at this point, to match her actions with her words, but she could only bring herself to wiggle her fingers over the animal's body. Myrtle took control of the situation and pushed her furry head against Carlotta's waving fingers before Carlotta could draw back. There. She had touched a cat. Let no one ever say that Carlotta had a fear of cats. The very idea.

Carlotta said, looking directly at Myrtle, "May I sit here?"

Everyone laughed.

"She doesn't understand English, you know, Carlotta," said Lorraine, adding sarcastically, "Try French."

Carlotta knitted her brow. Did she know the French for that? If she didn't, no one in this room would know the difference.

Carlotta addressed the cat: *"Je peux m'assoir ici, mademoiselle?"*

Before everyone could laugh again, Myrtle jumped off the chair, took three steps and gave a little shiver in her spine. She glanced once over her back at Carlotta and strode off toward the quiet and privacy of Margaret's bedroom.

While Margaret was lint-rolling the chair for Carlotta's use, and Mabel was good-naturedly dressing her wound in the adjoining kitchen, Ivy peered out of her purse-like pet carrier by the door. She perceived that Myrtle had left the room, and leapt out of the bag. Ivy greeted everyone with wiggles.

As Margaret brought the warm bread to the dining room, Mabel sat herself down at the head of the table. This seemed to bother Margaret not at all. *The shocking bad manners of this woman.* Well, it wasn't Carlotta's place to correct her. Everyone would notice, and it would serve her right.

"So you guys are fluent in French, huh?" said Mabel, shaking out her white napkin and tucking it into the neck of her sweatshirt. *Surprising that she knows how to use a napkin,* thought Carlotta, not enjoying her own meanness.

"I'm not," said Norbert. "I wish I did speak another language, but I only speak English. But the Club speaks French very well."

"Oh," demurred Lorraine, "not really. We know a little. Carlotta is fluent, though."

"Well," observed Mabel, "I guess French comes in handy for talking to cats."

The table laughed appreciatively.

It's not that funny, thought Carlotta. *Don't encourage her.*

"I don't speak French," said Mabel, splashing a piece of bread around in her bowl of soup.

Oh really? And you seem like the kind of person who would, thought Carlotta, wishing she could share her sarcasm with Lorraine, or even kick her under the table, but she was out of reach. Lorraine was not even making eye contact with Carlotta. All her attention seemed to be on Mabel Paine.

"Pero sí hablo español. Es más útil, el español, en Nueva York. Lo aprendí con mis amigos los boricuas—los puertorriqueños."

Mabel had everyone's attention.

"That's Spanish!" said Norbert, with confidence.

"It sure is, Norb," chuckled Mabel. She took a loud slurp of her soup and let out a satisfied sigh of approval.

Carlotta willed Lorraine to look at her, but she wouldn't.

"I studied Spanish in high school," said Norbert. "I have a couple of issues of *Reader's Digest* in Spanish, and I try to read them sometimes. It's interesting."

Carlotta turned to Norbert with the sensation that he was turning into someone she didn't know.

"The thing about Spanish," said Birdie, "is that it's so much easier to pronounce for English-speakers. Easier than French, for example."

"Yeah," said Lorraine. "That, and you know what else? The spelling makes sense. They don't throw in heaps of silent letters to throw you off the track. It's almost what you call a phonetic language, right, Mabel?"

"Well," apologized Mabel, "I don't know anything about the Phoenicians. I didn't go very far in school. I can't say that I did." She popped some soupy bread into her mouth and continued. "But I *would* say that anyone who really wants to, can learn to get by in Spanish. For one thing, native speakers usually help you out. At least, that's how it's always been for me."

Norbert leaned toward Mabel, showing the back of his head to Carlotta.

"Do you think you could teach *me* some Spanish, Mabel?" he asked.

Now Lorraine, Margaret and Birdie all turned the backs of their heads to Carlotta.

"And me? Me, too?" they all chorused.

-23-

It was the Club's newest project, and it was a smash from the very first day. Mabel's Spanish lessons were all anyone could think or talk about. Anyone except Carlotta, of course. Carlotta excluded herself on the grounds of being "too busy for Spanish." In the thrill of it all, no one even thought to ask her what was busying her so much.

Margaret's apartment filled with the music of Celia Cruz, as Mabel taught everyone to salsa. Learning how to salsa, in Mabel's opinion, was rudimentary to learning to speak the language. Norbert, as the only man, was very in demand as a partner, and he enjoyed his popularity immensely. He saw that he was not the only one who felt important in Mabel's Spanish class. Mabel was liberal with her praise, telling Lorraine that she had a natural gift for the language, enthusing that Birdie seemed to be picking it up with no effort at all, and affirming that Latin people everywhere would love Margaret for her naturally happy temperament. Everyone felt they were born to speak Spanish. Everyone looked forward to each lesson with excitement.

During a breathless pause in the music, Norbert asked, "Mabel, could you explain again how dancing will help us progress in speaking the language?"

"Sure, Norb!" said Mabel affably. "You gotta enter into the spirit of things. You gotta start with the fun part, that's what I say."

"You mean the *culture*," assisted Lorraine.

"Oh," said Norbert, who really wanted to know, "is salsa dancing a part of the culture of every Spanish-speaking country?"

"I don't know about that, Norb. I just know what my Puerto Rican friends like to do. They like to celebrate life, dance, and speak Spanish. So that's what *we're* doing."

Norbert nodded in approval. If his high school Spanish classes had started with salsa lessons, he thought, he might have taken a whole different path in his education. Instead of becoming an accountant, he might have become a translator. Or a dancer.

All the Spanish students in Margaret's apartment agreed. Spanish was fascinating. And Mabel was a lot of fun.

-24-

If Carlotta could not share her dark thoughts with any of her dearest friends, she could and did share them with the page. Her writing, which had been stalled due to a feeling that there was too much to say and no clear place to start, now became sharply focused on the topic of Mabel. The blue paper on Carlotta's writing desk filled with detailed descriptions of the gnome-like little crone. Although she was devoted to the art of exaggeration, Carlotta found it hard to exaggerate defects in one whose defects were already so exaggerated.

As she enjoyed her own genius flowing along on the pages of blue, she longed to share her work with her friends. She was torn between the excitement of having a secret and the admiration she was sure to gain by divulging to her friends that she was now a writer. How she would climb even higher in their esteem! Mabel, to be sure, could never write a book. Carlotta doubted that the Neanderthal woman had ever read one.

Carlotta invited the Club for tea. She had wanted to have just the Club: Lorraine, Birdie, and Margaret. But Margaret had said she didn't want to leave Mabel out.

Carlotta had said, "Of *course,* Mabel is welcome. If she really can't manage an hour or two without you."

"It's not that," Margaret had said. "She's very active and independent. Right now she's out walking with a seniors hiking group she found on the internet. It's just that Mabel has been including me in everything *she* does, and she does so *much.*"

"So why don't you take a hike?" asked Carlotta, knowing that Margaret wouldn't understand the dig.

"Oh!" breathed Margaret. "I can't keep up with Mabel sometimes. She has the energy of a sixty-year-old!"

Carlotta had decided that if Mabel was to be included, there was no reason not to invite Norbert. In fact, it occurred to her that there was every reason to invite Norbert. Carlotta felt the excitement of a New Idea dawning in her mind. On the periphery of the Club as Norbert was, Carlotta now had the magnanimous idea to confer membership upon him. That should shock them. The Club had not admitted a new member since Carter was president. While it was true that he would be the first gentleman to become a member of the Club, Carlotta was a forward thinker. There was no need to consult the other members. She was the leader. If they objected, she would tell them firmly that gender discrimination was definitely *passé*.

-25-

Norbert put down his man purse/pet carrier in the entry-way of Carlotta's home, and Ivy leapt out, ears down and tail between her legs, allowing Toutou to sniff every inch of her, which did not take long, as there was not much of Ivy. After that formality, Toutou greeted each human, and then went off for a nap in her immaculate bed under an end table.

"Dogs are great," approved Mabel. "Myrtle the cat is a good old girl, I can't say she isn't. But there's something about dogs." Mabel paused. She said, with sudden inspiration, "You know what it is? Dogs give you *unconditional love.*"

Carlotta asked, in pretend amazement, "Did you just think of that yourself?"

Lorraine looked at Carlotta over the top of her glasses, but no one else seemed to notice.

Carlotta seated her guests around the coffee table and poured tea. To her annoyance, each of them said, *"Gracias."*

"De rien," replied Carlotta, ever loyal to the language of Victor Hugo.

Before the eager Spanish students and their unlikely teacher could begin a basic conversation in a language she did not understand (which would be rude), Carlotta proposed a brand new idea that had occurred to her just that morning. If she knew her Club, they would snap at the scheme. If it turned out that the idea didn't interest Mabel, well, that would be her own problem, wouldn't it?

"So!" said Carlotta, "I have an Idea!" Her eyes glittered.

The Club leaned forward with interest.

"*An Oscar Wilde Reading Club!* We could get together once a week to read his plays out loud, everyone taking parts!"

Before her friends could respond, Mabel said, "Oh yeah? Or we could all just take a nap!"

Lorraine, always appreciative of a sarcastic remark, tittered unbecomingly.

"*A Woman of No Importance,*" Carlotta suggested, glaring at her old friend.

Lorraine called her out. "Who are you calling a woman of no importance?"

"*A Woman of No Importance* is one of Oscar Wilde's plays, Lorraine," said Margaret knowingly. Poor Margaret was so pleased to think that for the first time, she had caught a literary allusion that Lorraine had missed. She didn't see Lorraine and Carlotta exchange amused glances.

"Who would lead this reading club?" asked Mabel. "Oscar Wilde?"

"I'm afraid that would be neither possible nor pleasant," responded Carlotta icily. "He has been dead since 1900."

"Well," resumed Mabel, stuffing a cookie in her mouth, "I believe life is for the living."

Birdie looked as if she might object to that, but then sank back into a deep reverie.

Norbert said, "I never did get the chance to study Oscar Wilde's plays. I think it's a nice idea, Carlotta."

A nice idea? Talk about "damning with faint praise."

There was a pause as Carlotta waited for one of her loyal troupe to take up the cause of Oscar Wilde. The silence was disheartening. Wasting no time in defeat, she changed tactics.

"How about a little game of Literary Quotes?"

"I don't know that game," said Mabel, rubbing her hands together. "I like learning new games."

Carlotta exulted. Mabel was about to look very stupid, and she didn't know it yet.

Birdie explained, "This is a game Carlotta made up years ago. You have to think of any quote from a book or a poem. We take turns. We try to pick a quote that has something to do with what is going on, or with a quote that someone else just used."

"But don't be discouraged if you can't do it," said Margaret. "We've been playing this game for years. It's still hard for me. It's really only easy for Carlotta."

"I know lots of poems," said Mabel. Carlotta doubted this, with all her being.

Norbert said, "I've started keeping a notebook of quotes and reading it over, just to help me play this game. Lorraine told me they all keep notebooks, and have for years."

"That's right. It gets to be a little hobby," said Lorraine.

"Not for me," said Mabel. "I'm a *doer*—not a reader. You won't catch me reading books! Life's too short! But I do pick up poetry here and there. I'll try your game."

Mabel was revealing herself for the lowbrow that she was. She couldn't make it more obvious, thought Carlotta, with satisfaction.

"Okay! Let's go! Carlotta?" Lorraine was observing the rule that Carlotta always went first.

"Wait," said Mabel. "Do we put any money in?"

Everyone laughed, as if Mabel had made a very funny joke. Everyone except Carlotta, who discerned that Mabel was not joking.

Carlotta put her head back to regard the ceiling, as she began her recitation. She was well-prepared. She had been rehearsing it all day.

"'Blow, Blow, Thou Winter Wind,' by William Shakespeare."

"The bard," inserted Lorraine, with reverence.

"Blow, blow, thou winter wind,
Thou art not so unkind
As man's ingratitude;
Thy tooth is not so keen
Because thou art not seen,
Although thy breath be rude.
Heigh-ho! sing heigh-ho! unto the green holly:
Most friendship is feigning, most loving mere folly:
Then, heigh-ho! the holly!
This life is most jolly.

Freeze, freeze, thou bitter sky,
Thou dost not bite so nigh
As benefits forgot:
Though thou the waters warp,
Thy sting is not so sharp
As friend remember'd not.

Heigh-ho! sing heigh-ho! unto the green holly:
Most friendship is feigning, most loving mere folly:
Then, heigh-ho! the holly!
This life is most jolly."

The Club sat meditating on Carlotta's performance. Outwardly she was composed. Within, she was trembling with indignation.

"Huh," said Mabel with a wrinkled brow. "Sounds like a Christmas poem."

Carlotta was cheered by Mabel's ignorance.

Birdie, regarding her old friend closely, announced her poem:

"A Poison Tree, by William Blake."

"Birdie just loves William Blake," said Margaret in an aside to Mabel. "She knows lots of his poems by heart."

Birdie recited:

I was angry with my friend:
I told my wrath, my wrath did end.
I was angry with my foe:
I told it not, my wrath did grow.

"There's more to it," said Birdie. "That's the part I remember."

Another silence followed, while Carlotta sniffed at Birdie and looked away. Lorraine looked from one to another, perceiving their communication-by-verse.

Margaret said, "You and Birdie can go on and on. Lorraine does, too. How can you remember so many lines? I bet you make them up half the time."

Carlotta laughed with a merriment she did not feel. "Thank you for the compliment. If I could 'make up' poetry like Shakespeare, I'd be a very rich woman."

Mabel said, "You really think so? I don't. No one buys that old fashioned stuff anymore, do they?"

Carlotta opened her eyes wide, but before she could find words, Mabel proposed a poem.

"Hey, I've got one! Listen to this. This is a *good* one," promised Mabel, to distinguish her contribution from the drivel they had listened to thus far.

"There once was a young girl called Jana,"

"Stop!" cried Carlotta, putting up her hand. "We can't allow that."

Everyone looked at Carlotta. Censorship had never been exercised in this game before.

"We can't allow that," repeated Carlotta. "You are about to recite a limerick. Literary Quotes does not accept limericks."

"Since when?" challenged Lorraine.

"Since the beginning of the game," insisted Carlotta. "No limericks."

Mabel protested, "I don't get it. You're quoting poems. Why can't I quote a poem?"

"We," said Carlotta, "quoted poems by Shakespeare and Blake."

"And I," said Mabel, "am going to quote a poem by Anonymous." She ran a hand over her white hair. "Wait. Are you trying to say that your poems are better than mine?"

Carlotta smirked as she tried to think how to answer this, while remaining true to her democratic principles.

"Because," pursued Mabel, "a lot of people like this poem. It hung on the wall in Bugsy's Bar for *years*. It made everyone laugh. Especially after a few drinks."

Carlotta held fast. "Nothing off-color."

Mabel protested indignantly, "It's *not* racial. I'm not like that."

Carlotta, whose head was beginning to ache, said, "You have to understand the spirit of the game, Mabel. Literary Quotes is about literature. *You* were about to rhyme 'Jana' with 'banana.' Limericks are not literature, I'm afraid."

"So, if it's funny, it can't be literature?" asked Mabel, who really wanted to know. "Because if that's the rule, I'm not playing Literary Quotes. Because I *like* funny things."

Margaret burst out, "So do I!"

Lorraine said, "We all do! Think of Mark Twain, Carlotta. Think of Oscar Wilde. Even Shakespeare wrote comedies—you know that."

Carlotta remained firm. "Comedy is one thing. But limericks--."

"Were popularized by Ogden Nash," finished Birdie.

Margaret said, "Hold on! I just thought of a poem! Let me say it before I forget!" And Margaret began to recite:

Make new friends, but keep the old;
One is silver and the other, gold.

Carlotta questioned, "Title and author, Margaret?"

Margaret frowned. "Well, I guess it must be called 'Make New Friends.' And the author is ... Anonymous, I guess."

"Well, hey," said Mabel. "If one poem by Anonymous is okay for Literary Quotes, I don't know why another one isn't."

Margaret tried to help Mabel. "You do know that Anonymous wasn't an actual person, don't you, Mabel?"

"Wrong!" cried Mabel. "Anonymous was a woman. I read that on a bumper sticker."

Although Norbert and Lorraine hadn't had their turns yet, the group unanimously decided that Literary Quotes was over. There were so many thrilling things to talk about. Mabel had been teaching Spanish to Norbert, Lorraine, Birdie and Margaret twice a week, and they were full of praise for the fun-filled lessons. No books or papers. (Carlotta thought of the books and papers she had required for her French lessons.) Just salsa music and easy-to-pronounce words. They felt so *successful* with Mabel's Spanish. They'd also been playing poker. Carlotta had been invited but she had been busy each time.

And now, Mabel was researching where they could go for a hot air balloon ride.

"So I took the bus over to Upper Claremont, where they fly the hot air balloons." All eyes were on Mabel. "The young fella there says you have to book months in advance. They're all booked up until the end of October already. So *I* say, what about November? And *he* says, yeah, in November the balloons can fly, and there's some space in the calendar, but it's their slow season. Most people don't want to be freezing up in the sky on a cold winter's morning, he says. 'You probably want to wait until May,' he says, talking real slow and kind of loud, 'older people don't usually fly in the cold.' So *I* told *him*, me and my friends, we don't like to wait for things. We can take the cold. Then, he looks me up and down and asks me how old I am. So I told him, you want to know what I said? This will kill you. This is what I said: I said, '*You can kiss my ass in Macy's window!*'"

Norbert and Birdie chuckled, while Lorraine screamed with laughter, wiping her eyes. Margaret looked on at her "twin" with awe.

Anyone can get a cheap laugh by using coarse language.

"That surprised him, I guess, and he started talking to me more normal. 'I don't like people making assumptions about what I can't do,' I told him. He apologized. He was a nice young fella, I can't say he wasn't."

Lorraine, still snorting with laughter, asked, "So did you book a flight for us for November?"

Mabel opened her eyes wide in mock astonishment. "Aw, *hell* no. Who wants to freeze?"

The room filled with laughter again, and Carlotta thought she would explode with aggravation.

The moment had come for Carlotta to throw a bombshell into the group. It would give her a sense of power, and a sense of power was what she had been missing for some time now.

"Norbert," announced Carlotta during the first lull in the conversation. "I think it's time we made *you a member of the Club.*"

Carlotta waited for the impact of this announcement to register on the faces of her friends. She was fully prepared to defend her decision.

"Oh," said Birdie, distractedly, "I thought Norbert was a member already."

"Well, it's about time you made it official, Carlotta!" said Lorraine.

Norbert put his hand to his heart. "I am honored, Carlotta. Thank you very much. I humbly accept."

Mabel said, "I've been thinking about becoming a member of the Club myself. How much are the dues?"

-26-

Carlotta had ever been a believer in the popular wisdom of forgetting one's own troubles by getting involved in other people's. And Hope, in her imprudence, was willfully descending into trouble. If Carlotta could not stop her, she could at least find distraction by getting a close view of the wreckage that was about to ensue.

Upstate New York was refreshing in late summer, and there was a cool breeze blowing down Main Street. A couple of merchants—Maria from the salon and Dennis from the antique store--were sweeping their sidewalks, and Maude from Maude's Boutique was putting out a large pot of pansies and standing back to evaluate its effect. Carlotta knew all of these people and businesses: Flowers on Main across from the Art League, Jake's Bike Shop, Goofy's Ice Cream, and Butler's Books, which was just kitty corner from The Good Fortune Café. She greeted and was greeted by everyone who was out, and some shop owners waved to her from beyond their plate glass. If her Club had forgotten her, Gibbons Corner had not. Carlotta noticed everything with avid attention: the London plane trees lining the street, the new displays in the shop windows, and the mixed aromas of damp earth and brewing coffee.

Hope looked up from behind the counter as Carlotta entered the shop.

"Hey there, Aunty!" she called. There was warmth and gaiety in her voice.

Carlotta felt a surge of gratitude to think that she had not lost her place in *someone's* heart at least. Then she checked herself sharply for self-pity. Self-pity had one thing in common with the limerick. In Carlotta's world, there was no room for it.

The coffee shop was decorated with encouraging messages such as "Peace to all who enter here," and upbeat, popular music was playing softly. A few customers sat at booths, or in chairs by the fire, looking like subjects of hypnosis, their heads hanging and their faces lit by screens. Norbert sat in the back of the café, reading cards for a customer, who was looking at Norbert in deep concentration and awe, as if he were the Dalai Lama himself. Carlotta would have snorted, if she were the type of person to snort.

"Hello, Hope!" Carlotta approached the counter. "Any word on the--." Carlotta raised her eyebrows in lieu of finishing the sentence, because there were customers in the store.

Hope grinned. "It's not *that* top secret," said Hope in a low tone. "Yes, there is some movement there."

Carlotta sat down at the counter where she could enjoy a cup of peppermint tea and a little chat with Hope.

"I finished the 'Parents as Healing Hearts' course. That was an eye-opener. And then there were the parent panels to listen to. I've learned a ton, and it scared me, maybe a little," Hope admitted.

"Tell me all about it," said Carlotta, comfortably.

"They have this two-pronged approach. There's all this inspiration from parents who have made foster care and adoption their dedication, like, their way of life. And then there's all this warning about how hard it will be."

"How hard *will* it be?" asked Carlotta, innocently.

Let Hope be the one to say it.

"Well, I kept hearing, 'all of these children are damaged.' And 'There will definitely be behavior problems.' These parents and social workers talk about the kids' 'relentless pursuit of negative attention,' like, the kids keep on testing you even when you're trying to give all positive attention."

"What are the children testing the foster parents *for*?" asked Carlotta.

"To see if the foster parents will give up on them, like everyone else has."

Carlotta felt a pang. If there was one thing that Carlotta did not like to feel, it was a pang.

Hope went on, "The program keeps reminding you that your kid will almost for sure be far behind in school. And possibly aggressive."

"Ah," mused Carlotta. "It almost sounds as if they're trying to discourage you from doing it." She looked with intention into Hope's eyes.

"They're just trying to take the idealism out of us. While still being inspiring. I guess. There are two social workers. I have nicknames for them—not to their faces, of course, but in my head."

Carlotta nodded.

"One, I call Thundercloud. The other, I call The Wish Fairy. Thundercloud is all, 'don't say we didn't warn you.' The Wish Fairy is all, 'you'll never do anything in your life as meaningful as this.' The Wish Fairy says that sometimes these kids will surprise you, and make incredible gains. Then Thundercloud says not to bet on that."

Carlotta inhaled the aroma of her tea. Peppermint was so soothing.

"Well, dear, you know, you are not committed to this yet, are you? You could stop right now, and chalk it up to a learning experience, these seminars and panels and so forth. I mean, you didn't sign anything, did you?"

"Aunty." Hope put two plump elbows on the counter and looked into Carlotta's eyes. "I am going forward with this. With or without your blessing. But I do wish it could be *with.*"

"Hope, I've already told you I support you. One hundred percent."

"Thank you, Aunty."

"I just wish you would think about it a little longer."

Hope sighed.

"I'm just *saying.* Once you have a child, you're going to need to be able to get away from this café occasionally. Yes, you can find sitters for the child, but you must realize, when you are the mother, sometimes, especially after school and on weekends, you will have to leave work. Children create all *kinds* of inconvenience. You're always at the Good Fortune, taking care of everything yourself. You don't have anyone to rely on to handle things here in an emergency."

"That's true. I've been looking for someone trustworthy, someone who can take instruction. But I can't pay an assistant manager's salary. Someone who, as you say, can work after school and on weekends. I haven't found the right person yet."

Carlotta felt the pleasant hum she always felt at the beginning of any new project, large or small. If the Club was going to desert her now for Mabel, she would need to begin running something new. Perhaps she would find a way to insert herself into Hope's life. She needed to be indispensable to *someone.*

-27-

If Carlotta had remained the uncontested leader of the Club for fifty years, it was because she, and she alone, had had the energy and intelligence to satisfy the Club's insatiable appetite for excitement, learning, and new experiences. Mabel's effortless coup d'état was as unprecedented as it was inexplicable. She had marched in like a general and assumed the Club's full attention as if it were her due. Her audacity matched Carlotta's own. Carlotta would respect her if she did not despise her. If Carlotta would have looked beneath her despising, she would have found fear. But Carlotta did not like to delve too deeply into feelings. She preferred instead to observe how people managed to get what they wanted.

Studying Mabel's tactics from afar—for Carlotta refused to participate in any of the Club's activities which were not her own idea—Carlotta noticed some differences in the detestable woman's leadership style. Mabel had a cunning manner of appearing not to mind whose idea it was to have a poker party (Margaret's) or to go to have a picnic in the park by the beach (Lorraine's). She took up everyone's ideas with the cry, "Try anything once!"—as if poker parties and picnics were exotic adventures--and soon they were all crowing her trademark phrase like simpletons. Meanwhile, Carlotta abstained, hoping to set an example of disapproval. Her old friends encouraged her to join them, but when she didn't, they went on without her. Carlotta had the humiliating presentiment that they thought she was sulking.

When, at the Art League, they discussed their plans, Carlotta expected that her friends would ask her what was keeping her so busy these days, that she didn't seem to have time for them anymore. When they did ask, she would tell them that she needed "time for her writing," and wait for them to inquire with excitement, "What are you writing about, Carlotta?" And then she would smile and demur, and she would have to withhold the secret of her heart. And their curiosity would be ignited. And then she would have them back in hand once more. But none of this ever happened.

Instead, Lorraine, Birdie, Margaret and Norbert told Carlotta, in unnecessary detail, about all the things they were doing, and how much fun it was to have people everywhere looking from Margaret to Mabel.

"Whenever we go out," said Mabel, "people just can't stop *gandering* at us!"

No one corrected Mabel's malapropisms. They seemed to love her all the more for every silly thing she said.

Norbert reiterated, "Those two attract so much attention, you wouldn't believe it!"

The need some people have to attract attention is so...pitiful.

Birdie told the group, "There's an Escape Room in Buffalo. I think we should go."

What was this? Birdie, head-in-the-clouds Birdie, suggesting an activity? She never had, before. What had gotten into her?

"What's an Escape Room?" everyone wanted to know.

"It's a new thing," Birdie informed them with a lilt in her voice. "They're spreading all over the country. You go into a room, which is then locked, and you and your friends have to use your brains to get yourselves out. There are clues and things."

"That sounds *fun!*" approved Lorraine.

"What if we can't figure it out?" worried Margaret.

"Then they just leave you there!" mocked Lorraine.

"No," smiled Birdie. "It's timed. They give you one hour."

Norbert said, "Putting our heads together, we'll figure it out!"

"You all are something else! I can't even phantom where you come up with your ideas!" exclaimed Mabel. "Let's make the reservation! I've never done an Escape Room before!"

And the group took up the cry, "Try anything once!"

Although the idea for the adventure had been Birdie's, Carlotta observed that Mabel was still somehow in the position of leader. The group would have hoisted Mabel up on their shoulders, had they been younger.

-28-

Summer stopped by the studio after an oil painting class to walk her grandmother home. She'd had dinner with friends and wanted to walk in the fresh air, clear her head and poke fun at her revered ancestor.

As the artists were packing up, Summer saw Liam Hennessey's ginger head turned away from her, and she knew he was trying to hide.

"Hello, Liam! I didn't know you painted."

"Hi, Miss Moon," muttered Liam.

"Can I see your work?"

Liam stood aside, mutely, and let Summer study his underpainting of a bleeding eyeball.

"Just starting this one," he apologized.

"Well, I'm no artist, but I can see where you're going with this already. I guess my grandmother is a good teacher, huh? And you have talent."

Liam blushed fiercely and snapped his supply case closed. Grabbing his gear, he hurried to the exit.

"See you at school tomorrow!" called Summer.

"See you," mumbled Liam.

After all the class had left, Summer confided to Carlotta, "That boy Liam? He's got it pretty tough at school. Last week I saw a kid shoulder him real hard and push him against the lockers."

Carlotta frowned.

"Didn't you do anything to help him?"

"No, I pointed my finger and laughed. God, Gramma. Of *course*, I wrote the kid a detention slip and called the social worker to give her a heads up about it. What do you think? That I don't know my job?"

"Of course, Summer, I know you are an excellent teacher. It runs in the family. I think you get your instructional abilities from me. I'm just surprised that this kind of thing is going on in Liam's life at school. He seems very comfortable and even confident here."

"Yeah, with a bunch of old people, I guess he feels safe."

Summer might have been speaking of herself. She was never more at her ease than with Carlotta and her friends.

"Summer, not everyone in the class is old. You know that."

Summer looked around the studio, taking in the physical space, but also the ineffable feeling there, something her Aunt Birdie would notice, a sense of creative bliss and security. It was an atmosphere that her grandmother created, with her focus on her love of art, and her non-judgment. In the rest of her life, Gramma might be the most judgmental person Summer ever met, but when it came to painting, she was completely open and accepting. She truly enjoyed assisting others in the development of their gifts. Of course, a kid like Liam would be able to find comfort here.

"I'm glad you told me this, Summer." Gramma was getting that laser look she always got when she was coming up with a new idea. "What Liam needs is a real confidence-booster of some kind. Something to give him a sense of identity…. Let me give this a little thought."

Summer regretted having told her anything about Liam. Gramma was going to interfere with this kid's life.

-29-

Birdie materialized on the doorstep of Norbert's small stucco ranch house the following morning. As he let her in, Norbert was reminded of the day the year before, when she and the Club came to his home with their scheme to turn him into a fortune-teller. When at last he agreed, there followed tutoring from Birdie, Lorraine, Margaret and Carlotta in turn, to get him ready for the happiest career of his life. It was Birdie who had noticed his financial struggle in the first place, leading the Club to brainstorm this unique solution. He was grateful to her—and to all of them.

"Oh, Norbert," said Birdie, handing him a bouquet of asters.

"Is anything wrong?"

"Oh, put the dear things in water," said Birdie, waving vaguely toward the bouquet. "It can wait until you fill a vase. Their voices are getting weak. They're in a bigger hurry than I am."

Birdie often said strange things like this. Especially to Norbert, the sole possessor of her one great secret.

Norbert made the flowers comfortable on his dining room table.

Ivy lost no time making herself comfortable on Birdie's lap. She looked up at Birdie gratefully as Birdie massaged her with the tips of her fingers.

"The spirits in my house are restless, Norbert. Last night, when I got home from Margaret's, they were all lined up. They do that, whenever they want to get my attention—when they're warning me."

Norbert sat in the floral arm chair across from Birdie's striped one, and took a moment to envision the scene she described. He certainly did not believe in ghosts, nor any other psychic phenomena. But he did believe in Birdie. She had become a good friend.

"How do you mean, lined up?"

"They stand shoulder to shoulder. There are so many of them that the line goes clear through the first floor of my house and up the stairs."

Norbert chose to see Birdie's spiritual talk as metaphor.

"In other words, something is bothering you, Birdie?"

"Of course! What's bothering me is their message. This is how they tell me that I'm not paying attention to something in my life, something that I should be able to see clearly for myself."

Norbert smiled reassuringly.

"Well, then. This should be easy. What is it that you're not seeing?"

"If I could see what it is that I'm not seeing, then I wouldn't be not seeing it."

Norbert could see that this was so.

Birdie twisted her rings, and pushed her reddish curls from her forehead.

"Would you read my cards?"

Norbert was only too glad to oblige, if Birdie thought this would help to clear her mind. Birdie shuffled and handed Norbert the playing cards one at a time, and he began to lay them out on the coffee table.

"Five of Spades. That's a rift between friends, hurt feelings, damage that may be permanent."

Birdie's expression began to clear as she gazed off over Norbert's shoulder. She handed him the next card.

"Queen of Diamonds," said Norbert, "A controlling woman."

"*Carlotta,*" said Norbert and Birdie together.

"You can stop now, Norbert. I *see.*"

Norbert gathered the cards together and placed the deck face down on the coffee table. It never ceased to amaze him how people saw in the cards whatever they needed to see, and gave fortune telling the credit.

"Have you and Carlotta had an argument?"

"Never. Carlotta doesn't argue. Carlotta prevails. Oh, she'll have petty arguments. But if something were really and truly bothering her? The last thing Carlotta would ever do is address the problem directly."

"What's the problem she won't address with you?"

"What's the problem she won't address with any of us, Norbert?"

Norbert was stumped.

"It's Mabel! Carlotta feels like we've all ditched her for Mabel. She's terribly hurt."

"Oh," said Norbert, "I doubt that! Mabel's no threat to Carlotta. I mean, Mabel's a lot of fun--."

Both of them said, "*I can't say she isn't!*"

"But," continued Norbert, "Carlotta is the leader of the Club, for Pete's sake, and has been since before God was born."

They sat in silence for a moment, trying to imagine Carlotta with hurt feelings. It would have been easier to imagine a general with hurt feelings. Sentimentality of any kind was foreign to Carlotta, as far as they knew. She was always in command, and always the winner.

Norbert added, "She's just been very busy lately."

"You don't know Carlotta. That's exactly what she would say if she were hurt. She's not busy. She's pouting."

-30-

What an artist needs, reflected Carlotta, *is uninterrupted blocks of time.*

Uninterrupted blocks of time were what Carlotta had aplenty, now that the Club was following Mabel.

Carlotta wrote with passion from six until eight every morning, filling her blue pages with fluid black lines. She wrote of all she had done for her friends over their five decades together, providing them with entertainment and education. She wrote of her selfless dedication to their happiness and development. She included every favor she could remember having done for each of them. She wrote about their ingratitude and desertion. Sometimes as she wrote, the page ripped under the gouging force of her pen.

If Carlotta was not careful, she mused, she risked making Mabel, instead of herself, the main character of her novel, so intent had she become in showing the hideousness of this interloper.

The best art is borne of pain.

Carlotta gazed out her window where the yellow leaves against the blue sky created a Van Gogh color scheme. She wondered if this pain in her heart was making her book a work of art.

-31-

Hope sat across from Norbert the fortune-teller. Of all Aunt Carlotta's ideas, and she had had so many, the idea to bring Norbert into the café to read cards for customers was one of her best. Ever since he had come, not quite a year ago, Hope's business had begun to prosper as never before. Sometimes, she would ask him to stay after the shop was closed to the public, and she would take ten minutes to consult with this kind man.

Today, she did not have the concern for the numerous chores that awaited her. Her new assistant Liam was getting started on the end-of-the-day tasks. Aunt Carlotta's suggestion that she hire this shy high school student had turned out to be an excellent one, as her aunt's suggestions invariably were.

Liam Hennessey had seemed very awkward, and Hope had had her doubts, but within a few hours she was relieved to see his earnest focus on the work and his marked desire to please. Comically, he had even said to her, "you can rely on me, Hope," and then had turned three shades of red. Funny kid.

As Liam clattered away, Hope sat down opposite Norbert. She took the deck of cards from him, but put it to the side, unshuffled.

"When I was a kid," she said, settling into the comforting atmosphere Norbert created in his little corner of the café, "I always envisioned my future in a house filled with children and pets. That's all I ever wanted. I never could see a husband very clearly in this vision, but I assumed there must be one there, somewhere. But I could see all the kids. A child's face in every window, kids on the porch, kids swinging from the trees in the yard. That was supposed to be my life. And here I am, living alone, and forty-six years old. I don't know what happened."

Norbert, smiling, seemed to consider. "Well, John Lennon said--."

"Oh, I know what John Lennon said. But in my case, it's 'Life is what happens while you're busy being with the wrong man.' Men. One after the other."

Norbert confided, "Well, come to that, I never pictured myself being a fortune-teller. I was an accountant for forty years and never gave card reading a thought. So there we are. I guess we know life doesn't go according to plan."

"But in your case, it's like you've found what you were supposed to be doing all along! That's what I want."

"You've started on the road, Hope. It will certainly happen for you."

"The foster care thing is such a roller coaster. You can't imagine. I had a call last week, and it fell through. It was going to be a sibling group: an eight-year old boy called Deshon and his six-year-old twin sisters, Leesa and Mariah. I had four days to get ready for them. I set up beds, bought a few little things, but most of the activity was in my head. I *lived* with those children, without meeting them, for four days. I built it up, our life together, imagined it all in detail: welcoming them, taking them to the park, starting them in school, family dinners, tucking them in. Then the caseworker called and said the kids' grandmother decided to take them after all."

Hope looked through the thick lenses of Norbert's glasses, into his magnified brown eyes. She felt more peaceful.

"Maybe it's for their best; I hope so. But my dream of a family just burst."

Norbert was listening to her with great attention.

In a low tone, she added, "I feel discouraged."

Norbert motioned to the cards.

"Just shuffle, and pull one from the top."

Hope shuffled with focused attention. As she pulled one card, a second card flipped out of the deck and landed on the table. Norbert said, "There are no accidents! We have to take them both."

He flipped them both face up and placed them on the table.

"Queen of Clubs!" said Hope and Norbert together. "And Nine of Hearts."

"Looks like a young lady will be joining you very soon, Hope," said Norbert. "Looks like a young lady with a mind of her own, too. And the Nine of Hearts says that your dearest wish is coming true."

"How does it work, Norbert? How'd you do that?"

"It's not magic or anything," said Norbert, taking off his glasses and cleaning them carefully with a small white cloth. "It's odds, I guess. In a deck of fifty-two cards, there are twelve face cards. Odds are about one in four that you'll draw a face card. If you don't, any of the other cards will give a meaning that you will make fit your situation. Because it's human nature to see patterns and make meanings. But it's even better if you do get a face card. The Kings are males, the Queens are females, and the Jacks could be either one. So, you pulled a Queen. Okay. Maybe your chance of getting a girl foster child is about fifty percent? So now I have half a chance of being right. If you get a boy instead, you'll forgive me, and explain to yourself that the Queen was referring to someone else—a caseworker or yourself, for example. That's how it works. It's just our need to believe, that's all."

"Oh," said Hope, disappointed. She paused. "Wait. What about the Nine of Hearts, then?"

"That *is* the wish-come-true card, no doubt about it. But it just fell out of the deck. Some other card could have fallen out instead—one meaning a legal document, one meaning a period of waiting—almost any card, you would make it fit your situation."

"Oh. I wish you hadn't told me that."

Norbert was smiling. "In that case, forget about it. I actually have a strong psychic impression that you have a child coming to you very soon. A perfect match."

-32-

Carlotta had what they used to call a "brainwave." She was sure that Mabel did not speak fluent Spanish. Carlotta knew all about creating false impressions, and if she knew anything, this Mabel-woman was a fraud. If the Club would only see that, their servile worship of the venomous monster would end. Sure, Mabel could say some full sentences in Spanish, and even teach some lessons. That did not mean she truly spoke the language of Cervantes.

No one likes a faker.

A plan for exposure of the scam dawned in Carlotta's productive mind with the suddenness of a beam of light, and with the sensation of angels singing, "Ah!"

Her granddaughter Summer was a Spanish teacher, and she actually *was* fluent in the Castilian tongue.

"Summer, dear, since you and Hope are so keen to meet Mabel, I was wondering if we could compare calendars. I'm just going to have hors d'oeuvres—are you available this Friday afternoon, say, about 4:30?"

The 4:30 hors d'oeuvres party in Carlotta's gracious home didn't look like a steel trap, but that is what it was: a trap set to spring. Only Carlotta knew this. She missed the days when at least Lorraine would have been in on the plot. Everyone—Lorraine, Margaret, Birdie, Norbert, Hope, Summer, and the soon-to-be ensnared Mabel—thought they were coming for a congenial little pre-dinner party.

Carlotta had prepared a few favorites with charming presentation and had just finished setting everything out on the dining room table when her guests arrived, all in one prompt fell swoop.

Actually, a swoop is the descent made by a bird of prey, reflected Carlotta. It was she who would be doing the swooping this afternoon.

Norbert had already introduced Mabel to Summer and Hope as they all arrived on Carlotta's doorstep. They had just had time to say hello and make the obvious exclamations on the uncanny resemblance between Margaret and Mabel, when Carlotta opened wide her door.

As they came in, they brought with them a fly, which began to circle the rooms in a panic.

Carlotta smiled her welcome while Toutou wagged and wiggled joyfully, welcoming in the visitors. Carlotta let them have a little time to discuss whatever they liked and get comfortable, before she began the assault. She did it so innocently. No one would ever suspect her intention was to destroy.

"Mabel," said Carlotta. "You have been teaching Spanish to everyone."

"Everyone but you," said Lorraine. "You oughta join us. We're learning so fast!"

"Perhaps I will, someday," said Carlotta. "I've been so busy." Here she waited, willing to postpone her attack if any of her friends would like to ask her what had been keeping her so occupied lately.

"Spanish is fun!" enthused Margaret, who sat next to Mabel, as she always did now, enjoying the glances that bounced from her to her double and back again. "Mabel's a good teacher!"

Carlotta took in a gasp of air, very lightly; no one heard.

"Aw, teaching Spanish to you guys is easy. It's not like it's *rocket surgery*, or anything."

The woman doesn't even have command of her native tongue. Surely she can't be gifted in languages.

"Actually," Carlotta turned the full force of her toothy beam on Mabel, "we have *two* Spanish teachers in the room. My granddaughter Summer is a *real* Spanish teacher, a licensed one, at the high school."

She waited for Mabel to realize she was done for. Mabel seemed unaware of her doom, and smiled back.

Norbert, waving the fly away with one hand and with the other carrying a cherry tomato to his mouth, stopped and glanced from Carlotta to Mabel.

He must be getting a premonition.

"Summer, why don't you and Mabel speak Spanish together? I'm sure we'd all love to hear you. Spanish is such a ... well... such a *staccato* language, isn't it?"

Carlotta's secret opinion was that French was inherently somehow better than Spanish.

Summer, always glad of an opportunity to speak Spanish, began with a long rambling expression that seemed to end up as a question. Everyone was watching with interest, probably wishing that they could speak Spanish like Summer. With a friendly tilt of her head, Summer stopped and took a bite of her tomato and olive bruschetta.

Mabel, still chewing her potato croquet, held up a finger, so much as to say, she couldn't talk with her mouth full. A pathetic ruse that wouldn't last her very long. Carlotta tapped her foot. If Mabel hoped that someone would change the subject while she chewed, she could abandon that wish right now. Carlotta wouldn't allow her to escape her comeuppance.

Swallowing, Mabel clapped her hands together, and drew them apart. On one hand lay the limp carcass of the fly. On the other lay an imprint of fly blood and one fly leg.

"*Got* it!" she exclaimed. "I hate flies, don't you?" Mabel looked around at the group, who looked back at her, mouths open.

"Great reflexes, Mabel," congratulated Norbert, chortling.

Studying her hands with interest, Mabel said, "Now I have to wash." She held her hands up to Carlotta, who winced and signaled her toward the bathroom.

As Mabel left the room, Carlotta's friends guffawed in amazement. Not in disgust or contempt, as any right-thinking person would have done. What was wrong with all of them? The more ghastly the woman was, the more they all seemed to love her. And if Mabel thought that Carlotta would forget about exposing her lack of Spanish, she would soon learn with whom she was dealing.

Just as Mabel returned, chuckling about the fly, Hope's cell phone rang.

"It's Children and Family Services!" she cried. "Oh!" and she ran, clutching her phone, into Carlotta's kitchen.

"What's going on?" asked Lorraine.

Summer said, "It might be a foster child for Hope. But it's weird they'd be calling on a Friday night, isn't it?"

"Oh, yeah," said Lorraine, "the foster child that Carlotta volunteered us all to babysit—*that* foster child?"

Carlotta assumed a noble attitude.

"I can't imagine that any of us has anything more important to do than to help a child who has no home and no support in the world. I'm sure we *all* feel that even Spanish lessons and hot air balloon rides are not as *meaningful* as being of service to a child in need." Carlotta paused with the skill of a preacher sad-

126

ly regarding a sinful congregation, and then added, "Was I wrong in assuming that?"

Birdie, giving a belly rub to Toutou, said, "It will be good to have a child among us again. Children teach us so much."

Poor Birdie, always getting things backwards.

"Plus, kids probably love hot air balloon rides," contributed Mabel, showing herself to be irresponsible as well as ridiculous.

While the conversation concerning the role the Club would play with Hope's foster child—or children--went on in the living room, Hope was leaning against the kitchen wall, her heart beating fast, listening to Thundercloud.

A nine-year-old African American girl needed an emergency placement. Her current foster mother would not keep her a day longer. Could the child stay with Hope just for the weekend, until a new foster home could be arranged?

"We're only asking you to keep her for the weekend. But if it works out for both of you, you could have the option of fostering her long-term. Even adoption might be possible eventually, if you want. Her birth mother has already signed over her rights to let the girl be adopted."

Hope asked the obvious question, even though she knew she would take the child regardless of the answer.

"Uh... What has she done, that the foster family she has now won't keep her even one more day?"

Hope heard a long sigh at the other end of the line.

"Oh, *I* don't know. She's a little girl with a mind of her own. The usual behavior problems. Some people just can't put up with things." Thundercloud's voice became hard. "Do you want her, or not?"

Hope put her hand to her heart and closed her eyes.

"I want her."

Carlotta turned to study Hope's face as she rejoined the group in the living room. Everyone was listening closely to Mabel speaking fluent Spanish to Summer, and Summer was laughing heartily. Mabel seemed to be enjoying the bright rays of admiration from all of Carlotta's Club.

Vulgar people like to show off, thought Carlotta.

Carlotta was glad to interrupt Mabel's grandstanding.

"Hope, did you get some news?"

Hope announced simply to the group: "She's here. My daughter is here." And she told them all about the plight of this nine-year-old child who would be brought to her house in an hour.

Carlotta said, "It's too soon to call her your 'daughter,' Hope. Take the necessary time, to see how you get along."

"I feel it in my heart already. She's the child I've been waiting for."

Summer, laughing as if becoming a mother were an entertaining adventure, said, "Do you even know her name?"

"Yes," said Hope. "Her name is Queen."

The group, chewing and sipping in a contemplative silence, seemed to be visualizing a nine-year-old with such a name.

"I knew a stripper called Queen once," contributed Mabel. "I think it was her professional name, actually. She was a real nice girl. I can't say..."

Carlotta stepped in. "If this becomes a—permanent arrangement—you can change that name, I'm sure."

"I don't think so, Aunty. Her name, when you stop to think of it, is all she has that's hers, right? Anyway, it's a fine name. I have no problem with it."

"*Everyone* will have a problem with it, Hope. Think of her teachers at school. Who would saddle a baby with a name like Queen in the first place?"

"I don't know," said Hope, "Maybe someone who hoped her daughter would be respected, like a queen. Hard to tell what people are thinking. But her mom probably gave her the best name she could imagine, is my guess."

"But *Queen!* It sounds like she is in charge. That's just the problem with today's generation of permissive parents who put their children in charge. No boundaries, no respect, and no discipline. How will you even discipline a child called 'Queen'? 'Queen, don't interrupt adults.' 'Queen, go to your room and think about what you've done.' It's out of the question."

"Gee, I don't picture myself saying negative things to her all the time."

"Of course you'll have to say negative things. Didn't you say they all have behavior problems?"

"Behavior problems!" chimed in Mabel. "That's what *I* must have had when *I* was a kid. But come on, what kid *doesn't?* I mean, what kid *doesn't* leave a paper bag full of poop on an old guy's doorstep, set it on fire, ring the door bell, and then hide in the bushes to laugh when the old buzzard comes out stomping his foot on the bag of poop? Am I right? *I* did it, lots of times, and other things, too. Oh, man, I had *plenty* of behavior problems! Ha!"

Carlotta, vexed beyond reason, lashed out.

"And it seems you still have them!"

Before Carlotta could regret speaking in haste, Mabel doubled over in laughter, and everyone joined in, so glad to have some comic relief. You couldn't even insult the woman. It was beyond maddening.

"You ever get tired of dealing with those behavior problems," said the geriatric delinquent, "you send that child over to her Aunt Mabel. I bet we get along real good!"

Carlotta resolved then and there to never let this foul woman near her... let's see, her niece's foster daughter...that would make this little girl Carlotta's foster grandniece. Yes, so Carlotta was Queen's foster grandaunt.

So she had dibs.

-33-

From Queen's spiral notebook:

My name is Queen Serafina Jones & I burn bridges. That's what the social worker lady keeps saying Everytime she moves me. Burn bridges--means I don't care if people like me or not. I reely don't care At All.

& I don't have time for bossy forster mothers.

& I pack lite.

Hope stood outside in front of her ranch-style home on Ontario Boulevard, waiting for Queen to arrive with the social worker. She couldn't possibly wait inside, behind a closed door. Her heart was vibrating with happiness and sweet excitement.

It was Thundercloud herself who pulled into Hope's driveway. She lumbered out of the car as if it were very hard for her to move herself through space. She plodded around to the passenger door and opened it. A small girl stepped out. A pink backpack dangled from one hand and she stood, unsmiling, regarding Hope.

-34-

Carlotta had plotted to take Mabel "for a ride in the country," as people used to say long ago when they got rid of unwanted pets. This barbaric practice dated back to the decades before the existence of rescue groups, animal shelters, spaying, and neutering. One of Carlotta's saddest childhood memories was of her dad taking Pumpkin, her fluffy mixed breed dog, for such a ride. Pumpkin's crime was that she had a new litter of puppies every year, a fruitfulness which pleased Carlotta, but not her parents. This was in 1942. The common solution to canine fecundity was euthanasia (by drowning), or what was considered a kinder approach: taking the animal far from home, out into the country, and dropping her off near a farm house. As they drove away, people told themselves that the farmer and his wife would feed Pumpkin—or Scamp—because didn't farmers have so many animals already? They'd probably be glad to take one more.

When her parents told her they'd taken her little dog for a ride in the country, Carlotta asked, "When is she coming back?" Her parents had said, "Oh, she's having so much fun, she may never come back."

Years later, Carlotta still grieved to think her childhood companion had probably starved or been killed by coyotes. Taking an animal for such a "ride" was unpardonable cruelty. Informed, decent people today would never do it.

Taking Mabel for a ride in the country, however, struck Carlotta as a brilliant idea. It was the perfect way to get rid of Mabel.

Out in the country, just outside of town, stood a pillared mansion known as the Center for Deeper Understanding. It was run by Arnie's aunt, the eccentric Edith Butler, and was a mecca for every imaginable new age weirdness. The place had a cult-like atmosphere. Its instructors spouted astonishing beliefs, and then labeled them "miracle-facts."

Carlotta had no use for Edith and her Center, but Mabel, with her slogan of "Try anything once!" could probably be drawn in by Edith and her strange crew. The place welcomed eccentrics like Mabel, and Edith was always trying to pull people in. Carlotta could imagine Mabel on staff there, teaching a class in... something. The subject would be Edith's concern. With any luck, Mabel could become Edith's headache.

The way Carlotta lured Mabel into her car was this.

At the Art League, Carlotta opened her eyes wide and crooked her finger at Mabel, inviting her to come and take a gander at the catalog of The Center for Deeper Understanding. She intimated that she was sharing this with Mabel alone.

Mabel crowed, "Well, this looks real interesting! Let's get the whole gang in on it!"

Carlotta shushed her and said that the Club did not appreciate this fascinating place—in fact, they disapproved of it. That got Mabel's attention.

"Disapprove?" Mabel looked dumbfounded. "Well, I'll be a monkey's uncle."

Carlotta's imagination easily responded to that image, and she smiled.

Mabel smiled back.

"So," said Mabel, "it's just the two of us, then?"

"Yes," said Carlotta. "Just us two."

"That will be real nice," said Mabel, with feeling. "You know, I was beginning to get the idea that you didn't like me. And now you invite me to this interesting place! Well, which class is it we're going to take?"

Carlotta and Mabel turned the pages of the catalog. The two women perused, together. Carlotta had no intention of taking a class with Mabel. She would just get her interested in one of them, and sign her up.

Photographing Nature Spirits: An inexpensive camera or phone camera works best. We will gather in the flower garden for this class. Learn how to photograph the spirits and sprites that escape our corporeal view. You will be amazed at the images you collect.

Developing Intuition: In this three-part course, learn the steps to reading minds, predicting the future and connecting with the dear departed. This class will be held in the Third Eye Room.

Crystals for Deep Healing. Taught by Edith Butler. Do stones have spirits? Are crystals alive? How can crystals be used to heal the body? How can you use crystals for contacting the spirit realm? If you have asked yourself these questions, this class is for you!

Drumming Fun: Gather in a circle and drum for a non-stop two-hour session with instructor Daphne Cook. Participants report mental changes.

Fencing: Try this elegant sport. You will use a foil, and will begin with the "en garde," or "ready stance." You will learn basic footwork, simple attacks, and defense as you practice friendly fencing bouts. Instructor Stanley Oppenheimer is your challenging and knowledgeable teacher.

Mabel looked up from the catalog with a sharp intake of breath. To Carlotta's horror, she cried, "Fencing! *You* would really take the fencing class with *me*?"

Carlotta hesitated. This was not what she had in mind at all. Her vision was to drop Mabel at the door and let Edith deal with her—and swallow her up, if she wished. Then Mabel delivered the deciding blow.

"You're in pretty good shape for a woman your age. I can't say you're not. Of course, you're not as active as I am. But don't let that scare you, Carlotta. I'll go easy on you."

The nerve. The presumption. The aspersion.

Now she would have to put Mabel in her place.

-35-

It seemed that the little girl was mute. Had Thundercloud, in her weariness, forgotten to mention it? The child did not speak with her mouth, but her wide and expressive brown eyes took in everything, and there seemed to be a storm of emotions going on behind them. Her face, however, remained controlled and neutral. Hope rattled on, asking questions, giving information, and taking her new daughter on a tour of their home. With a stabbing pain of inadequacy, Hope suddenly realized: she had no idea how to talk to a child. Was there a special way to do it? She had thought she was so prepared, researching online and taking courses. Now she realized, she had rarely spoken to a child since she was one herself. Well, there were the children of friends and customers. But that was different. And there was her cousin Summer. When Summer was Queen's age, nine years old, Hope was nineteen. But Summer, as a child, was nothing like this little silent creature.

Opening the door to the small, ivory-colored bedroom that was to be Queen's, Hope stood back to observe the child for a moment. She had to force herself to stop chattering. The little girl did not look nine, in Hope's limited idea of what a nine-year-old should look like. She was so tiny; she appeared to be closer to six. Could there be a mistake about her age?

Hope watched as Queen stepped slowly into the bedroom, looked all around, and carefully laid her backpack on the white dresser. There was a dignity about this child, despite her narrow shoulders and her delicate little body. She wore very thick eye glasses with round frames, giving her the appearance of a miniature librarian. Her hair was in braids with colorful beads, and Hope wondered if she would be good at doing Queen's hair. She was afraid she wouldn't be. In addition to learning how to talk to a child, she would have to learn how to style a black girl's hair.

"This is your room, Queen," said Hope.

Hope stepped in and opened some drawers.

"You can put your clothes in here," she said.

Queen looked briefly at Hope, and then away, at the lace panel curtains, the white comforter on the twin bed, the stuffed monkey and bear linking arms in the white wicker chair. Hope could not read her feelings.

Hope showed Queen the white secretary desk, stocked with new colored pencils and drawing paper, and for the first time saw a glimmer of pleasure pass over the little girl's face.

"Is there anything you want to ask me?" asked Hope, wishing the child would speak.

The little girl looked around the room and sighed deeply. Without looking at Hope, she shook her head, ever so slightly.

"Well, that's okay. It's been a tough day for you, I guess." She tried to imagine what Queen must have experienced. The kid had woken up in one home, not knowing that she'd be spending the night somewhere else. And what had she done to deserve being kicked out? Hope still didn't know.

"You can take a bath before bed, if you want," said Hope uncertainly. Was she supposed to help a nine-year-old in the bath, or did children of that age bathe themselves? Should she leave Queen alone in her room to have a little peace and privacy? Or did the child need Hope to be present and reassuring? She despaired that she had no idea how to be a mother.

"Well, then," said Hope, "it's about nine o'clock. I'm going to start getting ready for bed, myself. Do you need my help to get ready for bed?"

Queen folded her arms and arched an eyebrow at Hope. Hope thrilled at this eloquent communication. It felt almost like talking.

"I'll take that as a no," laughed Hope.

She went into her own room across the hall from Queen's. As she opened her pajama drawer, she heard a voice at her doorway.

"Ahem."

Hope looked up to see Queen pointing to Hope's bed.

"I thought you said you live alone," said Queen, and her voice was sweet and stronger than Hope would have thought it to be.

"I do," said Hope.

Queen raised her chin in challenge.

"Then why you got two pillows on your bed?" asked Queen. Her tone said, *don't lie to me.*

Hope laughed with relief. They were talking.

"Why do I have two pillows? Well, I guess because it looks more balanced that way, don't you think?"

Queen did not have an opinion to share on that matter. Before turning back to her bedroom, she announced, "If I don't like it here, I will leave. Just so you know."

Hope sat up in bed, searching YouTube videos on her phone. "How to Style Black Girls' Hair." The African American mother-hair stylist on the little screen spoke smoothly, showing the steps as she went.

"Condition the hair well, with this apple cider vinegar mixture. You want to use liberal amounts, and make sure every single strand of hair has moisturizing conditioner. Just let that sit for fifteen minutes. Then, you rinse it out very, very thoroughly. Now, take your wide toothed comb and detangle. You have to section off the hair into pony tails. Be careful. Don't pull the hair too tightly."

Hope watched the little girl in the video standing patiently as the hair care routine went on and on. Would Queen let Hope do her hair like that? Would Hope get the instructions wrong and mess up the child's hair? If she messed it up, how would it get fixed? Did she need to find an African American salon in Buffalo? Did Queen do her own hair?

"Now," said the confident lady on YouTube, "you use this greasy-based pomade to lay the hair down. You use your little black rubber bands now. Watch how I twist and roll each little pony tail, all the way down to the bottom. Then I secure it with a cute barrette. That's all there is to it!"

The little girl in the video glowed with self-esteem, her hair done just right, by a woman who knew how.

Where, wondered Hope, did you find those little black rubber bands?

-36-

"The only reason Carlotta hasn't joined us in any of our outings with Mabel," said Lorraine, "is because she can't boss Mabel the way she bosses the rest of us. The way she's bossed us for years."

Lorraine and Birdie were walking buddies. Every morning at nine a.m., Birdie would appear on the sidewalk in front of Lorraine's house. Lorraine would hurry out and give her a hug and a kiss on the cheek, and they began their power walk through Gibbons Corner.

"Let's walk by the lake today," Lorraine had proposed. "There's not much wind."

The two old friends powered along the lake shore, huffing and puffing. Lorraine continued to pontificate.

"You know what Mabel is? I'll tell you what she is. Mabel is a great example of a person who is not controlled by other people, and not controlling, either. She has fun, and she doesn't even turn to see if anyone is following her. When we brainstorm with Mabel, it's *real* brainstorming, not like when Carlotta makes us think we're coming up with ideas, when the truth is, she's already figured out what she's going to make us all do."

"But I love Carlotta. I thought you loved Carlotta, too," gasped Birdie as she ran to keep up with Lorraine.

"Don't give me this right now, Birdie. *Love Carlotta.* Jeesh. Of *course* I love Carlotta. She's my best friend."

"Then why are you so resentful?"

"You know why I'm resentful? I'll tell you why I'm resentful. I am getting too old to put up with her manipulations!"

"—and her snobbishness?" added Birdie.

"—and her smugness!"

"—and her superiority?"

"—and her airs!"

"—and her insecurity?"

"Insecurity?" Lorraine laughed with scorn. "Now you're psychoanalyzing her."

"Of course, she's insecure. Why else...?"

"I don't need to look deep within, Birdie. I'm not like you. I'm just tired of Carlotta bossing everyone around."

"After fifty years, you're tired *now*?"

"Yeah." Lorraine grinned at Birdie. "Too patient for my own good, huh? I didn't know how irritating Carlotta was until Mabel came to town. We all have fun now, and no one has to be the boss or grab the credit. It's—it's restful."

Birdie considered. "Why not just talk with Carlotta about her controlling ways?"

"You know Carlotta. You ever had that kinda conversation with her? No! You know why? I'll tell you why. It's because she doesn't *listen*. She doesn't wanna *listen*."

"Still, I feel bad for her."

"Don't. She needs to learn a lesson already."

"A lesson?" Birdie frowned. "Do you mean a *life lesson?*"

"If it makes you feel better, you can call it that."

-37-

As Carlotta's Ford Fusion rolled along through the country-side, she glanced at Mabel in the passenger seat. She visualized a duel between herself and this short, energetic woman, and did not like the uncertain feeling it gave her. Carlotta liked competitions she was sure of winning, and those were strictly verbal ones. Mabel, for all her many defects, was agile. (*I can't say she isn't,* came the ready phrase to Carlotta's mind, and she brushed it away in irritation.) Carlotta prided herself on her own excellent constitution, her sharpness of mind and her svelteness of figure, even at eighty-one. But Mabel was one of those robust tomboy types. How would the two of them be matched in a fencing class? If the fencing students were matched according to height, Carlotta would be assigned a taller partner. Still, eventually, wouldn't Mabel want to work her way to having a physical duel with Carlotta? Wasn't that what she was up to, after all? In her place, that's what Carlotta would have been up to. All of these thoughts passed through her mind as she drove Mabel through field and forest and down winding roads, while Mabel jabbered on, frequently punctuating her monologue with the exclamation, "Where *is* everybody today?"

"This is the country, Mabel."

"The country makes me *nervous,*" said Mabel.

Carlotta smiled. Gibbons Corner and its environs were her turf, and it was satisfying to know that Mabel felt off-balance.

"It's so *quiet*. Even downtown Gibbons Corner, it's too quiet for me. At least there's the train passing through and blowing its whistle. If it weren't for that train, I think I'd lose my mind."

"Oh," said Carlotta, "we wouldn't want that."

Mabel agreed, "No sirree."

As Carlotta turned off Highway Four and onto the serpentine driveway lined with gingko trees, Mabel exclaimed, "Well, I'll be!"

The Center for Deeper Understanding was a white pillared mansion nestled next to woods on the east and within sight and hearing of the grey-blue whooshing waves of Lake Ontario. Behind the mansion stood apple and pear orchards and vegetable gardens.

Mabel declared, "Well! It's just like a castle in a fairy tale!"

Carlotta pulled the car into the adjoining lot.

"Just wait until you meet Edith Butler. You'll *love* her! She's... lots of *fun*."

In truth, Edith was an old rival of Carlotta's, and had been a member of Carlotta's Club decades ago. Carlotta resented Edith's self-importance and bossy ways.

As they walked across the flat stepping stones reading "Be the change," and "Breathe," Carlotta worked on the bait-and-switch that had just illuminated her brain.

"You know, Mabel, the more I think of it, I realize you absolutely have to get to know Edith. She's sort of a celebrity." Carlotta searched her imagination for the words that would ignite Mabel's interest. "She's probably the most famous person in town."

"You don't say!" said Mabel. She was beginning to catch the spark. Carlotta needed to fan quickly, before they reached the door.

"Oh, yes! People come from all over the country to meet her and learn from her, you know. She is a minister of sorts." Carlotta thought with disdain of Edith's title: the Reverend Edith Butler. Everyone knew she had just ordered that certification by mail. "She's… well, she's a *real hoot*, that's what she is. She's very busy, though. So I don't see how we could manage it."

As Carlotta put her hand on the ornate golden doorknob, Mabel, who had been frowning, lit up with the flame of an idea.

"Hey! Wasn't she in the catalog? Isn't she teaching a class this morning, too? What if we take that one, instead of the fencing?"

"Well…" hesitated Carlotta.

"Unless you'd be too disappointed. Were you really looking forward to the fencing?"

"Oh, no, that's fine," said Carlotta hastily. "Let's see if Edith's class has room for us." And although it nearly killed Carlotta to say it, she added, "You'll see! Edith's absolutely amazing."

-38-

The Synchronicity Room was filling with a motley gathering of spiritual seekers, and Carlotta led Mabel to the center of the room where a large table was covered with labeled baskets holding crystals. The labels said: *jade, amazonite, moonstone, crystal quartz, onyx, blue topaz, carnelian,* among others.

Mabel remarked, "These just look like colored rocks to me," and she looked back toward the door.

Carlotta, quickly manufacturing false enthusiasm, pulled Mabel by the hand toward the nearest basket. "Oh! But aren't they *pretty* colored rocks! Maybe we will make bracelets with them!" She ran her fingers through the light blue stones.

A young woman across the table said knowingly to Carlotta, "Ah! You are drawn to the Amazonite!"

"Oh, yes!" said Carlotta brightly. "I *love* pale blue, don't *you,* Mabel?"

"Well, it's okay," said Mabel, clearly wishing she were donning fencing gear right now.

"Amazonite," said the young woman, "blocks electromagnetic waves. You should put it next to your computer."

Carlotta, unable to resist such an easy quip, said, "Oh, I just use my aluminum foil hat for that."

The young woman, not to be distracted from displaying her esoteric knowledge, added, "And of course, Amazonite is also excellent for attracting fairies!"

Mabel stared at the young woman and let out a loud guffaw.

"Carlotta Moon!" crowed Edith's merry voice.

Carlotta spun around.

Edith, in her typical odd fashion, was draped in a saffron-colored sari over brown slacks and an orange tee shirt, and was hurrying toward Carlotta.

"You go straight to the Amazonite, I see! Ha ha!"

Was the odious woman making fun of her?

"Amazonite is the stone of the woman warrior! Of *course* that's the stone that drew you to it. Always engaged in some battle, eh?"

"Edith! How nice to see you again," lied Carlotta.

Edith's eyes twinkled with understanding.

"And Margaret Birch!" exclaimed Edith. "I haven't seen either one of you since your past life regressions. Margaret, you remembered your life as the soldier-poet, Joyce Kilmer, as I recall. *I think that I shall never see a poem lovely as a tree,* and all that?"

Mabel looked confused but entertained. She had no idea what Edith was talking about, but she was curious. This was good.

"No, Edith, this is not Margaret."

Edith stepped back dramatically.

Carlotta said, "Let me introduce you to my, uh, friend, Mabel Paine. She's from Rochester."

"You wouldn't kid me, would you, Carlotta?" Edith studied Mabel with astonishment. "So, you're Margaret's twin sister? I never knew she had a twin."

"No," smiled Mabel proudly, as if looking like Margaret were a stunt she had come up with out of her own cleverness. "We just happen to look alike. 'Everyone has a double, supposively,' as they say."

Carlotta winced at Mabel's made-up word, but Edith was staring at Mabel the way a talent scout stares at the next Big Thing.

Mabel was chattering on. "We just happened to *meet our* double, that's all. We're having a lot of fun with it. I can't say we're not!"

"Doubles!" Edith was clearly entranced by the idea. "What potential the two of you have for all kinds of things! I'll have to think how both of you could help me out here at the Center. Played right, it could really be a magnet for the public, to have psychic 'twins,' or something of that nature."

"Ha! That's not bad! At least it's better than that kid Liam at the Art League. His idea was that one of us could commit a murder and disappear. That would leave the other one--up a creek without a lasso!"

Edith and Mabel laughed jovially, and Edith shot Carlotta a look of appreciation for bringing her this diamond in the rough.

Edith glanced at the clock on the wall, and moved quickly to the center of the room. "Let us begin!" she declared, and she motioned the milling crowd to the chairs set in a circle.

"If you brought your own crystals from home, take them out now. If you need to use our crystals, just go on up to the table and grab four or five that call to you."

Carlotta, Mabel and several others returned to the table, while the rest remained in the circle, pulling stones from pockets and purses. Carlotta hesitated as she looked at the baskets, wondering what weird Edith could mean by suggesting the rocks would "call" to her. She grabbed five of the prettiest ones. Mabel, though, followed the example of others, who ran their hands through the air above the stones, back and forth.

A bearded man said to Mabel, "You'll feel warmth from the stones that are yours."

Mabel smiled coquettishly at the bearded man as she gathered her five specimens.

In the seated circle, one young man was saying, "Some of my crystals didn't want to come today."

"Oh, I hear you," said a heavily tattooed woman with straight black hair. "Sometimes, you just can't get them to cooperate, no matter what you do. You have to listen to their wishes, or they might just stop helping you."

"Oh, I know," replied the young man. "Since I've had my crystals, my third eye is getting stronger." He massaged the area on his forehead, between his two visible eyes.

"That is so cool," approved another young woman. "My third eye is helping me with every little decision lately! Yesterday? I'm, like, at the grocery store, shopping with my third eye, just trying to pick out some cereal? And my third eye is like, *no, no, and no.* Like, *I'm not feeling any of these.* I swear, I had to leave without buying any cereal."

The group laughed in support, and nodded sagely. They'd all been there.

Once everyone was seated again, Edith instructed: "Let's put our crystals together in the shape of a heart, in energetic vibration, so they can enjoy each other and draw energy from one another."

The black-haired woman contributed, "Sort of like a play date—for crystals!"

The group laughed in appreciation.

"And now," said Edith, "for those of you who would like to, let's express our thanksgiving to the stones."

Immediately, voices around the circle began to speak up, in turn:

"Thank you, crystals, for sharing your energy with us."

"Let our stones be filled with the healing energy of the universe."

"Thank you, crystals, for your spiritual gifts."

Edith's crystals class covered the topics that had been outlined in the course catalog: an exploration of the conscious being within stones, the meanings and uses of each type of crystal, the practice of using crystals to communicate with the dead, as well as a general Q and A session on anything the participants had been wondering about concerning their rocks.

The woman who had informed Carlotta of Amazonite's power to attract fairies, now brought up a relationship problem.

"I have a deep connection to my amethyst. Like, we're in sync. But there's a real communication problem between my turquoise and me."

As Edith guided her student toward understanding and resolution of this issue, Carlotta glanced sideways at Mabel. Was she drinking the Kool-Aid?

-39-

Queen sat on the white comforter on her bed, her feet tucked beneath her, reading *The Tale of Despereaux,* by Kate Di Camillo. Her lips moved as she read, and her finger ran across the lines on the page.

"What are you reading?" asked Hope, from the doorway.

Queen held up the book cover, as if needing to save her words.

"Is it good?" asked Hope.

Queen looked at her, unspeaking, and Hope imagined her thinking, *Now, would I be reading it, if I didn't think it was good?*

Queen's empty pink backpack hung from a hook on the wall. She had unpacked all her worldly belongings: one pair of pajamas, three outfits, the book she was reading, a notebook and a pen.

Hope thought with affection that Queen's coke bottle eyeglasses were just like the ones worn by Norbert. Those glasses, combined with her tiny body and her thin face, made her look fragile and vulnerable. But when she spoke, there was a determination about her that reassured Hope. As Norbert had predicted, Queen was a young lady who knew her own mind.

Hope came into the room and sat on the end of Queen's bed.

"So, how did you sleep?"

"I slept."

Hope had no idea what else to say to this little girl.

"How did *you* sleep?" asked Queen.

Ah. She's meeting me halfway now.

"Great!" said Hope. It wasn't that her sleep was that great, but it was great that Queen was talking.

"So, tell me a little about yourself, honey."

Down came the wall. It was almost as if Hope could see iron bars come down over Queen's irises.

"What do you want to know?"

Hope took a chance.

"Actually, I want to know why you couldn't stay in your last foster home. The caseworker didn't really tell me much. What happened?"

"Oh, *that*." Queen poked out her lips. "Usual thing."

Hope waited.

"I was too hard to keep track of. She said I was not her kind of kid. Said I was too smart for my own good…. I left a lot."

"You mean, you ran away?"

"Just for a day, sometimes, when she bossed me."

"Where would you run to?"

"Lie-berry," said Queen, in a tone that said, *duh*.

"Is that the worst thing you ever did, run away to the library?"

Queen studied Hope a moment before answering.

"One time I hit a caseworker."

Hope pictured this skinny, little girl hitting a caseworker—for example, one as substantial as Thundercloud. She had to suppress a smile. Hope wrinkled her eyebrows together, seriously.

"Now, why did you do that?"

"Didn't like all her questions," said Queen, with meaning.

-40-

Edith's class moved on to the important topic of How to Cleanse Crystals. As Edith explained, this may be done in a variety of ways, including smudging them with sage. The disadvantage of this method is that it leaves the stones smudged—with sage. Edith's favorite crystal cleansing methods were those that used sound: the bell, the gong or the drum. The sound vibrations cleansed the toxic energy that the crystals absorbed.

"It's a miracle-fact," she assured the gathering.

Carlotta put the tips of her fingers to her temples. This phrase was not her idea of meaningful speech.

Edith produced a bongo drum from beneath her chair, and began to beat out a rhythm, as the group gazed at the rocks lying on the floor in heart formation, visualizing the cleansing that was taking place. *Thump thump, thump thump thump. Thump thump, thump thump thump. Thump thump...* Even Carlotta began to feel the hypnotic effect of Edith's drumming, as it went on.

Mabel rose, and the spell over Carlotta broke. What was her guest going to do, here, in public?

Mabel began to dance, spontaneously, slowly, around the crystals. Edith's drumming began to speed up, and Mabel danced faster. She danced away from the circle, and she danced back in again. She turned her back to the group and shook her hips vigorously. The bearded man and the black haired woman were the first to their feet, to join in Mabel's dance. One by one, the entire class—minus Carlotta and Edith—were up and dancing, eyes half closed. Then the dancers joined hands, and as one graceful body, moved clockwise and then counter-clockwise around the heart shape on the floor. At last, Edith's drumming began to slow, and with her rhythm, she led the dancing to a smooth stop.

The group embraced Mabel, gently, and Mabel was suffused with joy.

Carlotta stared.

Before the entire group, Edith praised Mabel: "Some people have the inborn gift for calling in the Nature Spirits. Mabel Paine, you have the purest energy I have encountered in many a moon."

After the class broke up, Carlotta was torn between satisfaction on progressing toward her goal of getting rid of Mabel, and envy that Mabel was once again singled out as the most special person in the room. She dallied outside so that Mabel and Edith would have a chance to talk one-to-one. If only Edith would hook Mabel in, and Carlotta would have her Club to herself again.

When Mabel emerged, Carlotta congratulated her on her immediate popularity at the Center for Deeper Understanding.

"Goodness, Mabel, you made quite an impression on Edith Butler."

Mabel chuckled. "That Edith said the strangest thing! She said she wanted to *keep* me! *Keep* me, as if I were a stray cat or dog! She wants me to join her somehow, working at her Center."

"That's wonderful, Mabel! What an honor! What, uh, *fun* you will have, right? You know, 'Try anything once,' as you always say?"

"Aw, no. It was fun to try for one day. I told her that. I said, I had a ball, and I can't say I didn't. And I told her I'd try to get you to come back with me to take that fencing class some time.

But I told her, I said, I can't spare the time to get involved in working here, Edith. Because I'm real busy with my Club."

-41-

Hope and Queen sat in the breakfast nook having tea and buttered toast. The bay window looked out on Hope's small yard which adjoined other small yards, where children and dogs played. Queen didn't look at the frolicking with longing, but instead sat with a very straight back, nibbling at the edges of her toast, and blowing on her tea to cool it off before taking a sip. She seemed to be enjoying the tea quite a bit. She had put four teaspoons of sugar in her cup.

Hope had been about to stop Queen from putting in so much sugar, but the child had been talking at the time, and Hope did not want to stop the flow of conversation once it had finally started.

"I wish I could see my sisters. Tamika, she's six. Maya, she's five. You should see them. Ooh! Cute! And *very* well-behaved."

Hope had the fleeting impression she was talking to an adult who just happened to be small. She didn't talk like Hope's idea of a nine-year-old. Was it the foster care system that had caused her to grow up fast in some ways, and to seem so old for her age?

"Where *are* your sisters?"

"They got adopted by the foster family I had before this last one. I'm glad for my little sisters, I really, really am. I wish that family would have adopted me so we could be all together for-ever, but it didn't work out for me."

Hope, worrying she might be treading on thin ice, decided to ask anyway.

"Why? Why didn't it work out for you?"

Queen seemed not to be bothered. "I am too difficult," she said, simply.

"Difficult in what way?"

Queen looked Hope up and down, as if deciding how much more to say.

"Maybe I'm not that well-behaved. Let's put it that way." Queen dabbed at her mouth with her napkin. "Anyway, I'm glad my sisters got a family. I never wanted to be the reason they didn't get one. Every time we'd get thrown out of a placement, it was because of me. They never did anything wrong. So now, they have the family they deserve."

Hope felt tears welling in her eyes, and she willed them back down. She took a breath and spoke.

"*You* deserve a family, too, Queen, don't you think so? I mean, don't you think every child does?"

Hope wondered about Queen's self-esteem. Wasn't that important for children to have? Or, wait, were the articles online now saying that parents had gone overboard with self-esteem? This child had plenty of poise and self-determination, but maybe self-esteem was not the same thing. She thought she should try talking with Queen the way she had seen foster parents talk to kids in the educational videos at Children and Family Services.

"You know, Queen, you are very special; it's just that your mother is unable to take care of you."

Queen's eyes went dim with boredom. "That's what they keep telling me." She sighed. "In those exact words."

Hope felt a little silly. But she persisted. "Yes, but it means that it wasn't because of you, or anything you did wrong, you know. You are very…." Hope hesitated, and Queen watched her trying to think.

"You are very valuable, and you are good. That's all."

"Huh." Queen pursed her lips and stirred her tea. "I just got here. What makes you think you know me?"

-42-

When one project is not working out, take a break, and turn your mind to another. Carlotta was on her way to Hope's house to meet the little girl and change her name. While she was at it, she'd observe Hope and correct her early parenting mistakes. It was up to Carlotta to get things off to a good start. This day was shaping up to be a promising one.

Carlotta had the satisfaction of two missed calls from Lorraine, one from Birdie, one from Norbert, and one from Margaret. Her friends must at last be missing her and wanting to know what she had been up to. Let the Club wait. They had abandoned Carlotta for Mabel. Now let them wait for Carlotta to get back to them.

It was early September, a late afternoon, and Gibbons Corner was overcast and chilly, with a hint of rain in the air. She had recovered from her disappointment on the failed attempt to get rid of Mabel by taking her for a ride to the Center for Deeper Understanding. "Tomorrow is another day" was her motto. One of her mottos.

"Aunty!" cried Hope from her doorway, and came running down the walk to take Carlotta's elbow.

"I'm so glad you're here!"

Carlotta smiled and her heart filled with pleasure. Her guidance was needed. She was in command.

Hope ushered Carlotta into her house and reached out to take her raincoat.

"Oh, my dear," said Carlotta, peering into Hope's face. "It's not working out, is it?"

"Aunty," said Hope in an angry whisper. "Why would you *say* that?"

Carlotta had always been constitutionally incapable of whispering. It was as if she were possessed of the conviction that her voice was meant to be heard by all. Whenever she tried to whisper, she succeeded in whispering only the first word or two of her sentence. From there, the rest of her pronouncement came out loud and clear.

"Hope, I can read you like a book."

Hope shot a glance into the mirror that hung next to the door.

"Are you in over your head? If you are, you can tell me. You know I will support you in whatever you decide. But if you're feeling like you've made a mistake, you can just call Child and Family Services. You can have them pick her up."

"Of *course* I'm not going to have them pick her up!" Hope continued to whisper. "She's done nothing to deserve that!"

"I'm sure she hasn't, yet. I'm sure she's minding her p's and q's while she sizes you up. But think about it. What do you know about raising an African American child? Oh, don't give me that shocked look. Answer the question. What do you know?"

"What do I *need* to know?" Hope knitted her brows at Carlotta.

"That's just it! You don't even know what you don't know. Just to begin with, what about her hair? Don't you need to know how to braid it or something?"

Hope let out a groan and cast her eyes at the ceiling.

"It's called YouTube tutorials, Aunty."

A floorboard creaked in the hallway that led to the bedrooms, and both women stopped talking. They didn't need to speak aloud their realization that the child had been standing and listening to them. For how long?

"Well come on in, Aunty. It's silly to stand whispering by the closet."

"*I* wasn't whispering," asserted Carlotta truthfully, and she seated herself on the couch by the window.

The child called Queen came slowly into the living room, reading a book as she walked. She was very small. She didn't look like much of a "behavior problem."

"Aunt Carlotta, I want you to meet Queen Serafina Jones," said Hope. "And Queen, I want you to meet my Aunt Carlotta."

"Hello, dear," said Carlotta.

The child settled herself with dignity on the love seat, her feet dangling above the floor, and simply looked, unspeaking, at Carlotta. Maybe her intelligence was not all it should be. My, but her eyes were large, behind those magnified lenses of hers.

Carlotta spoke slowly and clearly. "You are reading a book. What is it about?" She smiled brightly to let the child know she was being friendly.

Queen held up the book to show its title. *The Tale of Despereaux.* On the cover were some rodents. Carlotta had a horror of rodents. She thought she would have to buy this little girl some suitable books. That is, if she would be staying for any length of time.

"That's quite a thick book for such a young girl," flattered Carlotta. "Do you understand it?"

Queen glanced at her open book, as if she longed to get back to her reading, and did not answer her elder. Carlotta made a mental note to instruct the little girl on the rules of polite discourse, at her earliest opportunity. Because it did seem that, against advice, Hope was planning to keep the girl.

Hope brought Carlotta a cup of herbal tea and they settled in for a nice visit, discussing the predicted storm for this evening, the booming business at the Good Fortune Café, the gratitude Hope felt toward her teenage assistant Liam for taking on increased hours at the shop while Hope got the child settled in, and circling back to Queen, who sat with her eyebrows in a V-shape, apparently absorbed in her reading.

Carlotta made a new attempt to draw the child out.

"Queen," began Carlotta, and the little girl looked up. "is an interesting name. But your *middle* name, *Serafina!* Now *that* is a truly beautiful name. I think I will call you Serafina—may I?"

The child put the book aside and sat up straight. Her voice was clear and strong.

"No. You may not."

"You don't like your middle name? But it's such a pretty one."

"Aunty," said Hope. "Her name is settled. It's Queen."

"Queenie, then," amended Carlotta. "That's a little better, isn't it? Queenie? I'll just shorten it to Queenie."

"Queenie is not shorter," observed Queen, as if patiently pointing out the obvious to a slow-witted child. "And it is also not my name."

This stalled debate was interrupted by the doorbell.

"Oh! That's your Club!" said Hope.

"The Club? What are they doing here?"

"They called this morning and asked if they could stop by to meet Queen. I knew you were coming, so I thought, the more the merrier. And I made sandwiches!"

And into the little living room filed Lorraine, Norbert, Birdie, Margaret and Mabel.

They were all carrying wrapped gifts.

-43-

Lorraine, the retired school teacher, grabbed the spot next to Queen on the loveseat, and immediately began to involve the child in a discussion about her book. Carlotta felt the sting of jealousy as she caught pieces of their literary conversation through the din of confusion the Club brought in with them.

"I like Despereaux," confided Queen to Lorraine. "He's in love with music and Princess Pea."

Meanwhile, Margaret was zestfully telling Hope all about their thrilling time at the Escape Room, and Birdie added that it had blown her mind. Carlotta reflected in bitter silence that Birdie's mind had been blown for years. Norbert asked Carlotta if she would come with them should they decide to try the escape room again.

Of all the ways to waste one's time.

"I'd love to," began Carlotta, "but lately I've been so...."

"Let's do presents!" crowed Mabel.

Carlotta felt the mortification of having come empty-handed, while all her friends had brought gifts for the little girl. It had never occurred to her to buy a present. She had brought with her only her intention to change the child's name.

Hope exclaimed that they all shouldn't have, while Queen's eyes gleamed with cautious interest.

Margaret extended her gift first, and as Queen unwrapped it and Hope continued to repeat that this was so unexpected, Margaret asserted, "How can you approach a little girl without a doll?"

Queen held in her arms a beautifully dressed African American doll. Queen plucked at the sparkly material of the doll's dress, and seemed unable to take her eyes from it.

"You're not too old for dolls, are you? You're still just the right age, aren't you?" fretted Margaret.

"I'm not too old," said Queen. "Thank you."

Mabel commented, "Margaret, how do you find such beautiful things? You have unpeckable taste."

Margaret laughed with pleasure. "Impeccable taste?" she corrected with subtlety. "Why, thank you! Yes, I do love to see a beautiful doll, even at my age."

Birdie extended her gift: watercolor paints and a block of watercolor paper.

Queen's fingers ran across the squares of color that showed through the top of the plastic box.

"I love painting. Thank you."

So far, the child's manners did not need correcting, reflected Carlotta. If anyone's manners were not what they should be, they were Carlotta's. Why hadn't her friends told her they would all be bringing gifts today? With irritation, she thought of all the missed calls she had not returned. They could have texted, at least, that they had conspired behind her back to bring welcome gifts. It was all their fault.

Lorraine gave Queen a copy of *The Secret Garden*, by Frances Hodgson Burnett. An old-fashioned classic. Would a modern child be able to understand such a book?

Lorraine summarized, "It's about a ten-year-old girl who lived a long time ago. Her parents are dead, and she goes to live in a big old house with an old uncle that she never sees. There's a hidden garden, a boy who can talk to animals, and someone is crying every night in one of the rooms, and she goes to find out who it is."

Queen observed Lorraine as she spoke, and then looked at the book in her hands, her interest clearly ignited.

Queen asked, "So she snoops through the house?"

"Well," considered Lorraine, "I guess the mean housekeeper would say she was snooping. She's really just finding out what she needs to know."

Queen nodded in approval. "I'll love this book."

Mabel was next: a box containing five shades of nail polish. *What is wrong with the woman? So inappropriate.*

Queen lit up with surprise and lifted each little bottle in turn.

The last gift was offered by Norbert: a Swiss army knife.

"Look!" said Norbert with enthusiasm, taking the tool back and demonstrating, "you have here a large blade and a small blade, a corkscrew, a can opener and a little screwdriver, a bottle opener, a hole punch, a key ring, tweezers—and a toothpick!" Norbert handed his gift back to Queen and sat back proudly. "I had one of those when I was about your age. It was my favorite thing."

Carlotta looked meaningfully at Hope, and Hope nodded her agreement to Carlotta. Clearly, Hope would take charge of that weapon when Norbert was gone.

Hope said, "Thank you, everyone. You didn't have to do this. We're very grateful."

Queen said quietly, "Thank you," and settled into the loveseat, her doll cradled in one arm and her other treasures all around her. She went back to reading *Despereaux*.

Mabel was wiping her chin, having finished her sandwich before anyone else had begun eating theirs. Stomach full, she launched into her next plan for the Club.

"I was just thinking, it's not hard to get on the local TV channel. Community television, you know. It's for everyone in the community. You just need to have an idea for a show, and of course, everyone needs to take the class to learn how to operate the equipment. That's a real quick affair, and you get certified. Then you come in with your idea, you book time on the schedule, and you're on TV!"

Carlotta watched Mabel wrap the Club in a new spell. They were all talking over one another, putting forth ideas for a program.

While Carlotta watched Mabel, she could feel Queen watching *her*. What an unusual child. But Carlotta's attention returned to the Club's impromptu brainstorming session. Carlotta knew what Mabel was up to. She was going to finagle a way to make herself the star of the TV show. That's what Carlotta would do, in her place. She watched to see how Mabel would work it.

Margaret suggested, "How about a psychic show? The Norbert Show! Norbert could read people's cards and make predictions for Gibbons Corner!"

Norbert balked immediately. "Oh, no. I couldn't read cards like that, on camera. No, I'm not your man."

Birdie said, "Then what about an interview show?"

Mabel said, "OK. Who would we interview?"

The Club ate their sandwiches and considered.

"Each other?" suggested Margaret.

"Or—hey!" said Norbert. "Interview the mayor! And the police chief."

"Sorry. Boring," vetoed Lorraine.

Mabel turned to Carlotta. "How about *Oil Painting with Carlotta?*"

"Ooh! A painting show!" cried Margaret.

Carlotta envisioned herself—just for a moment—as the star of a TV show. Then she shook herself free of the enchantment. Mabel would be her director. That was out of the question.

"I'm so sorry. I'm very busy these days."

No one asked Carlotta what was keeping her so busy.

"*I* know!" exclaimed Lorraine. "A cooking show! Everyone loves cooking shows, don't they?"

"Yes! *Margaret!*" exclaimed Mabel. "She's a fantastic cook! Margaret can cook, and the rest of us will operate the cameras, arrange the set, work the character generator, and all that stuff. There are plenty of off-camera roles to play. Then, at the end of the show, we'll all come in and eat and rave about how delicious it is!"

The Club took up the cry of: "Margaret! Margaret! Margaret!" until relenting and laughing, Margaret agreed to be the star of *In the Kitchen with Margaret*.

Outside, there were rumblings of distant thunder. The room grew dark, and Hope turned on the lamps.

Carlotta, a mass of dark reflections, felt herself being watched and turned to meet the owlish gaze of the little girl. Queen looked away from Carlotta, to take in the whole gathering.

Hope took advantage of the lull in the conversation to bring attention back to her foster child.

"Queen, you will be seeing a lot of all of these people after school and on weekends, while I am at the café. This week, I'm taking off every day after school just to help you get settled in. Starting next week, though, Aunt Carlotta will take care of you on weekends and pick you up after school Wednesday through Friday, and I bet she'll take you visiting sometimes. I'm sure she'll take you to the library, too."

Queen said, "No, thank you. She can just drop me off at the café with you. I'll sit in the kitchen and read and paint." She picked up the box of watercolors and gazed into it again.

167

Hope said, "Yes, you stay in the kitchen at the café on Mondays. That will seem like a long stretch for you, just reading and painting until I can close up. You'll see. You need to have different experiences, and get to know all your aunts and your uncle."

Queen's face was expressionless, unreadable.

Hope went on, "I bet Aunt Carlotta will take you to see Aunt Birdie. She has a parrot called Tetley and you can play in her pretty garden. And you'll visit Aunt Margaret. She has a cat called Myrtle and as you heard, she's a good cook! And Aunt Carlotta will take you to see Aunt Lorraine, who used to be a teacher, and you will learn lots of stuff.

"Now, on Tuesdays, you'll be with Uncle Norbert—that will mean sitting in the café again, near his booth, for few hours while he reads cards. But he will keep an eye on you and talk to you in between customers, and you can read and paint, like you said. But all the other days you'll be with Aunt Carlotta. Aunt Carlotta always has lots of ideas, so it will be sure to be fun."

"And Sunday is your day off," resumed Queen, "and we will be home together."

"No. I actually don't get a real day off. Not regularly. Once in a while I can get one, if I leave Liam in charge. But he's just a teenager, and the café is a big responsibility. I have to put in a lot of hours there every day."

"Then what happens to me on Sundays?" And although Queen's voice sounded challenging, Carlotta heard the vulnerability beneath.

Carlotta and Mabel spoke up together: "You'll be with *me*!"

A sudden, loud clap of thunder made everyone jump.

"That must have been close," observed Norbert, looking toward the window where the rain was now pelting with vigorous intention.

Mabel, raising her voice above the rain, said to Carlotta, "I don't think that's fair. You already have Queen every day but Monday and Tuesday. You don't need to take *all* the available days. What about the rest of us? We could divide up the week, and each take a day."

"The rest of you don't have the necessary energy to look after a child," said Carlotta, matching Mabel's volume.

"Well, that's a load of blarney," complained Mabel, looking around at the others for support.

"I believe you mean malarkey," corrected Carlotta with good cheer. She wasn't going to lose this one.

The Club was following this exchange with interest. Carlotta was glad to have them watch her winning something. And it was shocking to think that they would trust Mabel, who was, after all, a stranger, to look after a child.

"You are so busy with the Club, Mabel. And since Hope is *my* niece, that means that Queen is related to *me*. My foster grandniece. Blood is thicker than water."

As Carlotta left Hope's house, she basked in the gratification of having beaten Mabel out. And the little girl, surprisingly, was a reader, and that endeared her somewhat to Carlotta's guarded heart. However, this whole foster care thing was a terrible idea. She would just have to stand by her niece until Hope would see that for herself.

-44-

When the crowd had gone, Hope asked Queen, "What did you think of your new uncle and aunts?"

"They're not *my* uncle and aunts."

Hope took the armchair opposite Queen.

"They may be yours, but they aren't mine. And I'm not calling them 'aunt' and 'uncle,' either."

"Why?" asked Hope, with a sinking heart. "Didn't you like them?"

"Not a matter of liking," said Queen. "It's a matter of facts. They aren't mine. Not gonna call them aunt and uncle. That's it; that's all."

"That's fine," assured Hope. "But you will have to call them *something,* won't you?"

"Easy," said Queen. "I'll call them by their names."

"By their *first* names?" asked Hope.

"What else?" answered Queen. "I'll call them Lorraine, Birdie, Norbert, Carlotta, and those twin ladies—Margaret and Mabel. I think I've got them all straight already."

Hope explained that the two ladies who looked alike were not twins, but doubles. Queen seemed skeptical.

"Is that true?"

"Of course, it's true. Why would I lie?"

"People lie about all kinds of things. All the time."

Hope considered this. Of course, Queen was correct in her surmise. People did lie all the time. But a child of nine is not supposed to be so aware of the duplicity of adults.

"You're a quick learner," said Hope, "to get everyone's names so fast. But we may have a little problem to work out. You see, the older generation is not always so keen on being called by their first names by children."

"That still doesn't make them my aunts and uncle."

"Okay. But what can you call them, to show respect for the age difference?"

Queen reflected, interested in this conundrum.

"You mean I should call them something like 'miss' and 'mister'? Like, 'Miss Carlotta'?"

Hope shook her head vigorously. "Oh, no! Not that. That's too... southern plantation-y."

"Well, then?"

"You could call them the way you do your teachers, maybe? So: Mrs. Moon, Mrs. Walsh...."

Queen resumed: "Mrs. Andretta, Mrs. Birch, Mrs. Paine, and Mr. Zelenka."

"Good job! You even caught all their last names! But... is it too formal? I wish there was something else...."

"Like what?"

"I don't know. Something like, 'Mother Carlotta,' 'Mother Birdie,' you know, to show that it's a closer relationship."

Queen poked out her pursed lips and regarded Hope for a moment.

"I do not know what you're talking about, 'closer relationship.' Just because they brought me presents, now I gotta have a 'closer relationship' with them?" Queen had raised her voice suddenly and was levelling a hostile stare at Hope. She shoved her pile of treasure away from her. "They can take it all back then. I'm not calling them 'aunt,' 'uncle,' 'mother,' or none of that. *Now* what?"

"Right, all right, no family names, then." Hope agreed. "Well, we'll start off with Mr. and Mrs. Maybe someday you'll upgrade them all."

Queen made no comment.

Hope asked shyly, "And what would you like to call *me*?"

Queen, solemn, paused and considered Hope.

Hope hastened to add, "It's okay if you don't want to call me 'Mom.'"

Queen shook her head.

"You got any idea how many women I've called 'Mom'? And now, to tell you the truth, I can't even remember any of their faces. Maybe that's because I called them all the same name. They all blur together. You shouldn't call two people by the same name. A name is important. Now, my *real* mother, I call Mama. I have never called anyone else that. But all those women I called 'Mom'—I bet they don't even remember me anymore, either."

Hope swallowed her disappointment.

Queen seemed to sense Hope's feelings.

"Hope is a beautiful name," said Queen. And it *did* sound like a beautiful name, when Queen said it. "It's lucky when you have a name that means something. I would like to call you Hope. May I?"

"You may," Hope smiled. "And you'll see, the people you met today are very kind. You'll grow to like them."

Queen twisted her mouth and looked directly at Hope.

"I don't see any black people here. That's okay. I'm used to white people. But I can tell, you all aren't used to black people."

Hope paused to consider what might have happened in the visit to give the child this impression.

"Why do you say that?"

"I say it because it's true," said Queen simply.

"I mean, what makes you feel that we aren't used to black people here?"

"I can just tell. If you've been around a little bit, it's not hard."

-45-

On this sunny and windy September day, Birdie Walsh was inhaling the wet earth and walking to Carlotta's house, mentally rehearsing the opening to the conversation she intended to have. The trouble was that there was always so much spiritual distraction around Birdie that she seldom was able to really think anything through.

Wherever Birdie walked, she walked with unseen companions. They were the spirits of her departed loved ones, as well as the ghosts of random strangers who had come in with the antique items that furnished her home. *So many of them get in that way,* reflected Birdie, *if people only knew.* When she stopped and spoke to people in town, as likely as not she would see vaporous entities behind them, causing people to stop talking suddenly and look warily over their shoulders. For Birdie, there was no partition between the land of the living and that of the dead.

The red and orange leaves were floating, as if on unseen hands, down through the air all around her. Crows peered down from the trees and announced the passage of Birdie and her entourage.

Birdie had told Norbert that the spirits at her house were restless. Some of her friends jokingly said they suspected, but only Norbert had heard it from her, that she saw ghosts. It was, to Birdie, the most important thing about her, and at the same time the one thing she could not share. Lorraine would have laughed at her, Margaret would have been frightened out of her wits, and Carlotta would have wanted to exploit her for the Club's entertainment. She had to be on guard to not become another one of Carlotta's projects.

Birdie's sensitive soul felt Carlotta's pain. She knew that Carlotta felt abandoned by the Club she had led and nurtured for most of her life. Carlotta was larger than life. What if she *was* bossy, as Lorraine said? Hadn't they always accepted that about her? Didn't she have some right to be bossy if the Club had always chosen to follow her and benefit from her constant flow of inspiration? Who, after all, was perfect? Wasn't it heartless of them all to leave her now, just because Mabel had come to town?

What Birdie had in mind was a little chat to clear the air, and bring Carlotta back to the center of the Club, where she belonged. Lorraine had said such a talk was not possible. Birdie, hearing herself cheered on from the Other Side, would see for herself.

Carlotta smiled brightly as she opened her door.

"Birdie!"

They kissed cheeks.

"Come on in! I'll just close up my desk here so all these papers won't be in our way. I've been working all morning. I was starting to get writer's cramp," said Carlotta, with a light laugh.

If Birdie was supposed to ask what Carlotta had been working on, she missed the hint, because there was Ed, Carlotta's departed husband, nodding a greeting at her from his spot in front of the fireplace. At the same time, Toutou was wiggling in polite greeting at her feet, and Birdie kneeled to pet her and bury her face in Toutou's fragrant curls.

That was Birdie's day-to-day life: the spirit world merged with the real world. Was she delusional? She didn't think so.

She only knew what she saw and heard, and that it was different from what everyone else seemed to be experiencing.

"Just back from the groomer's!" said Carlotta cheerfully. "Look how proud she is! That's enough, Toutou. Go lie down."

Toutou hesitated, looking at her bed under the table, and then at Birdie.

"Oh, all right. You can cuddle with Birdie. It really is peculiar, the way all animals love you. You're an animal charmer, that's what you are!"

"It's been that way all my life. Animals seek me out and want to sit by me. I love that, actually. I always feel better with animals nearby. The only creature I've ever met who doesn't come to me is Myrtle. She seems to love only you, but...."

"Please! Let's not waste time talking about cats, for heaven's sake! I've lit the fire, as you can see, for our lunch. I don't know why, but it still seems so cold in front of the fireplace. Isn't that odd? It must be the cold draft, coming down the chimney."

Birdie was used to cold spots in houses, but did not remark on this. Ed rested his elbow on the mantel, smiling and shrugging at Birdie.

Carlotta had made buttered toast and lentil soup.

"Simple and warming," she said, bustling. "And tea for me, and water for you," added Carlotta, knowing that Birdie drank nothing but room temperature water.

"I like water," Birdie said, "it's so clear, energetically."

Lorraine, had she been there, would have made a wisecrack about that remark just to make Birdie feel silly. Carlotta only smiled kindly. What Birdie loved most about Carlotta was how accepting she was of Birdie's ways and observations. She never criticized or excluded Birdie, as most of the world had done before she met Carlotta. And now, here was Birdie, seeming to exclude Carlotta. Her remorse was deep and heartfelt.

Birdie, stirring her soup, launched right in, before she could forget why she came. Carlotta's mother was standing behind Carlotta's chair and singing a popular tune from the twenties, which made it hard to concentrate.

"Carlotta, it's a shame, what's happened, and I want to tell you that I am truly sorry."

"What do you mean, what's happened, Birdie? Has something happened?"

"Oh, you know, about Mabel and everyone being kind of excited about her."

"Oh. Are they? I've been so busy, I haven't noticed."

Birdie persevered. "I know it seems like Mabel is the center of things now...."

Carlotta conceded, "I *am* just a little surprised at Mabel's popularity with the Club, Birdie. Aren't you? She's rather crude and unintelligent, isn't she?"

Birdie paused.

"Actually, I don't experience her that way."

Birdie "experienced" people very much the way they experienced themselves. Judgment was foreign to her.

Carlotta's eyes opened wide in surprise. She changed the subject.

"Birdie! Do you know, I just remembered I have a pineapple upside down cake in the fridge. I almost forgot. I would have been so mad! I made it for our lunch. It's very moist. Let me tell you how I made it."

Carlotta recited the recipe and narrated each step in detail, filibustering to keep Birdie from discussing that which Carlotta would not discuss.

Lorraine was right.

Birdie, walking home again through the quiet streets and the autumn chill, said aloud, "I *did* try."

-46-

In the Kitchen with Margaret turned out to be an absorbing project for the Club, while Carlotta maintained her exile. They talked about it during painting classes.

At one o'clock on Wednesday afternoon in Birdie's Watercolor Class, they were all abuzz with their community television certification class lingo and plans for filming.

Mabel, who had tired of modeling for the art classes, was dabbing at her own abstract painting experiment while she talked.

"See," said Mabel, "if we were doing an interview show, or even a painting show, we'd just film in the studio. But if we do a cooking show, we'll need to film in a kitchen. Probably Margaret's kitchen. It's do-able. We'll have to rent a video camera...."

Lorraine said, "Carlotta, whatsa matter with you anyway? I can't believe you're not working with us on this. You're missing out. You would love it!"

Carlotta dragged a watery brush over her Arches paper and then laid down some dots of cool color and watched them expand into little stars. She shook some grains of salt over her paper to increase the star effect.

"You know," she said, "I've been very busy."

They aren't going to ask what you've been busy with. Just tell them.

"You've been wondering what I'm so busy with, so I won't keep you in suspense any longer." She paused. She took as long as she dared before losing their attention. "You will be surprised to know that I am writing a book."

Excitement broke out around the studio.

That's the way to get them back.

Carlotta thought with satisfaction that she had sprung the news on them at just the right moment.

"Oh, Carlotta," said Lorraine, with real feeling, "you always wanted to write that book! And now you're doing it! That's wonderful! I'm prouda you."

"Oh," enthused Margaret, her blue eyes sparkling, "*I've* always wanted to write a book, too. I'm going to write mine posthumously, though."

Lorraine smirked at Carlotta and said, "For that, you're gonna need a ghostwriter."

Birdie looked up with interest, and then gazed off into space, her default expression.

Carlotta felt warmly reassured by Lorraine's smirk. They were still friends, then.

Carlotta explained to Margaret, "You can't write a book posthumously. I think you mean to say, anonymously. You can write a book anonymously if you use a pen name. Posthumously would mean you would write it after you're dead. Which would be assuming an extra challenge. Writing a book while you're still alive is hard enough."

"It could be *published* posthumously, though," said Lorraine. "You could write it anonymously and then it would be published posthumously."

Margaret pouted, "Can we stop talking about death, please?"

Mabel asked, "Well, what's it about—this book of yours?"

"Why," said Carlotta, smiling her sweetest smile. "It's about all of *you.*"

The Club, ignited by self-interest, pressed Carlotta to tell them more.

"Am *I* in it?" asked Mabel.

"And *me?*" asked Lorraine.

Carlotta, expert in the skill of manipulation, knew that this was the moment to step back and withhold information.

"Now, didn't I just say I'm writing about *all* of you?"

"Ooh, what are you writing about us?" asked Margaret. "Good things, I hope!" She tittered.

"I'm sure you must know that a writer cannot talk about her work in progress. It kills the inspiration. You'll read it when it's published."

"You're *publishing* it? Whadda you—have a contract or something?" asked Lorraine.

Carlotta smiled her best enigmatic smile.

Let them feel that pull of unsatisfied curiosity. It would be good for them.

-47-

The following morning, Carlotta opened the door of her home to Arnie Butler, that dear young man. A forty-something balding fellow with a slight paunch can qualify as a young man when you're eighty-one.

"Arnie! Welcome! *So* happy you've come!"

Arnie, greeting Toutou and playing with her briefly, refused coffee, tea, scones, and anything else that Carlotta might offer, suggesting that they get right to her laptop.

Although he had never personally self-published a book, Arnie did take a look at the process on his own computer the night before. He was able to guide Carlotta through the easy steps toward creating a real book, one that would be available for purchase online, and one that he would be happy to stock for her at Butler's Books.

Carlotta felt a rush to the head, to see how simple it all was. She was vibrating inside, and had to take her own pulse. She was fine. She was just very excited.

Arnie tempered Carlotta's enthusiasm with some caveats.

"Now, you do understand self-publishing is not like publishing with a well-known house, right? You won't get the help with editing, promoting, and all of that. You won't get a review in *The New York Times*. It won't be a bestseller. You probably won't sell very many copies, in fact."

Carlotta waved her hand in a dismissive gesture.

"Arnie, *anyone* can write a bestseller. That's not what I'm after. My readership is above the masses. But you *will* carry it for me at Butler's Books?"

"Oh, sure. That is, if you'll pay for the copies upfront. Then I'll pay you for them as they sell. That's called 'on consignment.'"

"I know what 'on consignment' means, Arnie. You don't need to explain the obvious."

Carlotta was reassured. She didn't need a worldwide audience quite yet. If Gibbons Corner saw her book on display downtown, that was good enough for her. For now.

Arnie complimented her. "You have quite a lot of handwritten pages of manuscript already."

Carlotta rested her hand atop the blue stack, to prevent Arnie from reading any of her prose.

"I've had a few spare hours lately," she observed, trying not to betray her sour feeling about the ample time she now had at her disposal.

"Well, once you get it all finished and transcribed into a Word document, you have to edit it very carefully, of course. After that, you'll need a professional editor to look for errors and areas for improvement."

"Oh, that part won't be necessary," said Carlotta. The very idea of someone "correcting" her work was impertinent. Her memoir would be published just the way it rolled off the pen: natural and fresh.

"And then…" and Arnie showed her again the quick and easy steps.

"And how much will it cost?" asked Carlotta, ready to pay anything at all. To become a published author, she would empty out a Certificate of Deposit.

"Why, it's free!" laughed Arnie.

"How can it be free?"

"Because it's print-on-demand, you see. They don't print the book until one is ordered and paid for. When that happens, why, then they send the book out to the buyer, and they send you your portion of the money."

"No!"

"Yes!"

Carlotta went through the steps on her own with Arnie observing, just to make sure she really understood.

"Do you mean to say," said Carlotta, "that when I just press this button here, the one that says 'publish,' my book will be published?"

Arnie smiled and nodded, delighting in Carlotta's delight.

Carlotta sat, exultant, before the computer screen. The rush of power she felt was unlike any she had ever known.

-48-

Hope was deep into the famous "behavior problems" that Child and Family Services had warned her about.

Just when she had begun to doubt that Queen actually had any behavior problems, they burst forth in full force. One evening Hope, preparing an easy Mexican dinner, couldn't find tortillas in the refrigerator. Had she stored them in the pantry instead, contrary to her usual protocol? No, they weren't in the pantry. Wait. Neither was the box of Cheerios. Nor the bag of potato chips. The package of dried cranberries was missing, too.

Hope shut the pantry door with a sigh, and realized what must be going on.

Food hoarding.

Hadn't she learned about this in her foster parents' class?

Children who have experienced prolonged hunger sometimes develop a habit of secretly hoarding food, so afraid are they that they will one day be hungry again. It's not a "behavior problem," as such. It's more of an anxiety symptom. She would need to reassure Queen that she would always have food with Hope.

Queen did not take the reassurance well.

Hope sat on Queen's bed and told her that she noticed some food missing. Was there anything Queen wanted to tell her?

"Now," said Queen, her eyes wide and her voice loud, "what would *I* have to tell *you*? You're the one that came in my room. Looks like *you're* the one that got something to tell *me.*"

Hope had not expected this dizzying escalation.

"I'm not accusing you of anything, Queen."

"Okay. That's good. I'm not accusing you of anything either. So we're done, then, I guess."

Queen shot a heart-piercing look of scorn at Hope. Hope looked down at her feet. There was a cracker box sticking out from under the bed. She bent and picked up the box.

"I'm not mad at you, Queen. I understand. It's okay. I just want to tell you--."

"*I* don't know how that box got there. Don't look at *me*."

"Queen, you don't need to lie to me."

"Oooh!" yelled Queen, and there was surprising power in her voice. "*Now* you're making me mad! Don't you talk to me like this! Don't you do it!" Queen took some deep breaths, as if trying to control herself. Then, in a measured tone, she added, "I—am—using—my—words."

Hope considered. The child seemed to be using some anger management technique someone must have taught her.

Queen, regaining her composure, said, "We can forget all about this." She sniffed. "Soon as you say sorry."

For a moment, Hope was at a loss. She wished she could channel The Wish Fairy or even Thundercloud to tell her the right way to handle this unexpected blow-up. She felt that saying "sorry" would be a mistake. But then, what to say?

"Queen."

Queen sat with staring eyes and pursed lips, saying nothing.

"Queen, I just want you to know that you are safe in every way, including safe from hunger. You might not be sure if that's true right now, but in time, you will see."

Hope pulled the package of tortillas from under the bed. While she was at it, she gathered up the crackers, dried cranberries, and potato chips. She then left the child to think about their conversation while she made dinner.

Queen, in the meantime, went to her white desk and sat down to write in her notebook.

Forster mothers always like to tell you to sit & think about what they said like you got time to be thinking about them. I got my own things to think about like my Book which I am writting. They all might think it is just scribble scrabble or a journal. Thats another thing they Love to tell you write in a journal they say. No. This is re-serch for a real *book & I will publish it & people will read my book which will be called How to Sirvive Being a Forster Kid. & other forster kids will read it. & Bad forster mothers that I had will read it and they will cry and be sorry cause now there in a book & everyone will know how evil they are & they will wish they were Nice to me when they had the chance. This forster mother isn't evil yet but I am nipping her in the butt.*

Dinner started off quiet and pleasant. Hope had asked Queen to choose the music they would listen to, and to her surprise, the child had chosen a CD called Meditation Music. Hope would have expected her to choose some current pop star. The soft flute-y music was just the thing to calm jangled nerves.

"Do you meditate?" asked Hope, ready to be surprised.

"No. I just like the swirly blue picture on the case."

Whatever anger management technique Queen had practiced seemed to have worked for her, and Hope felt encouraged that they had just overcome their first bump.

She had a topic of dinner conversation to bring up. She had read online that chores were important to family life. Chores, assured the writer of the article, gave children a sense of importance and belonging in the household, in addition to teaching a work ethic. Chores helped children to understand that "in our home, we all work together to make our living space nice."

Hope presented the concept of chores to Queen.

Queen laid her fork on her plate and said, "I don't do chores."

Hope said, "But *I* do chores."

Queen answered, "That's because this is your house."

"But it's your house now, too."

"Not yet. I'm just trying it out still."

Hope paused. This little girl had such a need to be in control. That wasn't a bad thing. It was very understandable for a girl who had been sent from one place to another all her life. Still, Hope was the mother—no matter by what name. Aunt Carlotta had warned her about being too lenient, like "most parents today."

Hope smiled to let Queen know she was speaking from kindness. "Well, honey, while you are trying it out, you can help me with the dishes after meals. That's only fair, isn't it?"

She was not prepared for what Queen would say next.

"Don't tell me what to do, please. I don't like it."

"Excuse me?"

"You heard."

Queen left her dishes on the table and returned to her room. Hope cleared the table, and wondered what a real mother would do. She certainly wasn't a real mother, because she had no idea whether to nip this rebellion in the bud, or let it go this time.

After doing the dishes, she sat in the living room with her eyes closed and her headphones on, drifting into the calming meditation music. She hadn't listened to this CD in years. It was like therapy to her bruised spirit. Hope wasn't used to disciplining children, and was afraid she'd never be good at it. The parenting classes taught her that the kids needed patience, firm limits and unconditional positive regard. As a parent, she was supposed to separate the act from the child. It had all made sense in the class. Now she wished she had asked more questions. She wasn't ready to be a mom; she didn't know enough yet. She thought of consulting the fortune-teller at her café. He had never been a parent, but he was wise and kind. She floated on the strains of the flute, and the world around her dissolved. She didn't hear the front door gently open and close.

-49-

Carlotta sat hunched—she who had never hunched in her life—before her computer screen. She was transcribing her first blue pages into a Word document. She had taken a typing course in her youth, and enjoyed the mental and physical process of typing. She could not, however, take the leap to composing on the screen. She needed to begin by penning her prose in cursive. As she transcribed, she was able to edit. Publication was as near as her final revision. She was rushing to complete her narrative. *The Golden Bonds of Friendship* had been taking a darker turn at each writing session. The working title of her autobiographical novel would have to be changed. Carlotta typed: *How Sharper than a Serpent's Tooth.* She borrowed this title from Shakespeare's *King Lear,* where the suffering royal is shocked by the ingratitude of his favored and dearest. Of course, reflected Carlotta, King Lear was making a tragic mistake in judgment when he delivered his famous line: "How sharper than a serpent's tooth it is to have a thankless child!" It turned out that his daughter Cordelia was still as loyal as ever to him, and he himself was making a mess of things. The analogy could be stretched only so far.

She enjoyed seeing her thoughts fly from her blue paper, through her agile fingers, to land on the computer screen. There, in Times New Roman, her prose looked official and powerful.

Through all the decades, Regina Cassidy sacrificed unceasingly for her friends. Her every thought was for their benefit, their well-being, and their amusement. To think of her own interests would have been foreign to her generous nature. Regina poured into her friendships all of her considerable genius and creative energy. At times, she even put her friends ahead of her family. Never, in her goodness, did she suspect their moral bankruptcy. Never did she imagine the depth of their ingratitude and treachery. Her boundless faith in her friends was the great tragedy of her life.

Her friends would all need new fictional names. She herself would keep the name she associated with royalty: Regina Cassidy. *She* hadn't changed. But her friends would need names to reflect their false hearts. To Lorraine she would give the most traitorous name of all. Treachery, in American history, was associated with the name Benedict Arnold. Doodling, Carlotta assigned the name "Bernadette Arnold" to Lorraine. Dithery Birdie would now be "Debbie Dither." And as for Norbert, the fortune-teller, she would call him "Professor Marvel," the silly man.

As she sat before the written history of her Club, Carlotta had a sinking feeling that she did not care for one bit. She had never been a woman to despair. She would not sit at her computer and feel unpleasant things. Action was the solution to any problem. She would stand and take some step toward getting her Club back under control. She needed to talk to someone who could give her counsel. She would see Norbert.

Yes, she had just mockingly named him "Professor Marvel" in her book.

But he didn't know that.

-50-

Carlotta approached Norbert's booth at the Good Fortune Café with a light laugh.

"I just realized, Norbert, that since you have been in business here, I have never had a reading. I've come to support your little business." She generously gave him his twenty dollar fee, even though she should be entitled to a free reading, considering that she had put him into this career to begin with.

Norbert did not betray any sign of surprise. Smiling, he received Carlotta and her twenty dollar bill, and smiling, he laid her seven cards out in a horseshoe spread on the table.

He studied the cards as Carlotta looked about brightly, to give anyone who might be looking on the impression that she was having a lark, and did not care at all what the cards had to tell her.

Norbert's deep brown eyes behind his thick lenses looked compassionate.

Carlotta did not like that one bit.

Norbert said, "I must tell you something that will upset you."

-51-

Hope awoke to a vibration and knocking at the front door. She pulled the headphones from her head and ran to see who it was.

It was Jenny, from across the street.

"Hey, sorry to disturb you," said Jenny, and she looked pained.

"That's okay. What's wrong?"

From a tote bag hanging on her shoulder, Jenny produced a fistful of necklaces and bracelets. They looked familiar. They were Hope's.

"I found these in Angelina's room."

"They're—they're mine! How did Angelina get them?"

Angelina was only six years old.

"She said she bought them. With money from my wallet."

"Wait. What?" asked Hope. "How?"

"She said the kid that's staying with you—Queen, is that really her name?—she said Queen sold them to her yesterday. She said Queen told her to get the money from my wallet."

Hope took the jewelry from Jenny's outstretched hand. All the baubles were presents from Aunt Carlotta and her cousin Summer. Hope had no idea of their worth; she seldom had occasion to wear them. Material things did not mean much to Hope. Still, Aunt Carlotta and Summer both had expensive taste. Their gifts probably had value.

"Uh," said Hope, "how much do I owe you? How much did Angelina steal from your wallet?"

"Excuse me!" said Jenny. "Angelina does not steal!"

"Sorry, sorry. I just woke up. I misspoke. Sorry."

"It was three dollars," said Jenny.

"Right. Sorry. Let me get my purse." Hope hesitated. "Oh, come in. I don't mean to leave you standing there on the stoop. Like I said, I just drifted off. Kind of groggy."

Jenny stood in the foyer and looked curiously as far as she could see into Hope's house, as Hope rummaged in her purse for three singles.

Jenny folded the bills neatly and tucked them into her jeans pocket. She showed every sign of staying right where she was. Jenny was a talker. Most of her talk revolved around trying to persuade Hope (and everyone else) to come to "socials" and "open houses" at her church, but any subject would do.

"So, this kid. Where'd she come from?"

"She's my foster child," said Hope. "She just got here a few days ago. I'll bring her over to meet Angelina sometime soon."

Jenny recoiled. "Don't trouble yourself. They've already met." She tilted her head. "How long is she going to be here?"

"She's staying. I'm adopting her."

Jenny whispered, "Do you really think that's a good idea?"

Hope opened the door and, taking Jenny's elbow, propelled her through it. She shut the door and leaned against it, gathering her wits about her for a serious talk with her daughter.

-52-

Where *was* she?

Hope checked every inch of the house, and as she went, she moved faster, her heart rate accelerating and her voice calling louder. The bathroom, closets, and space under the beds yielded no Queen. She wasn't in the back yard.

Hope dialed her neighbor.

"Jenny!"

"Hope? What's up?" Jenny didn't seem to hold any grudge about Hope's abrupt dismissal of her a few minutes before. Maybe she was used to people pushing her out of their houses.

"Queen's not over there, playing with Angelina, is she?"

"What? No!" Horrified. "Wait. Let me check."

A pause that seemed to last an eternity.

"Hey! Angelina is locking all her dolls in the dog kennel. I said, what are you doing Angelina sweetie, and she said all her dolls are bad and she's putting them in jail. Isn't that cute? Wait a minute while I take a video to post on Facebook."

"No! I can't wait. Queen's gone. I gotta go. But text me right away if Queen shows up at your house, okay?"

"She's *gone?*" Jenny's excitement crackled on the line. "That's *awful*! You must be so *worried*!" With a hint of hysteria, she suggested, "Let's pray together right now that Jesus will bring her back to you, safe and sound."

"Sorry, gotta go find her. Thanks, Jenny." Jenny had an annoying habit of trying to convert Hope to her own brand of Christianity, never willing to believe that Hope's church was in good standing with God.

Hope recalled Queen telling her that she had a habit of running away to the library. She checked the time on her phone. It was 7:23 on a week night. The library was just a block and a half away; but she would have had to cross the railroad tracks to get there. Hope's anxiety doubled.

Should she call the library, or just run over? Should she call the police first, to get them started searching in case Queen wasn't at the library? She had the Wish Fairy's emergency number; should she call Child and Family Services? Police first. In fact, the Police Department was just across the street from the Gibbons Corner Public Library.

She drove, her eyes scanning the sidewalks for the tiny, braided child.

At the Police Department, Officer Curry, business-like, took down Hope's hurried account.

"We'll have all the officers out looking for her immediately," he said, and Hope could have hugged him. She wasn't alone. Someone would help her with this responsibility that she was clearly screwing up.

As she turned to run across to the library, Officer Curry offered encouragement.

"The good thing is, she'll be easy to spot."

Hope turned.

"A black child in Gibbons Corner, is that what you mean?"

"Well, yeah," said Officer Curry. "She might be the only one."

-53-

Hope stopped at the circulation desk. Roseanne, a fixture at the library for decades, was there.

"Roseanne! I have an African American foster child, a girl, nine years old, and I think she's in the library. Did you see her by any chance?"

"Well hey, Hope," said Roseanne, "yes, maybe I did see your young lady. I was shelving books in the teenage section, and she came up and settled herself in one of those red bean bag chairs, and just started reading to herself. Nine years old, did you say? Tiny thing for nine, isn't she?"

"Oh, thank you, Roseanne," and Hope wheeled around to run up the flight to the teenage section. Before she got to the stairs, she felt something warm touch her hand. Hope looked down to find Queen placing her small hand in hers.

As they walked to the car, Hope felt the adrenaline surge fading away and noticed that she was breathing again. Before starting the engine, she phoned the police so they could stop searching. She hung up to find Queen arching an eyebrow at her.

"You called the *police* on me?"

"Queen. You can never do this again. If you want to go to the library, you will *always* need my permission. Every time. And I will always have to *take* you, because I won't allow you to cross the tracks by yourself. It's dangerous for a nine-year-old."

Instead of arguing, as Hope expected, Queen sighed.

Hope stole a glance at the little girl and saw that she looked tired and stressed.

"I was so worried, Queen, because I care about you." Hope reached for Queen's hand, but Queen pulled her hands into her sleeves, like a turtle's head retreating into its shell. Apparently she had done all the hand-holding she intended to do for one day.

The car ride home was as quiet as it was brief.

Jenny and Angelina were standing on their lawn when Hope pulled into her driveway. They came running over. Jenny's eyes were alight with godly zeal.

"I *knew* Jesus would bring her back to you, Hope! Angelina and I prayed for Jesus to bring her back, and He did. The Lord is faithful! Thank you, Jesus!"

Angelina stood punching her mother in the thigh.

"I wanna go *home* now. I wanna watch a *movie. Mom*my *mom*my *mom*my…"

Throughout the child's abuse, Jenny valiantly continued her holy exclamations, bent on using the moment to evangelize her neighbor.

"It's been a long day, Jenny. Thanks for your prayers," said Hope. Holding Queen's hand, she turned toward her house. As she and Queen walked away, they heard Angelina whine.

"Mommy, are they both going to Hell?"

There was a furious "shush."

"But *you* said--."

"Shush!"

"Well, *are* they? *Are* they?"

Queen waited discreetly until they were in the house with the door shut, before she informed Hope of her own opinion of Angelina.

"That girl has entitlement *bad*. Ooh! You should just *hear* the way she talks to her mother. That child is *spoy-ulled*. Some mothers these days don't know how to do limits."

-54-

Norbert knew that his reading had annoyed Carlotta to no end.

Carlotta had drawn the Six of Diamonds, which told of opportunities for learning and growing. Immediately after it, however, she had drawn the Ten of Spades, showing a figurative wall. Norbert had told her that her old ways would no longer serve her, and she needed to open her mind and heart to new ways.

Carlotta, clearly feeling that Norbert was being presumptuous, had quipped, "Thank you so *much*, Norbert. Is that all?"

"No, there is something else. You have a blind spot."

"What on earth are you talking about?"

"There is a source of great love and satisfaction, very, very close to you, and you are missing it."

Carlotta had looked pensive for a moment, and then irritated.

"Thank you, Norbert, for the entertainment. I'm so glad I found time today to support you in your fortune-telling trick."

She was irked. Norbert knew he had given her something to think about.

-55-

Carlotta heard Hope's discouragement on the phone.

"I don't remember anything so scary in my life, Aunty. When she was gone, and I didn't know where, I felt so helpless. And stupid."

"Oh, no, dear. You handled it very well."

"Really? Because I feel like a total failure, every day. I hate feeling so incompetent. And whenever I do, I think of you, how you kept telling me that I didn't know what I was getting into. I was too naïve. You were absolutely right."

"No, Hope! I'm not always right about everything, you know." Carlotta wondered if she had ever said such a thing before, and wondered why she was saying it now.

"She crossed the tracks, do you realize? If something ever happened to her while she was in my care, I could never live with myself. She was walking around town without an adult, and in the meantime, I was relaxing in my chair, listening to music. I wasn't even able to keep her safe at home. Maybe I'm not qualified to do this."

"Hope, stop. You are doing it as well as anyone could. It's not that bad. She got mad at you and went to the library. You figured out where she was, and went and got her. Please. Don't make a tragic opera out of it."

"Well, when you say it like that," said Hope.

"It's all new to you, that's all." Carlotta noticed herself shifting in her stance. This whole foster-child-thing was becoming an interesting project, and if there was one thing Carlotta loved, it was an interesting project.

"She shuts down sometimes, Aunty. Did your kids ever do that? Like, stop talking, or like, burst out really angry sometimes?"

"Oh, who remembers?" said Carlotta with a light laugh.

She could feel Hope's resolve weakening. If Carlotta pushed her at this point, just a little, she felt she could convince her that she was failing this child, and was not fit for the task. Carlotta knew that Hope was experiencing normal doubts. After all, what mother didn't feel like giving up at times? What mother didn't feel, quite often, in fact, that she just wasn't cut out to be a mom?

Carlotta had vague recollections of long-ago children's temper tantrums, of her own tears of defeat, and of her perplexed searches for the library books that would tell her the secrets of perfect motherhood—those secrets that other women seemed to come by so naturally. A new mother is a fragile and vulnerable creature.

Carlotta needed to double back.

"Don't be discouraged, dear. Didn't I already say I would help you? The little girl and I will really get to know each other. And I want you to call me whenever you're feeling stressed about this. It's a good thing that you are doing, Hope. Good for *you*. And good for the little—uh, *Queen*, too. Stay the course."

"So, I'm not going to be an idiot as a mother, right?"

Carlotta found her throat growing tight with unaccustomed emotion, "Do *not* give up on this child." Carlotta could see Queen in her mind's eye, and felt a flash of loyalty toward this be-spectacled and dignified small person, although she didn't understand why.

"And, Hope, stop wavering. It's sounds as if you don't know your own mind. You've made a decision; it's a good one. Now: forward! March!"

In the silence that followed, Carlotta sensed she might have hurt Hope's tender feelings.

"I don't mean to sound harsh."

"What? No. I was just thinking that I never expected *you* to say, 'don't give up on this child.'"

"Did I say that?"

"Yes, you did."

"Well, then." Carlotta cleared her throat. "Wishy washy never won the war, my dear. Make up your mind. In, or out."

"Oh, I'm in. You're right. I shouldn't need anyone to encourage me."

"*Encouragement* –within reason– is fine. All mothers need it. But at the end of the day, are you committed to making this work, or are you just seeing how it plays out?"

"Committed."

"Good! I hoped you would say that."

There was a pause.

"I didn't tell you about the jewelry."

"What jewelry?"

"The necklaces and bracelets that you and Summer are always buying me for my birthday and Christmas?"

"What about them?"

"Queen took a big bunch of them and sold them to the little girl across the street for three dollars."

Carlotta visualized this entrepreneurial transaction. This was a resourceful child. She had no idea of the value of things, of course. But still, this was a girl with ideas of her own. And then, surprising even herself, Carlotta began to laugh. She laughed and laughed, until a tear ran down her powdered cheek.

-56-

An excerpt from Queen's notebook:
Snooping.

I am what you call a Snoop cause I need to be cause people don't tell you Everything you need to know about them they are liers & they don't tell you whats going to Happen but I know what I need to know cause I check droors cabinets & cell phones. & don't forget the glove compartment. Clews are Everywhere just Look!

It had been some time since Carlotta had entertained a nine-year-old. She'd bought a large box of crayons and a coloring book, and was prepared to take Queen to the park by the lake. But Queen was happy to stay home on this, the first day they would spend together, while Hope worked at the café. Queen roamed the house, running her finger across the spines of the lowest of the hundreds of books in the floor-to-ceiling book cases in Carlotta's living room, study and den. She seemed very impressed with the gold lettering on the books, saying, "Ooh. Hardcovers. *Pretty* ones." Whenever she hit a familiar title, she called out, "Hey! I *know* this one!" Carlotta let the child take her time, wandering the house with Toutou merrily following at her heels. Carlotta heard her footsteps overhead as the child poked her head into the bedrooms and all the corners of the house. In the meantime, Carlotta baked a batch of sugar cookies and brewed a pot of apple cinnamon tea.

What a storybook "grandaunt" I am, thought Carlotta, *serving warm, fresh-baked cookies to my grandniece.*

She would need to tell Queen that homemade cookies were just a once-in-a-while treat. It did not do to spoil children. The child would need firm ground rules, as every child did, and she would need to understand that Carlotta required polite and respectful behavior at all times.

The one good thing about children was that they were easy to control. On the negative side, children in general were inconvenient, messy, noisy, and slow on the uptake. They wore out their welcome quickly. The best way to deal with them was to settle them in front of the television, and wait for them to grow up and become good conversationalists.

Carlotta brought the still-warm cookies to the dining room. Queen and Toutou appeared at the table, Queen seated expectantly with her hands resting on the lacey cloth, and the little dog seated with equal expectation at her feet.

"Toutou seems to have fallen in love with you," flattered Carlotta.

"That's because I'm giving her graham crackers," said Queen, holding up the plastic bag of crumbs that had been resting on her lap.

"You've been trailing graham crackers all over my house?"

"Nah. Toutou gobbled them all up."

"But Toutou is on a special diet. She can't have graham crackers. Please don't give her anything ever again without asking me."

Queen studied Carlotta before answering.

"Toutou *loves* graham crackers."

It was Carlotta's turn to study Queen. The child's chin was lifted and her regard was direct.

"Be that as it may. No graham crackers for my dog."

"'Be that as it may,'" repeated Queen, softly, and then added in a stronger tone, "Be that as it may, I was only being nice."

In Carlotta's day, this would have been considered "answering back," and would have been met with strong discouragement, maybe even corporal punishment. Times had changed. People explained things to children now. Over-explained, in Carlotta's opinion.

Simply state what behavior is needed.

"Your continuing to discuss it is rude. I am your elder. When I correct you, you do not need to justify yourself. Simply say, 'I understand,' or 'Thank you for telling me.'"

The little girl sat with a very straight back and her eyes went wide.

"*Be that as it may*, don't correct me, please. You can correct *mistakes*. You cannot correct *people*. I am a *person*."

What an exasperating little girl.

Her attitude was completely unacceptable in any child. However, truth to be told, Carlotta was getting a tremendous kick out of her.

Queen added with emphasis, *"I am using my words."*

What a peculiar thing to say.

The two adversaries sat in stony silence, eating cookies. The skinny child had an extraordinary appetite.

Two copies of *The Tale of Despereaux* lay on the table. One was the child's; the other must have been Carlotta's copy, which she had left on her night stand. Queen must have been walking around in her bedroom, to spot it.

"Since you are so fond of Despereaux," said Carlotta, moving onto literary ground, "I picked up my own copy at Butler's Books. I'm not a fan of mice and rats; however, the book seems to have psychological depth."

Queen's expression became softer.

Carlotta tried to bring the discussion down to Queen's age level.

"Who is your favorite character?"

"Despereaux!" said Queen, with feeling.

"And why is that?" asked Carlotta.

"Because I like him the best," said Queen. She appeared surprised to have to state the obvious for Carlotta.

"But *why* is he your favorite? What do you like about him?"

"He's brave." Queen reflected, pushing cookie crumbs into a pile on her plate. "Did you read the part where he was born with his eyes open, and he should have had them closed?"

"Yes, dear. That's in the very beginning."

"Everything is wrong about him, but he's still the best one in the whole book." Queen lifted the plate and licked the pile of crumbs off, and Carlotta put a hand to her mouth, to prevent herself from delivering an etiquette lesson.

Queen continued, "His ears are the wrong size, *he's* the wrong size. He doesn't want to do what mice do. He wants to listen to music." Queen said shyly, "I love that."

Carlotta dropped her hand and regarded Queen intently.

"Go on. What else? What else about Despereaux?"

"No one wants him. I thought he would try to be like the other mice, to fit in. But he never does. He can't. Not even to make his mother love him, he just can't. He *knows* who he is. He's really perfect, *I* think."

Carlotta's breath slowed as she listened to Queen's analysis. She didn't want to miss a word.

"And the other characters, what about them?"

"Well, there's Miggery Sow!" Queen gave a short laugh, and Carlotta started, realizing that this was the first time she had heard the child laugh.

Queen went on, "I love that name, Miggery Sow. But that girl is *stoo-pid*. She thinks she can be a princess. She's so stupid, she'll believe anyone. But if you're born low like her, you can't be a princess. Never. But the real princess isn't that great her-self, anyway. It's not such a big deal to be a princess. It's better to be yourself. That's what Despereaux does. That's why he's the best one in the book, and so the book is about him."

Carlotta sat back in her chair, and experienced one of those rare instances in her life when she didn't know what to say. This little girl was a diamond in the rough. Carlotta determined at once to take over Queen's intellectual development.

Her first impression had been that Queen was a dim-witted child—probably due to Hope's description of what to expect before the girl arrived. She was pleased now to see that there was far more to Queen than she would have suspected. She felt an unaccustomed curiosity about this little girl. In Queen, Car-lotta intuited a fierce independence, a refreshing originality, and a superior intellect, in short: a kindred spirit.

Change, when it comes to a person, can happen slowly or it can happen quickly. It all depends on a person's readiness for that change to come and offer itself as a shining possibility, an opportunity to grow more fully into oneself. And it also de-pends on the person's connection to the catalyst for change. In this case, the catalyst was a vulnerable and dignified nine-year-old with a love of reading.

Hope's silly idea of fostering a child didn't seem so silly any more, now that Carlotta saw how she, herself, could have a starring role in this story. This little girl could be her disciple. Queen could grow to be a credit to her, and Carlotta could be admired by everyone for the natural educator and mentor that she was. Who needed a Club of old ladies of inferior intelli-gence, when one had a bright child to mold?

"Tell me, Queen, how did you learn to think about books and understand them as you do?"

"My mother used to read to me," said Queen.

Carlotta's assumption about Queen's mother toppled and shattered. A new image of the child's background was forming in her mind. A wise and nurturing mother, one who loved books and who knew the importance of passing on that love to her daughter.

"Did she, really?"

"Yes. Every night." Queen drank the last drops of her tea, and placed the cup in the saucer with care. "That was before she went to the Place."

"What Place?"

Queen's face puckered. "I don't like to say it."

Carlotta tilted her head and tried to imagine what Place Queen could be referring to.

Queen, tracing the lace pattern of the table cloth, whispered, "Prison." Emotions moved over Queen's face, until at last she said simply, "I call it the Place. I don't like that other word."

Carlotta's new image of Queen's mother faded and dissolved. *Prison?* Hope hadn't mentioned that the child's mother was in prison. No doubt she thought that this information would prejudice Carlotta against the child. As if Carlotta were in any way judgmental.

Should she ask Queen about her mother? But Queen had a question of her own.

"Be that as it may, Mrs. Moon. What is *your* favorite book, and why?"

-57-

The next morning, Lorraine burst in on Carlotta as she was putting away her morning's literary labors.

"The *show!*"

"*What* show?"

"*Our* show! It's on today. It starts in five minutes!"

Lorraine hugged and kissed Carlotta, and then pushed past her and hurried down to the den, with Carlotta following, saying, "And good morning to *you*, Lorraine."

Lorraine turned on the TV and sat on the couch, patting the spot next to her for Carlotta.

"Is your TV broken?" Carlotta was the sarcastic one today.

"What? No, of course not. I want you to see this." Lorraine glanced at Carlotta. "You don't mind, do you?"

Carlotta began to answer, but Lorraine said, "Shush."

To be shushed in my own home!

The music accompanying the opening credits was a banjo instrumental of "Someone's in the Kitchen with Dinah," while the title that rolled out over the yellow gingham background read: "In the Kitchen with Margaret." And then, there was blue-eyed Margaret, in her home kitchen, brightly describing the savory wonderfulness of the vegetable curry dish she was about to prepare, "for all of you out there in television land."

Carlotta folded her arms and leaned back, studying the production with a critical eye. Overall, it was an amateurish effort. The camera shook, giving the impression of an earthquake that the cook was ignoring in her determination to start her curry.

209

Margaret repeated herself often. She also left long moments of silence. The lighting was bad.

There was a break and a cut to the next scene, where Margaret, back to the camera, was talking while rinsing rice, and the water drowned out her voice. Margaret flipped off the faucet, turned to the camera with a big grin, and resumed, "*I can't say it isn't!*"

Carlotta leaned forward. "That's not Margaret. That's *Mabel!*"

Lorraine nodded and winked at Carlotta. "Isn't it a scream?"

"You put Mabel in one of Margaret's polka dotted dresses and took away her baseball cap."

"Yep!"

"What for?"

"For fun. It's fun, to see if we can pass off one as the other!"

Before Carlotta could share her own opinion, there was another awkward cut to a new scene, and on-screen Mabel called out, "Who's hungry?"

"We are!" called Carlotta's Club, and there they all were (with the notable exception of Carlotta herself), sitting around Margaret's table, eating vegetable curry and complimenting the cook. "Mmmm. Sure is good," said Norbert's voice. They were all so happy and busy without Carlotta. It was sickening.

From the TV, Mabel's raucous voice called out, "Well, that's all for this time. Bye for now!"

TV-Margaret whined, "Oh! That was *my* line."

Mabel reasoned, "Well you didn't say it. Someone's got to say it. Say it, then, honey."

Margaret put her face into the camera and said with satisfaction, "Bye for now!"

The credits rolled. Director: Mabel Paine. Producer: Mabel Paine. Talent: Margaret Birch. Camera 1: Birdie Walsh. Camera

2: Norbert Zelenka. Camera 3: Lorraine Andretta. Set design: Margaret Birch. Character Generator: Norbert Zelenka. A production of GBC TV, Gibbons Corner, New York.

Carlotta could feel Lorraine looking at her, proud that she had been on television and waiting for Carlotta to admire her.

"Well, don't worry about it too much, Lorraine. One comfort is, nobody watches community TV. No one will see it."

"Oh, no one will see it, huh?"

"Of course not. With four hundred channels to watch, no one will ever know about it."

"Oh, yeah? Even though this episode has already aired five times this week, in different time slots?"

Carlotta paused, uncertain.

"Because the young men at the station who decide on the scheduling like it so much, they are giving it lots of air time."

Carlotta opened her eyes wide, and put her hand to her mouth.

"Oh, dear. *Lorraine.* Do you think they are laughing at you? Elderly people making fools of themselves? They *wouldn't* be so cruel, would they?"

"Carlotta Moon!" Lorraine's eyes blazed. "Just listen to yourself! What's *wrong* with you?"

Carlotta didn't meet Lorraine's gaze, but found something absorbing to study in the corner of the ceiling.

"You know what, Carlotta? You could be having fun with us, too. You could be in the show. You could come to the Alibi with us after each filming. We all have a glass of wine. Well, maybe Mabel might have two glasses of wine. We have a nice time together, and we all want you to be part of it. But do you join in? No. You don't. You always pretend you're busy."

"Lorraine, I've already told you. I *am* busy. I am writing a book."

211

"And why is it that *I* can be happy for *you*, that you are enjoying writing your book finally, but you can't be happy for me, that I am having fun with our friends—yeah, *and* Mabel—while you write it? Tell me that, wouldja? I'm *prouda* you and the book you're writing."

Carlotta thought Lorraine wouldn't be, if she knew how she was portrayed as Bernadette Arnold in *How Sharper than a Serpent's Tooth.*

Lorraine resumed, "Is it just because you always have to be the one with the Big Idea? You always have to be the boss?"

There are some things that can never be forgiven. One of them is to be told an unflattering truth by a dear friend.

As Carlotta accompanied Lorraine to the door, they were both quiet, absorbed in dark thoughts about each other. Their old friendship was crumbling under the hurricane-like influence of Mabel.

-58-

Carlotta stood, well-dressed in a sky blue blouse, navy pants and good walking shoes, in front of Central Elementary School. She was following orders from Hope, to pick Queen up at 2:45. Carlotta thought it was ridiculous to pick children up. She stood among the young mothers in yoga pants who chatted among themselves and tapped at their cell phones while keeping watchful eyes on the school door. Why didn't children today walk home with their friends? Carlotta's house was only six blocks away. But Hope had insisted that Queen was still getting her bearings, and continued to need close monitoring, considering her penchant for "running away." Carlotta had insisted that going to the library was not "running away," but she had agreed to do things Hope's way.

"You are the mother," Carlotta had said. "I'm not going to thwart you."

"Thank you, Aunty," and Carlotta had heard the gratitude in Hope's voice. "Now," Hope had continued, "when she gets to your house, she'll need a snack, and then you go through her backpack and get her started on homework."

Hope had carried on giving instructions that Carlotta heard with disdain. Homework was children's business. What one wanted in a child was independence. Independence was fostered by staying out of the child's affairs, and putting one's attention on things more interesting to oneself. She had no intention of becoming one of those—what were they all being now—helicopters? No, she was not and never would be a helicopter.

Carlotta's musings were interrupted by the bursting forth of an unruly mob from the bowels of the school. Out poured children of all sizes, some hollering and laughing, some walking slowly with papers spilling out of unzipped backpacks. Chubby, skinny, exuberant and exhausted, there were all kinds of children. They all had one thing in common. They were all white. Except for one solitary black girl who stood still in the middle of the throng, blinking in the sun and looking around.

In the seconds before Carlotta stepped forward to claim Queen, she had the realization that she had rarely in her life considered race. Being a white woman in a white town, she hadn't needed to. She had never thought of anyone as particularly "Caucasian" before. But this afternoon, she saw before her a sea of Caucasian faces. From the corner of her eye she did at last spy—with a sense of relief—a sprinkling of Hispanics and a pair of Asians. But there was only one African American child in that entire horde of children: hers.

Carlotta walked away from the school with one hand holding Queen's and the other swinging a bag from Butler's Books. Lorraine had already bought the child one paperback classic. Fine. Carlotta had now bought three hardcovers. Classics, of course, every bit as good as Lorraine's choice. She anticipated Queen's pleasure on reading the titles: *Charlotte's Web, Alice through the Looking Glass,* and *Little Women.* An assortment of interesting and independent heroines. But, Carlotta now realized with a stab of uncertainty, none of these heroines was black. Why had the thought not occurred to her before that Queen might like a book about an interesting and independent black girl? *Were* there such books? Carlotta didn't know. She would have to make another trip to consult Arnie at the book store.

"Queen, you remember my friend Lorraine?"

"Mrs. Andretta?

Carlotta was pleased at this child's good manners. Sometimes she had the impression that the titles "Miss," "Mrs." and "Mr." were going away. That would be a terrible shame.

"Yes! Mrs. Andretta. She is not only my friend, but also my neighbor. We're going to stop at her house on our way home, just to say hello. And I have a little present for you," added Carlotta in a sing-song-y voice, "right here in this bag, and you can open it after we get to Mrs. Andretta's."

Queen smiled up at Carlotta.

"I already know. It's a *book,* isn't it?" She looked with interest around Carlotta, at the bag she was carrying.

"That would be telling," sang Carlotta.

Although she was still nursing a grudge against her old friend, she would be stopping by Lorraine's today just long enough to parade Queen in front of her, showing herself to be a young-at-heart, energetic caregiver of a nine-year-old child. And while she was at it, she could demonstrate that her own gift to Queen surpassed Lorraine's.

Lorraine lived in a red brick bungalow with leaded windows. On her stone front porch were stainless steel dishes from which she fed the feral cats in the neighborhood (as well as those outdoor cats who pushed in for an extra free buffet).

Peering around to be sure no felines were lurking in the shadows, Carlotta stepped up to the doorbell and rang. After waiting three seconds, she put a key in the lock and let herself and Queen in.

"Woo-ooo!" sang Carlotta in a forceful soprano.

Queen laughed. "Woo-ooo!" she imitated in exactly the same pitch.

Queen looked around at the arts and crafts-y style house, taking in the solid lines and abundant dark wood. "This is a pretty house," she commented to Carlotta, who tossed her head.

Lorraine emerged from her den at the back of the house, drying her hands on a towel. She had been painting, and was wearing a large white smock, stained with pigment.

"Well, look who the cat dragged in!"

Lorraine and Carlotta kissed cheeks.

"We're just stopping by, on our way home from school." Carlotta placed a hand on Queen's shoulder.

"What can I get for yooz?" Lorraine turned to Queen. "You want some cookies? I'll get out some cookies. Come on back."

Queen and Carlotta followed Lorraine through her living room and dining room, and into her kitchen.

"I'll put the kettle on for your Aunt Carlotta. She always wants tea. I never drink the stuff, myself."

"She's not my aunt."

"Oh. Well. All righty then."

"She's Mrs. Moon. And you're Mrs. Andretta. Hope wanted me to call you all 'aunts' and 'uncle,' too. But I decided to call you 'Mrs.' and 'Mr.' Except for Hope. She's just Hope."

"That sounds very appropriate, young lady." Lorraine put a plate of Girl Scout cookies on the table. "And whadda ya like to drink?"

"I like tea, like Mrs. Moon. With sugar, please. Thank you."

Lorraine arched an eyebrow at Carlotta, who understood her to communicate, *A little tea drinker, huh? Please and thank you already. I don't see so many behavior problems here.* They'd been best friends for a very long time, and a lot could be communicated by an eyebrow.

"Whatcha got in the bag?"

"Oh!" said Carlotta. "This? I picked up a little gift for Queen just before school let out. She hasn't even had a chance to open it yet." With a light laugh, she gave the bag to Queen.

Both Queen and Lorraine gave satisfactory reactions to the books Carlotta had selected.

Lorraine approved the title choices: "No child's library is complete without these!"

Queen said, *"Hardcovers,"* and there was reverence in her voice. "Thank you."

"You are very welcome, my dear." Generously, Carlotta added, "That was a nice book Mrs. Andretta gave you, too."

"I started reading it already. *The Secret Garden.* I like that title. I keep it in my backpack and take it out for silent reading time at school. I still haven't got to the part where she snoops to find the garden and the crying person. So far, looks like she's a girl no one wants, because she has a bad attitude."

"Some of the best protagonists in literature have a bad attitude," asserted Carlotta.

She was pleased with Queen and tempted to continue the book discussion, but this was not the time. When adults were speaking, children needed to be seen and not heard. Making a child the center of things was a sure way to wind up with an insufferable brat that no one would like. Children, believed Carlotta, needed to be able to entertain themselves. Life was not all Disneyworld all the time. Besides, Carlotta needed to speak to Lorraine privately, and give her an opportunity to apologize for the true and unkind statements she had made the day before.

"Queen, Hope wants you to get started on your homework after school. You can stay here in the kitchen with your tea and cookies, and get your work out of your backpack. Mrs. Andretta and I will be in the living room, talking."

Queen, heaping sugar into her tea cup, nodded.

The conversation in the living room began on the safe topic of literature.

"What are you reading?"

Lorraine brandished a thick black paperback. "You gotta read this. So maybe it's not so much your idea of literary. But it's *good!* A best-selling thriller! It's such a page-turner."

"Let me guess. An unreliable narrator? No one is who they seem to be? The bad turn out to be not so bad, and the good turn out to be the worst of all?"

"You've read it?"

"I don't need to, dear, do I?"

"Okay. I get it. Well, what are *you* reading then? Something so much smarter, right?"

"Lorraine. You make it sound as though I pick out books based on some wish of mine to impress people with my intellect."

Pause.

"It just so happens I'm re-reading one of my favorites: *To the Lighthouse*, by Virginia Woolf."

Carlotta, as it happened, was not re-reading that classic. She was neither re-reading it nor reading it. She had never read it. Her copy had sat undisturbed on its shelf for forty years. She *had* read a quick summary of it just that morning in *How to Discuss Classics You Haven't Read*, in case Lorraine would challenge her. Lorraine, however, appeared docile today, and ready to take Carlotta at her word. This was Lorraine's tacit—and inadequate—apology for her honesty of the day before: to pretend to accept Carlotta's pretension.

"Is that the one where she spends five pages talking about the drizzling rain, fuh crissake?" asked Lorraine. "You always pick the hardest books."

Carlotta laughed her tinkling laugh. "Oh, Lorraine."

Lorraine might fawn, but Carlotta had not gotten the apology she was after. Her resentment festered.

However, there was something more she hoped to get at Lorraine's: a teacher's informal assessment of Queen's intelligence. She lowered her voice, as best as she was able. "This little girl, now." She glanced through the dining room and into the kitchen, but Queen was no longer at the table. She must have got up to find the bathroom. "She's very interesting, isn't she?"

"She's a little smarty, that one," said Lorraine in a low tone. "Anybody could see that. I have a feeling she's gonna change things around here. She's the new generation. We need her. Because you know what, Carlotta? I'll *tell* you what: Life goes on. I've lost people, you've lost people…"

Carlotta did not like where this was going.

Lorraine, ever-sensitive to Carlotta's moods, made a U-turn. "And here we still are, and life goes on. Not to mention, this is not an ordinary kid. I taught fifth-grade, remember. I know a gifted child when I see one. First time I met her, I'll be honest with you, that's the impression I got. This kid is way up there."

Carlotta felt very pleased, as if Queen's brightness were, in some way, to her credit.

"Wait," said Lorraine. "Where is she?"

Lorraine stood and peered toward the kitchen. Then, stepping lightly, she walked swiftly back toward the bathroom and bedrooms. Carlotta remained on the couch.

From Lorraine's bedroom, Queen's voice bellowed, *"I hate you! I'll shoot you! I'll kill you!"*

Carlotta stood and hurried toward the commotion.

Queen was seated on Lorraine's bedroom floor with Lorraine's open wallet. Before Queen, on the rug, were bills and coins, stacked in neat denominations.

"You gonna *shoot* me?" asked Lorraine. "Whaddaya—gonna shoot me with your *finger*?"

Queen was stuffing the money back into the wallet. "I was just counting it. It's $37.42. You scared me."

"Oh, so now I *scared* you? While you're taking money outta my wallet I *scared* you? So I should be ashamed of myself? Or *what*?"

"Lorraine!" Carlotta found her voice at last. "Let's not talk about this right now. Let's get all the money back in the wallet, and just calm down first."

"Calm down? Calm down? I *am* calm. I don't need to calm down. *What?* I don't have a right to say, whaddaya doing, getting into my wallet? I shouldn't say that? *What?*"

"People don't like to be cornered, Lorraine. It's humiliating."

"Whadda you? Crazy? The kid was going through my *wallet!*"

"Oh! You just *love* to find people out, don't you? That's one of your faults, Lorraine. You should work on that."

-59-

Carlotta and Queen walked from Lorraine's house to Carlotta's in silence, letting their emotions settle. Once inside, Carlotta said to Queen, "Let's have a little heart-to-heart, dear."

"Uh oh. Here we go," said Queen, flopping onto the couch, with Toutou lying supportively at her feet.

"'Here we go'—where?" asked Carlotta.

"Here we go, back into the system," sighed Queen.

Carlotta regarded Queen, whose downcast eyes gave her a look of defeat.

"My, how you dramatize things," said Carlotta. "We simply need to talk, that's all. No need to bring 'the system' into it."

"Oh," said Queen. "You say that *now*. I know how this goes."

Carlotta reflected. *Did* Queen know how this would go? Would the child inevitably go back into the foster care system? But she hadn't done anything so awful. She had misbehaved, but every child does that.

"I wasn't trying to steal—you know that, don't you, Mrs. Moon? I wasn't. I said I was counting the money, and I *was* counting it."

"But why?"

"I just like to know what people have."

Carlotta nodded. *We all like to know that.*

"But you do understand—that's not allowed? Just because we 'like to know,' that doesn't mean we can get into people's purses." Carlotta thought it more tactful to use the first person plural, rather than put Queen on the defensive with the pronoun "you." "And another thing. Whenever we may be embarrassed or upset, we don't threaten to kill anyone. That really puts people off, you know."

"Mrs. Andretta hates me now. And Hope will, too, when she finds out. Because you're going to tell Hope, aren't you?"

"Oh, Mrs. Andretta does not hate you. She knows children are not good all of the time. And as for Hope...." Carlotta realized that Hope would be swayed by Carlotta's own attitude toward the incident. "Well, I'll explain to Hope that you are sorry and that you apologized to Mrs. Andretta. Because that's what you are going to do: call her and apologize, and tell her you will never do anything like that again."

Queen's temper ignited.

"*Apologize? I --wasn't --stealing!* Ooh, *you* all love apologies, but I don't ever hear any of you apologize for anything *you* do. Grown-ups lie and do all kinds of things, and never *ever* say sorry."

Tears of rage trembled in Queen's eyes, before spilling forward and trickling down her face, and dripping from her chin. She held the heels of her hands up to her eyes to try to stop the flow. Her mouth was contorted as she gasped to hold back the sobs that wanted to burst from her. Her nose began to run, and Carlotta handed her a tissue.

She realized that this child had had a volatile past, of which Carlotta was ignorant. She wondered how much Hope knew about Queen's previous life.

Queen, gaining control of her tears and straightening her back, challenged, "I bet *you* don't *ever* apologize, Mrs. Moon."

"Of course, I do, Queen. All the time," Carlotta lied. "It's the most natural thing in the world. I apologize, and so do you. All right-thinking people do."

Queen sniffed and hesitated. She wiped her nose with the tissue.

"Am I a right-thinking person?"

"You will be, when you apologize," assured Carlotta.

-60-

Hope stood over the recycling bin with the mail: pizza coupons and flyers from local stores. On the counter, she laid the bill from the sanitary district. And there was a handwritten envelope, addressed in a flowing cursive hand to Miss Queen Serafina Jones. Hope read the sender's name: Dahleeya Jones, Inmate #4482023. The letter came from the Compton Walker Correctional Facility in Shelton, New York.

The social worker that Hope secretly called "the Wish Fairy"—the nice one—had told her a little bit about Queen's mother. She was serving a twelve-year term, of which she had already served four years. Still, by the time she would be released, Queen would be seventeen. Ms. Jones had given up her parental rights so that all three of her daughters could be adopted and have some stability. The two younger ones had their forever family, but Queen had been harder to place. The Wish Fairy encouraged Hope to take Queen to see her mother, saying that it was important for the child's emotional health, but added that it was not a requirement, and maybe was a lot to ask. The prison was two hours away from Gibbons Corner.

Hope turned to find Queen watching her from the kitchen doorway.

"Is that for me?" she asked.

"Yes," said Hope, holding the envelope out to her.

Hope wanted to be the mother of this child, but the child already had a mother.

Queen opened the envelope carefully, making a jagged split with her finger down the side and sliding out two folded sheets of notebook paper which she opened and set on the table, smoothing out the creases. It was not a letter, but one blank page, and one sheet that displayed the tracing of a hand. In the palm of the hand were printed the words: "Remember me." Each of the five fingers contained a message: "Forever in my heart," "Do good in school," "You are smart," "Your mama loves you, always will," "Write to me."

Queen ran her own fingers along the drawn fingers, and then pressed her left hand against the larger left hand on the page. She looked up at Hope.

"My mama, every year, around the start of the school year, she sends me her hand. Then I trace mine, on the other paper, and send it back to her. She collects them, to watch how my hand is growing. She's making a scrapbook. It has all my letters to her. She says it makes her feel good to read them over and over. Do you have an envelope and a stamp you could give me?"

-61-

The next day, Queen, jostled by the throng of liberated children, emerged from Central School to see Mr. Zelenka waiting for her with his little white Chihuahua, Ivy, in his carrying bag. Tuesdays were his day. She would walk with him to the Good Fortune Café, where Hope would be bustling around. She would sit at a booth where he could keep an eye on her while she did her homework, and he would read fortunes with cards. People came from all over to get a reading from him. He was like that Madame Fifi on late-night TV.

Queen's last foster mother had been a fan of Madame Fifi, whose show came on at 2 a.m. From her bedroom door which was right across from the blaring living room TV, Queen would observe that foster mother smoke cigarettes, take little sips from a small glass with a golden colored liquid in it, and watch the "amazing television psychic that everyone is talking about," as the announcer asserted. Madame Fifi was a heavy woman with lots of black eyeliner and a French accent that seemed to come and go. She took calls from around the country. The callers asked questions like, "Is he cheatin' on me?" and "Am I coming into a lot of money soon?" After half an hour, sadly, Madame Fifi would tell her audience that she had to go off the air now, but they could—and should—still call her tonight, at the number on the screen. One night, Queen watched as her foster mother dialed. She heard as her foster mother read the numbers off her credit card.

Then she listened in.

"Is this Madame Fifi? .... It don't sound like you, Madame Fifi.... It is? You sure? Okay...." The foster mother stabbed out the stub of a cigarette in an ashtray and breathed out a stream of smoke. "Well, here's what I want to know, and if you're a real psychic, and I do believe you are, you should be able to tell me this: 'Where is my boyfriend right now?'"

Queen couldn't hear Madame Fifi's response, but she could tell that her foster mother was getting very mad, so she slipped back to bed. Wrapping herself in the thin covers, she lay awake, and imagined having the super power of knowing everything about everyone. Yes, that would be the super power she would choose for herself, if she *could* choose.

Today, as they walked together, Mr. Zelenka pointed out the trees and told her what kind they all were. They gathered a fallen, colored leaf from each species. He showed her the veins in the leaves, and said they were like the veins in a person's hand, carrying sap, which was like blood to a human. Queen noticed the veins on the back of Mr. Zelenka's hand, which stood out because he was old.

Queen asked, "If trees have blood, then where's their heart?"

Mr. Zelenka did not laugh, but paused to consider.

"Now, that is a very good question," he said, and Queen felt proud of herself for thinking of it.

Mr. Zelenka continued, "That question shows your mind is busy working." He tapped his temple. "Actually, trees don't have a heart muscle, like we do."

"I didn't think so," said Queen. "I was just playing."

Then he began to tell her about photosynthesis.

Queen was not interested in photosynthesis. She would have preferred to think of trees with beating hearts. While he spoke, she felt the kindness in his voice and she thought that he was a nice man, probably, and that he was not like the foster dads and granddads she had met so far.

At the café, Hope lit up with happiness when she saw Queen, and tried to give her a kiss, but Queen turned her face away, as she always did. She didn't need foster mothers kissing on her.

Then Hope brought her an avocado on rye sandwich and a glass of juice, and rushed away, busy with customers.

Norbert didn't have a customer, so he and Queen played rummy with a spare deck he had in his bag.

"That Ivy's looking at me," said Queen, with a giggle. "She's like, *'who are you?'*" Queen waved her index finger at the little dog.

Mr. Zelenka was smiling. One thing Queen noticed about him: he was always smiling, no matter what was going on. Did that mean he was always happy? Or was that just what his face did? She thought that was just what his face did. To know how he felt, she would have to look past the smile for another clue.

"Do you like your job?" asked Queen, conversationally, arranging the cards in her hand according to suit.

"Fortune telling? Why, yes, I do. I used to be an accountant, you know. I helped companies with budgets and taxes and things."

"That sounds boring," commented Queen.

Mr. Zelenka agreed, "I guess it does. I did like it at the time. I like things that make sense."

Queen nodded vigorously.

"But *this*—" He waved to indicate his booth in the café, "This is much better. I feel like I help people with their lives."

"Mr. Zelenka." Queen lay her cards down on the table. "What's it like, to know everything about everyone?" She rested her chin in her hands, the better to focus on his answer.

"Oh, my!" Mr. Zelenka, smiling, looked with interest into Queen's eyes, and set his cards down, as well. "Is that what you think? That I know everything about everyone? Oh my goodness, no."

Queen was disappointed.

"Then, you're a fake?"

Mr. Zelenka's eyes opened wide. "Oh, no, not that, either!"

Queen twisted her mouth and looked at him skeptically.

"Let me explain. A customer comes in and we lay out the cards in the horseshoe spread. While they are shuffling, handing me cards, and maybe telling me why they came, I am getting a sense of what they want or need in their lives, what would be good for them."

Queen folded her arms and pursed her lips, listening.

"It's not magic," Norbert went on. "It's not even ESP. I notice their clothes, their attitude, their posture—everything I can see. I listen to their words and their tone. It's just paying really good attention—plus the fact that I have lived a long time, so I've seen a lot of things before. It's like each person is a puzzle and I try to put them together while we sit here and look at the cards. And my goal is to help them see what they need to see, and to feel better in some way, to feel encouraged."

"So you are *too* a fake." And Queen had thought Mr. Zelenka was a nice man. "You say you are a fortune-teller, but really, you're just reading people."

"I *am* reading people—in order to help them. I'm helping them see things that they themselves are not paying attention to. When they sit with me and think that I have the answers from the Universe or something, they somehow become more honest with themselves. They tune into their own answers. I always tell them that—all their answers are already within them. But they never believe me."

Queen considered this.

"So what *you* do—you try to help people by having a conversation…. So, you're like a social worker, except instead of a laptop, you have a deck of cards."

"Something like that," agreed Mr. Zelenka.

In the front of the café, Hope was greeting a small blond lady who had just come in. She was wearing a brown tweed coat and tall boots, and looked like a white Skipper doll with freckles. It was Summer Moon, Hope's cousin and Mrs. Moon's granddaughter. Queen called her Miss Moon, because she wasn't married.

"Mr. Zelenka, hello! And Queen! How are you, honey?"

Mr. Zelenka, nodding toward Queen, said, "I'm keeping an eye on the little lady today," and he seemed proud to say it. "I was just thinking of closing for business and heading to the park with her. It's too beautiful of a day for a child to be sitting in a café."

"Ah, but first, you have a customer to read for."

Mr. Zelenka looked toward the counter, where customers had to sign in to reserve a time slot with him.

"Me! I'm your customer! Don't you remember last winter; you promised me my second reading?"

Mr. Zelenka shook his head.

"My first reading for you had such unintended consequences. To tell you the truth, I'm nervous to try again. If I do read for you, you have to promise not to do anything impulsive this time."

"Okay, I promise!"

Miss Moon slid into the booth opposite Mr. Zelenka and held out her hand for the deck of cards. Then she turned to Queen.

"Uh, this is a private reading. You don't need to be listening to us. So, why don't you move a couple of tables away, honey, and work on your homework while I'm talking to Mr. Zelenka. Get it all done, so you'll be able to go play at the park."

Queen didn't like this Miss Moon's attitude. She wasn't in charge. She was a bossy pants. Queen didn't like so many people acting like they could tell her what to do. She had all the bossing she could stand, between Hope and the old Mrs. Moon, and on Tuesdays Mr. Zelenka. Of the bunch of them, Mr. Zelenka pretty much let her do anything, as long as it was safe. But she didn't need for anyone to be in charge of her.

"I'll stay right here, thank you. I got all my stuff set up already. I'm not trying to hear what you all are talking about. Got my own work to do."

And without looking up to check if that was okay with Miss Bossy Pants, Queen went on about her own business. She had math homework to do, and it wasn't easy.

Of course, being a snoop, she kept her ears open. That was how you found things out about people. One of the ways. Miss Moon lowered her voice, but Queen's hearing was sharp. Miss Moon asked Mr. Zelenka about guys: this guy, or that guy, or maybe the other guy was better?

Queen sure was glad that Hope wasn't thinking about *guys*. Or was she? This inspired Queen to pull out her notebook and do a little writing.

If you are a forster kid reading this, one thing you do NOT want is your forster mother to get a boyfreind. Beleive me. Almost every forster mother always wants to get a man in the house. I do not know why because when he gets in the house life gets worst for everybody. When she gets a boyfriend they fight and he makes her cry. He might be nice but he probly won't. I never seen a nice one. He can do stuff to you and she'll be on his side. So you just stop him from getting into the house & I am serius. Serius as a harder tack. Do what you have to do.

-62-

The enthusiasms of young people were fleeting, as Carlotta well remembered from her own youth. Her granddaughter Summer, who had seemed thrilled at the prospect of Hope's plan to foster a child—or even a mob of children—had become strikingly unavailable since Queen's actual arrival. Summer's promise of support had apparently been an empty one. She was dating several young men; she was living her life. Meanwhile Carlotta, who had been much more cautious about the foster care idea, was now sharing a significant portion of the responsibility for the child with Hope. It was funny how these things evolved. If Summer thought that her social life was more important, so be it. That just left Carlotta with more time to study —and influence—this interesting child.

"We'll just stop by and see Mrs. Birdie Walsh today," said Carlotta as they walked down Washington Street toward Birdie's house.

"Mrs. Walsh is the one with the parrot," said Queen, with a skip in her step.

"That's right," said Carlotta. "We'll visit for a little while, and then I'll let you stay with her while I pop over to the bank."

"Did you bounce a check?" asked Queen, knowingly.

"Oh, heavens, no!" laughed Carlotta. "I just go and chat with the banker sometimes and we move money around. It would be boring for a child. Much more fun for you to talk to Tetley the parrot."

"Moving *money* around? Like, you have piles of coins and dollar bills in there, and you and the banker just move it all around? You mean, with a shovel or something? Actually, that sounds fun. I think I'd rather go with you."

Carlotta let out a hoot. She, who was not prone to hooting.

"You *do* paint a picture with your words, Queen. Unfortunately, it's not at all like that. You never see the money. It's just two adults talking, and looking at numbers on paper."

"Oh. In that case, I do prefer the parrot."

Tetley, who could be temperamental, was in rare form that afternoon. When Queen approached him, he cocked his head at her and sputtered, "Pretty Birdie! I love you! Mwah! Mwah! Mwah!" finishing his speech with kissing noises, and sending Queen into gales of giggles.

Trying to catch her breath, Queen said to Birdie, "Is he talking to *you*? Does he call you *Birdie?*"

Birdie laughed softly, seeming to delight in Queen's laughter. "He *does* call me Birdie, I guess, but only because I call *him* Birdie. 'Tetley' seems so formal."

Carlotta and Birdie spoke while Queen walked around, exploring.

"Behave yourself, now," reminded Carlotta, raising her eyebrows with meaning.

"Of *course*," said Queen, with dignity. "I'll just go to the powder room, if you don't mind."

After a nice chat with Birdie, Carlotta was on her way out the door, she called to Queen, who came running.

"That's a pretty powder room."

"You were in there quite a while."

Queen folded her arms, offended by Carlotta's air of suspicion.

"Be good, now." Carlotta gave one meaningful nod to the child, making direct eye contact with her. "I'll be back in less than an hour."

When Carlotta returned for Queen, the child had some thoughts to share in the car.

"Mrs. Walsh said a whole bunch of stuff."

"I'm sure she did," acknowledged Carlotta.

"She told me to open my hands up." Queen sat stretching her fingers back from her palms. "I usually hate it when people act like they got to tell me what to do, but Mrs. Walsh isn't like that, like a boss cow. She said, 'open your hands to receive life's blessings.' She said, 'when you keep your hands clenched, those blessings can't get in.' Mrs. Moon, what is she talking about?"

Carlotta smiled. "You just have to get used to Mrs. Walsh. She means no harm. She says funny things. Not ha-ha funny. But, well, a little strange. Her heart is in the right place."

Queen put her hand to her chest.

"Could a person's heart be in the wrong place?"

Carlotta laughed—not the tinkling, false laugh she tended to use with adults—but a real one.

"No, honey. I just meant to say, Mrs. Walsh is a very good lady. However, she may say things that don't make sense to you."

"But I feel like it does make sense, and I just don't get it. Do *you* get it?"

Carlotta, who typically ignored Birdie's whims, took this question as a challenge.

"Well, let's see. Clenched hands block blessings; open hands receive blessings.... Well, maybe it's not really about how you hold your hands. It's how you hold your mind. Open to re- ceive—that means you have a positive and hopeful attitude, and you are ready to consider new ideas. Clenched—that means, your mind isn't available to any new influence. You already know it all, or so you think, and so, you miss out."

Carlotta found herself loosening her tight grip on the steering wheel. Funny, she had never realized how tightly she held the wheel. There was no need. She allowed her hands to hold the wheel more lightly. That felt better.

An excerpt from Queen's notebook:

Mrs. Walsh says wierd stuff and I sware she gotta be on drugs but I didn't find any. Not in the medicine cabinet and not on the floor in the back of her closet either.

When you visit old ladies, try to look around at there stuff cause you will be supprised. Mrs. Walsh has some old timey brooches and some of them sparkel so pretty.

Wierd stuff Mrs. Walsh says: You can dream anything you want into the world. I said I want to dream a tree with a beeting hart into the world and she said if you wanted you could but thats not what you really want think of what you really want. I said I know what I really want but I'd ruther not say.

She said see it in your mind and feel it in your hart the happiness as if you already have it. I did it.

Then she taught me how to paint with watercolors the pretty way, the way real artists do. You shouldnt push hard on the brush that mashes down the hairs on the brush but hold it at an angel and kind of loose and I felt happy when I saw the water melt the blue and green lines into a blueish green stream.

Tonite when Hope said turn out your lite I said I will keep painting because I am inspired. Don't let your forster mother get her way all the time.

Sometimes Hope don't know what to do with me.

-63-

Mabel, wiping the beer foam from her lips, said, "I don't want you to take this the wrong way. I don't talk about people. Never have. But there's one thing I wonder about. How come Carlotta never joins in the fun with us? I'm not trying to gossip, because I hate that. I only want to know if it's something *I* did."

After another successful filming session of *In the Kitchen with Margaret*, the Club—minus Carlotta—was at the Alibi Bar. Below the glowing beer signs beaming from brown paneled walls, and country music playing from speakers, the little group was shifting uncomfortably. Norbert swirled his wine glass; Birdie looked in an unfocused way at Mabel as if she were seeing her aura.

Margaret tried to change the subject.

"Anyone want to order a sandwich? Or split one?"

Birdie reminded Margaret that they had all just eaten a delicious meal that she herself had prepared.

It was up to Lorraine.

"You wanna know what's bothering Carlotta? I'll tell you what's bothering Carlotta. And then maybe you can help us solve the problem and get her back in the Club."

Everyone looked at Lorraine. They were all loyal to Carlotta. No one wanted to tell Mabel, the newcomer, about Carlotta's insecurity and bossiness. But Lorraine encapsulated in a few words what the problem was, and appealed to Mabel.

"We've tried talking to her. It don't work. Whadda *you* got?"

"Well," said Mabel, "I'll do what I *can*. But don't get your hopes up. I always say, 'you can lead a dog to wander, but you can't make him'—oh, *what* is it you can't make a dog do? Anyway. Carlotta's gotta wanna come back to the Club herself, or nothing anyone else does is going to work. Now, *I've* never been much of a problem solver. I'm more of a problem *maker!*" And here she laughed heartily, but the Club regarded her soberly.

Mabel added, "I bet Carlotta's good at solving problems, though. She's a smart one, and I can't say she isn't."

Meanwhile, Carlotta was reading over the manuscript of *How Sharper than a Serpent's Tooth*. She held in her hands a stack of blue paper that had the power to decimate relationships; the power to burn bridges. If she were to publish this version of her life with the Club, she would have to be prepared to let go of her friends forever. It made her nervous to think of it. But the prose was so beautiful, so elegant and literary, she couldn't bring herself to destroy it. Not yet.

-64-

Hope stood in her kitchen after dinner, and held the landline to her ear.

A robotic male voice said, "You have a collect call from (pause, followed by a female voice) *Dahleeya Jones* (returning to the male recorded voice), an inmate at Compton Walker Correctional Facility. This call may be monitored. The cost for this call is $2.40 for the first minute, and $1.55 for each additional minute. To accept this call, please press zero. If you do not wish to accept this call, press five, or hang up."

Hope pressed zero.

The recording said, "Go ahead with your call."

"Hello? Is this Miss Hope Delaney?"

"Yes, it is. Am I speaking to Dahleeya Jones?"

"Yes. I'm Queen's mother."

"Yes, I know. I was expecting your call. We. We were expecting—I'll call Queen."

"Thank you. Thank you so much. I want to just thank you for accepting my call. I appreciate it. Is she all right? Is she behaving herself?"

The robotic voice interrupted the call to intone, "You are speaking to an inmate at the Compton Walker Correctional Facility."

Hope hesitated. "Hello?"

"Yes! Hello! You'll keep hearing that recording. They just feel the need to keep letting you know. Queen—how is she?"

"She's fine! She's doing well! She's a very good girl!"

"Oh, thank the Lord. Thank you, Miss Delaney. Do you think you could bring her out to see me sometime? I know it's far, but, it seems to be good for her to see me. *If* you could--."

"Yes, we're already looking at which day we could do it. I know you want to talk to Queen. Here she is."

Queen had come out from her room when the phone rang, as she did every time the phone rang, anticipating that it might be her mother.

Hope stepped out of the kitchen to appear to give Queen the privacy to talk to her mom, but stood in the dining room listening, with her lips pressed together.

"Yes, mama. I'm being good." There was a pause, during which Hope could hear animated tones coming through the line, from the prison to the little girl.

"Lasagna, garlic bread, and a green salad," Queen was naming the items in the dinner she and Hope had just eaten.

The voice on the phone went on, and then stopped.

Queen answered, "*The Secret Garden.* A lady here gave it to me. It's about a little girl that no one likes, and she finds a garden that no one takes care of. I know it sounds boring, but it's really good. Did you get my hand in the mail? I put a ring on every one of my fingers, like a rich lady." Queen laughed, and the tinny voice from prison laughed with her.

"I love you so much, Mama…. I will…. I will…. I do…. Yes, ma'am…. Can you talk longer?... Oh…. Okay…. I love you…. I will…. Bye, now. I love you…. Bye-bye."

-65-

When the Club was gathered for Birdie's watercolor class, Mabel put forth the proposition that she—Mabel—of all people—do a makeover class for all the ladies. She could give them a color analysis, telling them whether they should wear warm or cool colors, and she could do their nails and dye their hair, too.

"Now this is an idea that Carlotta, especially, is going to like!" declared Mabel, looking around at all the Club members and nodding, as if giving some sort of signal.

"And heck, Norb, you can be in on it, you know! I'll bet I could come up with something I could do to *you*!" Mabel winked at him, first one eye, and then the other.

Carlotta turned her appalled expression toward Lorraine at this bald innuendo, but Lorraine was filling brown pigment into the eyes of a dachshund, and did not break focus to look up at her.

"Oh, no," demurred Norbert. "You ladies go on ahead without me this time. I'll be content to sit this one out."

Margaret said, "Do you mean a makeover like they do on TV, when they give women a new hairdo and put eye shadow on them?"

Mabel nodded. "Yep! Did I ever tell you I used to be a beautician? In the seventies, I'm pretty sure it was."

Lorraine, with her eyes still on her painting, said, "It's an interesting idea, Mabel."

This was as good as a refusal, and Carlotta nodded her agreement, but again, Lorraine did not look at her.

Birdie said, dreamily, "Makeovers. Yes. Do-overs, re-imaginings and re-inventions. We get to keep re-inventing ourselves all our lives long."

Carlotta broke out, "What a dreary thought. Do we never get to stop?"

Lorraine, ignoring that remark, said, "Oh, why be closed-minded, right, Carlotta? Like Mabel always says, try anything once! Right? I've never had a cosmetic makeover before. It actually sounds like fun. Yeah, I'm in." Swirling her brush in a pot of water, she added mischievously, "But only if Carlotta's in, too."

Margaret joined her voice to Lorraine's, "Yes! Carlotta, even if you *are* writing a book, you still have time to get your hair done!"

"Come on, Carlotta," pushed Lorraine.

"Oh? Is Carlotta joining in, too?" asked Birdie, whose mind had wandered away into the mists.

"Yeah," urged Mabel. "It'll be just us girls this time! We need *you*, Carlotta. You're the most important one! Because I know I can make the most dramatic improvement in *you*. Come on, Carlotta! Let me see what I can do for you. I bet you could be a very attractive woman. You just need some help to make the most of yourself, that's all!"

Had Carlotta uttered such words, she would have intended them to cut. However, Mabel, as everyone knew, was as direct as a child, and meant no harm. That did not lessen Carlotta's irritation. In fact, it increased it.

"Mabel, don't be idiotic. Look at *yourself.*"

Mabel looked down at her grey sweats and clunky sneakers.

"What? This is my casual look. I do know how to get dressed up, you know. If you ever came to the Alibi with us, you'd know how I spruce myself up for a night on the town. Isn't that right?" Mabel looked around the group for support.

The room was quiet.

"I have a beautician's license. Or used to." Mabel was losing steam.

"Mabel," said Carlotta with firmness, "I don't mean to minimize your qualifications, but frankly, your qualifications are minimal."

There followed another awkward pause, during which Carlotta could feel the group's sympathy rushing toward Mabel. Mabel had been open and fun and had shown them all acceptance and a good time, and here was mean-spirited Carlotta. Being made to look mean-spirited.

Oh, it made her want to just spit.

"Okay," said Mabel cheerily. "Not every idea's gonna be a homerun, you know?" In an under breath, she added, "You can lead a dog to wander, like I said."

Why couldn't the woman get her idioms straight? In spite of Mabel's linguistic limitations, Lorraine and Margaret were smiling and nodding encouragement at her.

Mabel said, "Well, if Carlotta's not in, the whole makeover thing falls flat. What else have we got, gang?"

Incredibly, Mabel was just going to accept that the vetoing of her idea. Mabel would not keep cycling back with it until they agreed. The makeover idea was finished. Carlotta continued her painting, but her mind was on Mabel's personality, and her way of working with the Club. For all her loudness and uncouthness, there was nothing forceful about Mabel. She respected the will of others to do as they pleased, and did not find the Club's independence a threat to her power. In fact, she did not seem concerned about power at all. She just wanted to have friends, and have a good time.

Carlotta recognized, in the privacy of her own mind, that she herself *was* forceful. She was sometimes even described as "a force of nature." She felt it a threat to her power when any of the Club members made a suggestion that was as good as her own. And in an epiphany, it became clear to her that it was her very forcefulness and insecurity that was forcing the Club away from her and into the arms of Mabel, who held the Club gently. Mabel, coarse and ignorant as she was, had respect for individual differences and wishes.

Damn the woman. Why had she ever come to Gibbons Corner?

"Okay," said Mabel amiably. "So I got a joke for you. Stop me if you've heard this one before. It's about this nun. Don't worry, Carlotta, it's clean."

Carlotta felt called out for being a prude, and her resentment simmered.

"So this nun goes into a cloister and takes a vow of silence, okay?"

The Club was looking up from their work expectantly, ready to be amused. All except for Carlotta, who began to hum softly to herself, to show she wasn't listening. But she was. She was listening and humming at the same time.

"So the Mother Superior says, with the vow of silence, you can only say two words a year, and that's on your one-year anniversary. Other than that--." Mabel made the sign for zipping the lip.

"So the nun goes off to join the other nuns and lives in total silence for a year. On her one year anniversary, she comes back to the Mother Superior, who says to her, 'Today you get to say your two words. Is there anything you want to say?' and the young nun says, 'Cell cold.'"

Norbert folded his arms and smiled, and he raised his eyebrows at Lorraine in a gesture of mutual enjoyment. Lorraine jutted her chin at him with the beginning of a smile, and turned her attention back to Mabel. Carlotta felt provoked.

"So the little nun goes off to the cloister, and at the end of another year, she's back with the Mother Superior. This time, she says, 'Food lousy,' and the Mother Superior says, 'OK.' Then another year goes by. On the third anniversary, the nun comes back. She says to the Mother Superior, 'I quit!' And the Mother Superior says—get this— 'I'm not surprised. You've done nothing but complain ever since you got here!'"

The room erupted in laughter, with Margaret laughing the longest.

Then Margaret wrinkled her brow and said, "Wait. What?"

Mabel repeated the punchline.

Unsure, Margaret said, "Oh! I get it!" and laughed again. But Carlotta knew the joke had gone over poor Margaret's head.

Mabel was lit up with pleasure at the success of her joke.

"You're a good crowd. I can't say you aren't."

"Oh, Mabel," cooed Carlotta in a voice that was meant to be amused and amusing, "Honestly! Anyone who loves attention as much as you do should be on stage!"

"Well, I—."

"Or a psychiatrist's couch!"

Carlotta looked around to see if her joke had been as successful as Mabel's.

It had not.

-66-

Summer, rushing home from work to get ready for a date with her Jack of Hearts, blew into the Good Fortune Café with a gust of leaves, just for a quick chat with her cousin Hope. She wanted to advise Hope to send Queen back to Children and Family Services.

Hope greeted Summer with a hug and a kiss.

"Hey, kiddo! What can I get for you?"

"Nothing, really. Nothing at all. I just wanted to stop in and have a word with you."

"Oh." Hope lowered her voice. "Are you all right?"

"*I'm* fine. I just wanted to talk to you about Queen. Well really, about your whole foster child idea. I've been thinking. I just wonder if you've really thought through all the long-term consequences."

Summer's bright eyes were blue flecked with brown, giving the impression that when the freckles were spattered across her cheeks, some of the spatter got into her irises as well. The wrinkle between her eyebrows gave the impression of earnest worry.

"What? What's gotten into you? You were my biggest supporter!"

"Yes, I know, but, well, Gramma mentioned something to me."

"Oh." Hope felt disappointed in Carlotta. "She told you about the wallet?"

"What? No! Whose wallet? She didn't...."

"Oh, no, it was nothing. What did you hear?"

"Gramma told me," Summer looked around to be sure no one was close enough to be listening, "that Queen's *mother* is in *prison*. Is that *true?*"

Hope sighed.

"I didn't want everyone to know about that right away. I wanted people to get to know Queen first, before getting that image in their brains. But I guess Queen went ahead and spilled the beans."

"Hope. Seriously." Summer lowered her chin and looked Hope in the eye.

"What?" said Hope, folding her arms. "Didn't you expect that the mother of a foster child would be in some extreme situation? Or did you think she might just be away on a long cruise, or something?"

"You're trying to make light of it, Hope. It's not a light thing. And what is the hurry? You're just rushing headlong into this huge commitment. I thought adoptions take a long time. How can this be moving along so fast?"

"First of all, I've never been more serious in my life, so you're wrong: I'm not making light of it. Not at all. Secondly, it's helped that her birth mom has already signed over her rights. The sooner I can make the adoption final, the sooner Queen will have the stability she needs."

"Hope, think! If her mom's in prison, that means she committed a *crime*. Do you even know what the crime is? Did she murder someone? She probably has relatives who are—I don't even *know*. They might drop by your house some time. Have you pictured that? You're a business owner. They could think you have money. Something bad could happen to you. If you adopt her, you are forever connecting your life to the lives of people who—."

"You know what, Summer? Our lives are already connected. Reach out with love, or don't reach out with love—either way, we all live in this world, and our paths cross, and we affect each other. Like it or not, we are all connected."

"Wow. Really? That's something Aunt Birdie would say, we are all connected. Airy fairy stuff. This is the real world, Hope. You are putting yourself in danger by getting involved with this kid."

"What has happened to you, Summer? That day at Aunt Carlotta's, you were all about it. Was that just because you wanted to tease Aunt Carlotta? Why would you change like this?"

"Well, maybe it *was* fun to poke at the matriarch a little bit." Summer's eyes twinkled with the memory. "But the truth is, the reality of it didn't hit me at the time. I didn't know about the prison thing. I didn't think that there might be adults that could come into the picture along with the kid. This is a huge risk. I mean, it was one thing to *talk* about it. It's another thing when the kid is here, in the flesh, and you stop and think of all the baggage that comes with her."

"Summer, for someone so young, you worry an awful lot. Thanks for your concern. Now I'm going to have to ask you to stop."

Summer said, "I'm just...."

"Stop."

Summer opened her mouth, but Hope put up her hand.

"No more. I mean it."

Norbert and Queen entered the café, deep in discussion.

"I don't read for children," said Norbert. He had already repeated this sentence several times.

"But *why not?*" countered Queen.

"Because it's not helpful or appropriate for children. Adults have decisions to make, warnings to heed; adults have grown-up worries—and they come to the cards for help with their responsibilities."

"Are you saying that adults need more help than children?"

It was strange to be challenged by such a small child, and yet Norbert felt she was asking because she needed to know.

"I'm saying that children don't have the power to *make* any decisions or heed any warnings. Children just have to do what adults tell them, and deal with adults' decisions. I'm not saying it's fair, but that's the way things are—so there's no point in reading cards for children. Do you see?"

"Ooh. Now that makes me mad, Mr. Zelenka. *I* decide things every day. Every day. I wake up in the morning and decide what I'm gonna do. I decide lots of stuff. And worries? Looks like you forgot the worries you had, when you were a kid."

Hope set down a falafel wrap and glass of peach mango juice for Queen.

"Mr. Zelenka," said Hope with a wink, "did you know our Queen is a lawyer-in-training?"

Norbert sighed, vanquished. "How would you feel about me reading Queen's cards for her today?"

"As long as you give her the best reading you've ever given anyone yet, well, I would feel fine about it."

Norbert let Queen hand him cards and he set them out on the table between them.

Queen was delighted and then suspicious as Norbert enumerated the many blessings that lay in store for her. Yes, she would get good grades in the new school year. Yes, she would go to college. Yes, she would be the author of many books someday. Yes, she would live a long and healthy life. Yes, when she grew up she would have enough money to buy her birth mother a house and a car.

"How do I know you're not making all this up?" she demanded.

"I'm not making it up. I use a very special method. It's called the Self-fulfilling Prophecy Method."

Queen was listening with folded arms.

Norbert explained, "I give you a good reading, and you will make it come true. That's how it works."

"Huh." Queen was skeptical. "What about..." she looked over her shoulder to make sure Hope was out of ear shot. "What about Hope? Is she gonna get married or get a boyfriend? Because I'm not staying if she does."

Norbert gathered up the cards and looked with deep attention into Queen's eyes.

"I cannot see everything in the cards. But some things I just know. One thing I know is this: Hope is what you could call true blue. You can count on her to do what she thinks is best for you, every time."

Queen was not a happy customer.

"I didn't get all my questions answered," she said with a frown, "but thank you anyway for trying, Mr. Zelenka."

-67-

At the Art League Studio, it was just Carlotta's Club minus Mabel today: Norbert, Lorraine, Margaret, Carlotta and Birdie meeting for Birdie's watercolor class. Carlotta was gratified to hear the Club begin to rumble in discomfort as they painted autumn leaves. Birdie painted one huge red maple leaf that filled her Arches paper, while Lorraine painted a scattering of multicolored leaves of various specimens. Norbert's leaves were still attached to the branch he had brought in from outside. Carlotta had made a neat little bouquet-like bundle of leaves.

So difficult to make autumn leaves look tidy.

"Well, that Mabel, you gotta hand it to her. Even at her age, she's a partier."

"And I can't say she isn't!" wisecracked Norbert, who then basked in the laughter rewarding his successful imitation.

"But I don't feel so good today," concluded Lorraine.

"Neither do I," grumbled Margaret. "She's hard to keep up with. I just can't drink like Mabel. We look alike, but our constitution is not the same."

Lorraine said, "We don't want to disappoint her, and we sure don't want to be boring, so we hit the Alibi Bar after filming, and one thing leads to another...."

Carlotta painted in silence, listening to the group make their own observations about how "keeping up with Mabel" was serving them. The old Carlotta might have made a biting remark at this point, to embarrass them. Instead, she loosened the muscles in her hand, and held her brush lightly.

How different a watercolor is, she reflected, *when you hold the brush just a little more loosely. The painting has a chance to become what it wants to be.*

Carlotta smiled at the nonsense in her thoughts. There is a lot of truth in nonsense. Lewis Carroll knew that. And she thought, she must bring Queen up to speed on Lewis Carroll. The Alice books were an important contribution to juvenile literature; Queen couldn't do without them.

As Norbert and his little dog Ivy walked home from the Art League, Ivy stopped every once in a while to pounce and play with a windblown leaf as if she were a young dog again. Norbert was thinking about Mabel's influence—on him, and on all his new friends. Mabel's magic was that she lowered everyone's inhibitions: in her company, everyone wanted to try new things. And she added a lightness, a sense of adventure. Norbert had begun to look for whatever was funny in life, in order to share it with Mabel, Margaret, Lorraine and Birdie. They all were doing the same. As soon as Mabel entered the room, everyone lit up with expectant smiles, and hilarity ensued.

It was possible that Mabel's excesses were wearing the group down and becoming too much of a good thing. She was not an easy one to keep up with. And Margaret was looking tired and care-worn; sharing her apartment with Mabel seemed to be taking its toll.

Norbert saw that Carlotta had begun to change, too, since Mabel's invasion of the group had caused Carlotta to turn her attention toward Hope's little girl. Carlotta was becoming almost tender toward Queen. Carlotta was relaxing in some subtle way, and becoming a softer version of herself. She was growing into herself, at the age of eighty-one, as she was always meant to do.

-68-

Carlotta invited Hope and Queen out for a night of fine dining. Carlotta believed in bringing children to good restaurants to allow them to practice the rules of etiquette in public. This was one activity she remembered doing with her own boys when they were young. In fact, it was the only activity she remembered doing with them; certainly there must have been others. But it was a very long time ago. Charlie and Joey were children in the nineteen-sixties. What Carlotta remembered most about them as children were the clothes she put them in: mustard-colored jackets with wide lapels, shirts with Nehru collars, and those flared pants they used to call bell-bottoms. Oh, and black turtlenecks. She loved putting them in turtlenecks. They had protested they couldn't breathe, and she remembered laughing. They could be so dramatic.

Hope had asked for Summer to be included in their *soirée*, and Carlotta easily agreed. Hope could not be happy when there was conflict with any of her loved ones, and it seemed Hope wanted to smooth things out with Summer. They'd had some kind of tiff. Why young people had to continually have personal conflicts was beyond Carlotta. Life was too short for petty grievances. Still, she supposed she had been prone to the same silliness when she was young.

Fine dining in Gibbons Corner necessarily indicated Renata's Italian Restaurant, which was as fine as the town had to offer. Carlotta had always enjoyed the white table cloths and soft Italian background music.

Greg Thatcher, who had gone to high school with Hope, was the host. Carlotta tried to remember: hadn't Hope dated him years ago? He led them to their table.

"I haven't seen *this* young lady before," said Greg, nodding toward Queen.

"Greg," said Hope, "this is my foster daughter, Queen Jones. Queen, this is my old friend from high school, Greg Thatcher— Mr. Thatcher to you."

"Hello, Mr. Thatcher," said Queen, as Carlotta had taught her to do when being introduced to people, but she didn't smile. She looked away from Greg, at the fresh flowers in the little bud vases on each table, and the smoky mirrors that covered the walls.

Why *were* Italians so fond of decorating with mirrors? Perhaps because many Italian people were so beautiful, thought Carlotta, smiling with satisfaction at having figured it out. She checked her own image briefly, and was pleased to see how trim and stylish she looked in her tea-length charcoal grey cotton knit dress. Charcoal grey never failed to be fashionable, especially with that belt at the waist, giving the essential "pop of red." Her eyes were bright, too, and that was because she was with her girls, Hope and Summer. And Queen. Was Queen now also one of "her girls"?

As Summer, Hope, Queen and Carlotta seated themselves, Greg hovered for a moment. He whispered to Hope, "You always were the nicest person in our class. It would be just like you to take in a foster child. Not many people are as good as you are."

Hope answered, "I'm not good to do it. I'm *lucky* that I get to do it."

Queen was observing this exchange.

Hope repeated, "I'm lucky," and smiled at Queen.

Queen's eyes rested on Hope, and they seemed to convey some deep message. *My,* thought Carlotta, *but this child has expressive eyes. So much goes on behind them.*

Carlotta shook out her white cloth table napkin, and Queen did likewise. Carlotta perused the menu, and Queen did likewise.

Queen pointed to the big letters at the top of the menu.

"I think they spelled 'restaurant' wrong."

Summer said, "That's the Italian word for 'restaurant,' Queen. *'Ristorante.'* 'Renata's *Ristorante Italiano.'*" Summer, a Spanish teacher, had an idea of how to pronounce the Italian words with authenticity.

Queen repeated the words the way Summer had said them.

"You have a good accent, young lady," complimented Summer, looking at Queen thoughtfully.

"Gracias," said Queen. "That's the only Italian word I know."

"*Grazie,*" corrected Summer. She launched into a quick explanation of the shared roots of the Latin languages, which Queen attended to closely.

When the waiter came, Carlotta ordered a kale salad with mixed nuts and a roasted Bosc pear dressing for each of them. This was followed by *zuppe: pasta e faggioli* or "bean soup," as Queen was delighted to learn. Next, *pasta:* Carlotta and Queen shared pasta with broccoli, garlic and roasted pepper.

Carlotta, Summer and Hope enjoyed a superb Cabernet sauvignon, while Queen drank cranberry juice from a wine glass, swirling it and sniffing the bouquet.

Finally, Queen was almost too full for desert, but when assorted cut fruit arrived on little flowery plates, she discovered she did still have room. Plenty of room.

At a neighboring table, two women in their fifties had been glancing over at Carlotta's group throughout their meal. Finally, smiling in a friendly way, one of the women nodded toward Queen and said, "She's cute as a button. I just love those little barrettes in her hair."

"Thank you," said Hope.

The stranger directed herself to Queen, "Which one of these pretty ladies is your mother?"

Queen lowered her chin and pointed her finger at Hope.

The stranger asked Hope, "Is the father in the picture?"

"Ex*cuse* me?" asked Hope.

"Well, sometimes they aren't. Kids can still turn out good without a father. I really believe that." The woman dabbed at her mouth with a napkin. "Are you her real mother?"

Carlotta said, "I beg your pardon. Do we know you?"

The stranger's companion was trying to shush her. "I'm sorry," she whispered loudly. "The Merlot must have gone to her head. De*nise! Shut up!*"

As Carlotta and her girls filed out of the restaurant, Greg approached and apologized for the rudeness of the other patron.

"I heard what just happened. I'm so sorry she said that to you."

"Oh, that's okay," said Hope. "It's not your fault what people say in here."

"No. But people should think before they talk." Greg smiled at Queen, and then asked Hope, "So, how'd she wind up in foster care?"

Queen held up her small hand and said, "Sorry, no more questions. We're in a hurry." As if she were ending a press conference, Queen headed out the door with determination, and Summer, Hope and Carlotta followed.

Outside, Hope was reunited with Summer in a fit of mutual irritation. Summer was never so alive as when she was in a passion.

"Who did that lady think she was? Ooh, she's lucky she didn't say that to *me!* How do people get the idea—that Greg, too, he's another one—how do they get the impression that they can just come up to you and ask personal questions about your family?"

Hope said, "We learned about it in the foster parent classes. It's unbelievable, but this is what happens. People see an interracial family, and they feel like they can get personal for some reason. If you foster or adopt interracially, you just have to be ready to deal with it. It goes with the territory."

Carlotta, enjoying the shared bristling indignation of her young ones, joined in by observing, "Let it go. I, for one, have no time for ignorant people."

Queen added, "Me neither."

At home, Queen and Hope were getting ready for bed. Hope had come out of the shower and was toweling off her hair. She sat on Queen's bed as Queen pulled her pajamas from her dresser.

Hope said, "When that lady asked which one was your mother, you pointed to me. I was glad you did. But I wondered why."

Queen paused. She turned to Hope with her pajamas in her hands. Red ones with hearts. "I pointed to you, because you *are* my mother--out here. You care *about* me, and you take care *of* me, so you *are* my mother, I think. But I also have a mother that I was born from, and she cares *about* me, but she can't take care *of* me. So, to my way of thinking—I got that from Mary Poppins. I like how she always says, 'to my way of thinking.' To my way of thinking, I need two mothers. So, if you would like to be one of my two mothers, I would like to be your daughter."

Without waiting for a response, Queen ran off to take her warm bath.

Hope sat with her eyes closed, wrapped in a warm blanket of gratitude. Norbert had forecasted this for her. He was right again. Her greatest wish was coming true.

-69-

It was a Tuesday afternoon in October when that baldy-man with the big stomach came smiling into the café to sniff around Hope. Queen knew what he was up to.

This wasn't the first time. Queen had her eye on him. His name was Mr. Arnie Butler and he worked at that bookstore down the street. Why he had to come into the café and bother Hope while she was working, Queen did not know. He always brought a little book or something, and that was stupid, because Hope could buy her own books. He didn't have anything Hope needed, and Queen did not like to see his grinning face.

She watched Hope drying her hands on her apron and pushing a lock of hair off her forehead as Mr. Butler handed her the book and a little bag of candy corn. Queen thought, if Hope wasn't going to eat that candy corn, she would.

Queen left her spot next to Mr. Zelenka's table and casually skipped closer to Hope, so she could listen in.

"Sure, that would be great, Arnie. I'd need to see about getting my Aunt Carlotta or my cousin Summer to babysit."

Aw, hell no.

"Also, I hope you understand, but I don't like to leave her for very long yet."

That's better.

"We're still in the settling-in phase, and I have to leave her for several hours a week as it is because of the café. But just to get a bite to eat—sure! How nice of you to ask!"

"If you'd be more comfortable, why not bring her along?"

Queen grabbed Hope around the waist, giving her a big surprise. Queen had never hugged Hope, but this was a good time to start.

Queen looked right into the eyes of that man.

She told him, "We go everywhere together, *we* do."

As Hope watched Arnie walk out of the café, she could feel Queen's eyes upon her.

"I've got to get back to work. Just a couple more hours." She patted Queen's back, and the child skipped back to the fortune-teller's booth.

Hope was deep in thought as she returned to her work in the kitchen.

She didn't know if she just didn't like nice guys, or if there was something about her that turned nice guys into jerks. Maybe it was the star she was born under. Or some psychological imprint left from her childhood. Whatever it was, she was afraid of her old high school friend Arnie. Afraid of opening her heart to him. She had never thought of him "that way," probably, she told herself sardonically, precisely because he was a nice guy.

Or was she being too hard on herself?

Maybe it was all just dumb luck.

She had friends with lower self-esteem and worse childhoods than hers, and *they* seemed to wind up with loving and kind partners. Maybe it wasn't anything she did wrong, but just the way fate played out.

The point was, should she send Arnie on his way, or should she "give him a chance," as Aunt Carlotta kept saying?

Arnie was a good man; she felt that. She'd hate to turn him into a jerk, if that was the effect she had on good men. They all seemed good, at first.

He was a handsome man, regardless of Queen's opinion. He was a sweet and considerate person, but then again, Rudy had seemed sweet. They all had, until they were sure of her devotion. Then Mr. Hyde came out, every time. She just did not have the energy or inclination for any of that angst anymore.

On the other hand....

-70-

In the studio of the Gibbons Corner Art League, Carlotta was preparing for her evening's lesson. Tonight, she would demonstrate how to put the shine, dimension and shadow into an object. On her easel, she set a blank canvas. On a high table, she set a green apple. She had chosen the apple that afternoon at the Lucky Pig Grocery Store for the leaf that remained attached to its stem, making it more natural-looking, but also different from all the other apples on the shelf.

Art was all about noticing individual differences. Noticing them, and loving them, if it wasn't too fanciful to say so. Because as a painter looked at an object with great attention, she felt her interest deepen and grow into something that was very like love. Painting could open a person's heart to objects, to life. Painting a tulip that stretched its striped head toward the window, straining toward the sun, could not fail to make the painter feel with the tulip, long for the sun, be the tulip. She wouldn't say such things out loud, even if she did think them. These were things Birdie might say. But maybe Birdie wasn't always wrong.

Carlotta knew she was a good painting teacher. Her students told her so, all the time. As a teacher, she understood how to help people achieve their own aims without taking over. Why, then, couldn't she do that with the Club? Why did her grasp on her friends have to be so tight?

She knew the answer. It was because, with her friends, she was afraid. And here was another thing she would never say out loud.

She was afraid that if she did not control her friends, they would leave her. She had to control their interests and their actions. If she let go, they would drop her, because she was not, frankly, a very likable person. She must have decided years ago —she didn't know when—that if she couldn't be likable, she could at least be interesting—and commanding. If she couldn't appeal to people with sincerity and authenticity, then at least she could manipulate and organize them.

There was an awareness stirring in Carlotta. Like the tulip straining toward the sun, there was something straining in her. It seemed to have something to do with that little Queen. Hope's foster child stood in Carlotta's mind much of the time, even when they were not together. In Queen, Carlotta was surprised to see herself, and something better. Something she could aspire to. Like Carlotta, Queen was bright and curious. Unlike Carlotta, she was vulnerable; she had to be, as a dependent child. Yet alongside that vulnerability was an inexplicable confidence. The child had confidence in who she was, on a very deep level. She seemed to possess some self-knowledge. Self-acceptance, perhaps. Oh, it was hard to put into words.

Carlotta wondered if, at age eighty-one, a person could change in any way. Or were her lessons all behind her?

Carlotta's late and disappointing husband Ed had not believed that people could change. At least, he didn't believe that he could. "This is who I *am*, Carly. This is who you married. I can't change." How old was he when he had shouted that at her? Thirty-five? And yet, *she* had changed since then. For one thing, she had become a person that others didn't even think of shouting at. She had changed in dozens of ways. She had developed talents and accepted new ideas. She had continued traveling, reading, and learning. Perhaps she did still have some growing ahead of her, even now.

As her class filed in, Carlotta looked at each student thoughtfully, seeing their differences and beauty. What was happening to her? She was becoming soft. She wasn't sure she liked it. But there it was.

"Tonight, I've prepared an exercise for you. Feel free to paint along with me as we focus on making this green apple look as real as possible on our canvasses. Or, if you prefer, you can paint the apple your own way—as an abstract or a primitive— you are the artist. The interesting thing is, we will all paint the same apple, and yet we each have a different perspective, depending on where we are standing. Therefore, no two of us will paint the same apple."

-71-

Upstate New York in the fall was the most heart-soothing, glorious place in the world, even for a native. As Hope and Queen drove through the winding roads and up and down the hills, Hope felt joy and appreciation for the natural beauty all around them, and she and Queen pointed out to each other splendid things to look at: black horses grazing in emerald fields, stone walls, a red barn, and yellow and orange autumn woodlands.

"They'll make you go through a metal detector. That's the part I hate. One time, I made it go off with my belt buckle. When that happens, they act like you're a criminal. That was so scary."

They'd been driving for an hour already, having left at six in the morning to be able to arrive at the Compton Walker Correctional Facility by eight, when visiting hours began. They'd be able to stay until two-thirty, when visiting hours would end. They would get back home at four-thirty. Hope had left Liam in charge, and she worked at brushing away the worry about being out of reach of the café for a whole day. The good thing about this long drive was that it was loosening Queen's tongue, and she was chatting away, happy with the prospect of seeing her mother.

"Some of my foster parents didn't want to take me to see my mother. The Place is way far out in the country, far away from every foster home. So I didn't see her sometimes. That was terrible." Queen looked gratefully at Hope. "Thank you very much for taking me," she added, maturely.

After a pause, Queen added, "Would this be a good time for you to teach me how to drive?"

Hope turned quickly to see Queen observing her with a sly smile.

Queen shrugged. "It never hurts to ask."

Summer had argued against the prison visit. She had said, "But wouldn't that be teaching her that prison is normal? If she enjoys seeing her mother, wouldn't that give her a positive association with prison? Make her think of it as a possibility for herself?"

Hope had had to push back again, saying, "You know what, Summer? You didn't take all the classes at Child and Family Services like I did. Let me do the mothering here. The decisions are my responsibility. You just enjoy Queen for who she is, and I'll take the fall if I mess up."

And Summer *was* enjoying Queen, as the little girl had a passionate interest in learning foreign words and seemed to have a prodigious memory. Since that night at Renata's Restaurant, when Summer had seen Queen's potential for foreign language and then immediately had her righteous indignation button pushed by "ignorant people," she had flipped sides again. Summer had begun tutoring Queen in Spanish. Hope had never been able to remember her Spanish dialogs in school, but Queen had already started her own notebook dedicated to the study of Spanish, and was considering a career as a Spanish teacher or a translator for the United Nations. Summer thought she was funny and smart, and couldn't get enough of her. She was also out to prove herself as an outspoken advocate, looking for a fight with anyone who had a question about Queen.

"Now," Queen told Hope as they rolled along though paradise, "my mother's name is Dahleeya. It's kind of like the flower, the dahlia, but it's Dah-LEE-ya. Dahleeya Jones. Miss Jones to you. She doesn't like people she's just met to just go ahead and call her by her first name. And she will call you 'Miss Delaney.' Until she really knows you well. She's kind of formal that way."

Queen twisted her body to look in the back seat.

"My mama's gonna love that picnic lunch we packed. Those flatbread sandwiches with the roasted peppers and stuff? Ooh. My mouth is watering right now. Can I have one—just one?"

"Let's leave the picnic lunch in one piece, so it will be nice when your mother sees it. We have our smoothies and our blueberries and pita chips. That's a good breakfast for us."

Queen looked back at the picnic basket with regret, but said no more, sipping her smoothie and then resting it back in the cup holder.

"Can I ask you a question?" asked Queen.

"Sure."

"That Mr. Butler—the bald, fat guy, kinda ugly—do you like him?"

Hope smiled.

"He's an old friend from high school. He's certainly not ugly. He's a kind and interesting person; that's what I think. And I think he would like to be better friends. I really don't have much time, though, between the café and now taking care of you."

"That's what I thought. You don't have time for him." Queen seemed reassured.

"Let's play a game," Hope proposed. *"Things You Don't Know about Me."* She glanced at Queen, who was picking through a pint of blueberries. "So the way it goes is this: I say one thing you don't know about me, then you say one thing I don't know about you, and we keep going until we can't think of any more things."

"Okay," agreed Queen. "But do we ask questions? Because I don't like to be asked questions."

"No. We just tell the other one what we want to tell. No questions."

"Okay."

"I'll start. Let's see… Oh, I have one. You know I have allergies. But I bet you didn't know I'm allergic to flowers."

"I didn't know anybody *could* be allergic to flowers." Queen looked skeptically at Hope.

"Oh yes, they can, and the worst flower for me is daisies. Oh, I sneeze and my eyes water. I cannot deal with daisies. Your turn."

"Okay…. Maybe you don't know that I was five years old when my mama went away. Maya was just born, and Tamika was one. So they don't remember her like I do."

Hope did actually know that, but she was glad to hear Queen talking to her about it. For all Queen's objection to questions, she was now offering some information about her past. She seemed to want to start talking about it. But Hope would have to tread lightly.

"All right. My turn again. Did you know that I have always wanted to have a little girl like you?"

"Like *me?*"

"Exactly like you. Even when I was a little girl myself, I used to think all the time about the children I would have someday. And I always knew there would be a little girl, just like you."

"Is that for real?"

"That is for real."

"Huh. Okay…. Another thing you don't know about me. Well, when I was six, I was very bad. That's when I hit the caseworker. I did everything I could think of that was bad. Swearing, stealing," Queen lowered her voice. "The reason I was so bad all the time was because I thought if I did something really awful, I would get to go and live with my mama. Then I found out it's not like that. A social worker put her face right up to mine so our noses were almost touching and she said, real slow and real serious, that no matter what I did, that would never, ever happen. 'They don't put six-year-olds in prison with their mamas,' she told me. So I had to give up trying for that."

Hope's heart clenched and she turned to look at this child who had had to work through so much in her own little mind and heart.

"What do you miss most about your mom?" Hope asked.

Queen said, "Now, I thought you said we didn't get to ask questions."

They rolled along in silence for a while, taking turns pointing out the beauty all around them.

At last Queen said, "I miss my mama reading to me, riding bikes, telling jokes. My mama *loves* jokes. I have one here, in my pocket. I got this one from school and wrote it down on a piece of paper. She's gonna love this one."

-72-

As they passed the prison gates and drove down the long driveway, they left a world of color and life and entered a grey, dead world. The parking lot was almost empty. Although they had driven two hours to get here, now Hope did not want to go into the enormous brick building. She was surprised at how frightened she was.

Queen had told Hope about the metal detector, but Hope was not aware that the processing would take a full hour.

"Do you have anything in your hair?" asked a guard with cold eyes.

Hope took down her coiled braid.

She felt an irrational terror that now that she was in the prison they would never let her leave. She was overwhelmed with a sense that this was a place where terrible things happened.

Another guard intoned, "Please pull out your pockets and turn around."

After the metal detector was a series of large metal doors. At last, they entered a spacious visiting room containing tables, chairs, and vending machines. Some tables had board games on them. Pairs and groups of people were already visiting quietly. Each group had one member in an orange jump suit. Hope found herself studying them.

Queen tugged on her sleeve.

"Don't be looking at people," Queen instructed her.

They had to sit down and wait again. Hope tried not to look at people. Queen sat back in her chair, watching the door that led into the prison.

At last, a guard led in one more woman in an orange jump-suit.

"Mama!"

Queen ran to the prisoner and hugged her tightly, as if she would never let her go. They walked, Queen and her mama, to the table, where Queen introduced Hope.

Queen's mother was a slight woman, not tall, with beautiful large eyes like Queen's. Like the other prisoners, she seemed weighed down and cautious. At the same time, her face was radiant with the happiness of seeing her child. She held out her hand to Hope.

"Hello Miss Delaney."

"Hello Miss Jones."

Dahleeya sat down. "I want to thank you for taking care of my baby."

Queen climbed on Dahleeya's lap and buried her forehead in her mother's neck.

"It's my pleasure, really. Queen brings a lot of happiness to my life." Hope wondered if she shouldn't talk about her own happy life, knowing that the woman before her had no happi-ness.

But Dahleeya lit up even brighter than before.

"That's my girl!" she said with shy pride, patting Queen's head. "Now, look at those braids," she said, drawing her head back so she could see them better. "Baby, who did your hair like that?"

Hope felt stricken. Had she done something wrong?

"Hope does my hair," said Queen, simply.

"Well, she does a wonderful job!" smiled Dahleeya, undoing Queen's braids. "Really, a wonderful job, Miss Delaney. I don't want you to think I'm critical of how you did it. You did it perfectly. It's just that—well, I always braid Queen's hair when she comes. It's just something we do. Kind of a bonding thing, you know?" The open little barrettes were piling up on the table.

Hope didn't know that braiding hair could be a bonding thing. So far, for her, it was still a very hard thing, and she wasn't sure she was doing it very well.

While Dahleeya unbraided and re-braided Queen's hair, they talked as if Hope were not there. She was glad. She didn't want to intrude. She wanted them to have this time together, and would have asked a guard if she could sit in another room, if she had not been afraid of the guards. She stole a glance around. Most of the people there were black. She thought of the unfairness in sentencing articles she had been reading online that said that whites do not go to prison for the crimes that black people do. She wondered what all these women in orange jumpsuits had done.

Queen asked her mom, "Are you getting good food? What do they give you?"

Dahleeya detailed her diet of the last few days, and Queen seemed content.

Then Queen asked, "And your bed, is it nice?"

Dahleeya assured Queen that her bed was "good."

"And you, baby? Is your bed nice?" Dahleeya glanced conspiratorially at Hope, as if to say, *we're just talking; I know her bed is nice.*

"Mama, you should see it. A white headboard and a white comforter. And the prettiest little room all to myself with a desk for me to do my writing." Queen glanced at Hope, as if to say,

See, I'm telling my mama good things, and I appreciate what you have given me.

"You still working on your book, honey?"

"Yes, mama. Every time they move me to a new house, I make sure to take my notebook. I've been working on it for years."

Dahleeya smiled again at Hope, as if to say, *Years. Did you hear this baby say 'years'!?*

"And you're doing your homework, aren't you?" asked Dahleeya. Hope felt the weakness of this mother's position. How could she see to it that her child did her homework?

"Yes, mama. We have a *routine*. After school I get a snack, and then I do my homework."

Dahleeya turned to Hope.

"It's hard for her to keep up when she keeps moving from school to school. I'd like her to stay in one place and just focus on growing up and doing her school work. But she gets moved a lot."

Queen broke in. "Mama! I have a joke!"

"Oh, I do love a joke! Tell me!"

"Okay. Which dinosaur knew the most words?"

Dahleeya repeated the question, seeming to search her brain for the answer. Finally she said, "I sure don't know."

Triumphant, Queen declared, "The thesaurus!"

Queen giggled and Dahleeya and Hope smiled.

Dahleeya repeated the punchline, adding, "Well, I never would have guessed that. That's a smart joke."

Again, Hope felt she was intruding. She wondered how different their interaction would be if she were not there; how different it would be if they were not in a prison visiting room. She thought of the Wish Fairy social worker explaining to her, "children of incarcerated parents, you can't imagine how hard it is to see their authority figure disempowered. Do you understand? It shakes a child up." The Wish Fairy had also said, "When you are sitting in the visiting room of the prison, you'll see the dynamics. I think of it as 'public parenting.' The moms and kids can't be normal or natural with each other. Their behavior is being observed constantly, and they know it."

Hope felt intrusive observing Queen and her mother.

Dahleeya was saying, "Baby, you *know* this isn't your fault now."

Dahleeya told Hope, "Queen was acting up all the time in her foster homes. She never was like that before, when she was with me. She finally told me she thought it was her fault that I'm in here." Dahleeya turned back to Queen. "We've got that all cleared up now? You understand? That's my baby."

Hope asked, "Her *fault?* Why would she ever think that?"

"Oh, kids always blame themselves, you know. And in our case...."

"In your case?"

"Do you know why I'm here? They must have told you."

Queen began to hum, and then she wandered over to the empty table next to theirs to look at a board game.

Hope answered, "They said—I think it was—larceny, among some other non-violent charges."

"That's all they told you? So you don't know *how* I committed larceny? I'll tell you then. I claimed residence in another neighborhood. And that's called 'defrauding the taxpayers.' We were living in a rough part of town. I affirmed on a piece of paper that we lived in the wealthy area."

"Why?" Hope was dumbfounded. "I mean, why would you do that, and why would they send you to prison for that?"

"Queen was five years old. Smart little girl, all ready for kindergarten. Can you picture that? Now. What kind of school do you think they had in our neighborhood?" Dahleeya paused, to let Hope imagine. "Now. What kind of chances in life do you think my daughter would have if, instead of going to the crappy school, she could go to the quality one?"

"So you said you lived in the good neighborhood so she could go to a decent school?"

"You got it. I had a friend by the good school. I just listed her address as our own. Queen went off to school with her new backpack, all ready to learn. But I got caught. That's why she thought it was all her fault."

"Wait. You don't mean to say you're in here for that? That's outrageous! That's not a prison offense. It can't be."

Hope was turning this over in her mind. This was the worst injustice she had ever seen. She would talk to her Aunt Carlotta. They'd get a good lawyer for Queen's mother. They would fight this.

"Yeah, well. That's the system."

"But that's not fair!"

Dahleeya raised her eyebrows and a mocking smile played about her lips, but her eyes were haunted.

"That's all you did? Just lie about where you lived?"

"Actually, that's not all. I had a record for drugs from before."

"Oh." Hope stopped up short. She considered. "But you already paid for that?"

"Yes, but there were also some current drug charges. I was selling a little cocaine."

Dahleeya watched Hope process this.

"Miss Delaney, what I did was wrong. It was also stupid. Not the school part. I stand by the school part. My daughter has every right to a good education, and I know in my heart that is true. But the other parts. My own. Stupid. Fault. That's it, that's all."

Hope still suspected that if she herself had done the same things, she would not be wearing an orange jumpsuit. Dahleeya had to know this, too, but was not mentioning it. Even if she were angry, railing against white society to Queen's white foster mother wouldn't feel safe. She needed to stay on Hope's good side if she wanted to see her daughter. Which wasn't fair, either.

Queen had circled back and climbed up on Dahleeya's lap again.

"Can I just stay with you?"

"Now, you already know the answer to your own question. So why you got to ask? And you will never, never stay in a place like this. Do you hear me? You're going to college. You're going to make me proud. Are you doing your homework every day now?"

Queen said, "I already told you yes."

Dahleeya pulled her head back so that Queen could see her face very well, and gave her a look.

"Sorry mama. Yes, I do my homework, ma'am."

"That's better. I know, honey. I know you're my good girl."

Queen said, "We packed us a picnic lunch. We brought sandwiches from Hope's café. You are going to love them!"

They ate their lunch and talked about Queen's school, and the after-school hours when Mr. Zelenka and Mrs. Moon took care of her. They talked about Renata's restaurant and about Miss Summer Moon teaching Queen Spanish. They talked about the spoiled girl across the street and how her mother didn't know how to do limits. They talked about their ride this morning, and how beautiful the countryside was.

After lunch, they played a board game. Queen gave Dahleeya an update on *The Secret Garden,* and then she asked about her mother's school.

Dahleeya explained to Hope, "I'm pursuing a bachelor of arts in psychology. There's this program that links us with colleges on the outside. When I finish it, I'm going to pursue my masters."

Queen lifted her head high. "I'm going to pursue *my* masters, too."

"You sure are," said Dahleeya.

As the afternoon wore on, Hope began to feel less uncomfortable in the prison visiting room. She began to see Queen in a new light, compliant, affectionate, and respectful. Watching Queen and her mother, Hope understood the Wish Fairy's claim that these visits would be good for Queen emotionally. She had never seen Queen so relaxed, so unguarded. Hope wondered how many visits she would need to have to build trust with Queen's mother, so that she could broach the subject of adoption.

Dahleeya, as if reading her mind, said, "So, Miss Delaney, you want to adopt my baby?"

Hope felt her heart thump.

"A social worker from Children and Family Services told me you're a good match. And that you were interested. Since all three of us are here," Dahleeya seemed to be addressing Queen more than Hope, "I thought we ought to talk about it, see where we stand."

Queen shifted awkwardly and pressed herself closer to Dahleeya.

Grateful for this opening, Hope launched forward.

"Miss Jones, I've always wanted to have children. That's why I became a foster mother. I think Queen is adapting well in my home. She's settling into the school and life with my family. It's a good school we have in Gibbons Corner. Yes, I'd very much like to adopt her. Would you let me do that?"

Dahleeya smiled the widest and most beautiful smile.

"I've already signed over my rights, Miss Delaney. But I appreciate your asking my permission. And, yes, I think that would be wonderful. What do *you* think, baby?"

"I think it would be very nice," said Queen. "If you think so, mama."

Hope added, "There is one thing I worry about. There are no other African American children in our town, as far as I know. I know that's not ideal. But is it ok? I mean, do *you* think it will be a problem?"

Dahleeya studied Hope's face for a moment.

"Listen, Miss Delaney. I don't expect life anywhere to be perfect for my daughter. All I want is for her to have a fair chance, and someone who will have her back. I think she'll have that with you. That's enough. Going from home to home like she has been—even if some of them are with black people—that hasn't worked out so well for her…. I can see that you're making a stable home for my child."

Dahleeya stopped and stared hard at the table. Hope sensed that she was working on not crying, that she couldn't cry in front of guards and other prisoners. She mastered her emotions and resumed.

"That stability means a lot. That means everything."

"Don't be sad, mama," whispered Queen. "Nothing's sad."

Dahleeya smiled and took a deep breath.

"That's right, sugar. Nothing's sad." Dahleeya considered. She said to Hope, "Maybe it's hard for *you*, wanting to be a mother, and you have Queen here who has a mother already?"

She seemed to see the answer in Hope's eyes.

She continued, "Queen needs us both. She needs to know that I love her and that I think about her all the time, and I have dreams for her. But I'm gonna be in here for another eight years. So, at the same time, she needs a mother who is with her every day, taking responsibility for her every minute, a mother who can show her the way to reach for her dreams out there in the world. This child needs us both. Not one more than the other. Both."

-73-

Norbert's customer was a man in his mid-seventies, but fit, energetic, and bursting with an urgent question. He held the deck of cards in his hands, and hesitated before shuffling.

"Did you ever know a woman that you just could not forget?"

"Ah," deflected Norbert, "this is about an unforgettable woman."

"It sure is, my friend. Let me give you some background information before we start. Back in Rochester, years ago, I met an incredible woman. Her name was Mabel. Mabel Paine. The chemistry was amazing. We had wonderful times together, but we parted on bad terms. I've thought of her a million times over the years. I've never met anyone like her since. Well, back in June, I took a little vacation here in Gibbons Corner, and who do I run into in the Alibi, but--." He paused a moment to allow Norbert to insert a wild guess.

"Mabel Paine?"

"You got it! She was lit up like a goddam Christmas tree, thrilled to see me and catch up on all that's happened since our romance in Rochester. The years just melted away. We got to talking about the past and all the fun we had, and it was great, reliving old times. Then we got to the part about why we broke up, and we both remembered it differently, and she got mad at me all over again, see? But we had another drink, I thought the night ended on a good note, and I hoped to start seeing her again. Afterwards, I realized I hadn't gotten her phone number, or any way to reach her. I guess I'd had one glass too many. But I wasn't worried. I knew I'd run into her again in such a small town.

"The next day, I'm on the bus, coming back from Edwards Cove to Gibbons Corner, and who do you think is on the same bus?"

Norbert ventured a guess. "Mabel Paine?"

"Right again! Except, she said she wasn't Mabel! She gave me the brush off. She got all huffy and told the bus driver I was hassling her. Can you believe it?"

Norbert shook his head in sympathy.

"Well, she was so mad, I started to doubt myself."

Norbert's eternal smile was spreading from one ear to the other.

"You think my story's funny? There's more. I went back home to Buffalo. But after that, I kept thinking about her. I thought, that was Mabel, I'm sure of it. And I need to know why she blew me off like that. Then I thought, if that *wasn't* Mabel, then that *is* a woman I would like to know better, because she looks just like Mabel. I was going cuckoo with the whole thing. So I came back to Gibbons Corner a couple of days ago. I thought, in a town as small as this, I'll run into that woman, whoever she is, as sure as pie. So what do you think happened then?"

Norbert hazarded another guess. "You ran into her?"

"You bet!" The man checked his watch. "Hey, I know the reading's only twenty minutes. Let me tell you the rest, real quick, before I shuffle the cards. I only have one question."

Norbert nodded, and sat back to enjoy the rest of the story.

"I was sitting in Bailey's Irish Pub on Quaintance Court, eating a sandwich and drinking some Guinness, when who walks in?"

"Uh, Mabel Paine?"

"Hey, you're good at this! She walks right up to my table and sits down. So *I* say, why did you give me the old heave ho on the bus that day, and *she* says, get this, *That wasn't me, I swear.* And she's smiling like it's real funny. Then she says, maybe I dreamt it."

Norbert prompted, "And your question is?"

"My question is, does she have multiple personalities? Because I know I didn't dream it. So I need to know, does she have, you know, *alters,* I think they call them? You know, like in the soap opera everyone used to watch, you know the one?"

"I see. Well, I can't diagnose people, you know, but we *can* have a look at what the cards have to say about you and this impressive woman."

Norbert could not bring himself to break the doppelganger spell. He could so easily have disabused Walter of his delusion on the spot. But like Carlotta before him, he found himself helpless to resist the farce that wanted to play itself out.

"Great!" said Walter, "Let's get to the cards. And then, I just thought of my second question: should I marry her?"

"*Would* you marry her—if she had multiple personalities?"

"You better believe it, my friend! She's the most exciting woman I've ever met."

-74-

Carlotta and Margaret were coming out of Butler's Book Store after a successful shopping expedition for a novel with an African American girl as the protagonist. Arnie had assured Carlotta that *When the Black Girl Sings* by Bil Wright would be high enough in reading level and interest for Queen.

Margaret was confiding to Carlotta that her new roommate had begun to grate on her nerves.

"I don't know, Carlotta," sighed Margaret as they walked. "Maybe it's just that I've lived alone for so many years that I can't adjust to sharing my living space. But honestly, Mabel, bless her soul, just creates chaos in every room she enters. I'm beginning to resent cleaning up after her."

Carlotta, who couldn't imagine cleaning up after another human being, struggled to empathize.

"Have you asked her to find another arrangement?"

"I don't want to ask her to move out. You know how I am. I just wish she'd get the idea herself that she wants to leave."

Just then, a strange man rushed toward them, jay-walking—actually, jay-*running*—across the street from the direction of the Good Fortune Café.

"Mabel!" he shouted.

He seemed about to try to hug Margaret, who took a step back behind Carlotta.

"Oh!" cried Margaret in distress, "It's you again, from the bus!"

Gibbons Corner was a small town. It wasn't possible to avoid anyone.

"Ha ha! Mabel, are you going to start that again?"

"*I* am not *Mabel!*" asserted Margaret.

The man hesitated, obviously confused. Then, seeming to make up his mind, he stepped forward and made a grab for Margaret's hand.

Carlotta swatted him away as Margaret proclaimed, "Don't you dare touch me!"

The color had risen to Walter's lined face. "Then I'm leaving town, Mabel! You'll never see me again. I came here to find you and see if we could make it work. Just one more try. But if you're going to keep playing games, I'm outta here! There's only so much rejection a man can take!"

Passersby stopped and gaped, and a thirty-something woman asked, "Do you want me to call 911?"

"No thank you, dear," said Carlotta to the young woman. "We have everything under control here." Carlotta, sheltering Margaret with her arm, was struck by a sudden thought.

The young woman looked doubtfully once again and the oldsters, and then went on her way.

Carlotta said to the bewildered man, "Excuse me. You are--?"

Her sharp mind had begun to percolate. This man was the one who had bothered Margaret on the bus. This man was the "womanizer" that Mabel had referred to. This man was, in short, the answer to getting rid of Mabel.

-75-

"Let's just step around the corner to Willow Park," suggested Carlotta. "I think we can straighten out all this confusion in very short order."

Walter and Margaret matched Carlotta's brisk steps, while Walter shot reproachful looks at Margaret, and Margaret stared ahead icily.

The park, situated just behind Butler's Books, was quiet on this school day. The hazy autumn air was sparkling gold and warm. A good day for sitting at a picnic table, admiring the changing leaves, and manipulating people into doing what one wants them to do.

"Walter Strand," began Carlotta, who sat directly across from him with Margaret at her side.

Walter tore his eyes from the beautiful Margaret.

"Yes?"

"You are under the impression that my friend here is a woman called Mabel Paine."

"Oh, now if you're going to start that malarkey—."

"Please, hear me out. *This* is not Mabel. This is Margaret Birch. The reason for your confusion is that Mabel and Margaret are actually doubles."

Walter squinted skeptically. "Doubles? What do you mean? Twins?"

"No, not twins. They are no relation to each other. By pure coincidence, they look almost exactly alike."

The women watched the emotions pass across Walter's face as he doubted, considered, and doubted again.

"Look at Margaret's forehead. It's a little higher than Mabel's. And Margaret's nose…"

Margaret obligingly turned her profile to Walter.

Walter tilted his head. "Well. Well, I'll *be*."

"Exactly," said Carlotta. Now she could really warm to her work. "Of course, it's no wonder that you've been looking for Mabel. Mabel—oh yes, we know her, too—she is an extraordinary person. She is very… *popular*."

Walter frowned. "Popular? You mean she has a lot of boyfriends?"

"Oh no, no, no," Carlotta hastened to clarify. "In fact, she spoke of *you* to us, didn't she, Margaret?"

Margaret looked at Carlotta and nodded. Carlotta was on a roll, and Margaret was rolling along with her. Carlotta was going to solve her roommate dilemma, and Margaret was grateful.

"What *did* she say, do you remember, Margaret? Wasn't it something about 'the man she couldn't forget'—I think it was something like that."

Walter sat taller and smiled.

Carlotta and Margaret sang Mabel's praises then. What fun Mabel was! How exciting it was to be in her company! The uniqueness of Mabel!

When Walter could hear no more, he demanded, "Well, then, where *is* she?"

Carlotta said, "We *could* arrange a meeting. Would you like that, Walter?"

As Carlotta and Margaret walked toward home, they congratulated each other on their excellent team work regarding Walter.

"You said so many nice things about Mabel," said Margaret. "I had no idea that you liked her so much. I thought you kind of hated her."

"*Hated?* Oh, Margaret, you know I never hate anyone. Perhaps I *did* sometimes think she wasn't clever enough for the Club, I'll admit that. But she's been so much *fun!* Only now, everyone is tired of her, don't you think? *Now*, listen to me: you are going to have a good time bringing these old lovebirds together..."

"Oh!" said Margaret.

"*And* at the same time, getting your home back in order."

"Oh!" said Margaret again. "Everyone wins!"

"Precisely." Carlotta smiled widely. "You just have to play your cards right. You just do as I say, Margaret."

-76-

That evening Mabel and Margaret were quaffing their preferred beverages at the Alibi Bar. Mabel's was a bottle of beer, and Margaret's was a glass of fresh orange juice. She told Mabel she was "detoxing," and Mabel shrugged, taking a long swig of her Corona.

"All's you ever do is nurse one drink through the whole night. I don't know how toxic you could be, but, hey, different spokes for different folks, as they say."

Walter Strand was due to come along any minute. Margaret had called him and invited him to meet her and Mabel at the Alibi. As Carlotta had predicted, Margaret was enjoying being a matchmaker.

Mabel loved the idea of meeting Walter with her double at her side. She thought it would be hilarious.

Margaret remarked, "He's a very persistent man, I'll say that for him."

Mabel laughed. "Well, I can't say he isn't. Persistent and persuasive. And you know what else? He's ten years younger than me. But then, this isn't the first time I've robbed the cradle. I've never met a man quite like him. We didn't always get along. But I always considered him my soul mate. Whenever we were together, sparks would fly!" Mabel chuckled at her private recollections.

Margaret smiled, seeing that if she just followed Carlotta's instructions, she'd soon have her condo to herself again.

"He sure is a handsome man," encouraged Margaret.

Mabel, startled, took Margaret's measure, as if seeing her for the first time.

"Now. Don't you go getting any ideas. When it comes to my man, I don't like to share."

Margaret, taking inspiration from Carlotta's years of example on the fine art of manipulation, said, "Oh? Is he *your* man? Because he does seem interested in *me.*"

Mabel stared at Margaret, as one cat stares at another who has wandered into her territory.

"Are you saying you're going to try to take him?" Mabel set her bottle down on the table, just next to the coaster. She wiped her mouth with the back of her hand. "I'd like to see you try. It takes two to tangle, *I* always say."

Margaret always thought that it took two to *tango*, but she did not want to tango—or tangle—with Mabel. She just wanted Mabel to move out of her condo. And the way to make that happen was opening before her.

"Well," said Margaret, "I'm not *trying* to do anything. I'd say that *he's* the one doing all the trying, as far as I'm concerned." Fully aware of Mabel's growing indignation, she drew a pattern of moisture on the table with her frosted glass of juice. "And I don't know how you can say he's 'your man,' especially. I mean, you're not *married*, are you?"

As if obeying the law of synchronicity, in the background the strains of a country song on the theme of man-stealing began to swell.

Just then, the women's absorption in one another was broken, as Walter materialized beside their table. They had been unaware of his approach. He pulled out a chair and sat down between them. He took in first one lady, and then the other, while they both turned the full force of their charismatic beams toward him.

At last, he said, "Am I in Heaven, or what? *Two* Mabels?"

The two white-haired look-alikes laughed as if here before them was the most charming man in all the wide world.

-77-

Mabel and Walter left town the following day, going on a "road trip," to a destination that would be decided as they drove. Mabel's parting words to the Club had been, "Don't worry—I'm coming back! You can count on that! Ha ha! You know what they say: a bad pony always turns up!"

The entire Club seemed to take a huge breath of relief at Mabel's departure. They had not realized the tension that Mabel had caused until she was gone.

In the happy space that Mabel left behind, Lorraine turned her attention to Queen. The school teacher in Lorraine was delighted by Queen's obvious intelligence. She quizzed Carlotta on Queen's reading tastes and on her grades. Carlotta didn't know about her grades, but she was able to share some of Queen's reflections from their literary discussions. The child had an understanding beyond her years.

"Why isn't she in the gifted program at school?" Lorraine wanted to know.

Carlotta had no idea. She asked Hope.

"I never thought of it," said Hope. "Does Aunt Lorraine think she's gifted?"

"Yes, she's said so many times."

"If she's gifted, won't the school figure it out, and put her where she needs to be?"

"Lorraine says you need to advocate."

Thus it was that Carlotta, Lorraine, and Hope found themselves in Queen's classroom at Central School, face to face with Queen's fourth grade teacher, Mr. Fisher.

He smiled wearily on being informed that Queen was gifted.

"Another one?" he asked. "There are so many gifted children these days. This class is comprised of forty percent gifted students so far."

"Really?" asked Carlotta, astounded. "But that's remarkable! Forty percent?"

"Yep. According to their parents."

"Ah."

Lorraine said, "Mr. Fisher, we have good reasons for saying that Queen is brighter than average. You see, I'm a retired teacher myself--."

Mr. Fisher turned his kind eyes to Lorraine. "When did you retire?"

"In 1966. I know that seems like a long time ago, but--."

"It *was* a long time ago," put in Carlotta, beginning to feel that their visit to the school was without basis now. If everyone these days thought that their own child was gifted, then perhaps they were being just as vain as everyone else, and needed to go home and let the teacher do his job without interference.

Mr. Fisher said, "I am actually very glad you stopped in to chat. I'm especially pleased to see the kind of support Queen has at home, and I'd be happy to learn anything about her that you think will help me work with her here at school. To be honest, the first few days, I was beginning to think she might need special ed services."

"Why?" asked Hope.

Lorraine and Carlotta bristled, "Special *ed*? For *Queen?*"

"Well, you see, she didn't say a word. I saw in her paper-work that she was a foster child, so putting two and two to-gether, I began to wonder about her intelligence."

Carlotta began to wonder about Mr. Fisher's intelligence.

"But then, I was reading *The Wind in the Willows* aloud to the class--."

Carlotta relaxed slightly. The man knew his juvenile classics.

"For most of them, it's a reach to relate to the book. It's kind of old-fashioned. I always read to them above their own read-ing level, and explain as we go along. But Queen raised her hand one day—the first time I ever heard her speak—and voiced her opinion that Toad was lucky to have friends like Rat, Badger and Mole who cared about him and he should appreci-ate them, because they were like a family. I thought that was a pretty profound assessment for a nine-year-old."

The women smiled with pride.

"I've observed that Queen lights up whenever she's reading, writing stories, or talking about fiction."

The women nodded.

"Of course, she's got a lot of catching up to do in spelling, but I'm not worried about that. That will come. The greater concern is that she's very far behind in math."

The smiles and nods stopped.

"How far behind?" asked Hope.

"She's working at a second grade level right now."

"Oh!" said Hope. "I didn't realize. I mean, I know that I have to help her with math every night, but—*second grade*—you say?"

"Yes," said Mr. Fisher. "But it's understandable. I saw in her file that she has changed schools a lot. Really, it's surprising that she's as successful as she is in language arts. She must have got-ten a good foundation somewhere. As for math, well, we do differentiate for that these days." He turned to Lorraine. "I'm giving her work at her own level, and I can get some help from the math specialist for her, to see if we can bring her up to speed." Turning to Hope, he said, "I'll send a little work for you to do at home with her—not too much, just ten minutes a day on math facts; that's all we need. But as for her reading level, she's able to read middle school material already. She's my best reader."

The smiles came back.

"And the stories she writes! I've told her that I expect to see her name on the cover of a book one day."

After the meeting, Carlotta, Hope and Lorraine all agreed that, as a teacher, Mr. Fisher was gifted. Carlotta wondered aloud if he was married, and noted that he seemed to be completely charmed by Hope.

-78-

The Mexican Cantina was really pretty, with arched doorways and walls that were tangerine-colored and that bright yellow color of sunflowers. All around, there were ceramic suns with faces painted on, and the music playing was all in Spanish, but Queen didn't understand it. Someday, she would understand all the words in Spanish songs. She was learning fast with Miss Moon.

That Mr. Arnie Butler was treating Hope and Queen to dinner. After placing their order with the server, Hope had gone to the restroom, leaving Queen stirring her straw around and around in her ice water and looking hard at Mr. Butler. Mr. Butler just kept smiling, like he thought he could make Queen smile back at him, but it wasn't working.

Finally, he said, "Queen, let me ask you something."

Queen pursed her lips and let her eyelids come down halfway over her eyes, to give him a look.

"Does Hope ever talk about me? Have you ever heard her say anything?"

"All *I* ever hear is how she doesn't have time for you."

That wiped the smile off that man's face.

"She *said* that?"

He looked a little worried, then.

"I wonder if you would help me. See, I really like Hope, and I'd like to do something for her, or something, so she would know--."

"Oh, you mean you wanna give her a *present?* For her *birth-day?"*

"Her birthday?"

"Yep. Her birthday's Friday."

Mr. Butler calculated. "October fourteenth? That's her birth-day?"

"Ah hah."

"But I always thought she was a Taurus."

"No. She's a Methodist."

"I am really glad you're telling me this. Quick, before she comes back, what would she like for her birthday?"

"Well," Queen's imagination was offering all kinds of possi-bilities. "She'd really love it if you put stuff all over her lawn. Flamingoes? Ooh. She just loves flamingoes. You could put one for every year, for her birthday."

"That would be forty-seven flamingoes, then?"

"Fifty."

"No, I'm sure that's not right. We graduated from high school the same year."

"She was left back a few times in elementary school."

"She was?"

"Ah hah."

Mr. Butler looked doubtful.

"I don't know. Maybe I shouldn't do flamingoes. Maybe I should send flowers."

"Oh!" said Queen, inspired. "Now, that is an even better idea. And I know what her favorite flower is!"

Mr. Butler leaned forward, excited. He looked so foolish, he didn't even know.

"What's her favorite flower?"

"Daisies! Ooh, she'd be so happy if you sent her a huge whole bunch of daisies."

"Shh. Here she comes," said Mr. Butler. "Don't let on we've been talking about her."

Hope returned to the table.

"Now, what's going on here? You both look like the cat that swallowed the canary."

For the first time, Queen smiled at Mr. Butler.

-79-

Carlotta's pen hovered above her blue paper. It did not want to write. All new inspiration had to be written longhand, her thoughts following the line from her fertile mind to her nimble fingers, and flowing out onto the page in her own graceful handwriting. But Carlotta's zeal for her book had taken its leave. The inspiration that had gripped her mind only a few months before, now withdrew. She remained disciplined, reporting to her desk each morning at six o'clock; however, her thoughts stalled, her pen balked, and her paper remained as blue as her mood.

After all, what was the point? If a writer is to write with her ideal reader always in mind, Carlotta had to recognize that all along, her ideal reader had been her Club.

But the Club would never read her book. Once that awful woman came back to town, they would all be zip lining with Mabel. Well, perhaps not zip lining. But they would be doing whatever unexpected thing Mabel would come up with next. Their interest in Carlotta's memoirs would fade away. And this caused Carlotta's own interest to fade away.

Considering the nasty turn *How Sharper than a Serpent's Tooth* had taken, would she ever *want* them to read it? Was it a work she could be proud of? Yes, of course, it was beautifully written. A powerful book, in fact. But somewhere along the way, its power had become malignant. Carlotta was afraid of her own work.

She put her pen down at last, and watched the sun come up. Toutou climbed onto her lap and licked her face.

-80-

Now that Mabel was off on her road trip, Carlotta seized the opportunity to drop by Margaret's condo with Queen and pay a visit, Myrtle be damned.

The feline did not darken Carlotta's day. Queen reported that Myrtle was lying on Mrs. Birch's bed, giving Queen "the old stink eye," and apparently couldn't be bothered to get up today to harass Carlotta. As Carlotta chatted with her old friend, she was aware that Queen had slipped from the bedroom where she had been conversing with Myrtle, into the kitchen where she seemed to be opening cabinets and the refrigerator.

"Queen?" called Carlotta. "Come here, dear. Is it nice to poke around in other people's homes?"

Queen came to the doorway and narrowed her eyes at Carlotta. Instead of answering the question, she asked a question of her own.

"Did you know that I like ice cream?"

Carlotta informed Queen of the rudeness of such an inference, and then immediately rewarded her for it by suggesting to Margaret that they all go out for ice cream.

"Why not?" approved Margaret. "Who doesn't like ice cream?"

Outside, the maple trees were brilliant in orange and red. White and yellow chrysanthemums bloomed in the white ceramic pots that lined the sidewalks downtown. High in the sky above them, geese flew in formation, calling signals to one another to stay together.

At Goofy's Ice Cream Parlor, there were fanciful arrays of ice cream, and these included soy varieties. A strident-voiced woman ahead of them was giving the server a hard time. She wanted a taste of this flavor, and then that flavor, and made a disappointed face at each sample. She pessimistically selected a third flavor for her purchase, and then became indignant that the cones were so small. The teenage boy behind the counter shrugged and suggested that the woman could buy two cones.

"Oh yeah. Of course. More profit for *you* that way, huh?" grumbled the customer to the teenager.

As the glum woman stalked out of the shop clutching her displeasing cone, Carlotta, Margaret and Queen watched her with interest. Finally, Queen murmured aloud what all three had been thinking.

"Man. If you can't even be happy when you are picking out an ice cream flavor, when *can* you be happy?"

Heartily approving the sentiment, Carlotta said, "Hush now. We don't talk about people in public."

"Right," agreed Queen affably. "We talk about them in private."

That evening Hope got a phone call from Aunt Margaret.

"That little girl of yours is just the cat's meow. I'm still smiling about some of the things she said this afternoon."

"Oh, Aunt Margaret, thank you so much!" Hope lowered her voice, so that Queen, who was working at her desk in her room, would not hear. "I'm so glad to hear good things about her."

"Obviously, you are doing a wonderful job. She seems to be adjusting so well."

"You don't know how much it means to me to hear you say that. I sometimes wonder if I *am* doing such a good job. I'm finding this motherhood thing to be even harder than I expected it to be. Sometimes I don't know how to handle things."

"Oh, Hope! I still remember how hard it can be. As mothers, we have so many opportunities to disappoint ourselves."

Hope laughed with relief.

"Good to know! I wonder: when will I start feeling like a real mother, instead of like a screw-up?"

"If you feel like a screw-up, I'd say you already feel like a real mother."

"Aunt Margaret, you're the best."

An excerpt from Queen's notebook:

Here are some things I have learned about life:

1. People are liers but some dont lie that much
2. Dont be supprised when people act like thereselfs
3. Some people have cubberds and refigeraters full of food and they never get hongry.
4. I will leave blank spaces in case I learn more things
5. _____
6. _____
7. _____

-81-

"I like your life," said Queen to Carlotta. "When I'm an old lady, I'll be just like you, but black. I'll have a nice house, and lots of friends, and I'll be writing books. It's so cool that you are writing a book. Can I see it?"

Carlotta basked in the child's admiration. They were sitting at her kitchen table where they had a view of the fall colors and gamboling squirrels.

"I would love to show you my book, Queen, but it needs quite a bit of revision first. You see, it took an awkward turn, and I was even thinking of giving up on it. But now I have decided that I just need to bend it back to being the book I want to write."

Queen laughed. "Sounds like you're fighting with your own book."

Carlotta acknowledged that it felt that way to her.

"Be that as it may," said Carlotta, "let's get back to *Charlotte's Web*."

Queen pulled the novel toward her and ran her fingers across the illustration of the girl, the pig, and the spider web.

"As you read any novel, I want you to be aware of foreshadowing. At the beginning of *Charlotte's Web*, the spider, Charlotte, explained to Wilbur the pig that all living things die. As the story progressed, you saw that Charlotte herself died. So that part at the beginning was what we call foreshadowing. It is a *literary device*. It's something like a hint. The author is getting you ready for what is to come."

"Did *you* ever know someone who died?" asked Queen.

Carlotta allowed herself to be interviewed by the little girl, who looked at her unblinking through her round glasses, focusing as if she were taking mental notes. Carlotta told Queen the briefest of facts about her son Charlie, who had died in a car accident with his wife eleven years ago. And her husband, Ed, who died many years before that.

"Were you sad?"

"Well, of course, we're sad when someone we love dies."

"Which was worse—your son dying or your husband?"

"Queen, do you know, these are very personal questions now."

"Sorry. Did you know that Hope used to have a boyfriend? His name was Rudy. But she dumped that sucker's ass, and she's happier now."

"Queen! Really! Language!"

Queen hesitated. "Oh, sorry again. That's the way Hope said it. Dumped that sucker's ass. That's what she said."

Queen folded her hands and became pensive. She said, "I never knew you went through so many hard things in your life."

"Well, we all go through hard things in life. The challenge is to have 'grace under pressure,' as Ernest Hemingway said. You'll read him when you're older. But I don't know that my life is any harder than average. Actually, Queen, I'd say you have gone through harder things than I have."

Queen knitted her brow. "I don't agree. At least everyone that *I* love is still alive."

Carlotta had never encountered such a deep child.

Queen added, "It's so sad, that all living things have to die." She looked out at the autumn leaves floating on the hazy breeze.

Carlotta felt a softening of her heart. What a sensitive child.

"Yes, it is sad," she agreed, smiling tenderly at Queen.

"When *you* die," said Queen, "can I have your jewelry?"

An excerpt from Queen's notebook:

Foreshadowing. After I finish this book for forster kids I will write lots more I can just see a line of hardback books on a shelf with my name on them Queen Serafina Jones It looks lovely. I might write one called How to Start Your Own Countrey. I am foreshadowing that right here.

-82-

Hope phoned Carlotta seeking childrearing advice, and although it was pleasant to be asked for guidance, Carlotta was at a loss.

"It's been a long time since I've been responsible for managing children. I do remember that you were such an easy child, and so was Summer. Both of you responded to the 'stink eye,' as Queen calls it. You both *wanted* to behave. My boys, now, they were different. They created mayhem. But then, I had your Uncle Ed to help." Carlotta paused, trying to remember. "Spanking was his idea of helping, as I recall. That's what everyone did, when they didn't know what else to do."

"That's primitive! I can't understand why parents ever thought that was okay."

"It seemed to work, though, at least in the short term. It brought instant results."

"But doesn't violence just teach them that might makes right?"

"'Violence!' Really, Hope. I wouldn't call spanking a form of violence."

"Of course it's violent. What else do you call it when a person hits another person?"

"But spanking doesn't count as one person hitting another, does it?"

"Doesn't it? I'm sure you wouldn't suggest I try spanking Queen?"

Carlotta was shocked at the image.

"Certainly not! Your Uncle Ed was a blustering bully. I'm sorry to tell you that about your uncle, and I don't like to speak ill of the dead, but it is the truth. No, in this day and age, there must be a better way than spanking! Leave the child her dignity, no matter what she's done. Anyway, what *has* she done? I must say, she behaves perfectly when she's with me."

"She does? Wow. I wonder what that means. With me, it's like she's constantly testing and pushing. She defies me on a daily basis. I tell her it's time to work on her math facts, and she yells at me to stop bossing her. I tell her to go to bed, and she won't. She can be very sweet, too, sometimes, but she will not accept any direction whatsoever from me."

Carlotta searched her mind for something that might be helpful. The way she raised her boys was not the way parents were raising children today. If she had it to do over...she stopped that thought in its tracks.

There are no do-overs. There is only the present moment. Queen's childhood is here and now.

"Didn't you say, before she ever came, that children test their foster parents? I believe you said they are testing to see if you'll...." Carlotta paused, surprised at the knot that seemed to be forming in her throat. "To see if you'll give up on them. Isn't that what you said?"

Hope must not be allowed to become discouraged.

"Give her time, dear. She hasn't been with you long. It's only been one month! One month! It seems-- in a way-- like she's been here always."

Carlotta, receiving inspiration from she knew not where, put an air of authority into her voice, as if she were a radio psychologist: "I suggest that you stop directing, and simply propose things as possibilities, so that she can feel that she's got some control over her life. Instead of, 'It's time to work on your math now,' try, "Would you like to work on your math now, or shall we set a timer for twenty minutes, and you can start then?" I'll bet you anything she'll cooperate, just because you're giving her the chance to feel she has some say-so."

Carlotta added, "Queen doesn't like to be managed. No right-thinking person does."

-83-

On Friday, October fourteenth, Hope awoke at six-thirty in the morning to find her front yard full of pink flamingoes. She rubbed her eyes. They were still there. Wrapping her coat around her pajamas, she stepped outside. That's when she saw the large black number: "50." It was on sticks and facing the sidewalk.

Jenny, across the street, waved and called, "Happy fiftieth birthday, Hope!"

"Jenny! Did *you* do this?"

"Me? No! I didn't even know it was your birthday!"

She and Jenny would wake up the whole neighborhood shouting across the street at each other this way. Hope pointed to her own door, pantomiming that she had to go.

Jenny, always one for trying to prolong conversations, trumpeted, "You look great—for fifty!" as Hope closed her door.

Through gritted teeth, Hope said to the door, "That's because I'm forty-six."

Queen was watching her.

"Are you mad?"

"Well, yeah, I'm mad, except I don't know who to be mad *at*. Who would do such a thing? Everyone who knows me knows I don't like to be the center of attention. And my birthday is in May. So this has to be a joke. But I don't know anyone who would play a joke like this."

"It wasn't me," assured Queen, her eyes wide.

"Of course not! Where would you have gotten the money? No, I know it wasn't you."

As Hope made oatmeal, she called out, "I've got it! I bet it was just a mistake! Wrong birthday, wrong age: of course, they just got the wrong lawn."

The doorbell rang.

It was Flowers on Main, with a delivery: the biggest bouquet of daisies that Hope had ever seen.

The gift card read, "Happy birthday, from your admiring friend, Arnie."

"It's not a mistake! It's Arnie!" exclaimed Hope. At first she smiled. It was nice to have a man make a big deal about her birthday. Even though it wasn't her birthday. What a sweet thought. Her smile was short-lived.

"He thinks I'm *fifty?*"

Hope began to sneeze violently. Her nose began to run. Her eyes began to run. She shoved the flowers deep into the garbage and washed her hands.

Queen handed her a box of tissues and giggled. "You're okay, aren't you, Hope? Oh, those birds look ridiculous out there!"

After Hope took an antihistamine, they stood together at the window and looked at the flock of pink plastic flamingoes, hideous in the morning light. Hope's allergic distress had already lessened. She began to laugh.

Suddenly Queen's pleasure seemed to fade.

"I don't know what's so funny. Nothing funny about it. Uh-uh. It sure isn't funny to me. I'd be mad if I were you. I sure would."

In Mr. Fisher's class, Queen's head was bent over her math work, but her mind was on getting rid of Mr. Butler. Seems like instead of getting mad, Hope just thought the flamingoes and daisies were hilarious. That was not good. *A lady starts laughing at something a man does, and pretty soon he's moving in. He moves in, and that's when the bad stuff starts.* Queen had seen it all before.

What Queen needed was some advice from someone who knew everything about everybody. She wondered if that Madame Fifi was still on late-night television. Maybe she should sneak out of bed tonight to see. Hope always left her purse—with her credit card inside—on the dining room table. It was nice that Hope trusted her like that.

Red and orange leaves gusted around Hope's feet as she walked, hugging her long sweater around her. Orange Halloween lights lit up the window displays of Butler's Books. Inside, Arnie looked up with undisguised happiness at the sight of Hope.

She had left Liam at the controls of the Good Fortune Café to run over to the bookstore and thank Arnie for his gesture. While she was at it, she put him straight about her age.

"I didn't *think* you were older than me," he said. "I mean, you look like you're twenty-two."

Hope didn't believe him, but nonetheless she flushed with pleasure, and he gazed at her, enchanted.

"You *know* we graduated the same year," said Hope.

"Right. But Queen insisted you were turning fifty today."

"Wait. What? And she told you that today is my birthday?"

The light dawned on them both at the same time.

"Today is not your birthday, is it?"

Hope shook her head.

"And you do not like a whole bunch of stuff on your lawn."

Hope laughed and shook her head. "But it was really nice of you, anyway."

"Oh, wow. And...how do you feel about daisies? At least you liked the flowers, I hope."

"I'm terribly allergic to daisies."

Arnie was aghast.

"I am so, so sorry. You're *allergic?* Are you all *right?*"

"Sure, I'm fine. I just had to take an antihistamine."

"So this was a complete and total disaster." Arnie covered his face and peeked at Hope through his fingers. "I have been punked by a nine-year-old."

He looked so bewildered and embarrassed. And adorable, really. Why had Hope never realized how cute he was?

Looking into his kind hazel eyes, she began to laugh. She saw the relief in his face, and he began to laugh with her.

"But why?" asked Arnie. "Why would Queen set me up?"

Hope, still smiling, said, "I think she might feel threatened by you."

"Threatened? By *me?* You're kidding, right? What's threatening about me?"

"Nothing! But see it from her point of view. She has all my attention now. And maybe her past experiences with men haven't been so positive; I don't really know. She just doesn't want any more change in her life."

Arnie nodded. "I get that."

Hope knew he also felt encouraged that she was even talking about him changing things.

"I'm adopting her, you know. We've done the paperwork, and we have a court date. She'll be my daughter forever." In her mind, for some reason, Hope heard Queen adding, *just so you know.*

Arnie smiled.

"I can see how much joy she brings you. Congratulations."

"Do you know, you're the first person to congratulate me?"

"Hey, we should celebrate the adoption! I *would* have a bunch of storks or something put all over your lawn, but… how about we go out to dinner at Renata's instead? With Queen, of course."

"That would be lovely! Let's wait until after it's final. And this time, if I leave the table, don't believe anything Queen tells you."

She had to get back to the café. But first, she gave him a hug. And that felt really, really good.

-84-

Carlotta and Queen were muses for each other. Carlotta wrote down the droll things that Queen was always saying. Amusingly, Queen was also quick to write down quotes from Carlotta. It seemed the child was writing a book, bless her. She wouldn't let Carlotta read it; like Carlotta, she claimed it wasn't ready to be seen by others yet.

"Ah, it's still in rough draft form, then? Do you have a working title?"

"My title is always changing," said Queen. "Right now, I live in Gibbons Corner. So…."

Queen showed the front of her notebook where a label had been placed over several other labels. The top label read: *Queen of Gibbons Corner.*

Carlotta was suffused with pleasure at the charming title, but she had a correction to make.

"You need to put a comma after 'Queen.' That way, it means your name is Queen and you live in Gibbons Corner. Without the comma, it gives the impression that you are the monarch of this town."

"Monarch? Like a butterfly?"

"No. Monarch, like a royal person, like a queen with a crown."

"Huh." Queen reflected, drawing a comma with her finger where Carlotta had suggested it should go. "I like it better without the comma, then. I wouldn't mind being the monarch of this town."

Carlotta bit her lip.

A natural ambition, she thought.

Queen's eye was caught by an interesting book in Carlotta's house: *The Meanings of Flowers: The Study of Floriography,* by Flora Posey. She brought it to Carlotta.

"This book has all the flowers in alphabetical order, with their meanings. *I* never knew flowers *had* meanings."

"That is a very valuable resource, Queen. The French people are especially knowledgeable about the significance of each flower. You should never send anyone flowers without first knowing the meaning of what you are sending."

"Especially," resumed Queen, "if I'm sending flowers to French people." She leafed through the book, entranced by the illustrations. "I'm going to look up my mama. Her first name is Dahleeya, but that's just a different way of saying Dahlia. She was named after her great grandmother Dahlia, but her mother wanted to make it different and modern, so she made it Dah-LEE-yah."

She read aloud: "'The dahlia represents grace under pressure'—hey! Isn't that what you said the other day? Grace under pressure?" She continued reading. "'Inner strength, commitment to another person'—hey! That's *me*! She's committed to *me*! Let's see, what else: 'The message of the dahlia is to not be held back by the challenges in life.'"

Queen sat back and thought, gazing at the photograph of a dahlia.

"Well, now. That's just *like* my mama."

Carlotta, well aware of Queen's little practical joke on poor Arnie Butler, said, "Why don't you look up the meaning of *daisies?*"

Queen started guiltily.

"Oh. You know about that?"

Carlotta kept a straight face and nodded.

Queen turned to the next page.

"Ugh." She looked up at Carlotta. "Says here, 'true love and new beginnings,' and a whole mess of other stuff. I don't need to be reading about daisies. I sure don't."

An excerpt from Queen's notebook:

I snooped in Mrs Moons house and red her book I feel gilty cause I wouldnt like it if she red mine but I was soooo qurious. Now that I have red it I have a new prolem cause there is a disasster that is going to happen if any of her freinds snoop and reed that book like I did or if she publishes it like she said she might do. Mrs Moons book is going to burn bridges. Looks like she doesnt care cause she thinks her freinds desserve it but I know lotsa people desserve lotsa things don't mean you should do it. I want to tell her all this but then she will know I red her book and she will be mad at me. Oh. What shall I do? Alas! That is what they say in ferry tails when something is verry sad. Alas!

-85-

Mabel and Walter returned to Gibbons Corner on Tuesday, October twentieth, and burst upon Birdie's Watercolor Class with their usual raucousness.

"The chickens have come home to roast!" Mabel proclaimed as she and Walter entered the studio.

Everyone but Carlotta put down their brushes to take in Mabel's incredible accounts of her travels.

"It was just like a honeymoon, only without the wedding, wasn't it, hon?" she beamed at Walter, who beamed back, sleepily.

"And we brought each of you a little something from out west, where it's legal!"

From a blue Yankees tote bag, Mabel produced five dark chocolate candy bars and passed them around to Carlotta, Norbert, Lorraine, Birdie and Margaret.

"Oh, chocolate!" said Margaret happily.

"Whaddaya mean, 'where it's legal?' Chocolate is legal in New York, you know."

Mabel winked at her. "Not *this* kind of chocolate!"

Norbert read aloud from the label: "'Warning: this product contains a high level of THC. Not a food. Keep away from children.'"

"Edible marijuana!" cackled Mabel. "What'll they think of next, that's what *I* always say."

Carlotta said, "They put marijuana in *candy* bars?"

Mabel nodded, "Yep! And brownies, and gummy bears, and cookies! We tried them all, didn't we, Walter?"

Walter nodded slowly. He didn't seem to have much to say. He was very mellow.

Carlotta sputtered, "That's the worst idea I've ever heard of! It's irresponsible! Children are so attracted to candy. What if a child got hold of it?"

Mabel considered. "I never thought of that. Gee. That would be bad. Because these are very potent. If an adult my size ate half of one of these bars, she'd be knocked on her ass, hallucinations and the whole ten yards. Believe me. I know. Ha ha! But *we're* not children. We're responsible adults!"

Norbert handed the candy bar back to Mabel. "I appreciate the souvenir, Mabel, but it's not my sort of thing. I hope I'm not offending you."

"Not at all!" said Mabel, amiably. She stuffed the chocolate in Walter's shirt pocket.

Carlotta was next to hand her candy bar back to Mabel. She looked at Lorraine, Margaret, and Birdie expectantly, but they didn't follow suit.

Mabel instructed them, "Now, it takes a while to feel the effects, maybe even as much as an hour. So start with a nibble and wait; don't keep eating it, thinking it's not working. Ha ha! If you do that, you'll wind up in the emergency room like I did the first time."

Margaret was startled. "Oh, Mabel! The emergency room? What happened?"

"Well, I got real dizzy, see, and everything started going in real slow motion, and I saw some ducks and I thought they were talking to me. That wasn't the problem, though. I would have been fine, except then my breathing got real shallow, and I thought Walter here wanted to kill me."

Mabel gave Walter a hard jab in the side with her elbow, waking him out of his reverie.

"But *you* weren't trying to kill me, *were* you, hon?"

"Of course not," said Walter, blinking his red eyes.

Carlotta could not believe that her friends had not given back Mabel's nasty present.

"Lorraine. Margaret. Birdie. Be very careful here. It's been known for years that there is a link between marijuana use and the onset of mental illness. I, for one, still value my brain. This tainted candy is very dangerous."

Lorraine made a dismissive gesture toward Carlotta, "We can think for ourselves, Carlotta."

"If you want to talk about dangerous," said Mabel, "I'll tell you what's *really* dangerous. Trying to stay safe all the time. Taking no risks at all. Until you turn to *stone*."

Carlotta stared stonily at Mabel.

Birdie, moderating, said, "Carlotta is just concerned for our well-being. And Mabel just wants to offer us a new experience." She smiled serenely first at one, and then at the other. "I think it's good to always keep an open mind."

Carlotta countered, "Yes. But not so open that your brains fall out."

Birdie said, "I smoked quite a bit of pot in my earlier days. I haven't had any for decades. I just forgot about it, I guess. But at one time, I used it daily. I think. *My* brains didn't fall out."

Oh, didn't they, thought Carlotta. She tossed her head.

"We are all examples for a child now. Are you forgetting that? What if Queen could see you all, with your *marijuana?*"

Lorraine said, "As far as I can see, she's not here right now."

"Children perceive everything, Lorraine. You know that. Especially a gifted and sensitive child such as Queen. Nothing remains hidden."

"Yeah, right, especially when she wanders through houses and goes through purses."

"Exactly."

"Yeah, well, you might wanna teach her to not do that."

"And *you* might want to remember that New York is not Colorado, and you are holding an illegal substance in your hand, according to our state laws. You are in criminal possession of a drug."

Lorraine, Margaret, and Birdie, in synchronized motion, looked down at the candy in their hands, and stepped forward to give it back to Mabel.

"Aw, scared of getting busted?" asked Mabel. "Listen, at our age, nothing would happen to you. A night or two in the can, max. Slap on the wrist." Seeing the group unconvinced, she went on, "Or if they did send you away, we'd help you break out. We'd smuggle in a file or something. Ha ha!" At last, she shrugged and said, "Well, that's fine! More for us, huh, Walter?"

Mabel then turned to Margaret: "Listen, Margaret, I hope this doesn't hurt your feelings, but I'm going to move into Walter's room at the Harbor Home Bed and Breakfast. You don't mind, do you?"

Margaret's blue eyes opened wide with happy surprise.

"But," added Mabel, "can I leave some of my stuff at your place, just for a while, until we get a place with more room?"

"Of course, Mabel, of course you can!"

Carlotta knew that Margaret would have been happy to allow Mabel to leave any amount of junk behind her. The main thing was: Margaret had gotten rid of Mabel.

-86-

Hope and Queen sat perplexed at the kitchen table. Queen had an impossible school assignment. Tomorrow morning, she was required to bring in a baby picture of herself. No such picture existed.

"Looks like everyone but me has one. There's no proof I ever was a baby. So maybe I wasn't."

"Of course you were a baby, Queen."

"I don't *remember* being a baby."

"No, of course not. No one does. Our brains are not developed enough yet at that age to create memories. But some people say they remember being three or even two years old. What is your earliest memory?"

Down came the bars over Queen's eyes. While staying seated at the kitchen table, she retreated far, far away from Hope.

"Never mind," said Hope. "I just got an idea. Why don't we look at images of babies on the internet? We'll pick one that looks like you, and there you go, ta-dah! Your baby picture."

Queen was not amused.

"Will I have to lie?"

"If you want to lie, you have my permission. If you want to tell the truth, you do that. Mr. Fisher wants a picture? We'll give him a picture. What's it for, anyway?"

"We're going to look at our picture and write about ourselves."

"Oh! Well, then, Queen. No worries! The picture is nothing more than an illustration. It doesn't matter if it's really you or not. The important part is the writing. And that's your specialty."

-87-

On Tuesday evening, at Carlotta's Oil Painting Class, Margaret was troubled.

"A teenage boy approached me on the street, just as I was coming here," she confided to Carlotta, Lorraine, Birdie, Norbert, Liam, the teenage girl, and the young mother.

"Oh mercy!" cried Lorraine in pretend hysteria. "Are you all *right*?"

"Yes, of course, I'm all right," said Margaret, ignoring Lorraine's attempt at mockery. "I'm just confused. Lately, it seems people say the strangest things to me, and this one was *really* strange."

"What did he say, Mrs. Birch?" asked Liam.

"Well, he said, 'Do you still want to sell your nickel bag?'" Margaret's brow was deeply furrowed. "At least, I'm pretty sure that's what he said."

The teenage girl asked, "What did you say back to him?"

"I said, 'I don't understand you.' Then he looked over his shoulder, and just slinked off. Just like that. What does that mean?"

Liam and the teenage girl glanced sideways at each other.

Birdie said, "As I recall, that is a reference to pot. Five dollars' worth."

Margaret stood dumbfounded before the class.

"Are you telling me, that a teenager just asked me to sell him marijuana?"

Liam, who seemed to have become very fond of all the old people, said, "What's his name, Mrs. Birch? Do you want me to beat the crap out of him?"

Liam was small for his age, and it was alarming to imagine him starting a fight with anyone.

"Oh!" exclaimed Margaret. "Please, no! Don't even think of doing anything like that, Liam. I have no idea what his name is. I just wish strangers would stop coming up to me and saying such odd things."

Carlotta, wishing to draw her students' attention back to their easels, concluded, "I think you can easily piece together what is going on, Margaret. You have..." she paused, considering Liam, the teenage girl and the young mother, who were not privy to Mabel's recent nefarious activities. "You have a certain so-and-so to thank for your strange experiences. It's nothing we can solve in our painting class. For now, let's listen to *Eine kleine nachtmusik* and focus our eyes on our work.

"'Art washes away from the soul, the dust of everyday life.' Pablo Picasso."

-88-

Hope found her credit card bill in Queen's sock drawer while putting away laundry. It was Halloween, and Queen was singing in the kitchen, and declaring, "This will be my best Halloween ever!"

Hope opened the bill and scanned the charges. One stood out to her: the merchant's name was unfamiliar. "Two hundred and seventy-seven dollars!" she said aloud.

A floorboard creaked, and she looked up to see she was being observed by a three-and-a-half foot mouse. The mouse let out a surprisingly powerful bellow.

"Why do you hate me? You want to give me back to the social worker!"

Queen's head, above her mouse costume, was moist with tears and sweat, and she held her mask under her arm.

Aunt Margaret had sewn the Despereaux costume for Queen, working on it steadily for a month. Queen had visited Aunt Margaret several times for fittings and had been looking forward to this day with all her heart.

And now, Queen stood with tears dribbling down her face, as Hope held her credit card bill in her hand, looking from it to the distraught child.

"Of *course* I'm not going to give you back to the social worker. I wouldn't even think of such a thing. Of *course* I don't hate you, honey. Just—stop crying and tell me if you know what this charge is for. I don't understand."

Queen flung herself onto her white bedspread, face down, mouse tail dangling over the side of the bed. She cried hot, repentant tears, and Hope sat down next to her and rubbed her back. Queen did not pull away from her.

She turned her head to look at Hope from the side of her eye, as new tears flowed.

Hope waited.

"I-I-I-needed to talk to someone who knows everything about everyone. So I called Madame Fifi—do you know her? The TV psychic? While you were sleeping. Oh! I didn't know it was going to cost so much until I was hanging up. Then it was too late."

Hope's mind swirled with questions. She didn't know what to ask first.

But Queen went on, "I told her about that Mr. Butler. And that I want to get rid of him. Oh! And then Madame Fifi said, how do I know he's a bad man. I said maybe he's not exactly bad, but he wants to move in and change things, and nobody needs him. We talked longer and longer. I couldn't get off the phone because she wouldn't give me my answer. Finally, she totally ripped me off. Oh! She never did tell me how to get rid of him. She said the spirits were telling her that he was probably nice, and I shouldn't worry about it. I was so mad. She is just a liar-liar-pants-on-fire! I bet the spirits don't even talk to her. They probably know she's a fake. And then another person came on the phone and said $277.00 would be charged to my credit card."

Queen rolled over and sat up, her chest heaving from overheating and emotion.

"Are we poor now?"

"No, we're not poor now. We'll just cut back on extra goodies this month—like ice cream."

"Oh, Hope, I am so, so sorry. I will never do that again."

Hope, fighting to keep from smiling, said, "I forgive you, Queen. And listen. You don't need to worry about getting rid of Mr. Butler. You're my priority. We're not making any big changes around here unless both you and I agree. You understand?"

Hope opened her arms, and Queen hugged her, resting her head on Hope's shoulder.

-89-

An excerpt from Queen's notebook:

Today we went to Cort and I was scared cause when my mama went to Cort they put her in the Place but Hope said this is Adoption Cort wich is totally differnt and we had to go there so Hope could adopt me.

In the waitin room there was so many kids and babies with the grownups who were tryin to adopt them and there were toy cars, a play Kichen and some dirty old baby dolls kids could play with. Two kids had hearing aids but they were haveing fun anyway playing and I thought it would be hard to be them but then I watched them and I could tell they like there lifes.

Some of the adults had breif cases those were the Lawyers. The ones who wanted to adopt kids were nervous you could tell some of them were Smiling real hard not only cause they were nervous but they were so happy too.

Our Lawyer came then and Hope had to sign papers. Hope's been talking to this lawyer a lot. Hope said it was a hole mess of paperwork she had to do but she dosen't mind. Then while we were waiting some more, I had a supprise cause our freinds came in: Mrs. Moon, Miss Moon, Mrs. Birch, Mrs. Andretta, Mrs. Walsh, Mr. Zelenka, and that Mr. Butler came too. They were all wearing the same t-shirt as Hope: white, and printed on it said "I'm with Queen." Hope said it was to show how they were all Together to support the fambly Hope and I are making.

We went into the Cort and the Judge lady was waring a wig she was about one hunerd years old there was a young black lady next to her helping her cause she kept getting mixed up and I had to laugh I couldnt help it.

All our freinds had to raize thier right hand and sware to help Hope. I thought I relly dont think she's gonna need THAT much help, I basicly take care of myself But it was still Nice.

So now I am Hope's adopted Dorter hooray!

-90-

Mabel hooked her arm through Walter's and gazed into the blazing bonfire in Carlotta's back yard.

She declared, "The weathergirl said we'd have unreasonably warm weather this evening, and she was right!"

Margaret said tactfully, "Or she might have said, 'unseasonably warm.'"

Mabel chuckled, "She *might* have, Marg. Only I don't think 'unseasonably' is a real word."

Walter was now back to his jocular and extroverted self, complimenting all the women and laughing heartily at everything Mabel said.

Norbert and young Liam had gathered the sticks and started the fire. Norbert had instructed Liam in the Eagle Scout way to do it, and Liam took the instruction well. He was turning out to be a very good employee at Hope's café, very responsible for his years.

The reason for the gathering was the momentous occasion of Queen's adoption. To celebrate, Carlotta had invited Norbert, Margaret, Birdie, Lorraine, Mabel, Walter, Liam, Arnie, Hope, Summer, and, of course, Queen. They had enjoyed a potluck dinner, and had come out to gaze at the blazing sticks and the bright stars above. They all stood in a wide circle around the fire now, the flames reflected in their eyes. Carlotta had the odd thought that they resembled a tribe of yore.

The fire crackled in the autumn breeze, and Carlotta looked around the circle at her old friends. Life was good.

Queen hopped over to Birdie and said, "Mrs. Walsh! The visualization you taught me—just so you know—it *worked!*"

Birdie and Queen stepped out of the ring to chat, Queen very animatedly. Carlotta could hear Queen say, "Now, do you think it will work for something *else?*" and their conversation went on. It was lovely to see Queen developing relationships with Carlotta's dearest ones. Queen would always be able to consider them her extended family, and this caused a gentle fluttering of emotion in Carlotta, who was becoming accustomed to such flutters.

Hope and Arnie were side by side, and he was hanging on her every word as if she were his ideal woman. If only Hope would give him a little encouragement.

Lorraine interrupted the picture of budding love, and asked Hope, "So whaddaya need? What kinda support can we give you, hon?"

Hope said, "I definitely want Queen to see her mother once a month. I'll take her as often as I can, but as you know, it's hard for me to get away from work. If any of you would like to take turns to drive Queen out there, that would be the greatest thing you could do for us."

Carlotta volunteered herself and Summer for the next trip to Shelton.

Summer said, "Wait. *How* long did you say it takes to get there? *What* time did you say you have to get up?"

Carlotta chided her. "If *I* can get up in the dark on a Saturday morning, if *I* can drive two hours—at the age of eighty-one —I am sure it will be no problem for you, a girl of twenty-six."

Summer laughed, "I never thought I'd look lame next to my *grandmother.*"

Carlotta smiled firmly. "Well, my dear, you do look lame. Very lame. I suggest you get with it."

The gathering tittered nervously and looked around for someone to change the subject.

Mabel came to the rescue.

"I remember the days when we used to make s'mores over the fire. Anyone else ever do that?"

Carlotta, for the first time ever, supported Mabel's contribution. It was the only normal thing she'd ever heard Mabel say.

"That is an excellent idea. I'll just go in and get some marshmallows and chocolate."

Summer said, "The *vegan* marshmallows, Gramma. The ones I got you. And the vegan chocolate—the dark one. And vegan graham crackers. I'll help you."

As the party toasted marshmallows on sticks, they began to ask about Carlotta's book. It was very gratifying.

"I've been doing quite a bit of editing and revision as I go along. Some say, write the whole book first, and then go back to revise. But I get such pleasure out of reading my own prose that I find myself reading it— and improving it— as I go along. I really feel I've got something to work with now. It's exciting for me to write for hours every day."

Now they were all keen to know: when would it be finished? When could they read it? They pulled the gooey mess off the ends of their sticks and asked her a delightful barrage of questions. They really cared about what she was doing. They really loved her. They were still hers.

At last, wiping their fingers on moist paper towels, they all trailed in through the house and out the front door to sit on the wide porch and enjoy a glass of wine or hot cider.

It was sweater weather, and the group unanimously desired to stay outside in the fresh air for as long as they could. Carlotta noticed that Arnie finagled his way to sit next to Hope, and looking at the two of them, anyone would have thought they were a couple. They looked right together. Arnie asked Hope questions and seemed to admire everything she said. Meanwhile, Mabel was resting her hand on Walter's thigh, and he was bending his head to let her whisper in his ear. So unseemly in an older couple, Carlotta thought.

Lorraine and Summer talked about teaching, both amazed at how abandoned methods cycle back around in new packaging as the latest word in education. Norbert and Birdie were in a tête-à-tête, and Carlotta couldn't help but wonder how close those two had been growing without her even noticing. Now Liam and Walter talked passionately about the Buffalo Sabres, and who should be traded and who wasn't working hard enough. Margaret was raving about reviews for a movie that was showing at the Fine Arts Film Society, and asking if Carlotta wanted to see it with her. Funny, how Margaret was inviting her to a movie now that Mabel was busy with a boyfriend. Speaking of Mabel, where was she? Ah, she had only stepped into the house to use the powder room, and now she was back, twirling her baseball cap in her hands. Carlotta made a mental note to check the silverware later.

Not seriously, of course. It was just a thought she would have shared wryly with Lorraine, back in the days when she and Lorraine were wry.

Everyone was enjoying the fine art of conversation. It was a successful party, celebrating such an important event.

If Queen slipped out to the back yard while the adults were talking, if the dying bonfire suddenly burst into flames again, no one saw.

An excerpt from Queen's notebook:

I did it. I wouldnt want Some one to burn up my Book. But it was still the right thing to do. Mrs. Moon has freinds that are like fambly to her she is crazy enough to mess that up

-91-

Among her many virtues, Carlotta could list orderliness and attention to detail. She was a woman of systems and routines. Her neat stack of blue paper was always housed in the drawer of her secretary desk. She never stored it anywhere else. And yet, it was gone.

Someone had taken it.

But who? And when? And *why?*

She cast her mind back to the night before, and at once, the obvious villain emerged in her mind.

Mabel.

It must have been when they were all out on the front porch. Hadn't Mabel gone in to use the restroom? She was sure she had. That horrible woman had used that moment to pilfer through Carlotta's desk and steal her manuscript. She must have sneaked it into her blue Yankees tote bag. She stole it. She must have

"Why do you hate me? You want to get rid of me!" wailed Mabel.

The bartender's head bobbed up, and he looked attentive and displeased. It was a quiet hour at the Alibi, and he seemed surprised to see the old people acting up. They usually had their one drink each and left, no drama.

"Don't be ridiculous," hissed Carlotta loudly. "You're making a scene."

"*I'm* making a scene?" cried Mabel. "Now that's the cat calling the kettle black!"

Mabel, Margaret, Lorraine, Birdie, and Norbert were having their usual refreshment after a session of taping *In the Kitchen with Margaret*. Carlotta had come there to ambush Mabel, right in front of everyone. It was no more than she deserved.

"I'm not saying you stole it, Mabel. Maybe you accidentally mixed it up with your things. Just a mistake, I'm sure!"

Margaret interfered, "Carlotta! What proof do you have, to assume Mabel has your manuscript?"

Mabel downed the rest of her beer and looked with defiance at Carlotta.

"Yeah. The proof's in the pumpkin, Carlotta old girl."

Norbert and Birdie suggested uselessly that Carlotta might have misplaced it herself.

"I have never misplaced anything in my entire life," asserted Carlotta improbably. "There's no harm in simply checking Mabel's tote bag, is there?"

Mabel opened her eyes wide in shock.

"You want to *search* me?" She raised her voice again, and again, the bartender lifted his bald head. He put down the glass he was drying and walked with intention to the corner that was producing all the commotion. Putting his hands on their table, he bent down and said firmly but discreetly, "This needs to STOP."

Mabel, fury flashing in her eyes, shouted, "NO! This needs to HAPPEN!"

Norbert shaded his eyes, looking down at the table, while Birdie and Margaret reached for Mabel's sleeve. Lorraine folded her arms, ready to watch the show.

Mabel directed the full force of her hurt feelings toward Carlotta.

"I *tried* to be your friend, Carlotta. I tried and I tried. I even went with you to your crystals class at the Center for Deeper Understanding...."

"You guys went to the Center for Deeper Understanding *without* us?" interposed Lorraine.

Mabel was rushing on. "I even offered to give you a free makeover, like girlfriends do. You wouldn't be my friend, no matter how I tried. And now you come in here and call me a thief, right in front of my Club. You're a bully, Carlotta Moon. That's what you are. A bully!"

Carlotta's Club was banned from the Alibi Bar until further notice.

-92-

Queen observed Mrs. Moon searching her desk. It was sad, how she kept opening the same drawer again and again. Then she'd get up and wander around, poking in here, looking in there. She wasn't going to find what she was looking for. No one would ever find that stack of blue papers again.

Mrs. Moon sank into an armchair with a confused look on her face.

Queen pretended to be reading her book. That Mary Lennox in *The Secret Garden* sure was having herself a happy ending. She went from no one liking her, to now, having two good friends and a nice parent and a big old house and a beautiful garden. Queen sure did love good books like this: a bad-attitude girl gets a happy life. She liked that Mary Lennox, and how she was so tough with her friends. Like that boy Colin, he thought he was sick and dying and couldn't walk, and Mary figured out it was all in his head and she put him on blast. Pretty soon, he was out having fun in his wheelchair in the garden, and then he didn't even need the wheelchair. All because she didn't let him ruin his life. That's what friends did. Just like Queen did for Mrs. Moon.

Only now, Queen wasn't so sure.

She began to have that awful, sinking-in-the-stomach feeling that she had done something wrong again. It was just the way she felt when she hung up from talking to that liar Madame Fifi. Maybe she had made another terrible mistake.

Mrs. Moon took it pretty well.

"It's all right dear."

"It is?"

"Certainly. I'm glad you were honest with me, and told me you took it."

Queen felt proud that Mrs. Moon saw how honest she was.

But then Mrs. Moon said something awful.

"Just give it back now."

That sinking feeling came back to the pit of Queen's stomach.

"Can't."

"What do you mean, 'can't?'"

"It's all burnt up."

Mrs. Moon's mouth opened and she stared straight at Queen. Then she snapped her mouth shut. For a moment, she didn't say anything.

Before Carlotta's eyes swam the 270 pages of blue paper that recounted fifty years of her life events. That stack of paper covered in elegant cursive writing held the early, tentative sketches, the affectionate reminiscences, the sudden detour into Mabel's hijacking of the Club, her recollection of all the kindness she had shown her friends over the years, and all the ingratitude they had shown her in return, and then, the best and latest of her work, which she had just begun in the past few days: the releasing of resentment and the recognition of her respect and admiration for each of her friends and her appreciation for the lives they had shared—and still shared—together. With cross-outs and a tear stain or two, it was all there. And now, all gone.

Up in smoke.

Certainly, she had transposed some of it to her laptop... but only the first four pages of it.

Carlotta looked at Queen, who was biting her thumbnail and looking as horrified as Carlotta felt.

"Why?" asked Carlotta. "It's taken me fifty years to finally start writing my book, the book I've always wanted to write. You destroyed it in a moment... *Queen.* Whatever possessed you to do such a thing?"

Queen hung her head.

"Queen. Did you read it?"

Queen began to cry, softly, and nodded her head, not daring to look at Carlotta.

"I read the part where you said Birdie Walsh was 'lost in space,' and Margaret Birch was not the brightest crayon in the box, and Lorraine Andretta had bad grammar. I don't want your friends to hate you.... They're your fa-fa-family."

In a flash, Carlotta understood what had happened.

"You thought my friends would be angry, and they would all leave me. That's what you thought, isn't it?"

Queen sniffled, swallowed.

Carlotta, stupefied, gazed at the little girl, who was wiping her eyes and nose with her sleeve.

"Get a tissue, dear, please. Oh, my."

"I know now I shouldn't have done it," said Queen, obediently applying the tissue. "Even if I did see you were making the biggest mistake of your life maybe. It wasn't my decision to make."

"It certainly was not," affirmed Carlotta. "What you read, Queen, was a *rough draft.* I would never have *published* negative things about my friends." Carlotta conveniently allowed herself to forget that, until very recently, that is exactly what she had been planning to do.

Carlotta was silent again, seeing in her mind the bonfire, and the immolation of her memories.

And then she remembered her little file of index cards and colored tabs. No, her memories did not perish in the conflagration.

This debacle created by Queen was actually her opportunity for a fresh start on her book. Now that she had gotten the unpleasantness out of her system, she was free to begin anew, and write the book she had always wanted to write.

She would begin again, tomorrow morning, at six.

-93-

"Are ya *happy* now?"

Lorraine opened her door and greeted Carlotta with one of her favorite remarks of disapproval.

Ignoring her, Carlotta said, "I made extra zucchini-pasta casserole so I could bring you some today. Put it in your freezer. Freezing allows the flavors a chance to blend."

Lorraine took the casserole without a thank you and headed back to her kitchen, and Carlotta followed. Lorraine put the dish in her freezer and turned to face Carlotta. She put a hand on her hip.

"Well?"

"Well what?" responded Carlotta.

"Well, are ya *happy* now?"

"I suppose you're referring to the Alibi."

"I'm referring to *you*, Carlotta. So, you accuse Mabel of *stealing* from you, only to find out that it was Queen who took your papers. Cripes, Carlotta! Whatsa *matter* with you? We all feel so bad for Mabel, being called out like that in public for something she didn't even do. Something you would know she would *never* do, if you knew her at all. Did it ever occur to you to have some proof before you go accusing people? You owe Mabel an apology."

Carlotta chafed at this scolding, and even more at the suggestion that she apologize. Regardless of what she might tell Queen, she did not readily apologize. Not to people like Mabel, anyway.

Lorraine was not finished.

"I have never in my life been banned from a *bar*—or any-place else. And now, because of you, we can't go into that seedy joint anymore."

"If it's a seedy joint," reasoned Carlotta, "then why would you—"

"That's not the point, and you know it!"

Carlotta and Lorraine regarded each other with dismay.

And then Carlotta heard the cruelest words that Lorraine had ever said to her.

"Carlotta, I'm disappointed in you."

Carlotta considered how to make her apology to Mabel. She sat in her living room, with Toutou on her lap, trying first one phrasing and then another. Now that she was trying it for herself, she realized what a difficult thing it was she had asked Queen to do, when she had made her apologize to Lorraine. Apologizing was so humbling.

Toutou looked gently into her mistress' eyes, encouraging her to keep trying.

"Mabel," said Carlotta to Toutou, "I am sorry for accusing you. No. For asking if you had taken my.... Mabel, I apologize. It seems that I...." Carlotta stopped and sighed.

Oh, Mabel probably did not need an apology. She had prob-ably forgotten the whole thing already. She was one of those non-thinking, forgiving types. Ah, but even if she had forgotten, Carlotta's friends had not. The apology was for them, really, and not for Mabel. As Queen said, the Club was Carlotta's fami-ly. What they thought of her mattered more than she liked to think.

Should she call Mabel at the Harbor Home and Breakfast to make her apology? Or pop over there to do it in person? It was just down the street, only a block away. She'd take Toutou and walk over. Dogs were useful for lowering people's defenses. Maybe she'd catch the lovebirds at home. She was just taking Toutou's leash off the hook when the house phone rang.

It was Margaret.

Asking to be bailed out of jail.

-94-

Carlotta found the Gibbons Corner Police Department to be very interesting. With the cool objectivity of a writer, observing everything, she reported to the jail to bail out her friend.

But when she saw Margaret, ashen, shaken, and weak with the overwhelming emotions of the previous two hours, Carlotta's dispassionate view evaporated. Margaret, always effusive and bubbly, now seemed a different person, a traumatized person, with no words.

Carlotta drove her back to her condo and let her be silent.

They rode up in the elevator and went into Margaret's home.

Without asking, Carlotta put the kettle on and made them tea, while Margaret sat in her sunny living room, alone with her thoughts.

Myrtle lay in the sunniest spot on the carpet, blinking lazily. She rolled on her back and covered her eyes with one paw. Carlotta would not think about her. Margaret needed her attention.

As they sat with their tea cups, Margaret at last began to talk.

"My shattered nerves!" was the first thing that Margaret said.

It seemed that the mother of some teenager, on finding marijuana in his room, had pulled from him the description and location of his pusher. The boy did not know the name of the little old lady who sold the weed, but he was forced to tell what he did know to the police. He knew what she looked like, and he had been to her condo to make his purchase.

Two hours ago, the police had come to Margaret's door and asked if they could search, and she invited them in and offered them lemonade.

"Oh, Margaret! Don't you ever watch police shows on TV? They can't come in without a warrant."

"I know that, Carlotta. But they were such nice young men. And I have nothing to hide. Or, at least, I thought I had nothing to hide."

It turned out there was a baggie filled with "something that looked like oregano" in a backpack that Mabel had left in Margaret's spare bedroom. The police didn't seem convinced by Margaret's claim that she had a double. They took her into custody, assuring her she could explain it all to the judge.

She had to sit in the back of the cruiser, and walk into the police station with the officers, and they made her stick her fingers in black ink to make prints, and.... Oh, she shuddered to remember. The shame! She wished she could forget. Like Myrtle, she covered her eyes. It was the worst thing that had ever happened to her in her life.

Mabel, accompanied by Walter, went cheerfully to the GCPD, confessing to be the owner of the small stash of marijuana they had found in Margaret's condo. She and Margaret appeared together in court on the charge, where the judge, suppressing a smirk, soberly told Mabel that in view of her advanced age, she would merely pay a fine and promise to stay out of trouble.

Regardless of Mabel's assumption of responsibility, the Club had now undergone a distinct shift in its view of her. They were all deeply concerned about the shock and humiliation that Margaret had suffered because of Mabel.

It would not be going too far to say that the Club now urgently desired to get rid of Mabel.

They did not want to hurt her feelings. She had been a good friend. They couldn't say she hadn't. It was her very fun-loving nature that they had enjoyed, which had now become the problem. Mabel was just a little bit too much fun.

-95-

Queen's Baby Picture Essay for School:

This is not me when I was a baby this is some other Girl who has a diffrent life but be that as it may wherever she is I hope she grows up to be happy I am glad I'm not her becase to me there is nothing better than being the Girl I am. When I look at the baby in this picture I hope she felt loved cause that is what everybody needs. She probally liked to be held and talked to. Her mama probally held picture books up to her face and talked to her about the illustrashons and the storeys. I think that is what happend. A lot of things happend both good and bad. But if that Girl has a mama and a fambly it can work out good. That Girl is probally haveing a good life. And I am haveing a good life. Thank you for your atenshon.

On the long ride home from the Compton Walker Correctional Facility, Queen's eyes became heavy. Soon, her head was resting against the car window, and she was snoring softly.

Summer, in the front seat, whispered to Carlotta, so as not to wake the sleeping child.

"I really felt for Queen's mother when Queen showed her that essay she wrote about the baby picture."

Carlotta stage-whispered back, "And she had Queen read it to her *twice*... I'm actually very impressed with that young mother, going to college in prison and bettering herself. It's just what I would do, if I were in her circumstances."

"It's hard to imagine you in her circumstances, Gramma.... Hope thinks she would have had a lighter sentence if she were white."

"Hope said that?"

"Yeah. Racial inequality in sentencing, it's called. It's a 'thing.'"

Summer yawned and stretched.

They rolled along in silence through the most exquisite state in the union, their hearts uplifted by the fields, farms, woodlands and hills, all covered in a blanket of white, under a pale sky.

Finally, Carlotta said, meditatively, "She's been in that awful ugly place for four years and she's lost custody of her children. She sees her mistake now in getting involved in selling drugs. How much more can she be expected to pay?"

Summer, recognizing this as a rhetorical question, shrugged her shoulders and closed her eyes.

They cruised on, and Carlotta continued to think.

Every time Dahleeya Jones thinks of her three children, thinks that she cannot see them and hug them and help them, she pays for her crimes all over again. What if we all had to pay over and over again, for years, for mistakes we've made, after we've already learned our lessons?

... I wonder if there's anything about racial inequality in sentencing on Google? Or...maybe I could consult an attorney?

Carlotta saw herself, dressed in a smart business suit and stylish pumps, consulting an attorney. She would like that. She could empty out one of her little rainy-day funds. She'd never miss it. Her late husband, Ed, as disappointing as he was, at least was not disappointing in the financial sense. He had left her plenty of money, and she had always been a good steward of it. Now, she would put a bit of it to work. And if this should turn out to be an irresistible project that would send her Club running back to her, well, so much the better. Everyone would see how altruistic she was, and how unmotivated by self-interest. It would be thrilling.

As they drew close to the Gibbons Corner city limits, Queen stirred from her dreams and opened her eyes.

"Almost home." She yawned. She gazed out at the snow-covered landscape. "Next month is Christmas," she observed.

"Yes, it is."

"If it's not a rude question to ask, will I get presents?"

"You very likely will," said Carlotta mildly, knowing full well she had been having a wonderful time shopping for all the delightful things one can buy for creative and intelligent little girls.

"By the way," asked Queen, "where does Hope hide her Christmas presents, usually?"

-96-

Aristotle philosophized while walking, and so did Carlotta. This was called the peripatetic method, from what she could recall of her introductory college philosophy course. As Aristotle had his followers, Carlotta had her poodle.

Toutou's curly ears were flapping and she wore a wide doggy grin as she trotted along. Carlotta, more sober, was deliberating her personal philosophy of life and leadership. Her Club would soon return to her; somehow, she knew it. She sensed in the breeze that blew that a change was coming. She shivered. Whether she shivered from the wind or from the thought of changing, she could not discern. One thing was clear: when her Club returned, she would have to rule it differently.

Maybe I was a bit bossy. Maybe I didn't always allow input.

It was Carlotta's nature to bend life to her will. Her nature would never be extinguished entirely—nor would she desire it to be. As Mabel might have said, "You can't change the spots on a tiger."

Carlotta laughed softly.

However, she *could* learn to occasionally share her power and let others shine, at least some of the time. Carlotta paused at Ontario and Main. She'd just turn right and pop into the Village Shoe Repair to pick up her black pumps. But Toutou sat down stubbornly and looked to the left. She wanted to go north —toward the beach.

Carlotta sighed, and turned left.

After a stroll at the beach, Carlotta was inspired to stop in at the Good Fortune Café, and consult with her niece about her new social justice inspiration. She picked up her little dog, and tucked her under her arm. Who would complain about a little dog in a coffee shop, especially if her paws never touched the floor? It was mid-morning, and there was a lull in business.

"I *could* pay for legal assistance, if you wanted," Carlotta told Hope.

"Do you think it would make a difference?"

"Maybe not. We'll have no idea until we talk to a good lawyer. I'm sure it depends on the narcotics charges. What's needed is a top-notch attorney who has already had success with similar cases."

"That could run into serious money, Aunty. And maybe even after spending a lot of money, it wouldn't help."

"Don't let that be part of your decision, Hope. I'll take care of the cost. Consider it a gift from your Uncle Ed." Carlotta paused. "You decide, and let me know."

"It's not that I need time to think. I know that it's the right thing to do. It was just the cost that held me back. But if Uncle Ed is footing the bill, well, that's really generous of him."

"Money's nothing to him. He can't use it, where he is," Carlotta quipped. She turned serious. "Have you thought what it would mean if Miss Jones were released, as far as your adoption of Queen is concerned?"

"Of course! I've lived through all of that in my head already. Many times. She's signed away parental rights, and I've adopted Queen. Legally, Queen is my daughter. But of course, they'd want to be together. I think we'd wait some time first and let Miss Jones get on her feet. Maybe we could even help her a little. Maybe she'd live close by. Maybe we'd have some arrangement that develops. Maybe I'd adopt more children. Maybe I will adopt more children either way."

"Maybe," said Carlotta, "we cross those bridges as we come to them?"

"Exactly. You know what John Lennon said."

"Ah yes. *Michelle, ma belle, sont des mots qui vont très bien ensemble, très bien ensemble.*"

Hope laughed. "No! I'm pretty sure that was Paul McCartney's song. John Lennon said, 'Life is what happens while you're busy making other plans.'"

-97-

Mabel created one last sensation for the Club.

"Wedding bells!" she shouted joyfully at Birdie's watercolor class. "I've been married before, of course, can't say I haven't! But *this* time it's for *love!* I thought I'd skip the virginal white, you know. It's not like I'm fooling anybody. Ha ha! This might be my last wedding. So I'm wearing *red!* Margaret's my maid of honor. And Norb is best man. Queen is the flower girl. And of course, you're all invited!"

"*Who* are you marrying?" asked the young mother.

"Who else? Walter Strand! What a man!"

"Where is the wedding going to *be,* Mrs. Paine?" asked young Liam.

"At the Center for Deeper Understanding, of course. With the Reverend Edith Butler giving the last rights, or whatever they call it."

"Oh, wow!" said the teenage girl. "And *when* did you say it will be?"

"Right now! Come on, everybody!"

It wasn't as sudden as it seemed.

Margaret, Norbert, Hope, and Queen had had a day's notice. That was enough time for Margaret to create a lovely and simple wreath of red roses for Mabel's curly white head, for Norbert to go to the library and read up on best man speeches, and for Hope to buy a lacey pale pink dress for Queen.

Edith Butler fittingly reserved the Harmony Room for the nuptials. She had the room set up with chairs in rows and an aisle down the middle. The room filled with Carlotta, Birdie, Lorraine, Hope, Arnie, Liam, the teenage girl, the young mother (and her two irrepressible toddlers, who were pulling each other's hair and screaming), and the bartender from the Alibi, whose heart had been softened by the old couple getting married and who had already let bygones be bygones.

The couple had not required a wedding rehearsal.

"I've always just done what comes naturally, you know?" Mabel had said to Edith, who nodded and said she was a wild spirit child, or some such thing.

As the wedding march played on the sound system, Queen stepped with regal daintiness down the aisle, sprinkling red rose petals right and left. She took her place to the side of the altar, where the Reverend Edith signaled her to stand—next to Margaret in a pastel pink knee-length number and opposite Walter in a khaki-colored suit, and Norbert in his dignified grey suit.

That Edith was in her glory, officiating at a wedding with her mail-in reverend license.

Then, the strains of "Here Comes the Bride" announced Mabel's entrance. All heads turned.

"Ohhhh," everyone sighed.

When Mabel had said she would wear red, Carlotta had imagined her in an awful flamenco gown. But she had to hand it to Mabel for once. It was a long satin dress with a full skirt, and the only question in Carlotta's mind was, *How did a woman with such awful taste find such a beautiful dress on such short notice?*

As if reading her mind, Mabel paused in her march to call out to Carlotta, "It was the only thing they had in my size at the Goodwill!"

Everyone laughed.

This was Mabel's wedding, after all, and this was how it was going to go.

Edith opened a book, but before she could open her mouth, Mabel sprang her next surprise.

"Dearly beloved," she cried. "The groom and I have written our own vows! Haven't we, hon?"

Walter beamed at his bride and stepped forward to hold her hand, and the two of them faced the gathering.

Mabel cleared her throat.

She looked charming, with her rose head wreath and her crimson dress, Carlotta thought, generously.

Mabel began: "There once was a devil called Walter,"

Walter picked up: "Who took Mabel Paine to the altar,"

Mabel continued: "She thought he was fine,"

Walter recited: "Their friends drank some wine,"

Mabel concluded: "And he became her rock of Gibraltar!"

Edith lost only a millisecond in confusion, before adding, "I now pronounce you man and wife!"

Norbert, standing with a gold ring in his hand, seemed to realize he had somehow missed his moment, and rushed forward to give the ring to Walter, who, wiping a tear of sentiment from his eye, placed the ring on Mabel's finger.

Lorraine, at Carlotta's side, was sobbing into a tissue.

Mabel raised Walter's hand into the air and shouted, "Meet you all at the Alibi! The drinks are on us! Up to a point! Ha ha!"

The bartender turned down the pulsing music, and Norbert unfolded his paper and read his swiftly written best man speech:

"Mabel, you've brought us a lot of joy, and I can't say you haven't."

(Laughter.)

"Walter and Mabel, I know I speak for everyone here when I say that the two of you are perfect for each other. I foresee many years of marital bliss for you both. It was in the cards."

(Laughter.)

"Wherever you go in life, Mabel and Walter, know that you take with you our love and our sincerest wishes for lifelong happiness."

Did Norbert just say "wherever you GO?" Are they leaving? Carlotta sat up straighter. She turned to Hope for verification but Hope, like everyone else, was paying rapt attention as Margaret stood up.

Margaret began her speech:

"I'm not so good at speeches…. Even though you've made me a television personality. At eighty-seven!"

(Laughter.)

"I'm so grateful to you, Mabel, for all the good times. You've taught me *español*. *Un poco*. *Un poquito*. I love you like a twin sister. Happy travels to you both, Walter and Mabel. Don't be strangers. Come back to our little town. *Vayan con Dios.* Go with our blessings!"

They *were* leaving, then.

Carlotta applauded, with all her heart.

Mabel and Walter's wedding reception doubled as their send-off party. The Club felt nostalgia for all the fun times Mabel had brought them, but regardless of their urging the couple to come back and see them, they all fervently hoped that they would never see Mabel again. They longed for tranquility and intellectual stimulation. In short, they longed for Carlotta to resume her role as Leader of the Club.

And Carlotta, knowing her Club as she did, knew all of this.

While Walter and Mabel were feeding each other onion rings, at their own table, Lorraine, Margaret, Norbert and Birdie wanted to brainstorm their next Big Idea with Carlotta. As they turned to her, she felt their appreciation for her years of dedication to them. She and all the Club members had their home in one another. They created for each other that sense of belonging that all people strived for. Carlotta was deeply touched. She looked around at all of them with a loving heart and glittering eyes as she thought, *Tomorrow, I'll take them all firmly back in hand again.*

While Carlotta had softened enough to become mentor and champion of a child she hoped to mold and shape, and while she had learned to hold the reins of leadership more loosely, she was still herself. Carlotta Moon. And always would be.

"What about that Oscar Wilde reading group you mentioned a while back?" asked Lorraine, conciliatory. "That was a real good idea. We all love Oscar Wilde. He's funny."

"There are so many possibilities," said Carlotta, non-committal. Once an idea was rejected, it was never a good idea to return to it.

"Or French," said Margaret, amiably. "We could go back to our French."

Dear Margaret. Everyone knew she hated French with a passion. They were all being so careful of Carlotta's feelings.

Norbert said, "Or, what if we *all* started working on our memoirs? Then we could get together to critique and encourage each other."

Now, that was an idea with real possibilities. But again, did any of them really care about writing their memoirs, or were they just trying to placate Carlotta?

"Birdie?" asked Carlotta. "Do you have any ideas?"

Birdie smiled through the haze of her thoughts and said, "The Idea is coming. When it is here, we will all know. You will probably be the one to channel it."

Queen waltzed up to Carlotta and gave one spin. "How do you like my pretty dress? It's good taste, isn't it? I asked Hope if I could wear it to school, but she said no, it's too fancy."

"And right she is," said Carlotta, making a mental note to speak to Hope about this. Children outgrew clothes so fast; why not let them wear the best ones for every day? And where *was* Hope? Carlotta scanned the room and saw her laughing with Arnie Butler. Was there another wedding in the future? Hopefully, a more conventional one?

The bartender had agreed cheerfully to play Mabel's CD's and she was swirling and shimmying and singing along, and encouraging everyone to sing with her. She sang a song inviting everyone to fly up in a hot air balloon with her.

The chemistry of this party was heady and celebratory. Everyone was relieved to see Mabel leave town, whether by balloon or space ship, it mattered not a whit.

Mabel, clutching her dress with one hand so as not to trip over it, made the rounds, slapping everyone on the back, as Walter, starting on the other side of the room with his hands folded around his jacket lapels, did the same.

Mabel cornered Carlotta as the latter was fleeing to the restroom to escape the back-slapping banter.

"Hey, Carlotta! I wanna talk to you!"

Carlotta froze, caught.

"I don't like to leave with a bad smell in the air, you know? Listen, you and me, maybe we didn't always get along, but that's only because we're two peas in a pot. That's how I see it. We're just two women with strong characters. There's no reason to get our panties twisted in a wedgie."

Carlotta, trying not to envision a wedgie, agreed. "Mabel, I'm sorry if I wasn't always friendly to you. The fact is, now that you're leaving, I'll be sad to see you go." That was going too far, but what did it matter? She paused. "You *are* leaving, aren't you? I did understand that right, from the speeches Norbert and Margaret gave?"

Mabel lit up with anticipation.

"We bought a camper! We're going to live like nomads, out in nature, hit all the national parks. It'll take us the rest of our lives to get to them all. All night, everyone's been saying, be sure and come back. But to be honest, I don't know if we ever will."

"Oh, that's too bad," said Carlotta. She experienced a sense of gratitude to what Birdie would call "the Universe."

"But you never know. Ha ha! Life can surprise you! One day, you might be sitting in your back yard, enjoying the peace and quiet, and all of a sudden, you'll look up and see my face over the top of your fence. You just never know."

Carlotta's sense of gratitude to the Universe soured, just a little bit.

"Oh, hey!" said Mabel, "I have a parting gift for you. Don't go anywhere."

Mabel bustled across the bar and bustled back with her Yankees cap. She plunked it on Carlotta's head with an admiring smile.

"Looks good on you! Gives you personality! Something to remember me by!"

Carlotta tapped the brim of the cap. "Thank you, Mabel. It is a touching gesture. But there was no need. I would never be able to forget you. Your image is forever seared into my brain."

Mabel's blue eyes became soft and teary. "That is *so sweet* of you to say," she sniffed. "And now I realize something. You and me—we're a pair, Carlotta. And we will *always* be friends forever and ever. I promise you that."

DISCUSSION QUESTIONS

1. Explore the theme of belonging. How are Carlotta, Mabel, Hope and Queen all trying to get a secure sense of belonging? How do they all learn about belonging along the way?

2. How does Carlotta grow and change in the course of the book?

3. What does Carlotta learn from Mabel about leadership?

4. Discuss the parallel between Carlotta's desire to get rid of Mabel and Queen's desire to get rid of Mr. Butler. Compare how Carlotta sets Margaret up to how Queen sets Arnie Butler up.

5. Mabel is Margaret's physical reflection. Is she in another sense Carlotta's reflection as well? If other people can serve as mirrors to show us aspects of ourselves, consider also the mirroring going on between Carlotta and Queen.

6. Queen's superpower of choice would be to "know everything about everybody." Why would she choose this?

7. Discuss foreshadowing in this book, including how Carlotta explains it to Queen, and how Queen understands it.

8. Choose a character to invite for lunch at the Good Fortune Café. Who would you choose, and what would you talk about?

Acknowledgement

I wish to give deep thanks to my beta readers and informal advisors: Claire Smolinski, Tom Davy, Rosemary Davy, Susan Davy, Hilary Ward-Schnadt, and Jon Payne. I thank you all for your encouragement and your sharp attention to detail.

I am grateful to Maura Vivona for perspectives on adoption and to Sarah Lael for information on foster care-to-adoption.

Thanks to Rosemary Davy for assistance in getting this manuscript ready for readers.

Deepest thanks to all of the wonderful booksellers who have supported me in my writing and let readers know about my work, including Mary O'Malley, Jordan Arias, Alex Yount and Don Hailman at Anderson's Bookshop; Georgette Coan at Barbara's Bookstore; Pamela Klinger-Horn at Excelsior Bay Books and Valley Bookseller; and BrocheAroe Fabian at Riverdog Books.

I am grateful to the authors who have helped me on my way: Rhys Bowen, Lucy Burdette, Mary Kubica, Lynda Cohen Loigman, Benjamin Ludwig, Fredric W. Meek, Louise Miller, Phaedra Patrick and Lee J. Williams.

My agent, Danielle Bukowski, has my humble thanks for her early edits of the manuscript and for her belief in *Getting Rid of Mabel*.

A note from the grateful author to the esteemed reader:

Dear Reader,

If you enjoyed *Getting Rid of Mabel,* please review it on Goodreads and/or Amazon.

Your review makes a great difference. Reader reviews help the book to be discovered by other readers, and can even help writers in their publishing career. Thank you, in advance.

And if you would like to know about future books, sign up for my newsletter on www.keziahfrost.com.

I love connecting with readers like you!

Keziah